Worst Nightmares

SHANE BRIANT

Worst Nightmares

Vanguard Press
A Member of the Perseus Books Group

Published by Vanguard Press
A Member of the Perseus Books Group

Designed by Brent Wilcox
Set in 10.75 point Janson Text

Library of Congress Cataloging-in-Publication Data
Briant, Shane.
  Worst nightmares / Shane Briant.
    p.   cm.
  ISBN 978-1-59315-514-8 (alk. paper)
  1. Fiction—Authorship—Fiction.   2. Plagiarism—Fiction.   3. Writer's
block—Fiction.   4. Psychopaths—Fiction.   I. Title.
PR9619.3.B6933 W67 2009
823—dc22

                                                    2009001979

Vanguard Press books are available at special discounts for bulk purchases
in the U.S. by corporations, institutions, and other organizations. For
more information, please contact the Special Markets Department at the
Perseus Books Group, 2300 Chestnut Street, Suite 200, Philadelphia, PA
19103, or call (800) 810-4145, ext. 5000, or e-mail
special.markets@perseusbooks.com.

10 9 8 7 6 5 4 3 2 1

For Wendy, as always.

ACKNOWLEDGMENTS

First and foremost, I would like to thank Laura Blake Petersen. She is a literary agent to brag about. I do so on a daily basis. She's hung in there for me.

Also, a big thank you to Roger Cooper, Georgina Levitt, Amanda Ferber, Peter Costanzo—in fact all at Vanguard who have helped deliver what I believe is my best novel to date. I feel as though I've found a literary home.

Many thanks also to the best editing team around: the wonderful Wendy Walker, who forever urged me to be my best, and Francine LaSala, who, like a literary brain surgeon, cut to the heart of the matter with her editorial scalpel, doing her utmost to turn an overweight greyhound into a lean whippet.

I'd also like to acknowledge the input of Linda Writewatchman, who was so very helpful in a much earlier stage of the book's development.

Thanks to Tania Salvati, who came up with an extraordinary logo for me. Also Vanessa Ryan and Zoe Borecki at E.K.H.

My sincere gratitude goes to my old friend Jeffrey Bloom for being my "Mike Kandinski," though he isn't in fact a cop. He never told me to go hire an assistant. Also the lovely Carole.

Always thanks to Scott and Jennifer Citron, for offering a home away from home in New York.

Finally, I have to thank all those magnificent actors who were kind enough to offer their time and effort to take part in my lurid Internet promotional videos:

Jeffrey Bloom (Dream Healer), Katya and Barry Quin (Stakes Couple), Barry Langrishe (Agorophobic), my very own Wendy Lycett (Wheelchair Wanda), Janneke Arent (Scorpion Girl), Mary Regan (Superglue

ACKNOWLEDGMENTS

Lady), Alex Davies (Mouth Maiden), Danny Adcock (Drowner), and Holly Louise Greenstein (Bug Girl).

One last note. There were, as there will always be in the course of writing a novel, many wonderfully generous people who offered suggestions and told me scary stories, very often revealing personal details of their disgustingly morbid nightmares. I wish I could name them all here. Sadly it was not possible to include all their great suggestions in *Worst Nightmares*, though I relished all the input. They know who they are and I am very grateful.

PROLOGUE

"Your dream . . . tell me more, Miriam," the Dream Healer cooed at his computer. "Tell me more."

He sat cross-legged in the darkness of his shed atop the Stratten Building on Grand Avenue. His face was bathed in the bluish light of his laptop. The teenager on the screen was speaking quickly, her face vibrant with a mixture of fear and relish—as if she were talking to a best girlfriend.

"I'm asleep," the girl began. Speaking to a computer was as natural to this new-millennium teenager as speaking on the Bakelite phone had been to her great-grandparents in the forties.

"It's like . . ." She hesitated, her eyes gleaming at the exquisite remembered dream of personal violence. The Dream Healer could see her clearly, debating how best to describe her sado-sexual feelings. He knew she wanted to shock him. "It's like someone's dropped this tiny burrowing insect into my ear. I'm totally freaked!"

The Dream Healer smiled. This nightmare, like the insect, had legs.

The girl's pupils dilated at her extreme thoughts. "I can feel it scratching inside my head. And the noise . . . You know what I mean? It's awesome. Gross!"

The Dream Healer could imagine. So very easily.

The girl paused, closing her eyes. Her remembered sensations were beginning to scare her. The memory had stalled her breath. It was as if she was remembering reality, not a nightmare.

"Tell me more," the Dream Healer encouraged quietly, like a hypnotist.

The girl reacted immediately to his purring voice. Her eyes flicked back to the camera mounted above her computer screen. The faintest smile creased her cheeks as she opened her mouth to continue—the Dream Healer's voice was so very reassuring.

"It's like the sound of cornflakes. You know what I mean? When you eat them before they get soggy. Like . . . when they're still crisp and crunchy?"

"Mmmmm. Just the way I like them, too, Miriam. Crispy." He paused a second, then continued. "Tell me more."

The Dream Healer never ate cereal. Never had—he preferred oatmeal. Soft and warm, smooth and reassuring. But the girl's aural imagery intrigued him. The thought of an insect feasting on fresh brain tissue that crunched, crispy as a cornflake, was very original. Almost arousing, in fact.

He reached for the parchment paper that had previously wrapped his sandwich, and gently crinkled it next to microphone the computer.

"You see—" She stopped abruptly. "Hey, is that you?"

"Is what me?"

"Making that noise." A nervous tick under her left eye began to pulse.

"I don't hear any noise, Miriam. You must be imagining things."

The girl looked suddenly afraid and confused.

The Dream Healer watched her on his screen as she rose slowly from her chair and sank to the floor of her bedroom, her hands pressed to the sides of her head. She dropped to her hands and knees, inching across the floor like a wounded animal, ending up in a semifetal position just underneath her bed. She was moaning softly, clawing roughly at her ears with freshly manicured fingernails.

The Dream Healer crinkled the paper more vigorously. The effect was startling. The girl's limbs began to twitch violently, and her breathing now came in short snorting gasps.

"Oh, SHIT! It's moving faster! It's going to burrow right through! Right through my brain! Oh, my God . . . the pain! It's unbearable!"

There was now a fierce intensity to her voice. She was shouting, pitching her head from side to side like a cork in a storm. The Dream Healer rubbed the paper even more vigorously. Almost at once, she began to pull at her face, raking the skin of her cheeks harshly back and up, her hands covering what was left of her brutalized ears. She tried to deaden the appalling chewing noise, but the horrific aural images, that sound emanating from her computer, was like a virus. The imagined pictures were too much to bear.

Crunch, crunch, crunch.

CRUNCH, CRUNCH, CRUNCH.

"My head is *on fire*! It's going to *explode*!" she screamed.

On his screen, the Dream Healer watched as tears streamed down her face. Her body was jackknifing wildly, her feet kicking against the wall. She was still clawing at all that remained of her outer ears—shards of skin and bone. The flayed flesh looked like freshly ground beef in a supermarket meat tray. A yellowish fluid poured from both ears, spattering her blouse, pooling on the wooden floor between her legs. For a moment, she quieted, as though she was in some kind of a weird trance, her incoherent words a monotonic Buddhist mantra.

The Dream Healer smiled.

"I can hear it munching on my brain!" Her words changed suddenly to a high-pitched scream.

"Of course you can hear it," the Dream Healer cooed, crunching the paper hard and fast between his fingers. He closed his eyes briefly so he could envisage the horrific images of insect mandibles devouring pulsing brain tissue.

Miriam's eyes took on an insane glazed expression as her limbs temporarily slackened. Saliva drooled from the edge of her mouth. Within seconds she was convulsing again. "Make it stop," she mumbled. "Please! Make it stop!" Her legs twitched rhythmically in all directions as if zapped by a Taser.

"Perhaps you should think of dislodging this insect once and for all, before it takes a terminal hold on your mind," he advised.

The girl seemed to understand. She immediately thrashed the right side of her head against the wall. The fifth time her temple made contact, her skull cracked open. A mist of blood and tissue sprayed both the wall and the bed above her.

"Don't let it take hold, Miriam!" the Dream Healer urged loudly. "Fight the beastie!"

"My head's *exploding*!"

"Let it explode! Let the demon be burned!" the Dream Healer demanded harshly.

There was silence as Miriam's body finally went limp. She lay on the floor, blood spurting from her open temple. Her lips parted the barest crack, her words the softest almost indistinguishable whisper. "That's when . . . I . . . wake up . . ."

"Of course you do, my dear. But not *this* time," the Dream Healer replied with a short chuckle.

CHAPTER 1

Irish-born, good-looking, author-on-the-rise Dermot Nolan had it all. A British national, he'd won the Booker Prize two years earlier, and the Flannery O'Connor Award for Short Fiction the year before. His current *New York Times* best seller, *Incoming Tide*, was in preproduction in Hollywood, and up until just recently his bank balance had been high enough that his bills never concerned him. Nolan was the darling and cash cow of his feisty Jewish literary agent, Esther Bloom, and husband to Neela, his wife, whom he adored with a vengeance. Neela was highly intelligent, slim, and beautiful in a sculpturally angular way that reminded people of Audrey Hepburn.

For nearly two years, the Nolans had had sufficient money to buy whatever they wanted. Even a small yacht wouldn't have been out of the question. But such indulgences did not interest Dermot or Neela. They lived in an expansive converted warehouse in downtown Los Angeles, a place they shared with a fat marmalade-colored cat named Cheesecake. They owned just one car—a practical but unpretentious Peugeot 207 with tinted windows.

So one might have presumed Dermot was a happy man. He wasn't. Not now. Now his life was clouded by despair. He hadn't written a page of anything for an entire year. He'd lied to his agent, saying the pages were "flowing." The reality was that the pages were flowing with the consistency of molasses, and his real worry was that he'd been advanced a million dollars by his publishers and had already spent almost all of Dan Wasserman's money.

Esther had remained supportive and oddly content to wait for her favorite client to submit his new "masterwork"—one did not hurry Booker Prize winners, one nurtured them. But for Wasserman, head honcho at Gunning and Froggett, time was money. It was Dan's company that had made a fortune from Dermot's *Incoming Tide*, but now he'd been waiting eighteen months for a followup novel, and was beginning to wonder if he'd thrown his firm's money away on a promise that Nolan would never deliver.

The fateful day the diary fell into Dermot's possession, he had just returned from a visit with his stockbroker. No more buying—sell whatever I have left, had been Dermot's instructions.

He turned into Linley Place, a few blocks from Pershing Square, and saw an old man with a shock of lank orange-gray hair, wearing a filthy brown long-rider's coat, rummaging through his mailbox. As he drew closer, he could see that the man was struggling to shove in a bulky envelope.

"Hey! You!" Dermot called out, slamming his car door shut and running forward.

The old man turned, startled like a child scolded by an angry parent. Dermot shouted a second time, but the vagrant shuffled off at a surprising speed, leaving the fat manila envelope hanging half in and half out of the mailbox. The envelope was of a size and weight that screamed literary manuscript—the kind that publishers and agents had returned to him regularly before his first groundbreaking novel, *Beneath the Level*, had been discovered.

Dermot pried the package from the mouth of the mailbox and studied the front: "For Dermot Nolan." On the reverse, "From Albert K. Arnold."

Shaking his head, Nolan tucked the envelope under his arm and headed for his front door, where he punched in the entrance code numbers on the keypad. *Everyone thinks he's the next Hemingway.*

A former warehouse, stripped bare from its days as a clothing sweatshop, the Nolans' loft had been converted to a tri-level, state-of-the-art residence by world-famous designer Alex Popov. The floors were polished reclaimed Douglas fir, the walls cream colored on the entry level and white on both the upper floors. Downstairs was an open area, with the exception of a study, an oversized kitchen, and a guest bathroom. Eclectic artwork hung on the walls—a Scheeler, a Sciberras, two small Boyds, a recent Kamrooz Aram, and a decent-sized Pollock that Dermot had bid on and won after too many Veuve Clicquots at a Christie's sale. These were now all earmarked to be sold by Nick Hoyle, their closest friend and "art dealer to the rich and famous."

"What's the package?" Neela asked, emerging from the kitchen. Her sterile tone reflected the current state of their marriage.

"Don't know. Some weird guy was trying to stuff it in the mailbox. I shouted at him but he ran off."

"If it isn't postmarked, don't open it," she snapped, unprovoked.

"Dead right, Dermot." Nick Hoyle followed Neela from the kitchen, holding a bottle of New Zealand Marlborough sauvignon blanc and three glasses.

Nick had been his good friend since Dermot had moved from London to California and never looked back. Nick had the air of a daytime soap opera star, though no one could ever determine exactly which one. There was a haunting, earnest quality in his eyes, counterbalanced by a twinkle that indicated an ever-present humor. All this despite an injury to his right leg, sustained in Tikrit, during a tour of duty he had served in Iraq a couple of years back. During his tour, he'd earned the prestigious Medal of Honor for single-handedly rescuing five children from a burning school. Despite two operations to fix the leg, he had a permanent limp and walked with the aid of a silver-topped antique cane he'd picked up in the London Silver Vaults.

At UCLA, Dermot studied arts and sciences, Nick, visual arts, and Neela, media and sciences. Dermot and Neela met the first week of school and had fallen in love by midterms. Also that year, Nick had met Giselle, third-generation French, tall, lithe, dark haired, and graceful. She was studying writing, and her dream was to ultimately become a respected literary agent. Dermot, Nick, Neela, and Giselle became an exclusive band of four. They were inseparable.

Upon graduation, Nick set up business as a private art consultant to many of the richest businessmen in LA, managing the artistic investment portfolios of various companies and bidding on their behalf for hefty commissions. Giselle joined the literary agency Bloom & Associates and persuaded her new boss, Esther Bloom, to represent Dermot. The year Dermot became a U.S. citizen, he started his first novel, *Beneath the Level*—a contemporary take on Thomas Mann's *Death in Venice*, set in the Montana snow country—which got him short-listed for both the Whiting Writers' Award and the Hemingway Foundation/PEN Award. That same year, Neela became a junior curator at the Los Angeles County Museum of Art. Everything was on track. At least for a while . . .

"What do you want me to do? Call the cops?" Dermot shot back at his wife as he headed towards his office.

Neela didn't reply.

Once in his office, he grabbed his letter opener and slit the bulky envelope open. He was right. It was, indeed, a manuscript. But instead of being typed, it was scrawled in childish handwriting. Dermot immediately lost interest and let it fall to his desk. He had other things to worry about, such as Neela's disposition. From her aggressive tone earlier, he could tell it was going to be another one of those emotionally chilly days, tense, hostile, and unforgiving. When she crept in behind him, he knew he was right.

"Esther called. You left your cell at home so she couldn't get hold of you. She—"

"Wants pages. Yes, I know," Dermot interrupted. "She's going to have to wait."

"Hey, just the messenger here. Don't beat me up." Yes, the edge was there all right, same as usual, and for the same reason as usual. A woman in her thirties, Neela was ready for children; Dermot was not. He wanted to have a family, but preferred to wait till he was back on his feet financially. But if the future of Dermot's writing career was as bleak as the present, Neela was becoming more certain that the day would never come. One of the many reasons lately that he and Neela had started to drift apart.

"She seems to think you might have come up with something by now. Let's hope."

Dermot didn't reply.

"You'll have to give Esther some pages soon. Even a synopsis. It's been months since Dan's advance."

"Oh, right! What do you suggest? Return Wasserman's check?" Dermot gestured towards the newly renovated kitchen. "The money's gone, and you know it."

"Don't snap at me, Dermot. That's not fair to Nick. He's our guest."

"I'm a *friend*," Nick called from the living room.

Dermot managed a convincing smile. "Sorry, Nick. I apologize to you, too, honey. It's just—"

"So what was in the envelope, anyway?" she asked.

"Just the usual unsolicited horseshit. Forget struggling for years, just drop your manuscript on Dermot Nolan's doorstep and he'll pitch it for you—the poor bastard's got nothing else to do. Hasn't had a decent idea in a year."

Nick came into the office and held up a hand for peace. "Hey, you need a loan, you got it. You'd help me out if things were reversed. I know that."

Neither Dermot nor Neela replied, but their expressions indicated they'd soon be seriously considering Nick's offer.

"Look, if you like I can charge you interest—payable when you receive your next big literary award. Let's say two percent a year till you nail the Pulitzer?"

"Sure," Dermot muttered, a bit sullenly.

Neela walked over to Nick and hugged him. "You're the sweetest man. Maybe later? If things get really tough."

Dermot laughed hollowly. "She's talking tomorrow morning."

Neela tried not to let her annoyance swell.

"Well, the offer's there. It's just money—not a life or death thing. Better to share it with the only family I have."

Dermot and Neela looked at each other, embarrassed for a moment at their insensitivity after all Nick had been through.

"I have to get going," Nick said, placing his half-finished glass of wine on the desk. "I'm bidding on a Klimpt for a client, and he wants it badly. So I have to organize my 'couldn't really care less' expression to fool the other bidders down at Christie's. My client's only got a two million ceiling, and that's way too low for this one."

Nick picked up the packaged canvas he'd brought in with him and headed for the front door.

"Hey, what've you got?" Neela asked.

"Let's take a look." Nick pulled off the tape and lifted the small painting out of the paper.

Neela studied it. "Warhol. One of the *Absolut Vodka* series. Love it. Who's the client?"

"A well-known restaurateur who's fallen on hard times and needs the bucks to keep his place afloat."

There was another awkward silence. Money again. Then Nick continued in a lighter vein.

"I see a Warhol here. But Jerry Warschein sees the staff paid and a few weeks in Palm Springs."

"*If* it sells." Dermot wanted to think negatively. It was his form of self-flagellation.

"Hey, everyone likes vodka." Neela was doing her best to keep it light.

"He'll get a few weeks at the Villa Royale Inn if I have anything to do with it," Nick said. "And me? I'll get a week in Jamaica. The commission will help with the bar bill there if nothing else."

Neela smiled, but Dermot wasn't listening. Nick walked to the front door, leaning heavily on his cane.

"See you later," he called back to Dermot. "Always remember, I'm here for you two."

Neela picked up the wineglasses and left the office after Nick, but Dermot stayed behind. He picked up the manuscript once again. The pages were held together with a metal slide-bar down the left side. He read the cover page: *My Worst Nightmares—My Delicious Memoirs*, by Albert K. Arnold.

He let out a weary sigh. Horror thrillers had never been his taste in fiction. He casually turned to the first page as Neela re-entered the office. She looked at the envelope.

"So? What's it all about?"

"Give me a break, Neels, I haven't read anything here except the title, which I hate."

"Because it's too long? Who'd have thought *Midnight in the Garden of Good and Evil* would've worked? Talk about a mouthful. Or *All You Ever Needed to Know About Sex But Were Afraid to Ask*?"

"It's not that it's too long. It has a nastiness to it. Probably badly written by some pseudo-Brit academic wannabe."

Dermot began reading aloud to Neela. "'My name is Arnold. I am alone now. My intent was to bring suffering to others, equal in measure to that which I have endured. For through suffering cometh salvation. No one can ever know true sorrow without suffering true loss.'"

"See?" he asked. "Just a taste of the depraved rationale." Dermot tossed the manuscript into the wastebasket, glaring at it. "I tell you one thing, you asshole writer: The only suffering *you're* going to bring is on me for the time I waste reading this horseshit. I've got news for you—I pass, you sick fuck."

Neela opened her mouth to speak, but caught herself quickly. Dermot's mood swings had become more frequent lately, and he'd been deeply depressed for over a year now. He needed only the slightest lame excuse to get into an argument with her or whoever else might be around when his temper flared.

"What?" he snapped.

"Forget about it."

CHAPTER 2

Lucy Cowley's slim fingers tapped rapidly on her keyboard, like a bird of prey pecking at the carcass of a small rodent. Within seconds she was online at www.worstnightmares.net. The screen filled with images from Hieronymus Bosch's famous triptych, *The Garden of Earthly Delights,* as a seated bird, dressed in a delightful green jacket, devoured a naked human female while a flock of black birds flew out of her backside. Lucy had been both intrigued and terrified by the painting when she first came across it back in school, and wondered if the image had once been the substance of someone's personal nightmare, possibly even the creator's.

On a break from her job as a nurse at the Children's Hospital of Los Angeles, Lucy sat in the middle of the small utility room that served as her lunchtime hideaway, surrounded by oxygen cylinders, jars of ammonia, surgical spirits, boxes of rubber gloves, tall containers of liquid soap, and general hospital supplies. The room was tiny and had no windows. It was used very rarely during the middle of the day, so it was the perfect spot for some peace and quiet as she met her dream therapist.

She looked at her face in a preview pane on the bottom right of her computer screen—the same live image the Dream Healer would be watching. Her eyes then scanned the Web page. "Speak to me" was the link she wanted. She clicked on it.

The day before, a homeless person had handed Lucy the flyer outside the hospital. Lucy always made a point of accepting flyers from people less fortunate than herself, giving the literature a cursory glance before trashing it. On this occasion, however, she'd been intrigued by the design— Bosch's signature work had always been one of her favorites. She'd folded it neatly, slipped it into her purse, and promptly forgot about it. Later that night, she retrieved it from her bag and read it. "Are your dreams a source of pain and anxiety? Let the Dream Healer bring you peace."

Lucy did have vivid dreams—that was true—and many concerning fires. But there was one in particular that recurred on an almost weekly basis that was very different from the usual nightmares. She'd read on. "Share your worst nightmares with the Dream Healer. Expiate your fears—for I shall bring you rest." This site sounded better by the minute. Maybe this man *could* help. "I am a philanthropist, so naturally I charge no fee. To see you at peace is my reward." Perhaps the Dream Healer could help her to sleep dream free.

She had been tempted to go online right there and then, but was exhausted, so she'd opted to wait for her lunch period the following day.

Now in the utility room, the screen morphed from the Bosch to the dark silhouette of a figure, backlit the way undercover cops are on TV to conceal their identities. "I am the Dream Healer. Speak to me." The guttural voice was pure gravel.

Lucy giggled. If the Dream Healer was trying to spook her, he wasn't cutting it, though he probably scared a fair number of kids with his theatrics. Noticing her own image in the small preview pane, she swept a strand of dark hair off her forehead. This was going to be fun.

"Speak to me!" the Dream Healer barked a second time. Hardly the soft welcoming voice that would encourage a stranger to share intimate secrets, but one that immediately made you feel obliged to answer—like a parent demanding to know why you were late.

"My name is Lucy."

"So, Lucy. Share your dreams with me, my child. I will bring you peace." The tone had softened. Now the voice was soothing. Even encouraging. Lucy felt as though an arm had been placed around her shoulder by a kind uncle who was offering to help her through a personal problem.

But Lucy had no idea how to begin.

"Tell me your dream, my child. Have no fear of me. I am here only to bring you the sweetest night's rest you can ever imagine. I am your friend and savior."

She faltered, and then began. "I have dreamed the same dream since I was a little girl."

She paused, suddenly a little hesitant.

"Don't stop, my child," the Dream Healer continued in a reassuring tone.

"In my nightmare, I am completely paralyzed by fear. I try to move my limbs, even my tongue—" She paused again, swallowed hard, and continued. "My mother once asked a doctor about it. He told her it was sleep paralysis."

"I have heard of this. It is common. Continue."

"I wake up frozen in terror, unable to move—with no way to escape from the horror of my dreams. I am awake, yet still asleep. You understand? I'm aware I'm in the grip of a terrible nightmare, yet unable to move or waken."

Lucy glanced at the preview pane. She was surprised to see she no longer wore a relaxed expression, but rather a look of apprehension. She smiled in an attempt to hide her emotions, and stared directly at the outline of the Dream Healer.

She'd been wrong—this website *was* scary. Very scary. The Dream Healer made her flesh crawl. She felt his aura invade her very bones, like gamma rays at Chernobyl. She couldn't see his eyes, but she knew he was staring at her.

Seconds passed. Then Lucy addressed the motionless figure. "Dream Healer, what advice do you have for me?"

"I shall bring you peace, my child. Eternal peace. You may rely on it. For I am with you. And your spirit. We are as one."

Lucy was about to speak again when the door to the utility room opened sharply and the janitor entered. Lucy jumped, startled. The notebook computer slipped off her knees. She clutched at it, just managing to save it from falling.

"Sorry, don't get up." The janitor reached up for a box of latex gloves on a high shelf. He smiled, then turned and left, closing the door behind him.

Lucy's eyes went back to the computer screen. But to her surprise the screen had returned to the home page—the Bosch. She clicked on the link to get back to the Dream Healer, but she was instantly sent to the home page again.

Annoyed, she tried for several minutes to return to her conversation, but there was nothing. The Dream Healer didn't appear.

She looked at her watch. It was time to get back to her work. She'd try again later.

The rest of the day, Lucy couldn't get the image of the Dream Healer out of her head. There was something about him that fascinated her. Despite being unable to see his eyes, she'd been sucked into his eerie cyber world, just like Trilby entranced by Svengali. This man scared her. But the experience had been oddly enjoyable—similar to the thrill of watching a cheap slasher movie when she was a kid. She knew she had to speak to the Dream Healer again. It was now a pure compulsion.

Had she known what their next meeting would be like, she would have died of fright there and then.

CHAPTER 3

Dermot sat bolt upright in bed. His chest was heaving, his body bathed in sweat, as though he'd just hit the tape at the end of a marathon. He was immediately aware of the incessant ringing of the front doorbell as Neela raced from the bathroom.

"Jesus, Dermot! What's the matter? You were screaming. Are you okay?" She hugged him while the doorbell continued to ring.

"I'm fine, Neels. Just the nightmare."

He lay back again. "Hey, can you get the door? The sound's driving me nuts."

Neela slipped off the bed, an empty feeling of rejection uppermost in her thoughts.

The ringing stopped abruptly as she reached the bottom of the stairs. Opening the front door, she caught a glimpse of a man with almost fluorescent orange hair, wearing a brown long-rider's coat, shuffling off down the street toward Pershing Square. Looking back towards the house, she noticed a handwritten flyer wedged in the mailbox, its edges flipping in the morning breeze.

"Who was it?" Dermot called, now in the kitchen making coffee. Neela joined him, reading the flyer out loud. "'And therefore never send to know for whom the bell tolls; it tolls for thee.'"

"What's John Donne got to do with anything?"

"That's what's written here, honey. Some guy just left it in the mailbox. At least I think he did—I didn't actually see him put it there. It's handwritten."

"You saw him?"

"Sure. His back mostly. He turned to look at me quickly, then disappeared around the corner."

"What did he look like?"

"Late sixties, I guess. Maybe older. Wearing one of those cowboy long-rider coats down below his knees. Bright orange hair."

"Shit. It's the same weird guy."

"With the manuscript?"

"Yeah. Did you see his face?"

"Just a glimpse. That was all. Gnarled and weather-beaten. Probably a homeless guy. Had a week's beard. Reddish. Matched the bad hair."

"Come here a minute." Dermot walked into the office and picked the manuscript out of the wastebasket. He took the flyer from her and compared it to the cover page of the manuscript. "Look. It's the same writing," he said, showing it to her. "I tell you something, if I catch that fruitcake twenty feet from here again, I'll ram his fucking manuscript up his gnarly ass. 'It tolls for thee.' Jesus, what's with this guy, anyway?"

"Do you think he's dangerous? Maybe we should call Mike?" Detective Mike Kandinski was Dermot's North Hollywood Division police contact. They'd been casual friends for years; Dermot used him for research into novels when it came to law enforcement matters.

"Do you think you're overreacting?" he snapped.

She decided to let that one go. "Well, maybe the answer's in the manuscript?"

"Don't you think I've got better things to do than read someone else's stuff?"

"Right now? Maybe you don't."

The moment the words were out of her mouth she regretted saying them. "I'm sorry, honey. I didn't mean it that way."

"Sure you did."

The phone rang, and Dermot froze. "If that's Esther, I'm jogging."

Neela sighed. "You can't avoid her forever. You have to talk to her. Explain. Tell her how things are. You're not an automaton that can spit out a novel every two years. In his day Dostoyevsky was a fast act, and he averaged a book every three years."

She picked up. "Hi, Esther. I'm afraid he just left for the park. Jogging. I'll get him to call you back." She listened for a few moments. "Yes. Me, too. Take care. Bye."

She replaced the receiver. Dermot hugged her.

"Thanks. You have to keep the faith, Neels. Things'll work out. We'll taste the good life again soon, and then we'll have those babies. You have to believe me. That's all."

"I've never doubted you, honey. Not before the Booker, and not since."

Neela watched Dermot drop the manuscript in the wastebasket for the second time. "Can I take a look before you commit that mess to the garbage guys?"

"It's brutal, nihilistic, and sadistic—and that's my take on just the first three pages. But hey, knock yourself out. Me? I'm going for a walk. Maybe some air will get me inspired. Jaunts through the tundra worked for Tolstoy."

"Didn't he die of pneumonia?"

"But the point is *before* he died he was very productive. Besides, he lived in Russia, for Christ's sake. He walked around in minus-thirty-degree temperatures with no thermals. Had to die of the cold eventually."

Neela lifted the manuscript from the trash and took it into the kitchen.

CHAPTER 4

Lucy Cowley pounded the treadmill at her Studio City home. She'd just come off a seventeen-hour shift and was exhausted, but she was determined not to allow the overtime to interfere with her plan to lose fifteen pounds before her birthday in three months' time. She glanced down at the gauge. She'd jogged just under three miles.

When the readout clicked over to exactly three, she stepped off and headed for the shower.

Lucy wasn't exactly obese, though *she* certainly had that opinion. She'd increased two dress sizes in the past six months. She was currently a size twelve and wasn't happy about it. As a happy-go-lucky single nurse who'd just earned a big promotion, her life would have been perfect if she had a life partner. But there was no hurry—her work scarcely gave her time to think about what she'd have for dinner, let alone allow her an evening at the movies with a man. Finding one, she knew, wouldn't be too hard when she felt like going there—she was twenty-four, five-ten, had perfect skin, big hazel owl eyes, and a happy smile. Once she'd shed those fifteen pounds she'd have a damn good body, too.

As she rinsed the conditioner from her long brown hair she heard the front doorbell ring.

"Shit."

Lucy quickly toweled off and slipped hastily into a cream dressing gown.

The bell rang a second time.

Lucy opened the door a couple of inches, leaving the heavy chain attached. She didn't recognize the mailman. Maybe he was on vacation.

"Hi. You got something for me?"

"Sure have."

The mailman had a brown paper package eighteen inches long and five inches wide.

"You'll have to sign for this, Ms.—" he looked at the package, "—Ms. Cowley."

Lucy signed and took the package, which she placed on the living room table, then headed for the bedroom to change. She liked the anticipation of unwrapping a gift. It usually exceeded the joy of discovery—so she reveled in the various wonderful options.

Back in the living room, she clicked on the television and opened her mysterious gift. Under the wrapping paper was a wooden box, and inside that was a bottle of red wine. A Caymus Napa Valley cabernet sauvignon. She gasped—her favorite! Lying beneath was a card: "Congratulations on the promotion. Richly deserved. Now you can put last year behind you. Love Alex. XXX."

Alex, the registrar at the hospital, had befriended her some months ago, a beautifully warmhearted guy. Too bad for her he batted for the other team.

She mouthed a silent thank you to the card then walked into the kitchen to fetch a corkscrew. She wasn't about to share this treasure with anyone. She'd let the wine breathe; that went without saying. But a minute or so would be plenty!

Back in the living room, she sat down at her computer and poured some of the nectar into one of her treasured Riedel red wineglasses. She raised it to take a whiff. Heaven!

She then booted up and tapped into one of her "fun" sites— www.matchmakeme.com. While she wasn't necessarily actively seeking a partner, she found it amusing nonetheless to see who or what was out there. Scrolling down the profiles, she came across a diverse collection of oddballs.

"Too short," she murmured to herself and savored a sip of the wine. "Too fat! Jesus!"

She laughed. The guy looked to be the wrong side of two hundred pounds. Below Mr. Fat was a snapshot of someone else. His gnarled face belied his age. Eighty? The text underneath read: "I'm younger at heart than I look. I work out at the gym every day. I'm looking for a girl in her twenties. I'm very physical—I like to role play."

Lucy made a face. The mere thought of getting physical with this fossil made her flesh crawl.

She scrolled on further, reaching again for her wine and spilling some down the front of her fresh white T-shirt. She watched as the stain spread to the size of a golf ball. It had to be attacked right away. Red wine and beets—killers. "Damn."

Heading back to the kitchen to treat the stain, a sudden wave of nausea and giddiness flooded her body. She stumbled slightly, trying to adjust her bearings. How could just a few sips have buzzed her like this? Her eyes rolled back into her head and she pitched forward onto the floor.

When Lucy regained some semblance of awareness, she immediately wondered how long she'd been out. She tried moving her hand to look at her watch and was surprised that she couldn't shift it. Not even an inch. Maybe she'd fallen on a muscle and had a temporary "dead arm"? She tried moving a leg. Again, she found she couldn't budge it, not even a fraction of an inch.

It was then that she realized she was no longer on the kitchen floor but in her bed. Her head was propped up on both her pillows. "What the—?"

She was still dressed in a T-shirt and white panties, but not the same wine-stained white T-shirt. A tsunami wave of panic overwhelmed her. Who had undressed her while she was unconscious? Just the thought of foreign hands on her body made her feel nauseated. Her heart began to race. She tried moving her legs again. Dead. Each arm, separately. Nothing. Her mouth, even her lips remained slack. She wanted to scream, but even that wasn't possible; her lungs had almost shut down. Her chest was barely rising and falling.

Tears welled as her eyes swiveled and darted around, looking for any evidence of an intruder. Then she heard a deep, guttural voice. It echoed around the room.

"Does this feel familiar, Lucy? Does it bring back childhood memories?"

Inside her frozen body her heart leapt in terror. The room was empty, but the voice hung in the air above her.

"You wake from a bad dream but you are still a part of it? You can't move so much as a muscle? Your very words, my dear." There was a light chuckle. "Not even one of your little piggies, I'm guessing."

Lucy tried to gulp in sufficient air to speak. Her words came out like the softest slurred whisper.

"Who . . . are . . . you? I can't . . . see you . . ."

"Cast your eyes to the dressing table. You will see."

Lucy focused as best she could. Her laptop was open and the screen shone in the semidarkness. A dark figure was silhouetted there, backlit by a strong white light. *Oh my God! It was the Dream Healer!*

She'd been panicked before; now she was close to heart failure. She clutched at one final straw of sanity—was it possible she was actually dreaming? It was always like this in her worst nightmare—each time she was convinced she was experiencing reality until she awoke and the paralysis lifted within seconds. She prayed to God that it was so now.

"Remember your sleep paralysis, Lucy? 'I wake up frozen in terror, unable to move—with no way to escape from the horrors of dreams.' Remember, Lucy? They were your words."

Breathing was becoming practically impossible. Her lungs were shutting down completely. Lucy strained to suck in a tiny gasp of air so she might plead for mercy.

"What . . . have you . . . done to me?" she gasped.

"Well, you're in a better position than most people to understand what's going on inside your veins. You are a highly qualified nurse, after all."

There was a brief pause. A strained silence.

"Oh! Congratulations on your promotion! I almost forgot. Such a shame you'll never enjoy the fruits of your endeavors."

Lucy sucked in a thimbleful of air and was about to plead for her life when the Dream Healer continued.

"I have administered a drug, rendering you paralyzed. Succinylcholine—'sux' for short! You may have heard of it. A real beauty. A neuromuscular blocker. It's quite wonderfully immediate, and the effects last for eight to ten minutes. And while you're completely aware of what's happening to you, you can't even twitch the smallest muscle. Can't even blink. Isn't modern medicine a whiz? Just wicked? And it's so freely available on the Net—well, you have to search just a teeny-weeny bit.

"The good news? You have possibly just over a quarter of an hour to come to terms with your death. Not many people are granted that luxury. Most are struck down before they can make peace with their God. If they believe in that nonsense, of course. The bad news? This is a terminal condition."

"Why . . ." A feather dropping would have made a louder noise.

The Dream Healer didn't answer her question, instead replying, "Through suffering cometh salvation, my dear. Oh, one neat thing about sux that you need to know. You're paralyzed, but you can feel . . . everything. And listen up, I'm here to tell you that before you meet your maker, the pain's gonna be real bad."

"Please . . . make this stop . . . I beg you."

A second chuckle broke the silence. "Oh, believe me, Lucy. It will stop. But not as you expect."

The tiniest flicker of hope registered in her eyes. What did he mean? Would he reverse the process at the last second?

"Yes, it will stop. But not before it gets far, far worse."

Jesus Christ! Lucy felt a deep, yet discernible, pain in her chest. Presumably the drug stopped short of paralyzing her heart muscle. Perhaps she was about to have a heart attack. It'd be a merciful release. But what did he mean by "worse"? What could be worse that what she was currently experiencing?

She made one last attempt to speak, drawing in another impossibly tiny breath of air.

"I . . . I didn't do anything. I'll give you anything you want."

"But you are giving me what I want."

Lucy tried to draw another tiny breath, but it wasn't enough for speech.

"What was it your parents always used to say before you went to sleep, Lucy?" His voice became a graveled singsong croon. "Good night. Sleep tight. Don't let the bedbugs . . ." He broke off.

The pain in her chest grew worse. She began willing her heart to explode—death would be preferable to this torture. Then she noticed movement under the bedsheet that covered her lower legs. The sheet appeared to ripple, almost imperceptibly. Her eyes stared in horror as an enormous spider pushed its way out from under the sheet, the hairy forelegs probing her skin. The arachnid perched on her left knee, taking stock of its topography. Lucy's chest pain was now unbearable.

The giant goliath spider began to move again, tracing a path up her inner thigh until it rested on her belly button. It inspected the silver belly ring that glinted in the semidarkness. Then it continued upwards, choosing a precise path over, rather than under, her gleaming white T-shirt.

Had Lucy been capable of a scream she would have been heard several miles away, despite the traffic.

The spider braced itself on her neck. Lucy couldn't even hold her breath—she had little or no air left in her lungs. All she could do was watch.

She tried to close her mouth, but it hung open. She tried to close her eyes, but again the muscles didn't obey. Her gaze drifted toward her feet, where she felt another prickly movement. This time two tarantulas and a scorpion emerged from under the linen and began to wander over her body.

What the Dream Healer had said was true. She could feel every tiny footfall of the insects as they crawled over her skin—yet she could not move a muscle to escape.

A sharp pain in her neck brought her back to the first spider, which had bitten her on the jugular. The pain was deep and agonizing. She also felt a deep irritation in her mouth and left eye as the spider released a flurry of tiny hairs into the air. But that pain was in no way comparable to the bites that followed in quick succession seconds later. A tarantula bit her inner thigh—twice. The pain was obscene. Lucy was so concentrated on that particular pain that she never noticed the forward motion of the scorpion, which had quickly run up her torso to her face, pausing on the bridge of her nose. It gripped Lucy's lower eyelid and stabbed her in the right eyeball. The shock of this attack was more dreadful than the pain.

Lucy died fifteen minutes later while the scorpion feasted on the sclera, close to her optic nerve.

CHAPTER 5

"So?" When he returned from his jog, Neela had persuaded Dermot to sample the manuscript further. Even though she was trained as an art curator, she was also Dermot's editor and had a pretty good sense of what worked and what didn't. For that reason, as well as offering a gesture of contrition, he'd agreed.

"It's total crap. That's what it is. You just have to look at the handwriting," Dermot replied.

"What's handwriting got to do with anything? It's the content that matters. Everyone's voice is as different as a fingerprint."

"Sure. But this stuff? Some psycho deviant, whacking a bunch of people according to their worst nightmares? All the details, warts and all! I don't need this!"

"You've just trashed Hitchcock's *Psycho,* to say nothing of *The Omen* and *Silence of the Lambs*—" She was about to continue when Dermot held up a hand.

"Hey, Hitchcock was one of the all-time great thriller directors. To my mind anyway his craft remains unsurpassed. You can keep *The Omen*; I've seen enough of Satan movies. *Silence* was different—it was entirely original. This guy's not even in the same ballpark."

"That's precisely what I'm getting at. While you were out filling your lungs with fresh air, I read the first chapter and half of the second. I'll tell you something—this is different from any novel I've ever read. The website concept is fresh and original. The murders are scary as hell, because they're emotionless, impersonal, and horrific. And it's a diary. The narrator is absolutely fascinating because he has no guilt, pity, or compassion. I can't believe some of the vile things happening here."

"Tautology—pity, compassion."

"Not accurate. Strictly speaking pity is compassion aroused by another's condition. Compassion is pity inclining one to help or be merciful."

"I don't see the difference."

"That's why I'm your editor and you're the writer. If you have pity for someone you feel sorry for them, but if you have compassion you are inclined to do something about it—in other words, you act."

Dermot smiled. The truth was Neela *was* a great editor, and he attributed a great deal of his Booker success to her fine structural interpretation of his manuscript. Giselle may have received all the kudos as lead editor but this didn't matter to Neela.

"Fair enough. But judging by the first few pages, I can tell you it's not my taste. It's overly violent. In fact it's savage, with its calm, second-by-second deaths of innocent people as if they were cattle in an abattoir."

"That's fair. But there's more to it. The way I see it, the writer is stepping into the mind-set of a serial killer to demonstrate exactly how emotionally anesthetized a sociopath can be. And I think he succeeds brilliantly."

"But the content, the style, the choice of words, the structure? It's a literary nightmare."

"Sure, it is. But that's the whole *idea*. Would you expect a serial killer to have Truman Capote's voice? Or Stephen King's? No. Think Norman Bates meets Charlie Manson!"

"Serial killers are usually highly intelligent white males—people who are very precise about their murderous cravings."

"Right! I think that the writer here has these cravings, yet channels them through the actions of his leading character, a far simpler soul."

Dermot simply shrugged. "Look, this garbage might interest a psychiatrist or someone getting a doctorate in criminology, but it does nothing for me."

"But quite possibly it could 'do it,' as they say, for a great many other people. By that, I mean it could *sell*. And sell really well. Look at *In Cold Blood*."

"If Capote published a novel about the sexual proclivities of the muskrat I'd still go right out and buy a copy. But that's because it's Capote."

"*In Cold Blood* was based on fact. And don't be a literary snob, honey!"

"Hey, I have a Booker under my belt! I'm allowed."

Neela hugged him—he had finally made a good point.

"Well, all I ask is that you read a few more chapters. Who knows—it might strike some kind of a chord; give you some inspiration."

"So suddenly you think I should write horror schlock?"

"Not at all. But consider what I said about commerciality. You can't cocoon yourself in a literary world that doesn't take into account what the average reader will actually pay to read."

"Hey—"

"Sure, I know. You sold three million copies and won a Booker. But Stephen King has sold a hundred times that number because he knows his market. If you want the respect and approbation of the literary community, go ahead and wait another ten years for suitable inspiration. In the meantime why not take a year off and write something slightly less cerebral?"

Neela draped an arm around Dermot's neck, sat down on his lap and nuzzled. "Just read another few chapters." She kissed him gently. "Then tell me I'm wrong and I'll quit bugging you."

The touch of her lips stirred him, and he kissed her neck. "Okay. I'll read it. But just for you."

"Promise?" she asked, leaning on him more closely as her right hand drifted between his legs.

The warmth of her body, the smell of the Gautier on her skin, the scent of her hair. There was more on his mind than the diary, and also on hers.

Within seconds, they were stripped to their underwear, kissing passionately.

Neela turned to face Dermot and was straddling him fast, holding on to the back of his neck. She reached down between her legs and moved her panties to one side, allowing Dermot to slip inside her. After a second, he pulled out of her.

"Let me just run upstairs and get—"

"Hey, hey, hey—we don't need that," she whispered in his ear, sliding back on him and rocking her torso side to side.

"Neels. It'll just take a second."

In a hoarse whisper she replied. "It's okay."

"No, Neels. I mean it," he said, trying as gently as he could to pull away again.

Her motion stopped abruptly. She stared down angrily at him.

"I can't take this anymore, Dermot. I want babies. You hear me, Dermot. It's time. So if you don't want kids, you don't get to fool around with me anymore. Enough is enough."

She lifted herself off his lap and headed to the bathroom.

"Neels! You know the way things are. We're in no shape to have a child. There's nothing left—no money. We're in hock up to our eyeballs. Esther's screaming for pages, pages, and more pages that I don't have. Wasserman's up her tush telling her he wants to see the fruits of his advance—which, incidentally, is all spent, too—and I don't have a single original thought in my head! Can't you listen to reason? We have a problem here!"

As she reached the bathroom door she turned sharply to face him. "You're telling me! You may think you're some kind of literary Lance Armstrong who can win awards every year for seven years, but that's just not possible in the grand scheme of things. You may win another prize—most likely you will—but that could be years off. In the meantime, what we need is money! And more importantly, you need to fertilize one of my eggs before they reach their expiration date."

The sound of the door slamming was an explosion that shook the walls.

CHAPTER 6

It was a massive slice. The golf ball flew right and disappeared.

Bruce Major was treating himself to his monthly indulgence—a day at the Brentwood Country Club, and it was turning into a nightmare. Initially, he'd hit the perfect drive, two hundred and fifty yards down the center of the fairway. Then he got it into his head that he could reach the green with a three wood rather than playing safe with a two iron. Big mistake.

Bruce knew at once he was in big trouble. The ball had flown right, pitched once an inch from the rough, bounced up into the trunk of a massive elm, and ricocheted off behind some bushes towards a shallow ornamental lake.

"Tough one," came the teasing comment to his left.

Terry Butcher, Bruce's playing partner and fellow hospital security guard, smirked. Bruce was by far the better player, playing off a handicap of twelve, while Butcher was the weekend hacker, playing off twenty-six. He took in Major's pained expression, enjoying the moment.

"Looks like you're in the *water* hazard."

Butcher knew about Major's irrational fear of drowning, even in the smallest body of water. His phobia was common knowledge among the hospital staff, and the nurses and interns teased him mercilessly about it.

"You going to drop out, Bruce baby? Hit a fourth?"

Major smiled grimly and tried to mask his emotions. "Well, let's have a look-see. May not be as bad as we think. Maybe *you* should show me how it's done."

Butcher took out a five iron and addressed the ball.

"Five iron?" Major quipped. "Me? I'd be taking a three at least—you'll never make the green with that."

"I'm happy to lay up. Better than finish in a creek without a paddle—or should I say in a creek without a water wedge?"

Butcher's club came down and the ball screamed into the air. A magnificent shot? Not exactly. A compete fluke. Butcher had mis-hit the ball, but it flew with the trajectory of a one iron. That, coupled with the extreme force Butcher had applied to it, made the ball fly like an arrow towards the pin and trickle to within a few feet of the green.

"Not bad," Major observed sourly.

Butcher chuckled. "Wrong choice of club, you say? I should remember to use the five iron more often from two hundred yards."

"Whatever," Major mumbled, and trudged off to find his ball.

Major clambered through the dense shrubs to the ornamental pond. At its deepest the water was little more than eight inches, yet Major stared in horror at the wide expanse. He spotted his Titleist immediately. It was just two feet from the edge, sitting in water so shallow that half the ball lay above the surface. To anyone but the direst hacker, it was a challenge—but a reasonable one. Simply remove the shoes and socks, give the ball a good thrashing, and hope for the best.

For Bruce Major this was not an option. He would sooner have retrieved a ball from deep inside a wasp's nest with his bare hands than step into the water.

"Damn," he murmured, reaching into his pocket for another ball to drop out onto the fairway.

He never saw the blur of the clubhead. It was a sand wedge. It cracked into his temple from the left. Major went down like a felled buffalo, his face pitching forward into the shallow water.

CHAPTER 7

Dermot sat opposite Esther Bloom, doing his utmost to appear emotionally in control. Esther eyed him keenly. She was sixty, Jewish, five foot one, and nearly two hundred pounds. She wore her white hair in a ponytail that practically reached the small of her back. And she could smell a lie at a hundred yards in a stiff wind. She knew from the moment Dermot entered her office and gave her a hug that all was not well, despite his radiant, overly relaxed smile.

Esther was the top literary agent on the West Coast. She'd split from Manton Gray and Associates twenty-five years earlier to create her own agency, Bloom & Associates. There were no associates, but she liked the ring of the name. She'd left it up to her private coterie of authors to decide whether to join her or stay at their former agency. All but one had joined—the exception was the husband of one of the senior partners at Manton Gray.

Esther had a list of authors that was the envy of the world. Money was no longer a factor in her day-to-day working life—it was only personal kudos that interested her now.

"Esther, you know I can deliver pages. But I have to tell you, I'm not happy operating this way. They're just not ready. I don't want you to read work that's below par."

Esther ran a hand over the top of the antique desk that separated them as though she were smoothing a tablecloth. Her keen eyes never left Dermot's. She said nothing, aware of his discomfort despite his seemingly easy manner. The silence proved too much for him.

"It's all here," he said, tapping his temple. "Most of it is already written." What could he say next? "I mean the concept and structure are in place. The characters. Everything. I simply need a few months to flesh it all out on paper."

Esther didn't buy a word of it. How many times had she heard the same speech from authors? The fact was, she did sympathize. She believed in Dermot's brilliance. It was no accident he'd been short-listed for both the Whiting and the Hemingway prizes for *Beneath the Level* and had won the Booker for *Incoming Tide*, so she'd cut him a great deal of slack over the past six months. But now it was time to badger him—at least, just a little.

"We're talking a great deal of money here, Dermot. Wasserman feels he's waited long enough. One mil is one heck of an advance—keeping in mind the film was never made last time."

"Hell, Esther. How many intelligent award-winning novels make it to the screen nowadays? The average moviegoer is a fourteen-year-old kid who spends the day on a Game Boy and the evening watching *The Simpsons* or jacking off."

"True. But you can't hang on to Dan's money and do nothing. I agree with him—eighteen months is a long, long time. He's responsible to his board of directors, and that means you have to have at least *some* pages for him to show them."

Dermot took a pull at his Glenlivet single malt and shrugged lazily.

"Esther, I hear you. Believe me, I hear you. If Giselle was still around, the pages would have been in your hands three months ago. But she's not and, good as she is, Neela is not Giselle—she simply doesn't understand my voice sufficiently." He paused and smiled crookedly. "Of course if you ever tell Neela, I'll have to—"

"You'll have to kill me. A very tired joke." She paused and then finished her drink. "Look, Dermot, I know you've had it rough since Giselle died. You two were the best literary team I've had the pleasure to work with in years. And I know how close you were. But it's time to move on and realize that the chances of discovering another editor in her league are a thousand to one. Neela is good—albeit a bit of an amateur. I disagree about her not knowing your literary voice though—just give her something to work with."

Dermot nodded. It was all true. The year he'd spent editing with Giselle had been glorious. Every day with her had been a holiday. If he hadn't been madly in love with Neela at the time, he'd have fallen headlong in love with Giselle. Quite possibly he had anyway, and had denied that fact to himself. And there had been that one evening . . .

"How's Nick holding up anyway?" Esther brought Dermot back to the real world, one not scented with Bulgari's White Tea.

"Burying his grief in the art biz. Still dealing. Strictly on consignment, though, now. He's acting for people who have more money than they can spend in three lifetimes. He's made a sackful of his own along the way. Seems okay. But you know—calm above the water and paddling like hell underneath."

"And not waving, but drowning? Let's hope not. I have the greatest respect for him. The way he handled her passing. And then the tragedy with the twins."

Dermot was happy he'd steered Esther away from talking about pages. But now she was silent. He raised the Glenlivet to his lips, and then realized he'd already finished it. Esther continued to stare at him. Eventually she looked away to Dermot's alligator briefcase, which was only half closed. A manuscript caught her eye—Dermot had brought Arnold's diary with him to read on the subway.

"Are those the first crude pages you were talking about—the ones you don't want me to see?"

Dermot saw an immediate avenue of escape. A temporary one of course; but one that might buy him a modicum of time.

"As a matter of fact, they are," he lied.

Esther held out a hand. "May I—?"

"I'd really rather not. As I told you, they're not ready. Not even for you."

"Not even for me? So I'm a dumb literary agent who's incapable of distinguishing between pages, a rough draft, and a final edit?"

"No, that came out all wrong. They're not good enough for you, that's all. I want to surprise you with something wonderful, and I promise you won't be disappointed. Tell that to Dan, too—it'll be a license to print money."

"Then why did you bring them?"

"Sometimes I get an idea or a thought for a revision, and I can make notes right then and there."

"Fair enough. So I can't see them now? You're sure? Not even a small wee glance?"

"I'd rather you didn't. Just trust me, Esther."

She had to admit temporary defeat. "All right. Look, I'll hold Dan off as best I can for another three months. Then I'll *have* to see those pages. End of story. Make sure they're ready. Okay?"

What could he say? "Sure, Esther. Three months."

Dermot took the Red Line home from Wilshire/Normandie. He didn't feel like continuing with Arnold's diary, but since he had nothing to read other than the *LA Times*, which he'd devoured earlier, he reluctantly opened his briefcase and pulled out the manuscript, flipping to where he'd left off.

I will bring suffering to others, equal in measure to my own. Through suffering cometh salvation. You will never know true sorrow without suffering true loss.

Dermot drew in a deep breath. This stuff was such crap, it was nearly unreadable. But he'd promised Neela, so he continued.

When the train pulled into MacArthur Park, there was hardly anyone on the platform waiting to board. The doors slid open, but Dermot paid no attention. Instead, he continued to read. *Suffering. My watchword. Let others know the reality of extreme suffering. Let them watch the innocent suffer.*

Just as the doors were about to close, a man slid into the seat directly next to him, despite the fact that there were sixty or so seats available elsewhere.

Dermot tried to ignore the intruder and continued reading the manuscript, though his mind was very aware of the shadow at his elbow. The smell of rank body odor was intense.

I have watched my loved ones die. And now I may help others to appreciate the moment of their own death.

"Good read, huh?" the vagrant said suddenly, grinning like an idiot. "There's pictures in the back."

Dermot looked up. The speech pattern took Dermot completely by surprise. Although the man looked sixty-plus, and the timbre was a deep and guttural one, he spoke with the voice of a child. What pictures was he talking about? He hadn't seen any in the manuscript.

The train began to slow down as it approached the 7th Street station.

"Are you the person who delivered these pages to me?" Dermot asked, holding up the manuscript.

The old man continued to grin, revealing nicotine-stained teeth. He giggled like an eight-year-old. "Guess so," he replied.

The train stopped and the doors opened. Dermot and the old bum stared at each other, neither one moving.

"Did you write this stuff?"

There was no reply.

"Is your name Arnold?"

Just another grin and a half giggle.

Dermot was about to ask him more when the doors began to slide closed. In a split second the vagrant leaped up with an amazing agility, ran to the doors, and squeezed through them at the very last second.

"Catch me if you can!" he cried out delightedly, as though he was on some school playground.

Dermot jumped up to follow but missed the doors. The old man turned and pressed his dirty face against the glass. The eyes bulged, the tongue licked the glass, the teeth and gums were bared.

The train started off again. Dermot watched the old vagrant recede as the train plunged back into the tunnel, and the old man was nothing more than a speck in the distance. And he was waving.

"Then what?" Neela asked as she poured two glasses of Shaw and Smith sauvignon blanc.

"Then? Nothing. I jumped out at Pershing and headed back to Seventh, but there was no sign of him by then. I walked around for the better part of an hour looking."

Dermot took a gulp of wine and sat down.

"It was—" He couldn't find a word that suited his feelings. "It freaked me out. Reading scary sado-shit with that weird bum sitting right by me, staring at me like an imbecile. A hundred damn seats to choose from, and he wants to crowd me! Then he leaps up like a jackrabbit and makes a run for it," he scoffed.

Neela hesitated for a moment, trying to find the right words. "There are probably tens of thousands of homeless people in LA, honey. And you know how many of them hang out around Pershing Square? Hundreds. What do you think are the odds that he was actually the same guy who left the manuscript? Come on, let's face it—you saw him just once, and he was running away. Couldn't you have been mistaken?"

For an instant, Dermot thought of calling his LAPD pal Mike Kandinski to see what his take on things was. Then he dismissed it—better to keep everything close to his chest for now.

"Then why sit right next to me—crowd me in an empty car, for Christ's sake? He was ogling me like some dim-witted moron. How did he know my *name* if he wasn't the same guy?"

"You're a celebrity, Dermot! Get real." She paused, and then reconsidered her comment. "Okay. Maybe he *was* just loopy."

"Thanks," Dermot replied, acknowledging her little joke.

"You said he spoke like a simpleton—a child. How could he have written a novel if he was retarded?"

"Sure, go figure," Dermot admitted. "Had to be there, I suppose. But I still don't think a street bum would know a Booker Prize winner on sight."

Neela smiled, and it made Dermot ease into a smile himself. "Maybe I'm making too much of it. Maybe I'm just dumb," he said, relaxing a little, at the same time pulling Neela into his lap.

CHAPTER 8

At first Major was aware only of the terrible pressure in his head and an intense localized pain where the club had sliced through the skin on his face, separating his cheekbone from the rest of his skull. Trying to figure out where he was, all he could feel was disorientation and confusion. Why was everything upside down? And why was he swaying?

It was so dark he couldn't recognize any of his surroundings. The sensation was like floating in space. And it was cold—a stiff wind was blowing in his face. Was he dreaming?

Major desperately tried to kick his brain into gear. A golf course! Of course. His slice came to mind immediately. He must have dreamed it all. Butcher's stupid smiling face as he'd hit his fluke shot. But hold on—that had actually happened, hadn't it? That part hadn't been a dream . . .

Major ground his teeth in rage as he remembered Butcher's smug grin. Immediately the pressure in his jaw transferred to the open wound on the side of his head. He let out a small scream. Slowly his vision adjusted to the dark. Now he could focus on what rippled two inches in front of his face.

Water!

It was then that his brain cleared sufficiently to realize he was hanging by his ankles above what looked like a tank of stagnant storm sludge.

His heart began to pulse violently. His eyeballs bulged. If he fell he'd drown! But what was happening? How the hell could he have gotten here? It was night. The last thing he remembered, it was midafternoon and he was playing a round of golf . . .

Aware of an annoying speck of dust in his right eye, he moved to rub it with his hand. He quickly realized that both his hands were tied behind his back. Tightly. He tried moving his legs and torso and heard the gentle clanging of metal above him. His legs were wrapped in chains, and he was hanging by his feet.

His eyes adjusting to the dark, he could make out where he was. He was atop a water tower. The lack of any lights for miles around told him there were no houses between him and the horizon. He was alone.

His chest heaved with panic.

He craned his head upward to look at the sky. Storm clouds were gathering. He could just make out a crude gibbet running across the top of the tank. He was hanging from its center.

Distant thunder told Major that the weather was deteriorating. It was then he became aware of a persistent, scarcely audible sound. *Drip, drip, drip.* The sound came in two-second intervals. But where was it coming from?

He craned his head to the other side and upward. The blades of a primitive windmill apparatus were turning lazily above him in the breeze. It had been hooked up to a length of rubber hosing. The end lay in a wide metal tray attached to the rim of the water tank. The windmill was clearly designed to operate as a pump—the tray's function was to catch rainwater and funnel it into the tank.

Right now there was only barely a layer of water in the tray—hence the occasional drip sound he heard falling into the tank. But it didn't take a genius to realize that as substantial rain fell, the drips would translate into a torrent, raising the water level dramatically.

"You look as though you could use a smoke right now, Bruce. Maybe it'd help calm those nerves. Nasty habit, though. It's a killer."

The guttural tones hung in the air as though they had wafted out of the black clouds above him. Major couldn't breathe—he was stunned.

That voice—where had he heard it before? Oh, sweet Jesus! That crazy website! The link to that freaky dream guy! The creepy graveled voice!

Seconds passed. The wind was picking up substantially and it was about to rain. He sobbed some more, craning his bloated purple face to try to identify the source of the voice.

"Where are you? You've got to help or I'll drown. I'm up here . . ." His voice trailed off. With no one around for miles, he realized that the source of the voice could only be the sick bastard who had put him in this predicament in the first place.

He stared into the darkness as it started to rain. Not a great deal, but enough to feed the tray. The windmill was now spinning freely and a slow steady stream of water was pouring into the tank. The water level was rising, and soon was less than an inch from the top of his head. Lightning flashed and the rain began to pour down harder.

"Hmmmm," the guttural voice continued, idly assessing the climactic conditions, "looks like a change in the weather. Good for the farmers!"

Major couldn't speak. He knew a monster was out there. He knew he was being toyed with like a cat with a mouse. And the cat was clearly enjoying the game.

"Don't you just love rain?" the voice continued. "Personally I can't get enough of it. A rainstorm? I snuggle up in bed with a good book." He paused. "Or with someone who's read one." A short strange laugh followed. "I've always loved that joke!"

Major's sobs had become so violent now that they were tantamount to a midlevel scream.

"Hey, Bruce, that's some kind of a major boo hoo I'm hearing from you. So I suppose you don't agree with me about rain, do you? I can understand that."

"Please—" Major sobbed like a child. But the guttural voice continued. "Despite our differences, I've enjoyed our time together, brief as it was. You see, unfortunately I now have to leave. I forgot my umbrella and I'll confide in you, I'm fond of this suit. I've had it some time. Classic hand tailoring. Saks. Can't get the same quality now as you could even just a few years back. And heavy rain? Even with a first-class dry clean, rain this steady can damage the nap of the fabric."

"Oh, Jesus. Please—" Major pleaded. "You can't leave me like this."

"Oh, indeed I can, Bruce."

"Why me? What have I done to you?" It took every shred of the little energy Bruce had left to utter the last words that would ever emanate from his blood-engorged lips.

A huge crack of thunder shook the entire structure. The windmill's arms were now revolving as fast as an electric fan. Water was pounding through the rubber hose into the tank. The rain was now practically a monsoon.

"Hang in there, Bruce. I mean, literally." The laugh came again and echoed down into the tank.

There was a click, as if someone had switched off a microphone. The top of Major's head went under the surface of the water. He lifted his head one last time, trying for a few more seconds of precious life, but his body was so bloated with blood he couldn't shift his face more than an inch.

A few seconds more and his nose and mouth fell beneath the surface.

CHAPTER 9

Dermot turned off the closet light. He walked to the bed and climbed in next to Neela. He craned his neck toward her. "You're still reading that shit? I can't believe it. Since when are you into murder and mayhem?"

"I'm not, but that's the whole point," Neela replied. "The closest I ever got was that book on Ian Brady and Mira Hindley—*The Moors Murders*? Remember? Of course, that book was about real killers."

Dermot tossed his robe onto the chair at the end of the bed. "How do you know that this *isn't* real," he chided playfully.

"I don't *think* so," Neela said smiling.

"Why not?

"Come on! Just because someone writes about murder, it doesn't mean they *are* a murderer. How many serial-killer novelists do you know who are actual serial killers?"

"Well, how many serial killers have *you* come across in your life? Give me a break."

Neela just shook her head.

Dermot decided to leave it alone. He knew he was antagonizing Neela now, and she deserved better. He picked up a copy of *Vanity Fair* from his nightstand and flipped through it.

"Dermot, I have to tell you that this book is pretty scary. Primal, visceral stuff. I know the writing is on the far side of crude, but maybe that's what the writer is trying to do—communicate like a cold, calculating serial killer. And he's pulling it off. With every page, I feel more and more in the mind of a sociopath. Seriously. It's as close to real as you can get."

But Dermot wasn't interested in the minds of serial killers right now. He glanced down at his striking wife, whose nightshirt barely fell past her hips, exposing her gorgeous legs. He slipped his hand across the bed to rest it on Neela's thigh. It began to wander.

She halfheartedly batted him away. "Seriously, Dermot. You should take another look here. A closer look."

Dermot turned to face her. She looked delicious. Good enough to eat. He pulled the manuscript away from her.

Neela made a quirky face. "Hey, I was reading that," she said in a mock-serious tone. Dermot gently stroked her, and she felt warm and sexy.

"And you look so hot doing it," Dermot replied and moved in closer.

"Dermot," she said, playfully giving in.

"No, really. Just watching you flipping those pages—it'd make any Benedictine monk reach for a homemade liqueur."

She closed her eyes and he tossed the manuscript to the floor. She accepted his kiss as he flicked open a condom wrapper with one hand, a trick he'd learned to master over the years.

Aware of what he was doing, this time Neela didn't rebuke him.

CHAPTER 10

Abel Conway pulled over to the side of the road and parked the cab, craning his head upward as he looked through the windshield at the ugly housing project.

He usually avoided taking fares anywhere east of North Hollywood, but it'd been a slow morning so he'd accepted the call from dispatch. Now he regretted it.

He looked again at the tall building. No way could he simply honk the horn and wait. The old girl would never hear it up on the seventeenth floor. She wouldn't even hear it if she'd occupied a ground floor apartment facing the street—Artie had told him she was in her seventies, practically deaf, and couldn't take a step without her walker.

"Fuck," he muttered. Abel's face clouded. The seventeenth. You might just as well have informed him that a million dollars was waiting for him on top of Everest. Abel was terrified of heights. As a kid he never climbed trees, he avoided windows above ground-floor level, and never ever flew in a plane. Even climbing a ladder to paint the ceiling left a cramped, panicked feeling in the pit of his stomach. In a recurring nightmare he'd had as a child, he was standing on the top of a flagpole, and nothing was visible below him but billows of clouds. A light breeze blew in his face, making it difficult for him to keep his balance. As the wind picked up he felt more and more unstable, and fear turned to panic. Then to terror. The end of the dream varied. In one version, an Airbus screamed past him, the tips of its wings practically touching his face. In another, a giant condor flew into his face and he toppled backwards into the abyss.

"If you can't get to a damned taxi without my help—don't fucking call one," he muttered to himself and stepped out of the cab to look at the entrance to the decrepit building. It was so rundown in fact, he wondered why it hadn't been condemned, and why anyone would actually be living here.

Conway pushed the two big front doors inwards and walked into the lobby, where debris littered the hallway—empty soda bottles, pizza boxes, even a used condom. A line of dried urine stained the wall from waist height to a semidried crystallized yellow lake on the floor. It was only half evaporated.

Conway gazed at the elevator buttons. It was decision time. Take the ride and maybe make thirty bucks? Or forget it, and annoy dispatch sufficiently to leave him off the call list for the rest of the week? He took a deep breath and hit the Up button. An archaic whirr emanated from somewhere in the guts of the building.

"Tasco's sister takes it any way you want it!" a recently painted bit of graffiti stated. A cell phone number was scratched in the metal beneath it. "Ski junkie? Give Head for Xmas!" read another.

As he waited, it occurred to him that he hadn't seen a soul in the building since his arrival. But that wasn't possible. Surely Artie would know if the building were condemned? The old bat *had* to be upstairs—somewhere.

There was a dull thump as the ancient elevator hit the ground floor and stalled. The doors opened—painfully slowly.

Everything about this place was creepy, so much so that Abel half expected the doors to reveal a ghoul carrying a chainsaw that dripped blood. But the living dead he could deal with. Getting into the elevator and hitting that button and gliding up, that was another matter entirely.

The doors closed. Abel pressed the button for the seventeenth floor, breathing deeply and regularly—a friend had recently suggested that controlled breathing would relax him and help him deal with his phobia. The elevator crawled and shuddered its way upward. But despite the breathing, he was sweating like a pig. The sooner he was out of this place with the old lady in the back of his cab, the better.

The elevator shuddered again and stopped. He looked at the floor indicator. It had halted on the thirteenth floor. "Shit! And shit some more!" he said, hitting the seventeenth button again and again with no effect. The doors opened with a slight hiss.

Abel poked his head out into the corridor and looked around. He wasn't expecting carpet or fancy furniture, but neither was he expecting to see the window at the end of the hallway missing entirely—frame and all.

The wind blew in through the empty window, howling down the corridor and sending dust, scraps of paper, and other filth whirling around like tumbleweed in a dust storm.

What should he do? Head back downstairs? Walk up to the seventeenth floor and find the old lady? As he debated, the doors began to slide together and with some relief, he pulled his head back inside.

The car jerked and began to ascend. Abel smiled. It was plain dumb to be so scared. He tried to take his mind off the reality of his situation. He'd try being the devil's advocate. How often did elevators drop and kill everyone inside? About as often as jets crashed. But then, jets crashed someplace around the world almost on a weekly basis . . .

The elevator halted for the second time with such a lurch that Abel was startled. He looked at the floor indicator. This time it was the sixteenth floor. The doors slid open again.

"Fuck with me some more, won't you?" he said, craning his head out of the elevator and looking into the hallway.

This corridor was even dingier and filthier that the lower one. Graffiti covered all the walls; gang tags everywhere. An old garbage can stood next to the elevator and the smell of vomit was intense.

Abel decided to use the fire stairs to get to the next floor. As he stepped out of the elevator, he noticed that the window frame at the end of this floor was also missing. He pushed open the filthy door that led to the stairway and started up the cement steps.

The seventeenth floor was no surprise. It was the same as the previous two. No windows, wind blowing down the hall, litter everywhere. There was also a dead rat. Surely no one could live here. Maybe the old lady had no choice? He almost felt a twinge of pity as he made his way down the hallway, checking out the names on the buttons by the doors.

He stopped at a door and read a small handwritten nameplate. "Haven-camp. That's it!"

He pushed the bell under the name. He couldn't hear it ringing inside so he knocked heavily on the door and called out. "Miss Havencamp? Your cab's waiting!"

Still there was silence, just the wind blowing bits of garbage past his feet.

"Hey, snooze and lose, lady. That's what they say. Open up or I'm gone. You hear me?"

Just then he heard a deep growl down the hallway. His head whipped around and he saw them—two massive rottweilers. Their bodies were pulsating with excitement, waiting for a signal to attack. Their muzzles were stretched tightly upward, revealing razor-sharp teeth.

Abel stopped in his tracks and averted his gaze downwards—he knew that to lock eyes with vicious dogs would only make them more excited. He also knew he had no chance if they decided to go for him. What the fuck were two attack dogs doing on the seventeenth floor of a derelict building? How had they gotten there? And how was he going to get around them?

As if reacting to some inaudible command, both sets of ears pricked up and the pair moved several feet closer to Abel. Then they halted—again as if on command.

Okay, tiptoeing around them wasn't an option. Nor was confrontation—though the trash can might help him defend himself, if he could get to it.

Abel attempted an easy reassuring smile, keeping both animals in his peripheral vision. "Easy, fellas," he cooed, trying not to show fear. "Where did you come from, huh? Lost your daddy? What are your names? Boy, you both look cute as hell."

Inching to his right he grasped for the trash can. Very slowly he lifted it until he had it in front of his chest. The dogs didn't react. Twenty feet separated them. There was nothing to do but inch toward the elevator and hope against hope that this time it would function properly and allow him inside before the dogs broke and savaged him.

Ten feet. Nine. Eight. It was looking really good. Seven, six, five, four, three. Still the dogs remained motionless. It was looking better and better.

He reached out a hand, the forefinger extended toward the elevator button. Suddenly there was a loud *ping!* and the doors opened without his finger having made any contact. A rush of relief and gratitude coursed through Abel's body—the damned thing was working! Most probably it was still reacting to his command of several minutes earlier. He backed towards the open doors, still cooing to the dogs. "That's right, fellas. I gotta go *do* stuff. You have a good day, okay?"

It was only as his right foot touched inside the car that he heard the snarls behind him. Without turning he knew he was trapped—there were two more dogs behind him, inside the elevator.

Two dogs behind—two in the corridor, guarding the fire stairs.

"I hate my life," he murmured.

What the hell were his options now? None. Wait it out? Maybe. But that was simply waiting to be savaged to death. Clearly someone had to be orchestrating this macabre scene—but who, and why? Maybe his ex?

"Hey, Gina?" he called aloud. "Is that you? Look, I know I fucked up. I should have stopped when you said to stop. I know that. But hey, up to that moment it seemed to me we were both into it like—" He thought better about coming up with some asinine simile. "How was I supposed to *know*?"

There was no reply. All Abel heard were the low snarls of the hounds, the wind whipping in through the open windows and the occasional drip of rottweiler drool hitting the naked cement.

The window—that was his single remaining option. Abel could scarcely believe he was considering it. What was he going to do? Fly out like a bird?

Half a minute passed. Then the dogs' ears pricked a second time. Their bodies trembled and Abel knew it had to be the window. Hell, he was going to die horribly, anyway. Maybe he could leap to the opposite building. Had he been in a fire situation he'd have jumped through the window rather than burn alive—so what was the difference?

It took him two minutes to inch backward to the open window. He could feel the wind blowing on the nape of his neck. He made a slow half turn and glanced down. He may as well have been looking down from the viewing platform of the Empire State Building. There was no way he could contemplate diving out. No way. He was white with fear. He'd wait. He'd have to. Maybe the dogs wouldn't attack. Who knew?

Then all four dogs began to pad forward. There was no doubt about their intentions. They were coming in for the kill. What chance did he stand against them? One dog, maybe. Four? None.

Abel instinctively lifted a hand to his throat. That'd be the first target. He glanced out the window again. The building opposite was another deserted tenement. It was similar to the one he was in, but had a metal fire escape bolted to the bricks, leading all the way up and down the building. It was perhaps only ten feet away across the chasm. Could he make it if he jumped?

The dogs were only a few feet from him when he stepped onto the sill. His heart rate had risen to an explosive level. Abel balanced himself, bracing his arms against both sides of the open window. He focused only on the fire escape opposite his building.

Well, here we go. Abel crossed himself as his tears flowed. *Good-bye cruel world,* he thought with a wry smile.

The dogs broke and lunged at him. He leaped.

Abel flew through the air with exceptional grace—considering he was forty-five years old and out of shape. Self-preservation does strange things to the human body. Acts that appear impossible become feasible. His right hand made contact with the bottom rail of the metal ladder and his fingers curled over the rung. Then his left hand slid and lost its grip. He swung like a puppet left and right three times before he could secure his free hand to the ladder and hoist one leg over another metal rail. He couldn't believe he was still alive. He screamed with joy, completely oblivious to the one hundred and fifty foot drop to the sidewalk below.

Now his tears flowed freely. He had conquered his phobia. It was a magnificent moment!

Whoaaaaah!!! I fuckin' made it! I fuckin' made it. I'm never going to be afraid of heights again. No way. I can do anything now!!!

He looked up at the window and at the four hounds from Hades staring down at him, their jaws snapping, snarling with rage. "Guess I have to disappoint you, boys," he quipped at the animals. "Go eat Miss Havencamp—first door to the fuckin' left behind you," he shouted.

As Abel worked to hoist his other leg onto the fire ladder he heard a low, guttural voice.

"Very impressive, Mr. Conway."

The voice took him by surprise. He quickly looked around. *Who the fuck?* There was no one at the window, and no one at the windows below him or above him in the building he'd just reached.

"Given your age and weight, I honestly didn't think you were going to make it. But it made the day interesting. You surprised me."

Abel scanned every inch of both buildings to find the source of the voice. It was somehow disembodied. Then he saw a tiny speaker hanging from a windowsill above him.

"That was quite some circus trick. If I were a promoter, I'd sign you up right here and now."

"Who the hell are you? Help me, for Christ's sake."

"Who am I? Come on. Sharpen up, dumbo. I'm the Dream Healer, Abel. You remember *me*, surely."

Thoughts scudded through Abel's brain. The Dream Healer? *Who the hell?* Then it came to him. That guy on the Internet! The card he'd been given in the street. That strange online chat room with the dark spooky guy he'd figured was one sick fuck.

Breathless and exhausted, Abel hooked his second leg to the metal and called out. "You did this to me? Go fuck yourself! What the hell did I ever do to *you*?"

There was no reply.

"Look, you help me and I'll be your freakin' slave for life. Just help me inside, will you? Please."

"There's no way I would ever consider saving a driver as poor as you, Abel."

Abel was suddenly aware of the strange metal squeal above his head. He looked up and was stricken with terror. One of the metal bolts securing the ladder to the building was breaking off. Metal fatigue? Nah. A rivet popped out. Then a second. It was coming apart.

The fire escape began to give way. Abel felt his lifeline lurch beneath him as the metal broke free and he began to fall.

CHAPTER 11

Dermot was just finishing breakfast when Neela walked into the kitchen and lay the manuscript on the countertop.

"You still reading that trash?" he asked.

"And what kept *you* up all night?" Neela replied. Dermot had stayed up watching a late-night movie, then read till dawn.

"If I can't write anything intelligent, I might as well read something intelligent written by others. Something with a bit of intellectual credibility."

"And that was?"

"Margaret Atwood, not Crazy Harry."

"His name's Albert K. Arnold," Neela reminded him.

"Well, of course. A.K.A."

"Maybe it's a nom de plume."

"You don't say."

Neela could see he was in one of his dark sarcastic moods so she backed off, at the same time chiding herself. Why did men think that it was a wife's place to back down? It was really starting to bug her, how many times she gave in to his moody behavior.

"So what if he's calling himself A.K.A.?"

"Well, possibly he's hiding something?"

"Really? You think all writers who use a name other than their own have some dark secret? Mark Twain, Lewis Carroll, George Eliot, Anatole France—Molière, for God's sake? Do you take issue with Amandine Dupin calling herself George Sand and pretending she was a man? Maybe you think she was a sexual deviant."

"Don't be ridiculous. How can you talk of this idiot's attempts at writing and refer to Molière, Twain, and Sand in the same breath?"

Instead of jumping at him, like she wanted to do, she regained her composure again, and tried to switch the mood in the room. "You want some fresh coffee?"

"Sure. That'd be good."

She watched him. He was tense, no question. And he was getting worse. "Have you thought about calling Dr. Fineman?" she asked, offering Dermot his coffee with one hand and massaging the back of his neck with the other. She knew the question might irritate him, but it had to be done.

Dermot's answer was as dismissive as usual. "I don't need a fucking shrink, baby. Inspiration! That's what I need."

Neela continued to massage his neck calmly. "I'm just concerned, honey. It's been a bad few months, and I can see the pressure being heaped on you. So maybe it's best to just chuck this manuscript into the dumpster and relax."

She paused. "I don't want to lose you again."

Dermot looked up. "Christ, Neela, that was eight years ago."

He'd been two years into writing *The Devil and the Hindmost* and had run dry two-thirds of the way through. Esther had berated him for beginning a novel without the slightest idea how to conclude it, which only made things worse. After six months of emotional turmoil, Dermot vanished off the face of the earth. Neela had come home to discover he'd packed a suitcase and disappeared. Despite her best efforts, even hiring a detective, Neela hadn't been able to find him.

Then one day he'd returned, full of remorse and apologies. Where he went, they never knew, but he brought back with him the finished manuscript of his new novel. Dr. Fineman maintained he'd simply had an "episode," and had probably done the best thing he could by cutting himself free of everyone for a while.

"Besides, the novel made my reputation. Without it, who knows if I'd have won with *Incoming Tide*? You've got to be conspicuous to even be considered for awards."

He pointed to the manuscript on the counter. "So, what exactly are you suggesting here? You want me to write stuff like this?"

"You need to write *something*. Maybe you could try your hand at this genre. Just give it a try."

At lunchtime Dermot and Neela headed to the Flower Street Cafe and Sports Bar on Wilshire to meet Nick. The thrust of the conversation hadn't changed, so Nick danced around the delicate subject of Dermot's writer's block with incredible diplomacy.

"To a certain extent, I'm with Neela," Nick said, finishing a burger and shoestring fries. "Why not at least consider the genre. Stephen King's a very rich man. Suppose another truck nails him? He could go down for good. Somebody's going to have to pick up the torch." Nick chuckled as he took a sip of his pinot grigio. "It's the manuscript that weirdo sent you, isn't it?"

"Well, it got Neela thinking. She thinks it's clever. In fact, *very* clever—despite its primitive facade."

"Yes, I do," Neela rolled her eyes. "Go make a federal case."

The waitress came with the check. Both Nick and Dermot reached for their wallets.

"No," Nick said, "I'll get this one. My treat."

"No way Nick—we go Dutch," Dermot said good-naturedly. "I'm not completely down and out yet. When I am, I'll let you know."

"Okay, remember to do that."

The waitress smiled a big thank you for the tip they left.

"That manuscript's disturbing," Dermot continued. "I hate it more each time I dip into it."

Nick held up a hand. "Dermot. Hear me out. Suppose you write a book that disturbs *everyone*, but they just have to read it. They can't help themselves. What's that make it? A hit? A best seller? An Edgar award winner?"

"My point in a nutshell, Nick. It'd help a lot if Giselle were still here to help Dermot. I know, I don't do a bad job, but she and Dermot really made music."

A dark cloud passed over Nick's face. She placed a hand on his. "I'm sorry. I didn't mean to . . ."

"No, it's cool," he replied lightly. "I'd hate it if you felt you couldn't talk about her. Don't worry. I'm glad we think about her as often as we do. I do, twenty-four/seven. Minute by minute." He looked up at his friends. "I know I'd never have made it without you two. I'd have gone stark raving nuts. So now I'm here for you guys. Now and always."

"Thanks," Dermot answered. He couldn't think of a single clever thing to say.

CHAPTER 12

The Dream Healer sat in his darkened shed waiting for his computer to boot up. It flashed blue, then the desktop revealed itself—a closeup photograph of a dead man's face. The skin color was grayish blue. The eyes were open, and the eyeballs turned upwards. The mouth was open wide as if frozen in some rictus of sudden death—possibly a final terrible scream.

The Dream Healer clicked on Yahoo, then pulled down a list of favorites and chose www.worstnightmares.net. Bosch's triptych presented. A password, another click on a link and a young girl's face filled the screen. She was chubby, pretty, with full pink lips and the slightest touch of acne—but not enough to spoil her pubescent good looks. She looked fifteen, but could easily have been twelve.

"Speak to me," the Dream Healer cooed encouragingly.

The young girl's face positively shone with delight.

"Hi! Are you really there? Are you the Dream Healer? I've been waiting so long."

"You are aware there's a Dream Healer link for those moments I am not personally online? You can leave your message there as a video."

"Oh, yes—but that's not the same. That's not scary enough."

The Dream Healer chuckled and studied the girl's face. Not scary enough? Perhaps he should help her out—give her a scare she'd never forget.

"My name's Cheryl."

"Speak to me, Cheryl," the Dream Healer whispered.

Cheryl giggled. Immediately the Dream Healer's estimation of twelve dropped to ten. Much too young.

"Want to hear my nightmare? It's *real* scary. Something that'll make you hard and horny!"

So saying, Cheryl slipped her T-shirt over her head and her fingers unfastened her brassiere. She had huge breasts. The Dream Healer made a quick reappraisal. She had to be fifteen, or else have some congenital deformity.

The Dream Healer's finger hit the escape key, and Cheryl, along with the Bosch, dissolved, returning him to his home page.

"Shame on your parents," he muttered, linking back to the page of people waiting to speak to him online.

This time a Mediterranean-looking girl filled the screen. She was positively ugly. Thirty-something and gaunt, with what looked like an open sore on the side of her nose. "This is Wanda."

"Speak to me, Wanda."

Her drawn face actually almost lit up. Another desperate freak who'd been waiting to speak to him personally.

"Well, my dream goes like this—" She hesitated, unsure how to explain. "Maybe I should start by telling you about my friend, Damian?"

"If you like. Tell me about Damian, Wanda."

"Well, he was my best friend at school. Then he had the accident."

"What accident, my dear? It has some relevance?"

"Yes, it does. It's all sooooooo sad."

The Dream Healer didn't respond. He waited.

"He was windsurfing and he didn't know there was this sandbank. So there was an accident and he broke his neck. Now he's in a wheelchair. He can't move at all, like—" She searched for the correct word. "Like he's a quadriplegic? The only thing he can do is blow down a plastic tube. It's awful! But really. Gross."

The Dream Healer watched the tears pour down her cheeks. "So you dream of your friend?"

"No, that's the horrible thing. I dream about *myself*. In my dream I wake up and it's *me* that's in the wheelchair. First, I wonder what's happening— like, where is Damian? And what am I doing sitting in his wheelchair? That's when I try to move . . ." Her voice faltered.

"So what happens next?"

"I wonder why I can't move, and that's when I see I have no legs."

The Dream Healer smiled. *Original.* "Then?"

I try to reach down and that's when I see I don't have arms, either. I am just a blob—a torso with a head. I start screaming!"

The Dream Healer gazed at Wanda's grotesque face. "And let me guess . . . You try to wake yourself up but you can't."

"Right." Her tone was desperate.

"And you try to scream very loudly and nothing comes out?"

"Exactly! How did you know?"

"I am the Dream Healer, my dear. I know these things. And I can heal you."

"But how?"

"Before you go to sleep each night, you must say out loud: 'I am who I am. I have two legs and two arms. I can move any time I wish.'"

Wanda repeated the words exactly.

"Very good. Now, when you have this very same dream in the future, you'll awaken and see yourself as you really are."

"Oh, *please*, yes!"

"And each night before you go to bed you must say, 'Dream Healer, heal my nightmare world. Come to me in my reverie and give me peace.'"

Wanda reached for a ballpoint and began to write down his words. "How many times must I say this, Dream Healer?"

"Each time you go to sleep. You will not be cured overnight. But I assure you, you will receive rest—very soon. The Dream Healer will come to you."

Wanda managed to smile and snivel at the same time.

"I can't thank you enough, Dream Healer."

"There's no need for that, my dear. But now, I have to go."

The Dream Healer hit a key and Wanda was gone.

He hit the power button. Blackness.

CHAPTER 13

Dermot sat at his desk, reading Arnold's manuscript. Nick sat across from him at Neela's smaller desk, idly checking a sales invoice he'd taken out of his wallet.

"How much of this have you read?" asked Dermot.

Nick looked up. "I actually haven't read a single word—just listened to the passages Neela read aloud to me. What's it about?"

"He used the fear of impotence of some guy called Gareth Nash as a way to kill him."

"Sexual?"

"No. That's what makes it interesting. It's the terror of being unable to help save his wife. Here, listen. 'I have been watching Nash for some days. I've never seen such devotion of a husband for his wife. His nightmare is based on irrational fears. He tells me that sometimes he dreams he's on a cliff top watching his wife slip and fall, unable to reach out. In another, his wife's stepping off the pavement and Nash sees a truck barreling towards her, but he can't pull her back in time. Whoosh tack! She's pasted to the grille of an eighteen-wheeler.'"

"How does the guy twist this nightmare?"

"I'll skip down a few pages. 'I tied Nash and his wife to stakes while they were drugged,'" Dermot continued. "'I used succinylcholine. Works really well. The best part is that they are still conscious, can feel pain, but are unable to move. When I put them in the trunk of their car, I laid them face-to-face. This would be the last time they'd be close enough to kiss each other good-bye. Of course, actual kissing was out of the question—I'd taped their mouths just in case they decided to call out for help. It made me laugh seeing them staring at each other like that—all doe-eyed. I could smell the fear.'"

"Jesus." Nick's brow furrowed.

"Wait. It gets worse."

"You're kidding."

"'Nash was fat. It took a while to strap him upright to the wooden stake I'd prepared earlier. His body kept sliding down the pole. But I got him upright in the end. All the while he was just staring at me, pleading with his eyes. As if I was about to let him go! "Dream on fatso," I told him. "Look what I'm going to do to your beautiful wife." He looked crazed. Of course, he still couldn't move a muscle. I laughed out loud.'"

"How do people come up with these sick ideas?"

"It's a *book*, Nick. Some people thought Bram Stoker was demented when he wrote *Dracula*. But Stoker had literary style. This man has none."

"What happens next?"

"'So I start in on the woman, Laura. Not bad looking. I start taking her clothes off, and I can see Nash watching. At this stage he was getting some feeling back into his arms and upper body—I can tell, because he started to strain against the ropes.' You sure you want to hear more?"

Nick sipped his beer. "Sure."

"'She urinated, which annoyed me, but there was no turning back. I lifted her naked body upright against the stake and strapped her tight, same as her husband, so she could look directly across at him. Then I asked Nash how he felt. He's straining hard against the ropes, bucking like a horse, and his face contorted with rage.'"

"You're right. This stuff is revolting and it has no literary merit. What's the point of going on?"

"The point is that millions of people are fascinated by this kind of thing. People swept away by tidal waves, amateur footage of the bombings in Bali played again and again for no particular reason but sensationalism. You can buy countless sick DVDs out there—planes plowing into crowds of women and children at air shows, buildings collapsing on passersby. Look at the Twin Towers footage—how many times have you seen that? The Falling Man? My God, television current affairs shows now end each program begging viewers to send in sensational shots of disasters taken with their cell phones! So, yes—there's a real market for this. In that respect, Arnold knows what he's doing."

Nick didn't reply. He knew it was true. The story fascinated him in a grotesque way, too.

"You want me to read on?"

Nick nodded.

"'As the sun goes down, I lay a fire and break out the cooking stuff. Nash is moaning, and the woman hasn't stopped crying since I strapped her up. Her skin's been fried by the sun—her whole body's a nasty blotchy livid red. I eat a couple of chorizos. Pan-fried. My, they were good. I reckoned it was a waste of time offering any sausages to the Nashes—most likely they know they are going to die soon, so they won't have much of an appetite.

"'Around ten I wash up the fry pan. The woman's wailing is getting to me. I can't stand that kind of weakness. So I get out my bowie knife, pull out her tongue . . .'"

"Okay, I think I get the idea . . ."

Dermot laughed lightly. "Hey, it's only a book!" he said, imitating Nick's voice. "That's what you said before."

Nick shrugged his shoulders.

"Well, that's what Neels thinks I should write, so that we can afford to go to dinner more often."

"I don't think that's quite what she meant," Nick replied. "The way I see it, she wants you to write a hard-edged scary thriller in this genre but give it your own voice."

"Oh really?" Dermot snapped. "That's the way *you* see it?"

Nick could see that Dermot was becoming fractious. "Look, I've got to run. My client wants to see the Choma I bought today."

Dermot's edge immediately softened. "You sure you have to leave right now? Neela'll be home soon. She's going to fix some lemon calamari for dinner. Why not stay?"

"I gotta go. I'll call you later."

Just as Nick was heading for the door, the telephone rang.

"Dermot Nolan. Who's this?"

Half a second passed without a reply. Dermot cupped the receiver with his hand and called out excitedly to Nick. "Come back. It's him!"

Nick headed back as Dermot enabled the speakerphone. The voice had the same guttural timbre to it as before—like Jack Palance with a bad attack of bronchitis.

"My name is Albert, Mr. Nolan. Albert Kent Arnold."

"Was it you who delivered a manuscript to me?"

"Through suffering cometh salvation," came the reply.

"Yes, I know. It was in the manuscript."

"My diary. It's a day-by-day diary. Not a manuscript." The words came in a halting fashion.

"Okay, a diary then. Was it you who sat next to me on the train?"

"You will never know true sorrow without suffering true loss." The voice sang the line, as an Islamic cleric might call the faithful to prayer from a minaret. "You will never know true sorrow without suffering true loss."

"Yeah, sure. I know. Maybe you need a new stand-up routine. This one's getting old."

A slight hesitation. Then— "Mock me at your peril, Mr. Nolan."

"All right. I apologize." He shot a look at Nick, who was grinning hugely. Clearly he'd enjoyed Dermot's joke if Arnold hadn't. "What do you want, Mr. Arnold?"

"Publish my diary."

"Look, Arnie. I'm a writer, not a publisher."

Arnold cut him short. "Mr. Booker Prize Winner—get my diary *published*!" There was a moment's hesitation and a rustling of paper somewhere. "The written word belongs to everyone, not just to those who are connected, not just to big-time agents. Suffering is my watchword. Let ordinary people know the reality of extreme suffering through my diary. Let it help them appreciate the exquisite moment of their own death."

Dermot made a swirling motion with his fingers at Nick. *Blah, blah, blah.*

"What the hell are you talking about? You think I've got nothing better to do than spend my time publishing your diary? Dream on, buddy."

More background rustling paper noise.

"I know for a fact you have nothing better to do. You don't have one original thought in your head. That is your current suffering. Meanwhile, I have no mechanism to get my work published. Only you can ensure my words are brought to the world. It is up to you to convince your editor, your publisher, your publicist, your agents, your people. Do it!"

"Look, Arnold Kent, it doesn't work that way. And even if it did—"

Again the guttural voice cut Dermot short. "You call me Arnold Kent once more and you and your pretty wife will regret it. Respect me. My name is Arnold. As must be obvious to you, it is a pen name—and besides, my feeling is that you refer to me this way because you are patronizing me. Do *not* do so."

Nick made a gesture, coupled with an appeasing expression: Humor the guy—don't get his back up. Dermot nodded agreement. At the same time, he was seething at being threatened by this bizarre man. *You and your pretty wife will live to regret it?* If he'd been face-to-face with Arnold, he'd have punched the guy right in the teeth.

"Hey, you don't have much of a sense of humor, do you, buddy?"

More rustling of papers. What was this guy doing? Lighting a bonfire?

"Those who are about to die seldom smile," the voice spat out the words as if they were a famous quotation.

"Who said that?"

"I did."

"You are about to die?"

The voice didn't answer the question. "Meet me in front of the People's Bank Building on South Hill in twenty minutes. You will bear witness to my final statement. My worst nightmare—my life, that is—will be extinguished, granting immortality to my work, which will then be entrusted to you to shepherd."

Dermot's face darkened. He'd just about had enough of this crazy man. "Arnie? This conversation is over!"

"No, Mr. Nolan. Not yet. We haven't spoken of your wife yet."

Dermot's face blanched. What the fuck was he talking about now?

"That's right," the voice continued. "Maybe Neela should make a statement along *with* me."

Dermot's tone suddenly took on a harsh, panicked edge. "I swear, if you even touch my wife—"

A beat of silence.

"You'll what?" he replied. "Twenty minutes, Mr. Nolan. And please— no cops."

Dermot heard a click, then the drone of the dial tone. A second later he ran for the door, grabbing his cell phone from the desktop as he did so.

"Nick, stay here! If he's lying and she turns up, call me immediately."

Dermot was flying out the door as Nick called out to him. "You know where she is right now?"

"Should be at the museum. Try calling her. I'll do the same if I can!"

He ran to the car, ripped open the door, fired it up, and screamed off up the street, burning rubber.

Dermot hung a right onto West Fifth Street. He could see a red light ahead at the intersection. No time for lights—he snaked around three cars that were hitting the brakes, shot through the intersection on the red, causing two cars on the green to smack each other. Dermot didn't even notice the mayhem he'd left behind; one hand was on the wheel, the other hitting the buttons on his cell.

"Come on, damn it! Pick up, Neels. Pick up!!!" he yelled.

The lights were thankfully with him as he shot across Olive. He must've been doing over ninety. He made the lights at South Hill on the last second of yellow and wrenched the wheel right—not soon enough for the Peugeot, which slewed sideways until Dermot corrected the skid and barreled on up toward the People's Bank.

Finally he saw the impressive art deco People's Bank Building standing up ahead. He stood on the brakes; the ABS system kicked in and the car shuddered to a stop.

Dermot leaped from the car and ran across the street. There were a few cars parked, but little or no traffic. He stared upwards towards the top of the twenty-story building, scanning it from left to right. He saw no movement. Then he caught sight of a tiny figure standing on the parapet of the rooftop looking down. Against the skyline he couldn't make out anything more definitive than the fact that it was a human. There was also a faint shadow behind the figure—another person perhaps? Dermot's heart sank. He saw the fire escape at the far side of the building and raced toward it.

"Jesus! Please God, not Neels!" he cried out aloud as he clambered up the metal ladder, floor by floor, racing to the rooftop.

As he stepped onto the roof, his chest was burning from the effort. He stared around—no one.

It was then he heard the long, drawn-out scream from the far side of the roof. He ran to the edge, just in time to see a figure flailing past the final two stories of the building, legs and arms held out wide. The man hit the roadway below with a scarcely audible thump.

Dermot looked around the rooftop in desperation. Where was Neela? Could she still be here somewhere?

"Neela!" he screamed, racing back to the fire escape.

Twenty seconds later he was back on the ground.

Evidently no one else had seen the figure fall, so Dermot was initially alone beside the crumpled body.

The head had exploded, like a watermelon struck by a shotgun, sending brain and tissue in every direction. The dead man had bright orange hair and was wearing a brown long-rider's coat.

Dermot gazed at the remains silently. Then he became aware of people shouting from windows up and down the street.

Confused about what to do next, Dermot stood stock-still. There was no immediate hurry—mouth-to-mouth was hardly an option here. There was little or no discernible mouth left. The face was a paste of ground bone, sinew, and blood.

His cell phone chirped. Relief flooded through him and his knees nearly crumbled.

"Neels! Thank God. I've been trying to reach you. Where are you?"

"I'm just leaving the office." She paused. "What's going on? You sound panicked. What's wrong?"

"Everything's fine. *I'm* fine. Look, I'll tell you everything when I get home. Nick can fill you in. I'll be there soon."

He clicked off, slipped the cell phone into his pocket, and stared numbly at the body. Cars had now stopped in the street, and drivers were stepping out of their vehicles, staring in fascination. Dermot saw one young man on his cell, presumably calling 9-1-1—a response that prompted him to wonder why he hadn't done the same. It should have been an instinctive response to seeing someone fall from a building.

He heard sirens approaching and crouched down again beside the body. It was immediately apparent there was probably no bone bigger than a chicken's wishbone that wasn't broken. But the orange hair was unmistakable, as was the dirty brown long-rider's coat. It was the vagrant who'd delivered the manuscript all right—the man who'd sat next to him on the subway.

A voice behind him barked. "Sir! Please step away. Right now." It was a uniformed patrolman. Dermot backed away.

Dermot turned and faced the cop. A black and white was now parked across South Hill. An ambulance snaked its way past two more cruisers and came to a halt close to the corpse. Two paramedics ran to the body and crouched near the crumpled mess to see what they could do. A third cop car arrived and pulled up close to the ambulance. The uniformed cop studied Dermot as other police taped off the street.

"Did you see him jump, sir?"

Dermot's instincts for self-preservation kicked in. "No, I was walking by and I saw something hit the street. Then I saw it was an old man. That's all."

"You know this person, Mr.—?"

"Dolan. No, I don't."

"Right. Well, can you please stand behind the line? And sir, please wait a bit—I'll need a statement."

"But all I saw was the guy hitting the street," Dermot protested.

"Just try to help me, sir. What'd you say your name was?"

It was clear the cop hadn't recognized him. "Dolan. Thomas Dolan," Dermot replied. He then walked back towards the tape, slowly headed to his car, got in, and backed up the street. Seconds later he was gone.

CHAPTER 14

"You told them what?"

Dermot had been home less than five minutes. He was in the kitchen with Nick and Neela, and they had all just finished stiff drinks. Dermot was still trembling. "Why lie about your identity? I don't get it. It could land you in a heap of trouble."

"How? The cop had no idea who I was."

"But you were a witness, for heaven's sake. You saw everything. Where's your social conscience? If something had happened to me—like I'd been raped—and someone saw everything but decided to just disappear, what would you think of him?"

"But it wasn't you. And what the fuck did I see? I saw some street person fall from the top of the People's Bank and trash himself. I didn't see him pushed!"

Neela wasn't going to buy into this logic. "Oh, really? Just one guy was up there? And you saw him jump? Or had he already started to fall?"

"When I looked down he was already most of the way down."

"So he could have been pushed?"

"If he had been, then whoever pushed him would have been damn quick getting away or I would have seen him."

"But it's possible?" This time it was Nick asking the question. "Is there an internal stairwell?"

"I don't know. I imagine so."

"Whatever." Neela was upset now. "That man was a human being— you make it sound as though the death of a street person isn't important."

"I never said that, for Christ's sake!"

"But why say your name was Dolan?" Neela insisted. "Sounds to me as though you were already thinking of stealing the man's concept."

"Thank you so much! Your support is overwhelming. Now we're talking about stealing ideas. Just remember it was you who planted that seed!"

"Did anyone see you on the roof?" Nick asked.

"I don't know. I wasn't looking at anything except the man falling. I was thinking of Neela."

Nick placed a hand on Dermot's shoulder. "Hang in there, Dermot. I appreciate how you feel now, having seen what you did. But Neela's just asking why you didn't stop and tell the police what happened. And why you called yourself Thomas Dolan."

Dermot finished his Jack Daniel's and held the glass out to Nick. "Refill this and I'll tell you both. Okay?"

Nick gave him another three fingers of bourbon.

"My brain's seriously fucked up right now. I felt bad enough before when the only thing on my mind was bankruptcy, selling the house, and owing Wasserman a million-dollar advance. Then along comes some fruitcake with a crude Gogol-style Diary of a Serial Killer, and I'm reading stuff that chills the blood. The next minute I'm watching brains explode onto the pavement. How the hell would *you* feel?"

No one said anything.

"I wonder if either of you has any idea of the real the ramifications of this mess. Has either of you given it any serious thought?" Dermot continued, now on a roll. "Frankly it staggers me that you can be so naive."

"Okay, enough of the abuse," Neela said. "Make your point."

"The guy that jumped was the guy that put the manuscript in our mailbox, the same one that sat next to me in the subway and who called me here less than an hour ago." He paused for effect. "Am I beginning to get through here?"

"But that's not exactly accurate," Neela interjected. "The man you saw splattered in the road looked like the same guy you saw outside our house and in the subway. But his face was hamburger meat—right? How can you be sure it was him?"

"Give me a break, honey. The same coat, the same damn dyed orange hair? It was him!"

"But he also intimated Neela was with him," Nick interrupted, looking at Neela.

"Again not entirely accurate, Nick. We thought that at the time, but as I remember now, he merely suggested that Neela should make a final statement similar to his—not that she would actually be there with him when he jumped."

Nick had to admit that was true.

Neela prodded Dermot further. "Let's get back to why you lied about seeing nothing, and about your name. Why did you do that?"

"I don't know. I think I just didn't want any publicity. I didn't want to get involved."

"Bullshit, honey." Her tone was not so much angry as resolute. She simply wanted to understand Dermot's reasoning. "You know that's not true. Any publicity right now would be great."

"One time Booker winner witnesses suicide? That's going to help fire up my career?"

"Okay, I get your point. Then tell us at least what was going through your mind when the patrolman asked you those questions?"

Dermot sighed heavily and smiled. He felt like he was humoring children. "You still don't get it do you—either of you?"

"Okay. We're agreed. We just don't get it," Neela replied with a long-suffering tone. "Does that make you happy? Right. Now fill us idiots in, will you?"

"Ever since Arnold placed his manuscript—or rather his diary of bestiality—in our mailbox, you've spent every waking hour telling me it's the most commercial piece of shit writing you've ever read. The more I read, the more I tend to agree that while being gratuitously nasty and abhorrent, it might well appeal to a whole bunch of people who like to read that kind of pseudo-reality-based horror fiction. Then the guy telephones and asks me to publish it for him. Minutes later, he's strawberry jam."

Dermot paused for a breath. "*Now* do you see what I'm getting at?"

"You're thinking of asking Esther if she'll publish it as a posthumous homage to a madman?" Nick offered.

"Not exactly. No."

"You're thinking you might reinvent the basic premise?" Neela asked.

"Say what you're thinking, Neels. Rip off the guy's work? Well, yes. It's a thought I had."

Nick gasped. "Hey, have some respect. That guy's still warm on a metal tray down at the morgue, and we're having this conversation? It's not right. It's downright ghoulish."

"Oh, so we should now *respect* this guy? This vagrant-cum-derelict who's written a vile fictional account of how, in his nightmare world, he gets his kicks out of torturing people, cutting women's tongues out of their heads, inciting young girls to beat their brains against the walls? *That's* who we should have respect for? My God! Count me out, then. I'm gonna steal something that's maybe worth some bucks."

While Nick was disturbed by Dermot's sudden lack of compassion, Neela was more thoughtful, putting aside any immediate moral issues. "How do we know he didn't show his diary to a heap of *other* people?"

"A street person like him? It's highly improbable. You think he's registered it with the Writers Guild? I don't *think* so."

"Well, that's enough excitement for one night," Nick said. "For me, anyway. If you need anything, give me a call. Actually, if you hear of any more psychotic writers about to jump off buildings—your good self excluded—just leave a message."

Both Dermot and Neela managed a weak smile. Nick picked up his cane and walked to the door. Neela hugged him, and he was gone.

"What are you thinking now?" Neela asked as she turned back to Dermot.

"That you're still here. That I love you more than I can say." He pulled her close. "That I'm glad you're safe."

CHAPTER 15

Dermot couldn't sleep. Each time he closed his eyes, images of Arnold's head exploding against the curb like a soft vegetable filled his mind. The pictures were so vivid, so shocking, that he knew he'd have to get up and occupy himself with other things, somehow.

He slipped out of bed and made his way downstairs to his office. Something was bothering him about the structure and style of the diary, something he couldn't quite put his finger on. Some of the passages were dramatically different in style and content to others. Could Arnold—or whatever his real name was—have had help writing the manuscript? Were there two voices at play here? Or did it just boil down to the fact that Arnold wasn't such a great writer? If this was a first attempt at fiction some passages might work better than others. Either way, Dermot was curious.

He opened to a passage he thought peculiarly gruesome, one that involved a common fear—a fear of dentists. *The first time I saw her, I thought to myself this has to be the most perfectly beautiful face I've ever seen. I was stunned. It was as if I was looking at a photograph that'd been airbrushed to in-finity by a famous photographer. You know what I mean? The skin was so creamy, soft and blemish free. Amazing.*

Dermot immediately felt uncomfortable. Such perfection would be short-lived.

She told me online that she was a model, and had just returned from a photo shoot. I was curious as to what her worst nightmare was going to be? Rape? Dying in a plane crash? No, hers was far more obvious. She was afraid her teeth might crumble and fall out of her mouth. Every few nights she dreamt about waking with a mouthful of broken teeth. A very common nightmare really. She explained that when her parents had died she'd spent her inheritance at the den-tist! She'd paid a king's ransom for the teeth. Can you believe it? You'd swear the caps were the real deal. That's when she started modeling. She made a lot of money, she said.

Dermot could imagine how this angel looked.

I remember her laughing; her entire face lit up! Those teeth—they were quite something. "In my nightmare I'm in the dentist's chair, and he's drilling a molar out without any anesthetic." I played along with her. "Unbelievable! Root canal? And you can feel every nerve in your jaw?" So I calmed her down a bit and told her that soon her nightmare would be over, and that she would find peace.

Late one night, I followed her to her car and stabbed her in the backside with the thermomuscular blocker. She didn't cry out. She just looked at me for a second or two and fell into my arms. I carried her to my car and put her in the trunk. All the tools for my primitive dental surgery had taken me some time to arrange, but it was worth every minute of my time and trouble.

Arnold described how he had set up the guts of his dental surgery in a wooden shed he'd stumbled across out in the middle of nowhere. He had the chair, the lights, the spittoon—everything. He'd even brought a gen-erator, which sat outside at the back.

When she woke, I already had her in the chair with her mouth wired open.

She was aware she didn't have any feeling in her arms and legs—I could see that in her eyes. I could see her eyeballs looking at them one by one as she tried to move. But she couldn't move a muscle. Of course she must've been aware that she could still feel every nerve ending in her head! I made damned sure of that. So I took the drill and turned it on. It was one of those old-fashioned ones: the type that grinds, rather than whines. You should have seen her face as I dipped it into her mouth and began to drill out her front teeth.

Dermot took a sip of his Jack Daniel's and forced himself to read on. How on earth was he ever going to lend his voice to this horror? "You bastard," Dermot mouthed to himself. This was truly a monumentally sick story, yet somehow it sucked him in. Had he sworn at Raskolnikov? Had he shouted and insulted Vlad the Impaler, or Hannibal Lecter as he read about their cruel deeds? He had to admit the diary had him hooked. It shocked and horrified him, yes, but he'd hung on every word.

CHAPTER 16

Cheesecake ate her tuna morsels in prawn jus noisily, sending shards of flaked fish flying onto the glass bifold doors that separated the kitchen from the garden. Neela made bacon and eggs for herself and Dermot.

"I just don't get it. Why did he send it to you, anyway? Why not try a publisher? Or an agent?"

"Maybe he did."

"Well, I can do some careful checking if you like. Without disclosing too much about my interest. I bet I could find out."

"Could you do that?"

"Sure. Why not? Of course there's no point in doing a name search. Albert K. Arnold? A.K.A.?"

"I could ask Mike if they found any ID on the body."

"But you'll have to tell him you lied about your name to the police last night."

"Not at all. All I have to say is that the cop misheard me, and that I stuck around as long as I could, but he never got back to me. I can tell Mike I just saw the guy hit the ground. There's no way I'm going to tell him I met him before—that'd be plain stupid."

Neela thought about the logic. It made sense.

"By the way, you're right about the style of the book, Neels. Written like a hack, but boy does it get into your bone marrow. I was calling the guy names out loud last night in the middle of the night. Can you believe it?"

"Sure I can. Same reaction with me. Sucks you in like a leech—you just have to read on; every damn word. It's seriously 'high-concept.'"

"Oh, please! Don't give me that movie bullshit."

"No, really! The concept is dynamite. A website called worstnight mares.net. The antihero selects his victims from those who visit his website. He analyzes the nightmares that appeal to him most, assesses the chosen victims' mind-sets, then seeks them out so he can visit their worst nightmares on them—magnified tenfold in horror. I'm not sure if I've ever read anything like it."

"Hey, I haven't finished reading it yet."

"Have you reconsidered getting involved with it?"

"Let's put it this way. I *have* reconsidered to the extent that I think the cyber concept's outstanding—very now and in your face. Kids would love it. But as for suiting my purpose? That I don't know. I won the Booker because I wrote an intelligent, well-crafted novel. I wonder what Esther's reaction would be if I offered her a novel in this genre. It's not her taste, and she'd hate it—but that's not the issue. As for Wasserman, he'd love anything he thought would turn a buck, and there's every chance this might make a very scary movie. But whatever I decide, one thing's certain—I'd have to rework the entire manuscript and put it into my own voice; filter it through my own language. It has to read like a book I could have written, not appear to be the work of some grammatically challenged psychotic. I'd have to clean it up, change some of the names, and make it my own. As it stands now, no one would believe I'd written it. It's simply too shabby."

Neela let his words hang in the air for a few seconds.

"Dermot?"

"Yes?"

"You can't leave any clues as to the provenance of the story."

"Sure. That goes without saying. And we've got some serious research to do as well. For starters, you do all you can to check with agents and publishers to see he hasn't run it by any of them. Meantime, I'll go see Mike and see what the police have found out about Mr. Arnold. If they have identified him then I'll check out his background, his friends, his family—if he had any that are still alive. There are a whole heap of things that need checking out before I can commit. But on the upside, the manuscript is written longhand, not typed, so the chances are it's the original draft and there are no copies. And the other major plus is the author is dead."

"Sounds kind of heartless when you put it that way."

"What way?"

"That it's a plus that he's dead? Maybe he had a tragic life. Few friends. Let's face it, he was living on the streets, and that's no fun at all. And he entrusted you with his manuscript, hoping you'd publish it in his name."

"His pseudonym. Not his real name. It might just as well be my name."

Dermot stood up and stacked the dirty plates in the dishwasher. He felt better today. More optimistic and reinvigorated, actually. Quite possibly he now had the chance to turn his writing life around.

"I had a thought last night about how I could rework it into something more my own."

"And that was?" Neela asked, reaching for her coat.

"I thought I'd add a nightmare to the mix. One of my own invention."

"God knows you have enough of them. You wouldn't need to invent too much . . ."

"I can't help what goes on when I dream."

"Well, maybe it's time you got help for it."

Dermot shrugged off her remark. "It's no big thing."

"But you wake up screaming."

"It's a nightmare, honey—it ain't gonna happen."

Dermot chose to change the subject. "Just remember, Nick knows about Arnold and the diary."

"There's no way he'd breathe a word. You know that."

"Okay. But no one else can know."

"Absolutely." Neela took a breath. "One thing's kind of odd."

"What's that," Dermot asked.

"Most of the so-called victims have names, but two are referred to as Ms. A and Mr. B. Why do you think that is?"

"Your guess is as good as mine. I'll give it some thought."

Neela headed out the front door, but Dermot called out to her.

"Hey, wait a minute . . ."

"What is it?" she called back, unwilling to be held up.

"Come and look at something. It's important."

Reluctantly she closed the front door and walked back into the office. Dermot was staring at the computer screen. He had a search engine open; the screen read: "Safari cannot find the server."

"Interesting," Neela murmured. "Of course this could mean many things."

"Like?" Dermot had never been a geek.

"It might mean the site was online once, but it's no longer active. It might also mean the site's down for maintenance, or the person who runs it is uploading something."

"Or it could mean that the site doesn't exist—possibly it never did."

"Wait a second. What's a street person doing with a website, anyway? How could he possibly have set all this stuff up? Remember, there are continuing fees for hosting. And how's he going to keep tabs on it—you think he had an iMac stashed somewhere? Or was spending two bucks an hour in some North Hollywood Internet café? I doubt it."

"You think maybe he heard about the site and borrowed the idea for his diary?" Dermot asked.

"That makes more sense. Either way, we need to keep an eye on the website; see if it comes on again. If it does, then someone else is pulling the strings, and Mr. Arnold loses credibility as a mass murderer. Meanwhile, I'm off. See you later?"

"Sure," Dermot replied, rather relieved that the site wasn't available—at least not at the moment.

Half an hour later, Dermot was still rereading passages of the diary. As he read, he mentally rewrote the text in his own words. He actually enjoyed the exercise. As he mouthed his own version, the work seemed to come to life. It was better—much better. The words were crisp and well chosen, the tension far greater. At least to him.

It was only when he closed the manuscript that he noticed the back page was a good deal fatter than any of the others. He examined the edges and immediately saw that one edge had been crudely sealed with glue. He reached for the letter opener on his desk and slit it open. Inside were several sheets of rice paper. He pulled them out carefully. When he read the top page, a feeling of horror chilled him.

The Mouth Maiden, the Superglue Lady, the Drowner, the Plastic Bag Man, the Flyer, the Bug Girl, Ms. A, Mr. B. Nicknames for the victims.

And the list went on. Under each heading was a primitive, almost childlike drawing in charcoal and crayon. Was this group of drawings what Arnold had been referring to in the train—the "pictures"?

All the victims had their own drawings. The Mouth Maiden's drawing was a close-up of a mouth, wired open, blood spurting outwards, with a pair of workman's pliers reaching inside. The Drowner looked liked a hangman game suspended over a pool of water.

Dermot's pulse rate was sky high. If the text had affected him, the drawings were even more frightening. Yet he continued to look through them.

Each victim had an exact location detailed at the bottom of his or her file. Dermot stared at the directions and almost stopped breathing. Almost all were within two hours of the center of downtown LA—some in the Santa Monica Mountains, some inland north of Malibu, one in the Sierra Nevadas.

He reached for his cell to call Neela, but thought better of it. Why worry her now? Besides, before he jumped to conclusions, it was better to think things through logically. Why were there drawings? Just for the fun of it—to bring a harsh reality to the text perhaps? Depictions of how Arnold imagined his characters would meet their end? But why did he detail the exact topography? Why had he described the locations so succinctly? So ghoulish readers could visit the fictional crime scenes and wallow in their imagination? The details were not simply "in such-and-such Creek." One actually said, ". . . two miles past the cinder block restaurant on Folsom Falls Road, you'll see a big stone. Turn left here and drive two point six miles directly towards the eagle-shaped hill. Look for the ring of stones. He's buried there."

He snapped the book shut. It was deeply disturbing to read details of burial sites. But looking at it all logically, it was quite possible that Arnold was merely adding a little verisimilitude to his manuscript. An illustrated novel? Coupled with these skillful drawings, the idea was a visual nightmare as well as a written one. Of course it was.

CHAPTER 17

Dermot's Peugeot 207 was parked down the street. As he climbed in, he noticed a stray dog walk up to his house, sit, and gaze at the front door. Dermot couldn't take his eyes off the hound—in this part of town, there weren't too many stray dogs walking the empty streets. It reminded him of Toto in *The Wizard of Oz*, except skinny, sad, and malnourished.

He was about to drive off when he glanced again at the poor mutt. It was still standing there. He switched off the engine, opened the driver's door, and walked back toward the house. As he got closer, the dog turned its head and stared at him, a baleful look in his weepy eyes. He looked hungry. The desperately lonely face tugged at Dermot's heartstrings.

"What's your name, fella?" There was no collar. "You hungry?"

The dog continued to stare at him forlornly. Dermot made some lip-smacking noises. The mutt seemed to catch on to that idea very quickly. A little tongue protruded from his mouth as he licked his own doggie chops. Then he sniffed the back of Dermot's hand and licked it. Cute.

"How about this? I take you inside and see what I can find for you to eat. When you're through eating whatever Neels has in the fridge, you can come with me for a ride, or take your chances on the street. But you'd better watch out for Cheesecake. That's our cat. You treat her with respect or she'll pick your bones. She can be one mean pussycat. How's that for a deal?"

The dog barked once. Dermot took it as a positive sign. This was turning into a good day—for both of them.

Twenty minutes later Dermot was on the Harbor Freeway heading southwest. The dog—whom he'd christened "Scarecrow" after Toto's straw pal—was in the passenger seat.

As he drove, passages of the diary kept reverberating in his head. *Let ordinary people know the reality of extreme suffering. Let them watch innocent children burn.* As these thoughts ran through his brain, Scarecrow bounced up and gave the side of his face a delicate lick.

Dermot had been on the road for just under an hour. Traffic was light on the Santa Monica Freeway. Arnold's diary lay open on the seat beside him, and Scarecrow's head was hanging out the passenger window. He was sucking in the air, his ears flying backwards.

Dermot slowed down, picked up the top sheet of the flimsy paper and glanced at the directions. He wondered whether there actually was a Cedar Line Road—he hadn't found anything like that on his map. If there was no such turnoff, it would mean the directions had simply been fabricated to intrigue the reader, and that the manuscript was pure fiction. He really hoped that was the case.

Then he caught sight of the sign for Cedar Line Road and his heart sank. At that precise moment a tractor unexpectedly pulled out onto the road from behind a thick stand of trees. Dermot braked hard. The Peugeot slowed to a halt, inches from the trailer that was hitched to the rear of the tractor. It was stacked with farm rubbish.

Dermot lowered his window and called out.

"Hey! Watch where you're going. You could have killed us both!"

An old weather-beaten farmer stared at Dermot with a disdainful look. *Asshole.*

The farmer laughed and drove on, doing his best to make passing impossible.

Unwilling to give in, Dermot leaned on the horn and snaked around the tractor, taking a chunk of thick hedge with him, the outside wheels gouging deep into the bank.

As soon as he was past, he waved to the old curmudgeon just to annoy him. This time the farmer raised his middle finger at him, swirling it around a few times for good measure.

Dermot began counting off the miles on his odometer. Five miles down the dirt road he saw the lake.

Driving into the area that served as parking for picnickers in summer, he headed for the top right-hand corner, as directed. Then he cut the engine.

Scarecrow looked at him, pleading for a rest stop. Dermot reached across and opened the passenger door from the inside. The terrier jumped down, ran to a bush, and lifted a leg for an interminable time.

"Who would have thought this little dog would have that much piss in him," Dermot mumbled, deliberately misquoting *Macbeth*.

He looked around. There was no one else around, and there was a definite chill in the air. Looking at the sky, it looked like a heavy rain was heading his way. It wasn't a time to be walking in the Topanga State Park without a raincoat.

Glancing at his compass, Dermot headed due east, counting strides that he hoped approximated Arnold's. Scarecrow followed obediently at his heels.

After about fifty yards Dermot came to a barrier of thorn bushes.

"Hell," Dermot muttered. Nothing in life was easy. But the screen of bushes did make sense—if you were committing a murder and burying bodies, you'd hardly do it in plain sight of a parking area where people might be watching.

He covered his head with his jacket to avoid getting scraped by thorns and waded through the dense brush, still counting his strides. Scarecrow snaked through behind him.

At three hundred paces the brush thinned and progress was easier. At seven hundred and ninety strides he came across a wider area where there was little or no vegetation at all. Then he saw the twin stakes. They were a short distance ahead—one slightly taller than the other.

Scarecrow ran forward and lifted a leg on the taller stake.

Dermot examined the stake closely. There were circular indentations in the wood at about head height—marks you'd expect to find if someone had been roped around the neck and secured to the stake. There were similar marks at ankle level. Interesting.

He crouched down and examined the baked earth in front of the stake. The dust was stained black. He was reluctant to touch it, but at first sight it did look very much like dried blood. Of course it could just as easily have been something *other* than blood, but right now every instinct he had was telling him it was the blood of a human being. Unless the whole thing was a macabre setup to fool him into believing people had in fact died here. Arnold could have deliberately placed the stakes here, brought some animal blood with him, and staged everything. *But why?* Maybe this was the weirdo's idea of a grim joke. If so, he'd succeeded in raising the hairs on the back of Dermot's neck.

He walked across to the shorter stake where Arnold had allegedly tied up Laura Nash. At the base of this stake was a length of rope lying on another dark patch of earth. The rope had been cut through. Dermot pulled it free and looped it around the stake. It was several inches short. Even allowing for the knot it was clear someone had cut out a section of the rope and removed it.

The words of the diary were still so fresh in his mind. *That's when I cut out her tongue. All that screaming was getting on my nerves. The temperature was beginning to fall. I'd had plenty to drink but they had nothing. I can see Nash's tongue lolling out of his mouth. Dehydration's a fierce thing. I know, I almost died in the desert once—I know what it's like when your brain screams out for water. So I fetch a pitcher of water from the cooler in the car, and walk over to the woman. Her naked body's shaking—she's practically unconscious. It's the reaction to the sunburn. But when she sees the pitcher of water, the reaction is magnificent: the power of thirst, I suppose. So I lift it up just above the stump of her tongue, as though I'm going to pour some into her mouth. She strains her head up and opens wide. Like an obedient child. That's when I stop, walk back to Mr. Nash and pour all the water over* his *head! "Give it to* her*, you animal! Give it to* her*!" he screams, like he's demented. So much rage. You should have heard him scream. My God! That was something. Real fury. You see? Impotence. There was nothing he could do except watch her die.*

Dermot stood by the stake and found himself conjuring up a picture of Laura Nash straining against the ropes, staring blindly at her husband with the full knowledge that a psychopath was about to cut her throat. The thought chilled Dermot to the marrow. Again, Arnold's words mentally assaulted him. *The woman's body has taken a real beating by the sun. In fact, more than I would have imagined. She's shaking pretty violently now. I look at my watch—I've missed the ball game, but who cares? I'm out of beers, so I decide to end it for them both. So I cut Mr. Nash's heart out. Right out of his body. Laura shakes like a butterfly when I hold it up and show it to her. Quite amazing.*

The chafing marks were also present again on her stake, at neck height, and again around the base where her ankles would have been lashed.

He crouched down to examine the dried black earth. Scarecrow stayed about twenty paces north of Nash's stake. Dermot looked at the dog—wasn't he sitting at the exact location of the grave detailed by Arnold? Dermot looked again at Laura's stake. A vision of Arnold pulling out her parched tongue and severing it with a bowie knife flashed through his brain.

Scarecrow was whimpering. Odd. Dermot walked over to the dog.

Dermot eased Scarecrow to one side. The ground wasn't by any means freshly tilled, but it certainly had a very different consistency compared to the hard-baked earth elsewhere. Dermot estimated the shape of the softer area to be roughly seven feet long by four feet across.

He was looking down at what could easily be a grave. If Arnold was pulling his leg, he'd done a convincing job with the detail.

He cursed himself for not bringing any digging implements, but he'd never seriously thought he'd come across any crime scenes—not if the book was fiction. The last thing he ever expected to encounter was a shallow grave.

The woman's naked body is caked with dried blood. Her mouth's kind of gaping, so I can see the blackened stump of her tongue quite clearly. I reckon she may die of thirst even before I finish her.

The words were now stapled to Dermot's memory.

He sank to his knees and scraped at the earth. One inch down he saw it was surprisingly soft—just the initial top crust was baked a little harder.

He'd dug down about five inches when he heard Scarecrow howling behind him. He jumped. Scarecrow was standing by Laura Nash's stake, chewing on a piece of cloth.

"Hey, Scary! Stop that!" Dermot called. The dog sloped off toward the car. Dermot continued to dig as best he could with his fingers. He looked around for a stick—anything to help him dig. But there was nothing.

Thunder rumbled in the distance. He noticed the rolling black clouds. The rain was closing in. Maybe it was time to stop digging—better to come back some other time with a proper shovel. Anyway, at the rate he was progressing with his fingers, it would take him five hours to get down two feet.

He walked back through the thorns to the car. Scarecrow was already on the floor in the front of the passenger seat—he'd jumped in through the open window. He looked frightened. His wide eyes fixed on Dermot as he got in and slammed the driver's door shut. Both man and dog were clearly spooked.

He was halfway down Cedar Line Road when he met up with the old farmer again. Their eyes locked. Dermot slowed and edged past him. Why goad an old man? But the farmer wasn't in a mood to pull over and let him pass. He deliberately moved to the left, then to the right to keep Dermot from passing.

At the intersection of Cedar Line Road and Canyon, the farmer pulled over. It was getting dark. Dermot parked at the side of the road and called Neela's cell. When she didn't answer, he left a message.

"Hi, Neels. Look, the time just got away from me and I'm really tired. I think I'll find a motel for the night. Love you."

A short distance down the road a motel came into view. Three gas pumps were the centerpieces of the place. Behind them stood the motel. A sign to the left of the main building read, The Gullet—Breakfast Burgers 'n Stuff. Sputtering neon letters atop the hotel proclaimed it to be Dusty's Motor Inn.

Dermot pulled in.

Scarecrow was sitting on the front passenger seat again, animated and ready to leap out of the car at the earliest opportunity to look around. "No way, Scary. Now's the time to hide. I've got to sneak you inside or you'll have to sleep in the car. So stay down and be good."

The reception area stank of cigarettes and body odor. A pungent smell of urine was an indication of how often the toilets were cleaned.

He pinged the old-fashioned bell. The voice of Jerry Springer echoed from a back room. He pinged again. A voice called out from the back.

"Oh, Jesus Christ! Hang on!"

A few seconds later an obese man ambled into the reception area. The remnants of some kind of hamburger were encrusted in his wiry beard.

"What can I do for you, buddy?"

Dermot was tempted to reply that he was a nuclear physicist searching for weapons of mass destruction. "You have a room available for the night?"

"Sure thing, buddy. Forty bucks. Up front, here an' now. You get a tee-vee, an' a video." He gave a sly wink. "An' a choice of some interestin' house videos to select from—just say the word. I keep 'em back here be-hind the counter. There's coffee, tea, and sugar substitute, soap an' all in the room. Everythin' a discernin' world traveler could possibly require." The human mountain smiled and raised his T-shirt an inch. He scratched at his hairy gut.

Dermot pulled out his wallet and took out two twenties. He placed the money on the counter, and then showed the manager his driver's license.

"No need for that, buddy. Cash transaction. Know what I mean?" He lifted a key from one of the pegs. "Cabana 12."

Dermot thanked him and took the key.

The cabana was made of cinder block. There was a bedroom with a soiled threadbare carpet, and a small stinking area off it that passed for a bathroom. Inside were a sink, a toilet with no seat, and a shower. The tiles were green with some kind of fungus. It was even less than Dermot had ex-pected for forty bucks.

He retrieved Scarecrow from the car, set him down on the bed, and shut the door. It was close to six-thirty, so he tried Neela again. He told her how he'd spent the day, without getting specific. "Whoever Arnold is, he certainly planned things pretty well," he told her. "But to go to all this trouble to play a prank on me? Why? What the hell did I ever do to this guy to make him want to scare the daylights out of me? It's unbelievable."

Neela was thoughtful. "I won't even ask how that old guy could have managed all this."

"Beats me," was all Dermot could manage. Then Scarecrow barked. "Shut up, Scarecrow. Unless you want to sleep in the car!" Dermot ad-monished him.

"Who are you talking to?" Neela asked. "Was that a dog?"

"Uh . . . I . . ." He searched for a decent reason for adopting a second pet. "I came across the cutest dog outside the house. Just like Toto in *The Wizard of Oz*, but thin and scrawny. A truly pathetic case." Scarecrow turned his head toward Dermot, as though he was challenging the de-scription. "Looked like he hadn't eaten in days, so I gave him some food."

"Are you telling me you fed our cold lamb to some mutt? I'll have to di-vorce you. You know that."

"He was ravenous—it saved his life. Isn't that enough to justify the loss of a few leftovers?"

Neela calmed down. "We'll discuss the dog when you get back. I'm not having him upset Cheesecake." There was a pause. "Where are you?"

"Some incredibly shabby joint called Dusty's Motor Inn. North of Topanga State Park."

"If you plan to spend the night there, wear your coat to bed. And don't shower till you get home."

He left Scarecrow in the room and headed to the Gullet, where he bought five hamburgers, a small pizza, and a can of Coke. Returning to the cabana, he separated the patties from the soggy buns and gave Scarecrow a good meal of what passed for meat. The dog drank thirstily from the bathroom sink and then went to sleep on the pillows. Dermot sat next to him, opened the diary at the chapter after the Stakes Couple, and positioned a map of California next to it. Which fictional crime scene would he hit next? He scanned the pages again and stopped at the chapter titled "The Superglue Lady," whom Arnold had named Marla Nestor.

Nestor was middle-aged, late forties. Blowsy. Big tits that hung down at half-past six. She'd been a hooker all her life. Made a decent living till she reached forty. Least, that's what she told me online. After that she found it hard to inter-est the opposite sex. Well, with arms like pork chops and sagging bazookas, who'd want any part of that action?

Dermot took a swig of Coke and read on.

She had a thing about the environment and how the big corporations were messing up the world. Told me she liked to protest—lie down in front of eighteen-wheelers stacked with timber logs and chain herself to chemical plants and that sort of thing. "Corporate fucking greed. Look at the way they're raping the countryside," she kept telling me. "Anything for the almighty buck. And chemicals, Dream Healer. Look at what they do to the world." I remember wondering how I could get a hold of some yellowcake uranium and stuff it in her mouth—you know, make her eat it.

Dermot found the charcoal sketch of Nestor's face. In the drawing her mouth was shut tight—a white crusty substance coated both lips. Her expression was one of abject terror. *Those who are about to die* was scrawled under the sketch.

Arnold had supposedly killed Marla Nestor in a small town a few miles from where he was now, in a motel room above the Lazy Lizard, a bar she used for her sex trade. Dermot stroked Scarecrow. "What do you think, Scary? Wanna check out the Superglue Lady?"

Dermot wrapped Scarecrow in his jacket and placed him in the car. Then he walked to the reception area and pinged the bell. The sound of game-show applause resonated from the back room. Dermot hit the bell again.

"Jesus Christ! Hang on!" Then the human mountain appeared. "What can I do for you now? It's late." He picked at a tooth with his pinkie and was rewarded with a piece of gristle.

"Anywhere close I can get a beer?"

"Get as many as you like at the Gullet," he replied. "No hard liquor though."

"Any bars close by? I heard there was a joint around here called the Lazy Lizard."

"Sure. That's up by Shute."

"How far?"

"Ten minutes, I'd say." He grinned. "Is that all I can do you for right now?"

"Yeah. Thanks."

The fat manager grinned some more. "Ladies in the room's extra. Another ten bucks."

"I'll keep that in mind," Dermot replied, straight-faced.

The Lazy Lizard was a shabby bar-cum-rooming house. A fluorescent sign outside was missing the second L and the final A, but it didn't matter; the sign just added to the picture of shabby degradation.

Inside, the men were young, the women were mostly middle-aged tramps, and the booze was flowing freely. Dermot looked out of place; something not lost on the clientele. He stepped up to the bar.

"What can I get you, stranger?" the barman asked, with all the immediate charm of Charles Manson.

"Large Jack Daniel's and a beer chaser," Dermot replied.

Within seconds a woman close to sixty slid onto the stool next to him. "You from town?" The usual hooker's intro—let the mark ask for sex; she wasn't about to get busted by some undercover vice cop.

"That's right," he replied.

"How'd you like to make that a *pair* of Jacks, big boy?"

Dermot saw the barman was waiting for the call, the bourbon bottle hovering over a second glass. "Sure. Why not?" Dermot looked at the barman. "Make that two, please."

The barman set down the drinks, and the woman traced his inner thigh with her bony fingers. "Care for a little companionship later? Be my pleasure," she whispered into his ear.

"No offense, sweetheart, but just tonight I think I'll pass. But it was a nice offer. Thanks." Best not to get on the wrong side of the locals. Not if he wanted information.

She frowned theatrically. "My, you just broke my fucking heart." Then she grinned. She was missing a tooth, bottom left front. Bluebeard's mistress.

Dermot scanned the crowded bar. Several tough-looking bikers sat at a big table. One was leaning forward, staring at him and talking out of the side of his mouth to his ugly friend as the others listened. When they all laughed, Dermot knew it was at his expense, but he didn't care—provided they weren't planning on beating him to death later, just for kicks.

He drained his Jack and walked to the far end of the bar, where the barman was cleaning glasses.

"Any rooms for hire?" he asked. The barman eyed him up and down. "Not for right now," Dermot added. "Another time maybe. I'm a salesman. New to the area, but I'll be passing by on a regular basis. Useful to know these things for next time."

"Sure. We got rooms by the hour and rooms for the night. Clean and decent enough. Like to see one?"

The barman took a bunch of keys down from a shelf, selected one, and handed it to Dermot.

"Out back and up the stairs."

"Thanks. Won't be long."

"Take as long as you like. Just don't make me have to come get you."

As he walked through to the rear of the bar, Dermot glanced back at the hooker who had tried to get his business. The ready smile had evaporated. She looked ten years older—tired, alcoholic, and hopeless.

It didn't take a whole lot of questions to find out where she hung out. I think she thought I'd buy her a few drinks and pay for some sex.

Looking at the pathetic woman at the bar, Dermot wondered if she knew how lucky she was not to have been sitting there the night Arnold had walked in. Immediately he reminded himself again that Arnold's diary was fiction. If Arnold had visited the bar and checked the place out, he could very easily have written the chapter based on his experiences.

He moved through the door, closing it behind him.

He was now in a darkened hallway. Cigarette and soft-drink vending machines stood next to each other in the spartan area. Wooden stairs led up to the first floor landing.

A line of filthy carpet ran the length of the upper hall, room doors leading off it every twelve feet or so. They were numbered. Dermot opened Arnold's diary to refresh his memory. *She led me to room number 10. I stood right behind her, sniffing at her hair. Smelled of peroxide and beef stew.*

Dermot had been given the key to room 8, but he tried 10 anyway. It was unlocked, so he walked in and flicked on the light switch.

There was a bed on the right-hand side and an armchair next to the bed with all the stuffin' hangin' out one side where someone had slashed it with a knife.

He stared at the bed, then the armchair. The research was certainly accurate; horsehair *was* spilling from the left hand side of the chair. And some kind of hard substance stuck to the right arm.

The room was quite cozy, considering the rest of the place. She started taking off her clothes, like she was in some kind of a hurry. I took out the small bottle of whisky I had in my pocket. She smiled, fell into the chair, and held out a hand. How was she to know what I'd mixed in with the booze? It made me laugh—she was so desperate for a drink!

Dermot picked at the hard stuff on the arm of the chair. The image he had of the woman reaching out for the glass of whisky laced with fast-acting glue was horrific.

You've no idea how quick that stuff worked. She chugalugged like she'd been walking in the desert for a week. Half of it was down her gullet before she knew what was happening. There was quite a bit of it hangin' off of her lips and this was already bonding fast. She just managed to part her lips for a second, as if she wanted to scream, but the stuff was in her mouth and down her windpipe so she couldn't take any more air in. Then she started clawing at her mouth like a crazy woman. Her fingernails were those stick-on things. I watched them break on her teeth as she twitched in the chair. I saw a big gobbet of glue spray onto the arm of the chair. I left it there.

Dermot stopped picking at the glue.

I knew I couldn't leave her where she was. So I watched her die, then put her in a sack and carried her down to the car. I drove her a few miles and put her in the ground in a grave I'd dug the night before. Check it out.

"You finished up there, mister?" the barman called from downstairs.

"Sure," Dermot replied. "Be right down."

The hooker was still at the bar when he returned. A young man in a plaid shirt and jeans, young enough to be her grandson, was sitting next to her. She was ruffling the soft fluff at the back of his neck as Dermot walked by.

As he headed out, he saw her pulling the eighteen-year-old behind her toward the back stairs. She winked at Dermot and disappeared.

When he arrived back at the Peugeot, Scarecrow was sitting obediently in the passenger seat, ears pricked. He let the dog out to stretch his legs and take a leak while he checked out the coordinates for where Arnold had specified the body of the hooker was buried—if in fact there was a body. The location was 4.3 miles due west, but it didn't seem like a smart idea to go trawling for dead bodies in the dead of night without a flashlight or shovel.

As he reparked outside his cabana at Dusty's, Dermot could just make out the curtains at the reception area window being pulled discreetly to one side. The fat manager's face presented itself, probably hoping for the extra ten bucks for "ladies in the room." Dermot waited for the curtain to fall back again before wrapping Scarecrow in his jacket and taking him inside.

Lying on the bed, he thought about calling Neela again, but it was late already. He'd call her in the morning when he had a better sense of whether or not the diary was fact or fiction—though he still believed it was the latter.

Dermot woke in the middle of the night to the sound of a familiar engine firing up in the parking area outside. He looked at his watch—it was just after three in the morning. He padded quickly to the window and pulled the curtain to one side. As his night vision began to kick in, he saw a Peugeot 207 cruise past his window, traveling very slowly; the revs low, so that it made as little noise as possible.

Wearing nothing but his skivvies, Dermot wrenched his cabana door open, and ran out into the night after his car, shouting obscenities. The response was instantaneous. Whoever was driving the Peugeot floored the accelerator and the car shot toward the highway, where it was lost forever in a cloud of smoking rubber.

"Shit!" Dermot's chest was heaving from the exertion. "That's fucking *great*. Now I'm stuck out here in the boonies with a fucking dog and no fucking wheels."

He walked slowly back to the entrance of the motel, trying to catch his breath. The manager was now standing outside reception, wearing an undershirt and shorts, and carrying a strong flashlight. Lights had been switched on in a lot of the cabanas and occupants were standing at their doors wondering what the shouting was all about.

"You got a problem?" the manager asked.

"Yeah. Someone just stole my car," Dermot replied. "*That's* my problem. You get a lot of cars stolen out here?"

"Never had a vehicle stolen since I been here. That's eleven years. Guess you're just one unlucky dude." He smiled.

"You have a number for the local cops?"

"Sure. But first of all, you sure that was *your* car? You checked?"

"I know my own car when I see it."

"You saw who was driving?"

"The windows are tinted."

"But you saw the plates, right?"

Dermot opened his mouth, then stopped. He hadn't, but what were the chances there were two identical Peugeots in the same parking lot?

"How's about we both take a walk through the lot 'fore we call the cops out at this hour of the night?"

"Sure, why not."

When they reached the parking area, the manager ran his flashlight over the cars. Dermot saw his car almost immediately.

"Shit . . . It's there. There must've been two the same."

"Well, why don't you go check out your little twin car while I get back to bed. Then maybe find another way to make an ass of yourself." He stalked back to reception as Dermot unlocked his car and climbed inside. It looked the same as when he'd left it. A few minutes later Dermot was back in his room. He pulled the curtain closed. What were the odds of an identical black Peugeot 207 being parked in the same motel parking lot? Dermot closed his eyes for a second, savoring the relief he felt. He still had the means to get out of this hellhole in the morning. Before he knew it, he was asleep.

CHAPTER 18

Several hours later, a paw on his cheek woke him. It was already way past ten o'clock; he'd wasted the best part of the day. Twenty minutes later, he and Scarecrow were on the road. The rain had stopped, but looking at the sky, he saw it was most likely the calm before the next storm.

The diary was open on his lap at the chapter titled "The Drowner." Dermot thought he knew exactly where he was headed. But after about an hour's hard driving he knew he'd taken a wrong turn and had to retrace his steps. One more hour wasted. A further two and a half hours later, the topography began to resemble a desert landscape. He mentally factored in the extra miles to his odometer reading so he'd still be on track.

There were hardly any trees; just a few low bushes and a bit of scrub. Occasionally balls of dried grass rolled across the road, driven by the ever-increasing wind, a scene somewhat reminiscent of a third-rate Western.

Dermot slowed when the odometer clicked over to 132 miles. Then he stopped and checked both the diary's directions and his own map in case he'd missed the turn. He saw it should be just another mile on the left. He pulled out again onto the highway. Sure enough, as the odometer clicked over to 133, there was a very narrow track off to the left. Unless a traveler was looking for it, he'd miss it. It was all exactly as Arnold had detailed.

Dermot turned left and started slowly down the track.

Two point three miles. Look for the farmhouse on the right. Then look right again. There's a water tower. You can't miss it.

Twelve minutes later, Dermot arrived at the farmhouse Arnold had described. On closer examination, it looked as though the front door was missing. He stepped from the car, leaving Scarecrow inside, and walked to the building. There was no door and also no window frames—the farmhouse was derelict.

Back at the car, he opened the passenger door for Scarecrow, but the dog didn't want to get out. Instead he slunk into the rear seat and curled up on the floor in front of it.

"Don't you need to pee, Scary? You've got some major bladder control there."

Ahead Dermot could see the water tank, positioned exactly where Arnold had indicated. It loomed like some sinister *War of the Worlds* alien machine right on the skyline.

At the base of the tower, Dermot looked up. The stanchions were metal and looked in reasonable condition—just a little rust, which you'd expect. It'd easily bear his weight. A metal ladder headed to the top.

Just as his head cleared the top rim of the water tower a deafening clap of thunder resounded directly above him. It startled him so profoundly that he nearly lost his footing on the metal rungs.

From the top, he peered inside at the water collected in the tank. The surface was about seven feet below. Running across the tank was a wooden plank that didn't seem to have any practical function. It was just as Arnold had outlined. Dermot could see chains hanging down from the center of the wooden plank. Could this be where Arnold had envisaged the Drowner hanging? Closer examination of the plank revealed a scrap of paper nailed to its central point.

Dermot screwed up his eyes, but he was too far away to make out the words; all he knew for sure was that it was handwritten. But what did it say? He had to know.

It wasn't easy, but he slid himself up onto the rim of the tank and positioned his upper body along the wooden plank. It was a good two inches thick and seven or so inches wide, and the wood looked sound enough.

He inched forward just as the heavens opened in earnest. The rain started to beat down. Heavy didn't begin to describe it; monsoonal was more accurate. Drops as big as grapes pounded down on his head and body; his clothes were drenched within seconds. Despite this, he continued to inch forward, but now with extreme caution—the last thing he needed was to fall into the pit of stagnant filth below.

He was only a forearm's length from the nailed note when he heard the prescient groan of distressed wood for the first time. He immediately froze, breathing as shallowly as possibly. *Go back*, his brain screamed at him. But he couldn't retreat. Not yet.

Twenty seconds later he got to the note and read it in shock. It was in Arnold's signature childish script . . . His mouth was suddenly as dry as the Gobi desert as he read the words: *Mr. Nolan. I didn't think you'd get this far. But since you have, take a look at the cut on the far side of this note. Arnold.*

Rank terror surged through Dermot's veins. He focused on the spot the note had indicated, and saw the plank had been cut three-quarters of the way through. His heart began to pound so desperately that the board actually vibrated.

He then heard the pistol crack of wood as the plank gave way. He felt himself falling. Dermot had just enough time to reach out with one hand to try to grip the side of the tank. No luck. His effort just left a shallow gash in the side of his left hand. He was almost horizontal as he plunged into the ten-foot deep water. Underneath the surface, the liquid had the consistency of raw sewage.

The shock of the cold water and the instinctive fear of drowning took over. Dermot flailed about, trying to ascertain which way was up. As he'd fallen, he'd closed his eyes and mouth in anticipation; but the foul liquid had still forced its way up into his nostrils as he clawed for the surface. He fought for orientation and pushed and clawed at myriad objects floating in the tank. He could feel rotten branches of trees and the carcasses of dead birds and rodents around him. His panic only pushed him deeper into the sludge.

In desperation he opened his eyes—he had to see where he was so he could make for the top and fill his lungs.

It was then he saw the head.

It was suspended in the murky water, just a few inches from Dermot's own head. The putrescent eye sockets still contained some white aqueous residue, and, oddly, the milky eyeballs appeared to be staring right at him.

Dermot opened his mouth in a silent scream of terror. A natural reaction, but hardly a smart move under the circumstances.

He lashed out with his undamaged hand at the head, kicking violently upwards. Three further wild thrashes of his strong legs and his head broke the surface. He gasped for air, gagging and vomiting at the same time. The rain was still pounding down. The windmill apparatus now had a waterspout gushing from the catchment tray into the tank, and the surface level had already risen several inches. But on the plus side it made reaching the rim of the water tank easier.

He grabbed at the rim with both hands and pulled himself onto the edge by the metal ladder.

The sky was black as pitch. Lightning scissored down every few seconds, followed too quickly by deafening claps of thunder. The storm was directly overhead. The wind was howling like a hundred banshees. And the rain? It was now a near-solid wall of water tumbling down on top of him.

He stepped gingerly onto the first step of the metal ladder; his hands were frozen claws. He held on for dear life to the side rails like a crazy man. He was vaguely aware of Scarecrow howling from the car.

He clambered down the last few rungs of the ladder, and ran flat out to the Peugeot, leaping inside and firing up the engine. Two seconds later he'd made a U-turn and floored the accelerator.

As he passed the abandoned farmhouse his peripheral vision took in what he thought was another black Peugeot 207—one identical to his own. It was parked outside the front door. The nerve endings in his spine exploded—like he'd been struck by lightning.

As he reached the highway, he pulled out his cell phone. "That's it, Scary," he breathed, more to himself than the dog, "I'm not suffering through any more of Arnold's shit! No way! I'm calling the cops as soon as I get home."

It was only then that he noticed the water dripping out of his Nokia phone.

Fuck, fuck, fuck!

He threw the soaked cell phone into the backseat in frustration, crunched the car into gear again, and raced on into the night.

The rain was still pelting almost horizontally when he finally turned into Linley Place. He'd been on the road for nearly three hours and his clothes were still soaked, stinky, and slimy, despite having had the heater on full blast.

Several blocks around Pershing Square were in the grip of an electricity failure; emergency crews were everywhere trying to get the power restored. The traffic lights were out and there were no lights in the windows of the buildings that surrounded his house.

He parked, grabbed Scarecrow under his arm, and raced for the front door. As he turned to close the door behind him, he caught the briefest glimpse of a black Peugeot 207 cruising by. He stared, transfixed for several moments, unable to comprehend the coincidence. Dermot slammed the door shut and padded to the kitchen, where he put Scarecrow down. He then lit a couple of candles and a paraffin lamp. A quick search of the fridge revealed nothing any self-respecting cairn terrier would choose to eat, so he filled a bowl with Cheesecake's dry food. Scarecrow practically inhaled the cat food and lay down obediently on a rug that Dermot placed in the corner of the kitchen. Dermot then padded upstairs softly, showered in the guest bedroom, and put a Band-Aid on his cut hand. Finally he tiptoed into the main bedroom. Although it was a couple of hours before she normally turned in, Neela was asleep. Possibly she'd had another of her migraines. Dermot very gingerly slipped in beside her. He was unconscious in less than a minute.

CHAPTER 19

Neela shook Dermot as hard as she could—he was screaming. Cheesecake was on his pillow biting his head, certain that an aggressive reaction was warranted by the violent outburst.

"Wake up, honey! You're dreaming again! It's okay. I'm here! Everything's fine!" Neela hugged her husband as tightly as she could. Dermot opened his eyes, and stared wildly about him. The gasping stopped.

Cheesecake sank her teeth into the crown of Dermot's head one last time, Neela gave her a smack on the butt, and the cat jumped off the bed and ran downstairs.

"Okay . . . let me go. I can hardly breathe."

Neela laid him back on his pillows and stroked his forehead.

"You have to seek help about these nightmares. I'm not sure if I can take them anymore."

"It wasn't *that* dream . . ." Dermot replied, as his breathing gained equilibrium. "Not the usual."

Neela caught her breath and held both his hands in hers. Suddenly Dermot began to sob uncontrollably. Neela couldn't believe it—she'd never seen him cry like this before.

"Tell me what's wrong. You're scaring me."

Dermot's mind and body were full of conflicting emotions and random thoughts. He tried to rein in his emotions as he prepared to level with Neela about the truth. "I went to check out some of the details in Arnold's book."

Neela nodded. "Yes, so you said."

"But it never occurred to me that the manuscript or—" he hesitated, "or diary, *whatever* you want to call the damn thing, was anything more than a work of fiction."

"Go on."

"Well, the more I read the book the more the descriptions made my flesh crawl, and the more upset I became. Remember when I was yelling at the bad guy as I read?"

"Sure."

"The thing is, though, I wasn't prepared to admit to myself that there was any possibility this diary could be real."

"So?"

"But the more I read, the more I had to know if any of it was based on truth, or had, God forbid, actually happened."

"You mean you were actually beginning to think that this weird manuscript was based on *actual* murders?"

"Because if these people actually had been butchered we'd *have* to tell the authorities."

"Well, of course we would. That goes without saying."

"But then something else occurred to me. It came right out of left field—and showed me a side of myself that scared me a little."

"Honey, you'd never do anything that was reprehensible or unethical. It's not in your nature."

"Oh, right, you think so? Well, as I was driving to all these spots, I got to thinking that even if this psycho *had* actually murdered all these people, he was dead wasn't he? I'd spoken to him on the phone, listened to his words of contrition, and seen him take his own life because he couldn't live with himself anymore. So . . ."

Neela cut in, now confused. "What are you trying to say?"

Dermot's tone became a little more edgy. "Can't you tell what I was thinking, for heaven's sake? I was cold-bloodedly thinking that it didn't matter a damn if all those people *had* actually died. I wasn't responsible for putting matters right. I'd done nothing wrong. None of this mattered because the diary was pure dynamite and I still wanted to steal it!" He took a breath. "Don't you see? I was still thinking of ripping it off—plagiarizing the work of a dead serial killer. Without one single thought about any closure for the families of any of the people he'd hacked to death, drowned, suffocated . . ." He began to shake.

"Hey! Steady." She handed him a glass of water. "Drink this and tell me what exactly made you think Arnold's diary was real. What did you find out there?" ·

Dermot thought about how to spin what he had seen without letting his wife know everything.

"Well, I found the exact coordinates. He scribbled down everything on extra pages that he stuffed in the rear cover of the manuscript and sealed. I found the stakes, just like he said. There were rope marks at head height. And a big black stain that looked like dried blood where Mr. Nash's feet had been. Same in the dirt at his wife's stake. I guess it could have been animal blood."

"Have you ever seen real dried blood? I mean lots of it. How would you know it was pints of the real thing?"

Dermot was annoyed. "Are you trying to be clever here, Neels? No, I haven't seen much dried blood, human or animal. But I've seen plenty of fresh stuff. Spattered everywhere, just recently if you recall!"

Neela realized she was only winding him tighter, and tried to change the course of her comments. "Have you considered that maybe this guy Arnold was only toying with you? That he knew—"

"Of course I have! It's the first thing I thought."

"You were there, too?"

"Didn't I tell you? I thought I had." A confused look creased his face. "Yes, I looked inside the room where Marla Nestor supposedly died. It was exactly like he wrote it. There was even a hooker in the bar who could have passed for the Superglue Lady herself. Or her twin."

"Maybe the hooker you saw was her and she's not dead. Maybe he just used her as a model. You know, to tell a ghoulish story."

"Maybe. But I went upstairs and looked around. In the room he describes there really was dried glue on the arm of a chair."

"But no evidence of blood or a body."

"Of course there wouldn't be a body! A rotting putrescent corpse with maggots crawling out of her eyeballs hanging around in a motel room?

C'mon! Besides, he said he buried her. I didn't go look because I didn't have a shovel and it was pitch black outside. Besides, I was spooked by then. I wasn't about to dig for bodies after what I'd been through."

"Then we have to check whatever records we can find. See if anyone went missing near there."

"That makes sense. What doesn't is how he'd been able to get her into his car without anyone seeing. He was old—he had to have been struggling."

"We could check whether there was a hooker who took a client upstairs recently and never came back down."

"She could have left with the guy—slipped out the back door. Doesn't mean . . ."

He was about to continue when a bark came up from downstairs followed by a low caterwaul from Cheesecake. Neela jumped up. "We'd better go save your dog."

In the kitchen, Cheesecake had Scarecrow cornered up against the fridge. She looked as though she meant business—her back was arched like a longbow, her tail straight out like a dagger behind her, her teeth bared and oiled with spit.

Neela picked up Scarecrow, opened the door to the yard, and gently tossed him outside. Then she fed Cheesecake and made some coffee.

The doorbell sounded.

"Who the hell could that be?" Dermot was still really wired.

"The clairvoyant in me says it's Nick. The pessimist says it's someone with a letter of foreclosure from the bank. The optimist says it's an employee from the Lotteries Commission to tell us we won thirty-three mil. How about I go see?"

Dermot didn't smile. He was mired too deep in images of death.

"Hi, Dermot," Nick said, in a happy-go-lucky voice. "How's things? Hope I'm not intruding?"

"You never intrude. Just having coffee."

Nick sat down opposite Dermot at the kitchen table. Nick sensed the tension in the air. "What's up? Nothing too personal you don't want to share with me?" he asked lightly.

Neela shot a glance at Dermot and could see he'd clammed up. So it was up to her. "Dermot went off on a fishing trip, but he found more than just fish."

Nick smiled, even though he had no idea what she was talking about— Dermot had never gone fishing in his life.

"He found some sketches in . . ." she paused and put on a spooky voice, "the weird one's diary. Details of the places where he said he buried bodies."

Nick started to reply but Dermot held up his hand. "I know. It's a book, for Christ's sake. It's fiction. Would I be stupid enough to rush off to see where Stephen King's murderous desperado or Patricia Cornwell's assassin said they buried the bodies? Makes no sense, huh?"

"Well, I have to say . . ." Nick conceded, "that was what I was thinking."

"The thing is, this damned manuscript has seriously gotten under my skin. Sure, I know it's written in a shithouse way by a rank amateur, but as you get into it, you'd almost believe it's the real deal. Some parts of it don't feel right, but others chill you right to the marrow."

"What do you mean some parts don't *feel* right while others do?"

"Some of the killings sound like the writer is just having deviant fun, while others sound as if he was seeking some kind of revenge."

"I'm not sure I follow you, Dermot," Nick said, as Neela handed him a coffee.

"How can I put it? There's the Drowner . . ."

"The hydrophobic?"

"Yes, him. I wanted to check him out because it read like Arnold had a special interest in this guy. He hated him and seemed to take the greatest pleasure in watching him die. Then there's the Superglue Lady . . ."

"The one with her lips glued together?"

"Yes. Her death seemed more like a seriously weird practical joke. There wasn't any sense of personal involvement—it was more like she was a victim chosen at random just to amuse him. Anyway, I decided to do some research to see if anything was out there that could prove once and for all if this was fact or fiction."

"How did you know where to go?" Nick asked.

"There were some directions pasted in the rear cover," Neela explained. "Dermot drove to the spots where Arnold said he killed and buried some of his victims."

"You actually went to see the places Arnold wrote about?" Nick looked incredulous.

Neela and Nick exchanged glances. Dermot was becoming increasingly unhinged.

"You see, I tried digging at the location of the Stakes Couple, and it took me an age to get down just a few inches."

"So, what happened?" Nick prompted.

"So next morning I went to take a look at the water tower."

"Where the Drowner was murdered?"

"That's right."

Neela refilled their coffee mugs, and Dermot continued his strange story.

"So what made you think Major was still in the tank?" Neela asked.

"Arnold wrote he'd cut him down after he'd drowned, and watched the body sink. He didn't say anything about removing the Drowner's body from the water or burying him. The *water* was his grave—that's what he said. So I figured . . ."

"But if—" Nick started to say.

Neela raised her hand to stop him. She wanted Dermot to tell the story his own way. "Exactly what did you see when you got up there?" Neela asked softly.

"Well, there was the windmill just like Arnold said. And there was the note. I crawled across the plank to get it."

"What plank?"

"There was a piece of wood stretched across the top of the tower."

"You're telling me you *stood* on this piece of wood?" Nick interrupted, unable to remain silent. "That's nuts. It could have given way."

"No, listen to me! There was a note nailed to the middle of the plank! With a message. And it was in his handwriting! Arnold's!"

Neela shot a glance at Nick.

"Don't do that!" Dermot shouted loudly.

"Do what?" Neela asked, annoyed.

"Look at Nick as if I'm some mental patient."

"But it doesn't make any sense."

"Jesus Christ! Does *anything*?"

Neither Nick nor Neela replied—they could see that Dermot was breathing hard and working up a sweat.

"The note turned out to be a booby trap. The plank was fixed so it would support my weight until I neared the middle. The other side was nearly sawed through."

"What was written on the paper?"

"That he knew I'd fall for the bait, and I was seconds from falling."

"I guess he was playing a cat and mouse game with you, then?"

"Depends what you mean by a game. He was certainly playing with me. But I'd say it was a lot more than just a scary game. Anyway, next thing I knew the wood gave way and I fell into that stinking pit. That's when I nudged something and opened my eyes without thinking and . . ."

Dermot's pupils were huge, staring.

"You *saw* something?" Neela asked, fearing what he'd say.

Dermot paused and took a breath. "I saw a head. A human head. It was just a matter of inches away from my nose. It was suspended in the water— sort of . . . hovering, watching me. The eyes were milky white. It must have been in that filthy water, putrefying, for weeks!"

Neela was totally freaked now. She glanced at Nick, who looked shaken, too. "Are you sure it was a *human* head, Dermot? You were scared and trying to get out of that muck. Maybe you just thought you saw a human head. It might have been a sheep? Or a coyote? We have to be sure."

"The truth is, I'm not sure." Dermot caught his breath. He'd been talk- ing like a machine gun. "But I think it was Bruce—Bruce Major."

"I'd prefer to think it wasn't Major's head," Neela said, finally.

"But why would he do that?" Dermot now figured the more he insisted the head was human, the more Neela would take the opposite view. "Why me? One minute Arnold's asking me to publish his book, and the next he's trying to drive me nuts."

Neela refilled the coffee mugs. "Look, I've listened to all these facts and I don't think you discovered anything to suggest that there are real dead bodies out there. Everything you saw was circumstantial. Arnold could have researched real murders and then directed you to the setups to scare you, and give himself a big laugh."

"Well, he did that all right."

"So let's do some research and see what we can find out about these murders—if they're real or not," offered Neela.

"How about we divide up the scenarios and see what we come up with?" Nick directed.

Dermot had lapsed into a dream state again. "There was one other spooky coincidence . . ."

"What's that, honey?" Neela asked gently.

"I keep seeing a Peugeot 207. Same as ours. Like a twin. I've seen it a couple of times now. Maybe three. At the motel, out at the abandoned farmhouse, and maybe somewhere else—I can't recall exactly now."

He related the incident at the hotel where he thought his car had been stolen.

"C'mon, there must be hundreds of Peugeots in South Cal," Nick retorted.

"With tinted windows like mine? Same year? And at the same locations where I'm doing some investigating? Pretty major coincidences."

"Honey. Arnold's dead. You saw him. Are you thinking maybe he had an accomplice, now? Someone who's out there stalking you?"

"I just don't know."

CHAPTER 20

Neela set out to investigate the deaths of Meredith and Noam Zersky and see if they had any connection to any of the other victims. In the diary, they were known as "the Free Fallers," and Arnold had listed the location of their demise as Van Nuys Airport.

Neela Googled their names but came up with nothing. The same was true for obituaries in all South Cal newspapers. Then she tried Googling Van Nuys Airport incidents, but the only recent fatalities were a Fox 11 chopper that crashed in 2001 and a Cessna Citation that fell out of the sky, killing two passengers, in January. Finally she used Nexis.com, the search engine she knew stored articles from almost every periodical known to mankind. She waded through all the newspapers the day after Arnold said he'd killed them. And that's when she came across the story. It hadn't been listed as a crash statistic because, strictly speaking, it wasn't. It was a triple murder.

Referring back to the story in the diary, Neela learned that Noam Zersky had admitted to the Dream Healer that he had a nightmare of being in the business class cabin of a 747 when the ceiling blows off, and the pressure rips his seat from the plane and sucks him into the sky, before plunging back to earth headfirst. When asked, he admitted that his wife also feared flying, and he told the Dream Healer, "You'll never catch either of us in a plane."

The Dream Healer had other ideas. *I followed them home on the third day I'd been watching them.. They lived in an apartment on Olympic, and I decided to pay them a visit. Mrs. Zersky came to the door. I told her who I was, describing myself as Noam's dream therapist, and she called out to her husband. He said something to her and she opened up the door. He was delighted to meet me and was too preoccupied with questions to ask me why I was making house calls. Mrs. Zersky even made peppermint tea. When she went to the bathroom I stuck Noam with the syringe and he went down quick. When Meredith returned, I stuck her, too. Then I bagged them both and put them in the trunk of their old Lincoln.*

Neela couldn't help but wonder how he'd gotten a pilot to fly the plane, but as she read on, she got her answer. Of course, Arnold had already thought of that.

I'd known Corey Hamilton a few years. Weird guy. Bit of a loner. Thought I was gay. Said he'd been biding his time as far as putting the hard word on me— said he'd screw any man regardless of age or beauty. What a maggot. Anyway, I was a big letdown in the sex stakes. When he told me he flew small planes part time—that's when I got the idea.

At four in the morning, I drove them to the airport and loaded them into Hamilton's plane. Then I called Hamilton and told him I wanted to go for a dawn joyride, and that I had plenty of cash to pay for it. And just in case he wasn't greedy enough for money, I put a sexy gay come-on into my voice. The fag agreed and met me at the airport. Of course he had no idea about the cargo he was carrying, all gagged and immobile in the rear of his plane.

Once we were airborne, I pulled out a gun and told Hamilton what was about to take place. Hamilton threatened to crash the plane. But when he realized I didn't give a damn whether we all lived or died, he pleaded for his life and said he'd do anything that would see him on the ground alive.

Once we reached jumping altitude, I pushed the gun in Hamilton's face. I told Hamilton to level out and cruise as slowly as possible. Said I'd blow his brains out if he didn't obey, and we'd all die. Then I gave the Zerskys a wake-up call with a needle full of adrenaline. I'd bound their hands behind their backs and they were lashed together, face-to-face. I'd duct-taped their mouths earlier to muffle any screams—but now they were up so high it didn't matter, so I ripped the tape off. Besides, listening to the wild screams would be a real blast.

Meredith Zersky immediately started screaming. "Stand up!" I shouted.

That's when I opened the door of the plane. The wind rushed past with a dull and consistent roar. It was sheer heaven!

The Zerskys knew they were only a few minutes from oblivion. But I couldn't help but relish the moment, allowing a full minute or so to pass so I could watch them take sneaky peeks at the open door and the abyss.

He kept asking me what I was going to do, like there was something else I had in mind other than push them through the door. Really funny. Anyway, I finally prodded Zersky in the back of the neck really hard with my Sig Sauer pistol—and they shuffled forward to the opening like a couple of second-rate tango dancers. Then I kicked Zersky very hard in the ass and they both went flying out the door. Boy, did she scream on her way down. He did too, as a matter of fact.

Neela drove to Van Nuys Airport to check out the report she'd read in the *LA Times*. Things had changed since Arnold was last there, because now security had been beefed up big time.

Inside the main building, Neela asked if she could book a joyride and was directed to a company called Up, Up and Away. It was in a reasonably sized prefabricated building a hundred or so yards from the gate. She drove through some secondary boom gates and parked outside the hut.

Sitting behind a reception desk was a gum-chewing girl in her thirties with the worst psoriasis Neela had ever seen.

"What can I do for you, honey?" the girl asked, cracking her gum loudly. "You want to take a ride in the sky?" She sounded as though she rehearsed the lines each night before bed.

"Well, maybe. Can I ask you a few questions first?"

"That's why I'm here. Ask away."

"Safety's a big concern of mine. You see, I want to take my kids up. Show them a fun time on their birthday—they're twins. Ten years old. So I need to be sure it's safe."

"It's safe. Take my word for it."

"Well, the thing is, someone told me that six months ago a couple died here. They went up in a plane and fell to their deaths. No parachutes. The man was dressed in a suit and his wife had on a skirt and blouse. No safety gear at all. *And* the pilot was killed, too."

The girl's face clouded. She eyed Neela intently. "That was the murders. Got nothing to do with safety here at Van Nuys. If you want to fly with your kids, chances are there'll be no murders that day. We don't get those very often." She smiled, pleased with her little joke.

"So the story's true?"

She nodded. "Well, yes. There were murders here. Some months back." She paused. "Mind if I ask you where *you* live?"

"LA."

"No. I mean where in Los Angeles?"

"Downtown, actually."

"Well, there you go! I'd say there are more murders in a week downtown than in ten years here at Van Nuys airstrip."

Neela ignored her challenging tone. She let a few seconds pass.

"Do you remember their names? The dead couple? Does the name Zersky mean anything to you?"

The girl thought about it, then nodded. "Sure . . . Zersky. Times two. Husband and wife. The pilot was Corey Hamilton. Weird guy."

The news story on Nexus had been brief with few details—but it all added up. The question now was, had Arnold committed the crimes or simply incorporated the newspaper details of the deaths into his diary?

"Was there any closure on the case? Did they ever catch the guy that threw the pair out of the plane and then shot the pilot?"

"Sure was. They caught him all right. He's locked up tight, waiting to go to trial."

The girl stopped chewing and stared at Neela. "But how do you know all that stuff? About him wearing a suit and her wearing a blouse and skirt? That wasn't in the paper. Far as I know, anyway. The cops deliberately kept all that stuff a secret. I know 'cause I dated one of the cops, and he got real chatty sometimes."

"My friend told me," Neela said, recovering. "She was working as a secretary in a police station somewhere."

"Well, your friend should've told you it had nothing to do with safety issues. So what's all this about?"

"Look, thanks for helping me," Neels ignored the girl's question. "I'll get back to you about the birthday ride. Have you got a brochure?"

Neela drove home feeling concerned, but not overly so. Okay, three peo-ple had died. But someone other than Arnold had been charged with the murders. That was wonderful news. It surely suggested Arnold had merely *heard* of the crimes, and had just included them in his book. If Arnold had made this one up from a story in the newspaper, surely he had made the others up in the same way. She couldn't wait to get back and tell Dermot. What a weight off his chest the news would be!

CHAPTER 21

Dermot sat opposite his old friend and sometime research assistant, Detective Sergeant Mike Kandinski in the North Hollywood Division. A forty-something junk food addict, thirty pounds overweight, married to a solid working class Canoga Park woman, he was a committed Catholic, had two kids, was a dedicated Mustang driver, and, best of all, was a straight cop.

"You just curious, Dermot? Or are you thinking there may be a novel in it somewhere?"

"Just curious. It was the most horrific moment of my life so far—seeing a human being fall out of the sky right in front of me. I thought you'd know the whole story by now—who he was and why he jumped."

"Not even sure he jumped right now. Could've been pushed. All we know for sure is he looked like a street person. Some booze involved; not a lot, but enough to affect his equilibrium. He was a real mess—mostly pulp. Not that it matters. Street people don't tend to have dentists anyway, if you know what I mean."

A beefy detective with a buzz cut and an ill-fitting suit poked his head around the door. "Sorry, Mike. I'll come back later."

"No, come on in. Jim, this is Dermot Nolan. He's a famous writer. Dermot, meet Detective Jim Hansen."

Hansen was six-three, two hundred pounds, and an obsessive bodybuilder. His shirt stretched tight across his chest, abs, and biceps, like the Incredible Hulk's preripped vest.

Dermot held out his hand. "Pleased to meet you, Jim."

"Pleasure's mine," he said, as he gave a hearty shake.

"Dermot was right there when our John Doe died," Kandinski continued. "The Stratten jumper."

Hansen eyed Dermot. "Is that so?" He thought a bit. "Beat cop must've made an error. Said your name was Dolan. Said he asked you to stick around. But I guess you had something urgent to do." He hadn't taken his eyes off Dermot, nor blinked. Dermot felt unsettled.

"I did hang around for quite some time, but no one approached me, so I thought I'd come in here now and see what help I could be."

"Sure. That's good of you, Dermot," Mike interposed. "Can I get you some coffee?"

"No. But thanks."

"Wise decision. It's sludge," said Hansen.

Dermot sensed they were both waiting for him to say something, but he had no idea how to begin.

"So, you saw the old guy jump?" Hansen asked.

"No. No, I didn't. The first thing I knew was he was hitting the deck just a few yards in front of me."

"Shame," Kandinski said. "Would've been useful if you'd seen anyone else up there on that roof with him."

"Did anyone else see anything?" Dermot asked, as casually as he could.

"We're still door-to-dooring. No one yet."

"He wasn't carrying any ID?"

"No. But it's seldom people remain John Does for long. There's always something that'll tell us who he was," Hansen said, opening the office door. "Look, I got to go do stuff, Mike. I'll be at my desk filling out paperwork if you need me. Nice to meet you, Mr. Nolan."

Hansen closed the door behind him.

"Anything else I can help you with, Dermot? You got a new thriller on the boil?" Kandinski asked. "About time, I'd say," he quipped.

The comment hit a raw nerve, but Dermot didn't let it show.

"Yeah. Been a long time between drinks. But, yes, I'm working on something kind of different."

"Well, let me know if I can help you with anything. Just call me, huh?"

"Thanks, Mike. I will."

CHAPTER 22

The Flower Street Cafe was full. Dermot and Nick sat at a table at the rear of the restaurant. Dermot toyed with a chicken salad; Nick ate a focaccio like a starving man.

"Far cry from Traxx." That was Dermot's favorite restaurant.

"Don't worry, the good times will be back and soon," Nick replied cheerfully. "If you could eat like a king every day, life would be dull."

Dermot smiled. "You really think so?"

"Sure. I was talking to the guy who bought the Jackson Pollock I represented. His teenage daughter walked in and the father introduced her to me. Sexy in an obvious, anorexic, Kate Moss kind of way. He asked her where she'd like to spend the weekend. She pouted. He says, 'Paris?' She drawls, 'Oh, Dad, I'm *so* over Paris!' Then she starts in about global warming and all the jet fuel they'd use to get there. Private jet, of course."

"Brat."

"Sure. But if she had to holiday on Brighton Beach a few times she'd be looking forward to one day in Malibu."

"Sure."

Nick saw there wasn't much he could say that would lift Dermot's depression. "So what did you find out today?" he asked.

"A forty-something woman named Marla Nestor went missing near Shute about the time Arnold says he killed the Superglue Lady."

"A missing woman? So what? Doesn't mean she's dead. Anyway, Nestor was a prostitute. She probably just moved on."

"What about the glue on the chair?"

"Do you know that it's glue? Have you had it analyzed?"

"No, of course I haven't. But I think I know dried glue when I see it."

Nick looked dubious. "Sure you do. I bet that blob could have been any number of things."

"Then how did Arnold know about the rooms, and the chair with the stuffing falling out the side?"

"He went there, dumbass," Nick replied with no animosity. "Research. You know, like when you're a writer!" He paused and finished the last bite of his sandwich. "Dermot, you're asking me questions you already know the answers to. Ease up. Fact is, you still haven't convinced me that Arnold did anything other than base a story on a lot of real-life events he read about somewhere. Maybe some old newspaper he found in a dumpster. Then he set things up to scare the shit out of you."

They sat in silence for a while.

"How about I treat us all for dinner at Traxx tonight. I just made a deal on a Klee and I'm fully cashed up. What d'ya say?"

Dermot was about to respond when he saw Neela enter and walk towards them. She kissed Nick on the cheek and took a seat next to Dermot. "I've got some good news. Our troubles are over, I think."

"You won the state lottery? Or better yet, you robbed a bank?" Dermot said with a sarcastic edge.

"Neither. But I can tell you one thing you *will* want to hear. Remember the Free Fallers? Meredith and Noam Zersky?"

"Pushed out of a plane, and the pilot was shot and killed."

"That's right. Well, the DA has brought charges against the alleged killer, and he's on remand, awaiting trial!"

No one said anything immediately.

"Didn't anyone hear what I just said? The man who killed the Free Fallers is in jail right now, which proves Arnold was lying when he said he did it. And if he lied about this one, who's to say he didn't lie about everything?"

Dermot just shrugged. "How do you know they charged the right man?"

"I doubt if the DA would send the guy to trial unless the cops convinced him there was a case to answer."

More long seconds passed.

Neela looked deflated. "What's the matter with you, Dermot? I come here with some real good news, and you just shrug your shoulders and look for problems. Are you going to tell me you got some *bad* news today?"

"No. I guess not."

"Then as far as we know, the police have found three of the bodies mentioned in the diary—and those three deaths have been attributed to someone else. Sounds like good news to me."

"So now what?" Dermot grudgingly asked.

"So now we know that Arnold's diary is a work of fiction—one that has probably not been copyrighted or even Xeroxed by anyone. The bottom line is you can do whatever you want with it. Shred it, rewrite it. Whatever! What you just don't do is whine about it—because you've got no reason to. You have a real opportunity here."

Instead of annoying Dermot, Neela's words seemed to cheer him up. That was, until Nick spoke again.

"So what about the Mouth Maiden? Did you check her out? I seem to recall that she got free. Am I right?"

"You're absolutely right," Dermot replied. "That particular chapter ends with Arnold hunting the girl down and dragging her back to the shed he'd set up in the countryside."

"You think she could still be alive?" Neela asked. "Somewhere out there? Maybe tied to a dentist's chair? That's one hell of a thought for lunchtime, isn't it?"

"No," Dermot replied sharply. "He'd have finished her off for sure. We just don't know how and when."

"Could have been a few days ago for all we know. She could be dying as we eat," Nick observed. "He doesn't say he did finish her off. Which means he either didn't, or he doesn't know whether she died or not—presuming he made up the episode or based it on someone else's handiwork."

"If anyone had been found dead with all their teeth pulled or drilled out, it probably would have made the news," Neela interrupted.

Dermot and Nick nodded. It made sense. That kind of torture in a homicide was God-given front-page news.

"So why not check it out?" Nick suggested.

"Go out there again? Jesus, Nick! Don't ask me to do that." Dermot stared at Nick. "Unless you'd like to come with me," he challenged.

"No fucking way," Nick chuckled. "I'm the biggest scaredy-cat around."

Dermot laughed for the first time in days and pushed his plate away.

They sat in silence for a while. Then Neela spoke. "I think . . ." she hesitated, "I think we have to come clean with the police. At least get Mike's opinion. Arnold's pseudo confession to the murders of the Zerskys and Hamilton throws doubt on the guilt of the man they're holding for those killings."

"No!" Dermot's outburst was so loud that the people at nearby tables turned and stared. Dermot glanced around, then spoke again, this time softly, but his tone remained urgent.

"How the hell can we do that? What can I say? That a guy I said I didn't know sent me a diary in which he detailed how he'd killed a dozen or more people? That he gave directions to where he buried all his victims and I didn't say anything to anyone? I just went out to see if there actually *were* any bodies out there? And that's not even owning up to coming eyeball to eyeball with a decomposing head."

"You don't know it was human."

"Oh, Jesus, Neela. It doesn't matter! I already lied to Mike."

"But if that girl with no teeth is out there dying right now, the police need to know. They have a better chance of getting to her before you. Maybe they can save her."

"She's got to be long dead by now. How long would you last if someone drilled out every tooth in your head and drugged you stupid with succinylcholide? An hour? A day? No damned way you'd hang on any longer than that."

Neela suddenly began to see a somewhat desperate side of Dermot she'd never seen before, and she was concerned. She glanced at Nick and saw he was thinking the same. Their exchange of looks wasn't lost on Dermot.

"So I'm just some callous bastard am I? Is that what you're thinking? Well I'm *not*! Okay? I'll do what you want. Just to please you both! I'll go look for Phoebe Blasé. Right now. Will that make you both happy? I hope so, because it'll most probably scare the daylights out of me—but who cares? I might end up with a novel after all—who the fuck knows? Right?"

Dermot opened his wallet and tossed a twenty on the table. He looked at Neela.

"You ready?"

Neela couldn't believe Dermot was behaving in such an abusive way.

"I'm still eating. Can't you see that?"

"Well, I've got things I have to do. Maybe someone's life depends on it." He laughed callously and turned to Nick. "Can you give Neela a lift home?"

"Of course," Nick replied, taking her hand under the table. "I'd like another coffee anyway."

"Thanks," Dermot replied offhandedly. His mind was already on other things.

As Dermot disappeared onto the street, Neela burst into tears.

CHAPTER 23

Dermot saw the car the first time when he took the on-ramp to the Santa Ana Freeway from West Temple. He was still considering Nick and Neela's arguments on the moral issue of not telling the LAPD about Arnold's whole sorry tale. That's when he caught a glimpse of the Peugeot. Five cars and a truck separated them. Same model Peugeot. Black. Tinted windows.

All moral and ethical considerations immediately left his mind as he focused his attention on the car. Had he noticed it before? Had it been ahead of him as he left North Grand Avenue? It could hardly have been tailing him from the front.

Got you, you bastard. This time I see you clearly. I'm not dreaming—you're real.

He slipped out of the slow lane and began to pass the traffic until just one car and the truck separated the two Peugeots.

Logically, the twin car *had* to be more than coincidence. It had been in various locations, in the country and in the city. It was the same color. The same year. It had the same tinted windows. Now he had to check it out.

He passed the truck and snaked in behind a Mercedes 55. The Peugeot kept a consistent speed, just under the speed limit. The driver's window was down about four inches. It was tempting—perhaps when he overtook it, he could sneak a look inside.

Overtaking the Mercedes, he accelerated enough to position himself directly behind the Peugeot. Now, the adrenaline rush was taking control of common sense and a wave of road rage was kicking in. He flashed his lights several times at the Peugeot in front—high beam. Then he leaned long and hard on the horn.

The effect on the other Peugeot driver was startling. The car swung violently across two lanes of traffic, almost taking out a Saab coming up in a center lane. It then took off at high speed.

You want to race? Okay. You got it! Dermot stood on the gas pedal and took off after the other car.

Since the Peugeot driver had taken him by surprise, the doppelgänger vehicle immediately gained about eight car lengths. But Dermot had always fancied himself an excellent driver; he floored the accelerator.

The doppelgänger exited onto the Harbor Freeway and Dermot followed. Both Peugeots were doing eighty, maybe ninety-five miles an hour, weaving in and out of the traffic like maniacs. However, Dermot was the better driver, so foot by foot he began to gain.

Soon he was just twenty feet back. He flashed his high beams on and off several times. The Peugeot simply put on more speed. Soon they were barreling along at close to a hundred. Dermot felt reasonably comfortable at that speed, weaving in and out of the traffic as cars swerved to avoid him. The question was how comfortable was the other driver? What would his reaction be?

As they sped under the Wilshire overpass, Dermot inched up and made another move, pulling out to overtake the Peugeot. That's when he saw the window go up. No chance of eyeballing the driver this time. *Shit!*

Adrenaline was now gushing through his veins, so he snaked back in behind the Peugeot, flashing his lights again and leaning on the horn. The other Peugeot swerved violently and took the exit onto West Eighth

Street. Dermot followed right behind. The Peugeot reached the first set of red lights at Columbia.

Would the driver take a risk here? Absolutely!

The car flew across the intersection. Dermot was twenty feet behind—far too close, but close enough to avoid contact with the Beemer that had taken off with the green light to his left, missing its rear bumper by a hair.

Dermot stayed right behind the renegade Peugeot as the driver stood hard on the brakes and skidded right back onto West Seventh. Dermot felt quietly confident—this guy wasn't such a great driver when it came to side streets.

The Peugeot shot around a corner and was lost to sight for maybe two seconds. Immediately, Dermot heard sirens behind him and glanced in his rearview mirror. Two patrol cars had appeared out of nowhere and were closing in on him. They were maybe fifty yards behind him, with lights flashing and sirens screaming.

Dermot barely held the next corner at Bixel; his concentration was now on the cops following him. He hit the ABS brakes and his Peugeot juddered to a halt, just inches to the right of the other Peugeot.

Without giving the police a second thought, Dermot jumped from his car and ran toward the other Peugeot. When he was several yards from it, the driver's door flew open and a woman about thirty jumped out, screaming hysterically and waving her arms at the police. Dermot stopped dead in his tracks and stared at her.

"My daughter's still in the car!" she screamed to the cops. "Help her!"

Four officers were now advancing cautiously on Dermot. All had their weapons drawn; one was pointing his at Dermot.

"On the ground! Now!"

But Dermot wasn't listening. He stared at the woman, who was still screaming, standing between Dermot and her car. The lead cop yelled out again. "Face down! On the ground! Now! Put your arms out, palms down. Don't move!"

Dermot lifted his arms high and knelt down, then prostrated himself, palms down. *What the fuck have I done now?* His face made contact with the roadway.

The cops slowly walked towards him. Out of the corner of his eye Dermot could just make out the figure of a small girl as she jumped from the second Peugeot and ran to the outstretched arms of her mother. Both were crying hysterically. The cops cuffed Dermot and put him in the back of the lead patrol car.

Back at Hollenbeck Police Station, Dermot was processed and then interviewed by a Detective Sergeant Aaron Sassine.

"What made you think you were being stalked by a car identical to your own, Mr. Nolan?" Sassine spoke slowly and soothingly—his usual initial routine.

"I've seen a similar car several times the past couple of days. Enough for me to know it wasn't a coincidence."

"Mr. Nolan. Let's get one thing straight—you didn't know *anything* for sure. And on this occasion it did turn out to be a coincidence. Right?"

"This time, yes. Look, I'm really sorry for scaring that woman and her daughter. I thought they were someone else."

Sassine leaned back in his wooden chair, but said nothing. He stared at Nolan, but Dermot said nothing. The detective glanced down at some sheets of typewritten paper in front of him. "You have no priors, Mr. Nolan. Not even a speeding ticket—not till now, anyway. That's in your favor."

"I abide by the law and respect authority. I was merely provoked by someone who drives a similar car to that lady—provoked to such a degree that I simply had to do what I did. I thought it was the guy who's been stalking me. I had to find out who was at the wheel."

Sassine regarded Dermot coolly. "The driver's daughter was smart enough to use her cell phone to call us from the car. She thought you were going to force her mom off the freeway into oncoming traffic and kill them both." He paused. "Why *would* someone be stalking you? Do you have enemies? Am I missing some domestic issue here? Are you having an affair with someone else's wife? Someone you know have a violent nature?"

"No. Of course not. Nor do I owe any loan sharks money—apart from my publisher."

Sassine clearly did not get the joke.

"I'm a well-known writer. Some people might think of me as some minor celebrity. That can bring out the worst in people. I'm constantly being bugged by people who want me to look at material they've written. But I don't have the time, so I usually throw it away. This often results in bitterness. People think I'm ignoring them and get angry. That's what I thought was going on here."

"Sounds like this has happened before, Mr. Nolan? Has it?"

This question stumped Dermot. "Well, not to me personally, no. But I know plenty of writers who *have* been stalked."

"Can you give me an example? Of writers who've been stalked?" Sassine wasn't about to let Dermot off the hook. "Just so I know what kind of event was bothering you enough to warrant tailgating another car at high speed for several miles and risking a serious accident and loss of life?"

"Well . . . I've read about this kind of behavior many times in the newspapers over celebrities. Tom Cruise, Nicole Kidman. Princess Diana, for heaven's sake!"

Sassine stared at Dermot. Then he smiled and leaned across the interview table. "Mr. Nolan. There's something going on here that you're not telling me. That's my take, anyway. Nevertheless, your driving record is clean and you have no priors of any kind. And a colleague of mine tells me you're a stand-up guy, so what I'm going to do is cut you some slack. As far as the road rage part of this incident goes, I'm going to give you the strongest possible caution. This caution will remain on record, should you ever think of repeating this kind of behavior. You've got your speeding ticket—take it home with you and think about what you did. You're free to leave."

Dermot said a silent prayer to Mike Kandinski, grabbed his belongings, and left.

CHAPTER 24

After lunch at the Flower Street Cafe, Nick took Neela to Sotheby's to see a painting, one he was going to bid on for a client. Later, he dropped her at home. He wasn't surprised to see there was no sign of Dermot. "You think he decided to drive off and dig up bodies? Surely he couldn't have been serious?"

"Who knows?" Neela replied wearily. "He's been getting more and more unstable. Like before . . . I wish I could slip some Prozac into his Jack Daniel's without him seeing."

She walked through the living room and into the kitchen, then unlocked the sliding plate-glass bifold doors that opened onto the garden. She headed for the small garden shed and noticed the shovel was still there. Her relief was huge—had it been missing she'd have known Dermot had gone off digging for bodies. But where the hell was he now? Nick called from inside the house. "Neels, he's back."

She immediately walked inside, relieved. She was shocked when she saw him.

"Give me a drink, Nick," Dermot said, sinking into an armchair. His face was ashen. His tie and jacket were hanging over one shoulder.

Neela fetched three fingers of bourbon in a crystal old-fashioned glass.

"What the hell happened? Did someone carjack you?"

"Nah. I got arrested. That's all."

"That's all? Arrested? Are you kidding me?"

"Was it DUI?" Nick asked, attempting to calm them both down.

"No. Road rage. What can I tell you?"

Neela sat close to him, irritated by his flippancy. What the hell had happened? Dermot was treating everything as a big joke.

"Are you going to tell us? Or is this an annoying question-and-answer session we're having?" she asked.

Dermot heaved a sigh. "I saw another Peugeot on the Santa Ana. I thought it was the Peugeot that'd been tailing me before—you know, the one I mentioned. So I changed roles. I tailed the Peugeot. It turned out—after a pretty interesting ten-minute Indy-car chase—that this car was being driven by a terror-stricken young woman taking her daughter home from ballet class. She thought I was a madman planning to kill her," he took a long draw of his drink. "So, I'll cut to the chase. Four armed cops arrested me. I was handcuffed and taken to the Hollenbeck cop shop." He looked at Neela, then Nick. "Okay? Is that enough? Or would you like more of the gory details?"

More silence.

Neela fought to hold back her emotions again. Was Dermot totally falling apart? Were these crazy kinds of antics going to become a regular part of their lives?

She worked hard to sound calm. "Did the woman press charges?"

"No. And neither did the police. I called Mike Kandinski and told him what had happened. He said he'd do what he could. Said he knew the detective."

"That was a stroke of genius," Nick remarked.

"Sure was. Last thing I need right now is a history of violence on a police rap sheet."

Dermot chugalugged his drink. "Can I have another? Yes, I know. *Yet* another. I won't be driving again tonight."

"Sure, honey. I'll get it." Neela took his glass.

"So you told them about the Arnold business?" Nick asked.

"No fucking way, Nick!" Dermot's outburst shocked Nick and Neela both. "What the hell are you thinking? Jesus Christ, man! I told you in the Flower Street Cafe—I've already kept important facts from the police, facts that I should have told them. I've already lied to them. So what am I supposed to do? Sit there a few minutes after they've taken off the cuffs, after acting like some crazy man, and tell them I thought the driver was the accomplice of a serial killer who'd sent me a diary of his recent atrocities? I'd be in some psychiatric ward by now, doped up to the eyeballs, with you two trying to get to my bedside."

"But Dermot—" Neela began, but Dermot didn't allow her in.

"Besides, it was *you* who told me this diary was the key to the reinvention of my career. Now listen up. If I find Arnold acted alone—or at least feel comfortable with the *thought* that he did—I plan to rip the bastard off as best I can and try to save us from the poorhouse. Okay? I've made my decision. End of story. So shut up about it all!"

Nick reached for his walking cane and stood. "That's up to you, Dermot," he said, walking to the front door. "But me? I have to get some shut-eye. So I'll see you later. You take care, okay? If you need any help on the road tomorrow, let me know. I'll go with you."

Dermot was suddenly embarrassed. "I'm sorry, Nick. I'm just really tense now. Add to that I've never been arrested before, and you get one deeply screwed up individual."

Nick smiled. "Hey, don't worry about me. Just give your wife a hug, huh? She deserves one after today."

Dermot did as was suggested, glad to have her arms around him.

CHAPTER 25

Dermot was up before dawn. He hadn't slept more than an hour or two. Most of the night he'd tried to figure out what he genuinely believed, that the diary was a work of fiction jumbled together from various news reports, or an actual detailed confession of a serial killer.

He weighed both sides of the case as he took a mental inventory of what he had found. The head in the tank? It was an animal's head—sure it was. The stakes and the graves? Well, the timber stakes were certainly where Arnold said they'd be, but if Arnold had only been playing a sick game with him, then that's the way the site *would* look. And now a man was in prison charged with the murder of the Free Fallers and the pilot. So if Arnold had lied about the Free Fallers, logic dictated that he'd probably also lied about all the deaths in the diary, just as Neela had said. Nick was right about the glue on the chair. It could've been anything at all.

Making sure he didn't wake Neela, Dermot slipped out of bed, dressed, and made himself a coffee in the kitchen. He fed Scarecrow and Cheese-cake, fetched the shovel, and was in the car before seven.

As he filtered onto the San Gabriel River Freeway, Dermot felt a good deal more relaxed. The sun was shining and the sky was bright blue. Scare-crow's hairy face was hanging out the window, his ears swept back flat to his skull. The diary and its addendum lay on the passenger seat between them, open to the Mouth Maiden chapter.

Dermot took the 210 and turned into San Gabriel Canyon Road at Azusa. Fifteen minutes later, he spotted the small lakes Arnold had de-scribed, and continued to follow his directions. He passed a Kemps Creek sign and saw the track Arnold had written about. It was narrow and deeply scarred by potholes, as though washed out by heavy rain. Dermot wove his way around the deep gouges. Scarecrow smacked his head a few times on the window frame as the car bounced, before deciding it was a smarter move to pull his head back inside the car.

When you reach the tree line, you'll see the shed. But when Dermot reached the tree line, there was no shed in sight.

Dermot pulled up, leaned across Scarecrow, and opened the passenger door. Instead of jumping down, the terrier stared at the ground for a few seconds, then slunk into the backseat and lay down on the floor of the car. Dermot studied the hound with a wry smile—dogs, gotta love 'em. He picked up the diary and stepped out of the car, whistling to Scarecrow to follow. But the dog stayed put.

Where was the shed? Maybe Arnold had sent him on a wild goose chase this time. No shed meant no murder scene.

He walked toward a copse of trees directly ahead. It measured no more than fifty by a hundred yards and was surrounded on all sides by open ground. About thirty yards ahead, Dermot noticed an indentation in the ground. It looked like a prefabricated shed had once stood there. His heart sank. It was about four times the size of a portable toilet. The ground in-side the indentation was hard as a rock; the ground outside looked com-pletely different, as if washed away by rain.

He crouched down and studied the indentation carefully, running his fingers over the scuffed earth. If this was where the shed had stood, why had it been moved? And who had moved it? An elderly derelict like Arnold? This finding lent even more weight to Neela's theory that if

Arnold was indeed a killer, he must have had an accomplice. However, Dermot didn't feel like following that line of thought yet—far better to suppose Arnold had acted alone. An accomplice, after all, suggested Arnold was indeed a murderer.

As he pushed down with his right hand to stand, he stirred the ground on one side of the indentation. He looked down. His fingers had uncovered what looked like a small white pebble, no larger than a child's fingernail. He picked it up and examined it closely. Actually, it didn't look like a stone at all—it was more like a piece of ceramic. He disturbed the ground some more to reveal three more shards of white ceramic-like material. His gut told him exactly what he'd just found: teeth.

A knot was developing in the pit of his stomach. He turned the fragments over, studying them carefully. If they were teeth, that didn't necessarily mean that they belonged to Phoebe Blasé. Nor did it mean the girl had even been here, let alone been murdered here. Another of Arnold's cat-and-mouse games? Dermot quickly did a bit of intellectual spinning. The shed wasn't there now because it never *had* been there. It was an easy task to gouge out marks that would lead him to believe it had been. And all Arnold had to do was scatter a few pieces of broken teeth in the earth to convince Dermot this was where Blasé had been tortured and killed. He carefully slipped the white shards into his shirt pocket and continued walking around the tree line.

The damned generator was dry, so I walked to the car to get some more fuel. Must've been then she decided she had enough strength to slip past me. I should have stuck her again with a needle, but she looked like a sad sack of potatoes when I left her, so I didn't think it was necessary. Fact was she fooled me. She was smart—had to give her that. But I was smarter. She didn't get far.

Dermot tried to imagine which direction Blasé would have headed. He'd parked his own car in the most logical spot at the head of the track. Presumably, Arnold had, too. It was logical to assume she'd stumbled as best she could in the opposite direction—toward the bushes to hide.

It was black as shit when I got back to the shed and saw the door hanging open and the girl gone. So I stood very still and listened. After a few seconds I heard the brush moving ahead of me, then it was still. So I guessed she'd decided to lie low.

Dermot continued walking. About thirty feet away, he spotted a patch of ground where the vegetation was beaten down.

Only took me about three minutes to spot her. She'd curled herself into a ball and had squished her body deep into the mud. The rain was still comin' down like an open tap, so maybe she thought I'd miss her. But I saw her. I had to hand it to her, she was one gutsy girl. Anyway, I thought I'd have a little fun, so I called out to her, like we were playing a game of hide and seek. "I seeeeee you," I cooed, like I was her daddy. Just to see if she'd move. She didn't, so I moved a step closer and called out again. And again. Must've scared her to death, because I was getting closer and closer every time. It wasn't till I was a few yards from her that she moved. Just a twitch. Caused by the pain in her mouth, I'd say. Anyway, I stamped down on her leg so she wasn't going any place; then grabbed her hair and dragged her back to the shed right through the mud, caveman style.

It was time to go. There was something evil about this place. He was shaken up and wasn't afraid to admit it. He was trying desperately to believe that Arnold had borrowed some police scenarios and news reports, but it was becoming clear that the old man had indeed committed at least *some* of these crimes.

Scarecrow was curled up on the floor in front of the backseat, whimpering. Dermot knew the dog would need to pee, so he opened the rear door and tried to pull him out.

"You're getting out, Scary. I mean now. I'm not having you pissing in my car."

But Scarecrow resisted—his body actually shaking with fear. No way was he getting out of that car.

Dermot stared angrily at the dog, reminded of horror movies where canines know when they're in the presence of a devil, werewolf, or demon—and humans don't.

He looked around. Nothing. The sun was out and the countryside looked lovely. In fact, everything looked so peaceful that he calmed down, deciding he'd revisit the Stakes Couple. He hoped they would reverse his new fears that Arnold was a serial killer.

The sun was slanting down when he caught sight of the twin stakes again. On the journey Scarecrow had returned to the front seat and seemed to have forgotten his imagined fears. Life was good again. Not so with Dermot. Once he saw the twin stakes, all the familiar demons came back.

He stood in front of the taller stake, holding his shovel and looking at the rope burns and the almost-black stains at its base. He crouched and took a small sample of the black earth, spat on it, then rubbed it between his thumb and forefinger. It turned from black to a deep red. Just like dry blood would if it got wet.

Dermot stood up quickly. He'd felt something graze against his leg and he jumped—but it was only Scarecrow. The dog sat about five feet away, staring at him. Dermot smiled, reminded of the *Lassie* television shows when he was a kid: *Over here! Look over here! Woof woof.*

Okay. Dermot decided to play the game. "What's up, Scarecrow? You want to show me something?"

Scarecrow raced off and sat right on the spot Dermot had found the last time he'd been here—the grave site.

Dermot dug for about an hour. It was hard work, but he had to be sure he hadn't missed anything. Scarecrow got bored after about ten minutes and snuffled off into the undergrowth.

He was three feet down and had excavated the full length of the area that was supposed to represent the grave when he decided to quit. No bodies. End of story. Several minutes later, he was driving back down the track, trying to avoid the deep craters in the road. He felt much happier that his dig had revealed nothing. More grist to the mill that Arnold was a scammer, plain and simple. It was only then he saw Scarecrow in the rearview mirror, obscured by red dust, running like crazy after the car.

Shit. I forgot the damned dog!

He braked hard and opened the passenger door. Scarecrow jumped in, carrying a small piece of cloth in his mouth. Dermot tried to take it from him, but Scarecrow started playing the "see if you can get it" game. He was exhausted. He wasn't about to play doggie games now.

As he headed down the highway, another thought entered his brain. Why had Arnold named some victims and not others? Why say Ms. A, rather than Alice Andrews? He glanced down at the diary pages, focusing on the drawing and directions under her name. Her site was only about fifteen minutes from where he was now. At Yellow Rock.

He floored the accelerator.

As he neared Ms. A's location, habitation became sparser. The landscape was reasonably lush and green. At last he found the turnoff from the main road that indicated Singles Ridge Road.

Take the Purvines Road turnoff all the way down to Fogg Road. Then you go off-road due south. One mile. Then park. Walk down the pathway to your right then look upwards to the top of the grassy bank.

Dermot didn't have to tell Scarecrow to stay in the car. He followed the trail on the other side of the gate, as detailed in the notes. He walked for several minutes, until a rising bank, previously hidden by a hedge, appeared on his right. He stopped and stared up at the crest, where a large object was shadowed by the sun. The closer he climbed, the clearer it became to Dermot that the object was a wheelchair.

Standing beside the chair, he happened to glance down to his car. There was a second car parked next to it. A Peugeot 207—identical to his own.

The fucking second Peugeot! Jesus H. Christ!

He watched, rooted to the spot, as a man stepped out of the second car and opened the door to Dermot's car. He took an involuntary step forward and stumbled, clutching the back of the wheelchair for support. Then he ran headlong down the grassy slope, temporarily losing sight of both cars as he neared the high hedge.

By the time he reached the gate the second car was gone. He pulled open the driver's door and looked into his own car—no sign of Scarecrow. Where the hell was the dog?

Then he heard a short muffled bark. He crouched down. Scarecrow was under the chassis, his chin pressed to the earth.

"Great guard dog you are," he said, as Scarecrow crawled out to him and licked his hand.

Maybe it was time to go.

He looked back up the hill. A wheelchair? Was that all that Arnold could tease him with this time? No blood? No body parts? He wasn't falling for this one.

There was one last crime scene he wanted to visit. If he didn't find any bodies there, he reckoned he'd be home free. The next step would be to write his own version of the scary diary. He could almost taste the money.

His name was Joey Farrell and his nightmare was pretty ordinary. But it was a compound nightmare, so it made it all the more interesting to me. Something I could really spin well—you know what I mean?

First time I saw him, I knew he was a nerd. Skinny. White skinned—like he'd lived under a stone for years. "I suppose you could describe it as claustrophobia," he told me online. "But that's way too simple. I've had asthma since I was five years old, and breathing's a thing I think about twenty-four seven." The skinny young guy kept pumping his Ventolin inhaler, and I had to wait for him to start speaking again. Pissed me off. I've got better things to do than watch a guy fight for air. But as I watched him heave and pump his little plastic venti-thingie, I drew an image of his face—the way he was going to die.

Dermot was always amazed how Arnold's words stuck in his memory. The images were so crisp and yet so revolting. Lips glued together? People plunging through the clouds.

Once I got him out of the trunk of the car, I roped him to a rock. Well, there weren't too many trees around, and I knew the rock would be heavy enough to hold him. It took him a good thirty minutes to come around. That's always a fun time, because you can see the first slow realization creep into their eyes—but so very slowly. First it's "What the fuck?" Then it's "What the fuck am I doing here?" Then it's "Oh fuck!!!!" It's like the various stages of coming to terms with alcoholism. Like denial and acceptance and all that crap.

While he was out I'd put a heavy-duty clear plastic bag over his head. I tied it tight around his neck and had this thin rubber hose hanging out—one end inside the bag, the other connected to the oxygen bottle.

As I saw his eyes flick open I watched his reaction. It was the best thing I'd seen since I pushed the Zerskys out the door of the plane and saw their eyes bulge. That was something else.

Farrell looked around and tried to figure out where he was. He was very scared indeed. I could see him trying to move his arms but he couldn't. He must have realized he was tied up and in major trouble.

I looked him straight in the eye and gave him a wide wonderful smile. Then I switched the tap off and reversed the flow. I watched his reaction very closely.

A fraction of a second later, the plastic was clinging to his face like a second skin. The best thing of all was that he tried to open his mouth as the plastic shrank. This meant he couldn't close his mouth at all! I could see right down his throat. Then I opened the valve and let the oxygen flood in again. The effect was fantastic! He must've taken in five lung-fulls—gasping in and out! And all the time he stared at me, pleading for mercy with his eyes.

Dermot stopped the Peugeot by the side of the empty road to look again at the directions to the Plastic Bag Man. He'd been driving for the better part of an hour northwest on a dirt road and was approaching Tujunga Wash. The sun was beginning to set. He'd have to drive fast.

I carried on for about an hour. One minute he was nearly dead—the next I was giving him life. It was entirely up to me. And all the while I totally knew what breathing meant to this jackass.

Dermot parked at the designated spot. Opening the trunk, Dermot reached for the shovel. Once again, Scarecrow wouldn't get out.

At the top of the hill, he caught sight of an oxygen cylinder and hose, both deeply corroded by the elements. Another nice touch. Arnold had sourced the correct equipment and laid it out for Dermot to find.

Very faintly, he heard a whistle in the gathering gloom. He looked carefully around but saw no one. Seconds later, Scarecrow was running madly toward him, his ears flat to his head. The animal looked terrified, crouching down close to Dermot's heels.

"Decided to have a bit of an adventure, did you? About time, Scary."

He opened the pages of the diary.

I got bored after a while. One second Farrell was about to lose consciousness; the next the bag was filling with the delicious, crisp, heady elixir of life. So I finally said good-bye to the nerd and waved to him. He died two minutes and five seconds later. Not bad for an asthmatic. I buried him eighteen paces away on the far side of the hill.

Dermot began pacing it out, but Scarecrow was way ahead of him—already pawing at the loose earth. Shooing the dog away, he started to dig. It was cooler now, so it didn't take him as much effort.

He didn't notice the ragged fold of plastic at first. It was only about six inches square. But it was Scarecrow's reaction to it that set his mind racing. Scarecrow sniffed the earth that contained the fragment and stiffened. Then he howled.

Dermot knelt down and picked up a much larger piece of plastic that he found next to the first piece. It felt wet. The stench was appalling.

Gagging, Dermot let the plastic bag fall, pulling out a handkerchief from his pants pocket and placing it over his nose. He looked more closely at the section of bag. It certainly was big enough to accommodate a human head—but no more—and it was open at one end. Inside was some kind of a pulp. It looked as though any solid matter such as a cranial bone had fallen out, leaving human tissue clinging to the sides of the plastic.

He started digging again. Almost immediately the shovel hit something hard right below where he had found the plastic bag. It was the size of a small football.

Dermot knelt down and carefully brushed the earth from his find. There was no need to uncover anything more—it was a human skull, infested with moving larvae. A wave of nausea swept through him and he staggered to his feet. At that instant he knew his life had changed irrevocably.

He filled in Farrell's grave without giving it a second thought. He knew he'd made a final decision. No one would know of this grave. No one would know about Arnold and his diary.

"Let's get out of here, Scary. We won't be coming back. Not ever."

The Dream Healer watched Dermot's car drive by. The tree foliage he'd cut down an hour before camouflaged his twin Peugeot 207 perfectly. He laughed lightly at Nolan's expression as he drove past. Confusion. Total confusion, coupled with abject horror. The plan was working. He'd found the wheelchair, but no body. And the identical car had sure spooked him.

It was such fun to use exactly the same model car. There'd been no special motive for it. It was simply another way to drive Nolan nuts, trying to figure out reasons why it was happening. People always assume there are reasons. But the Dream Healer knew better. People lived and died for no reason whatsoever. The Dream Healer had seen the innocent die for no reason. He'd watched them suffer terribly. So . . . was there a God? No way.

He heard a faint thumping sound coming from the trunk. Another miscalculation on the correct measure of succinylcholine. Now was the most appropriate time and place to give her another shot.

He prepared the syringe and walked to the rear of the car, opening the trunk. Wanda Bell stirred—it was most probably just a reaction to the breeze; she sensed someone had opened the trunk.

She was well bound. Her hands and elbows were tied behind her and her knees and ankles were tied tightly as well. Gaffer tape covered her mouth and eyes—the Dream Healer didn't want to spoil her surprise, everything had to be perfect before the blindfold was removed, revealing her most intense nightmare ever.

It took him only ten minutes to return to the car park at the end of Fogg Road. The area was deserted. He pulled Wheelchair Wanda from the trunk of the car and slung her over his shoulder. She was unconscious, so there was no issue with any thrashing of legs. He had a good twenty minutes to get her ready.

The wheelchair was lying on its side when the Dream Healer reached it. He laid his charge down beside it and righted the chair with gloved hands. He'd seen Nolan touch it with a bare hand. This was a *huge* bonus.

Lifting Wanda into the chair, he placed her right hand on the electric controls, and her left on the arm of the chair. Next he tucked her feet up onto the twin footrests, pulling four lengths of cable wire from his pocket. He then began with the ligatures—one just below the shoulder of each arm, and one at the top of each leg in the groin area.

He pulled as tightly as he could. The cable dug deep into the flesh, but he made sure it didn't cut the skin—he merely wanted to shut off the blood flow completely, not make a mess. Then he secured her body to the chair, made certain the gag could not shift, and stepped behind the chair so that he could be sure of the exact view Wheelchair Wanda would enjoy as soon as she opened her eyes.

As the light began to fade, he studied the color of her limbs. They were becoming a bloated, deep red purple. She would have lost all feeling in them already. He wondered how long it'd be before gangrene set in. It wasn't particularly relevant—she'd most likely be dead of heart failure by then.

Eventually he saw her eyelids flutter. He could see her face—a mask of agony. The Dream Healer watched her thought processes kick in. *Where am I? Can't move. Strapped down. Legs. Arms. Oh my God!* Finally, she became aware of the shiny wheelchair.

It was time to leave Wheelchair Wanda. The Dream Healer patted the top of her head and made his way down to his car.

CHAPTER 26

It was nearly dark by the time Dermot reached home. He had decided to make a stop at a bar for a couple of hours to have a drink or two and calm his nerves before facing his wife. Neela had yet to draw the curtains, so Dermot could see into the living room from the street. He saw Nick talking, holding up a painting and showing it to Neela. He was smiling—Neela was laughing. He decided right then that she would never know of his decision to descend into the darkest world of ethical nihilism.

Dermot stood outside for several moments looking in at the happy faces of his wife and best friend. Life would never be the same.

Cheesecake was sitting on the arm of a sofa close to the window, staring out at Scarecrow—she didn't miss much, and was probably waiting to finish him off.

"Can you take the dog through to the kitchen, honey?" Neela said as he stepped through the door and Scarecrow led him inside. "Cheesecake's been in a snit all day."

"Sure," Dermot responded with the best attempt at a smile he could muster. "Hi, Nick. Hey, what've you got there?"

Nick and Neela followed him into the kitchen.

"It's a deliciously naughty Norman Lindsay. I was telling Neela how much certain aspects of it reminded me of her. Of course she asked which aspects I was referring to. 'The smile,' I replied. What else?"

Neela laughed. "Let me get you a drink. You look exhausted." Neela watched him empty two small cans of cat food into a soup bowl for Scarecrow.

"You need to get him some proper food, sweetheart. Dogs don't eat the same thing cats do. And get him a bowl while you're at it. That is if he's staying, which I hope he isn't." Her comments weren't meant to annoy him, but they did.

Back in the living room, Dermot sank into a soft armchair; Neela sat at his side, while Nick stood by the mantle.

"How did it go today? Find anything new?" Neela asked. Dermot hesitated, shooting her a questioning look.

"Look, if it's private, I can disappear," Nick said. "No problem."

"No way, Nick," Neela said. "Just more of the Arnold thing. Dermot was out checking some of the details in the diary. How did things pan out today, honey?"

Dermot was suddenly very aware of the tooth fragments in his shirt pocket. He felt as though they were the size of medium-sized rocks and their outline had to be obvious to the eye. He placed his left hand over his right shoulder to cover them.

"Arnold's clearly gone to a great deal of trouble to convince me that his diary is based on reality, but I can't find anything to substantiate it as more than anything but an elaborate hoax."

"But why would he bother doing that?" Nick asked.

"Maybe he thought if I actually fell for his ploy and believed it was all true, a publisher might be more inclined to publish it. You know, 'Based on true events.'"

"But if that were the case," Neela argued, "why not send it directly to a publisher in the first place and lie, saying he was the serial killer responsible. Then commit suicide. They'd surely take him seriously until they did some serious digging and found it was all just pure fantasy."

"Or based on real cases—ones he'd researched," Nick added.

"I have no idea. However, I do know that no publisher would ever read that kind of unsolicited material. But coming from me? That's something else entirely. If I convinced the publisher that everything happened, and Arnold was in fact a real psychopath, then maybe a publishing house would buy it."

No one said anything for a while. Then Dermot wrapped up his case. "Either way, I didn't find a damned thing today. I went to the spot where the Mouth Maiden was supposed to have had all the teeth in her head ripped out, and there was no shed, no chair, no dental tools, nix. I dug around the place where the Plastic Bag Man was supposed to have died and came up with nothing. None of Arnold's stuff stacked up."

"That's wonderful news, honey."

Dermot's bowels had the consistency of water.

"This must be a gigantic load off your mind, Dermot," Nick said. "Mind if I help myself to another scotch? I feel like celebrating here."

"Sure, go right ahead."

"Anyone else for a refill?" Nick asked. Dermot and Neela shook their heads.

"He must have been a very weird guy, Dermot," Nick said as he poured his drink. "I mean, to go to all this trouble. I suppose he got his wish in the end. Now you'll have to show it to Esther won't you?"

The directness of the question took Dermot completely by surprise. He should have seen it coming, but he didn't. He hesitated for a microsecond.

"As his work? You have to be kidding, Nick. That man's been leading me by the nose, lying to me, frightening me, using implied threats to Neela—threats that almost stopped my heart beating. When I saw him dead, I have to say I was relieved. Who knows what he might have done next? He could well have stalked Neela for months. Showing his gruesome treatise to my publisher in the hope that he might gain some sort of notoriety from his scribbles is *not* on my list of priorities."

"One way or another I think it's worth publishing. It smells like money. The question is, who should get it? All that money, that is."

CHAPTER 27

Dermot sat at the end of Santa Monica Pier, staring out at the gentle ripples of the Pacific. The air was still and the sun was warm.

He'd painted himself into a corner. Now he could wait for the paint to dry or pad out of the room, leaving footprints everywhere. But it wasn't this particular aspect of his situation that so deeply disturbed him. Rather, it was how his actions might impact Neela. He had now upped the ante and lied to her as well as the authorities. He should have told her everything, but he'd deliberately not done so. Why? Because he feared she would insist on an ethically correct course of action—one that he now found impossible to follow.

He was now convinced the diary was an accurate, minute-by-minute account of a mass murderer's horror fest. The thought chilled him to the bone, and at the same time strangely fascinated him. Was he ethically bound to give the manuscript to the police? Of course he was. Yet the murderer was dead—he could do no more harm. And the "accomplice" scenario carried little weight. What good could come of any revelation of the diary to the police? Closure? No. His and Neela's lives were more important right now.

He closed his eyes and fought back tears. Selfish self-interest, literary success, and suitcases of money—*they* were more important than closure to the families of countless victims? What kind of monster had he become?

Yet even if he told the police everything he knew, they'd have no one to charge with the crimes. The perpetrator was dead! But what of the man charged with the murders of the Zerskys and Hamilton? That was a much greater concern. Somehow, he'd have to arrange to make it abundantly clear to the authorities—sometime along the line, he mused—that there was reasonable doubt as to that man's guilt. But that was something he'd think about later. Besides, it was always possible the man was guilty of those particular crimes.

He also chose to ignore the second Peugeot, at least for now. It was an inconvenient glitch.

Yet, try as he did, the "closure" aspect nagged. Was it better to know that one's loved ones had died horribly—tortured to death in an unimaginable way? Or was it preferable to believe they may still be alive?

Dermot thought of how any unexplained disappearance of Neela would affect him. He imagined he'd initially be hugely shocked that she'd vanished without a trace. He'd certainly think foul play was involved—after all, he knew she loved him as much as he did her, so there'd be no way that she'd simply walk away from their marriage without at least leaving a letter. But which was the better alternative in the long run? Never knowing what had happened to Neela, possibly to forever harbor doubts that he'd misjudged her affections? Or be confronted with the reality that she'd been gang-raped and given the death of a thousand cuts?

One thing was certain: it was much too late to explain his actions to the authorities. To do so would be to lose his next novel. His two research visits to the murder locations would have to be a secret that he, Neela, and Nick would take to their graves. If the police ever knew of his trips they might even view him as a murder suspect! After all, he'd tampered with various crime scenes, hadn't he? And what about all those people who had seen him in the vicinity of the murder sites? Would the barman at the Lazy Lizard remember him? Had anyone seen him on the road?

Another important question loomed. Could he persuade Neela and Nick to keep his secret? He was almost sure he could. If he was right, he could shred the diary and pretend he'd never seen it. He could maintain

Arnold had never delivered it to him, and hope that no one had seen him do so. That was possible. But what if Arnold had told someone of his intentions, and at some stage this person came forward? He would have to deny everything.

His second option was to develop the diary further, translate Arnold's crude words into his own personal voice, and end up with the pages he desperately needed to deliver. Sure, horror fiction didn't appeal to him, but the diary was very high-concept indeed. It was hugely commercial and would make big bucks. If he could accomplish transposing Arnold's crudely wrought scribblings into the kind of genre that Truman Capote had made acceptable to literary critics, he could well be onto a winner.

He felt a hand on his shoulder. Then he smelled Gautier. It was Neela. He leaned his head back onto her arm. She always knew where he headed to think things over quietly.

"I love you, Dermot. Always know that," she said. "If you ever acted cruelly to animals, I'd have to rethink. But barring that, I'll be there for you forever—whatever the cost."

Dermot drew her close and kissed her hand.

"I love you too, Neels. You are everyone and everything to me."

Dermot and Neela looked deeply into each other's eyes. To Dermot, she seemed to be looking directly into his soul.

She smiled as she pulled a little notebook from her purse and flipped it open. "Let's go over what I've been doing while you've been relaxing on the beach here twiddling your thumbs." She smiled again. "As you know there's someone already charged with the murder of the Free Fallers—that's the Zersky couple, and their pilot, Corey Hamilton. There was also a missing persons report in the *LA Times* about a Lucy Cowley—the Scorpion Girl?"

"I know."

"Well, she's still missing.

"How did you find that out?"

"*America's Most Wanted*. The website. You can search for anyone. By first name, second name, hair color, geography. You name it. It's a giant jigsaw."

"What if whoever it was that went missing was a loner—with no one to miss them?"

"Well, then they probably wouldn't be listed. But to get back to where I was, no one ever found Lucy. So my guess is that Arnold looked her name up and said he'd killed her—but he never did. They say tens of thousands of people just vanish every year in America and are never found. A great many others turn up living different lives with different identities in another state."

"Okay, so who else? The Stakes Couple?

"Can I do it in my order, master?"

"Sure."

"I tried to trace Bruce Major next. In the missing persons' report it said a man by that name inexplicably disappeared from a golf course. It didn't say where he lived or what he did, so I checked phone records going back three years and called a few numbers. The only man his age with his name worked at a hospital as a security guard. Someone else is living in his apartment now. Seems he just skipped town and left everything behind."

"That looks bad."

"Sure. The cops thought so, too. But there was no evidence of foul play, so he's just another missing person. The lady who lives there now told me the cops told her what happened."

Dermot gaped. "You actually went to his apartment?"

Neela looked stunned by his sudden outburst. "Why not? I was being thorough. What's your problem?"

Dermot quickly gathered his thoughts and emotions. "Well, if you think about it, surely it's better if there's no link to either of us if I decide to base a book on these events."

"But if you did decide to go ahead rewriting Arnold's diary, what harm would there be in saying that your story was inspired by actual events. There's no need to mention that Arnold sent you his diary. It'd be a piece of cake just to say you researched a few missing persons cases, added news reports of some actual unsolved murders, and then based the novel on that research."

Dermot could hardly breathe. He'd woven such a tight web that to extricate himself was fast becoming impossible. How could he counter Neela's logic? Were it not for the fact that he *had* found what appeared to be actual evidence of dead people, why not agree to this course of action?

A cute shih tzu appeared from under the bench and nuzzled Neela's leg. An owner called out and it ran off.

"If, and I emphasize the word *if*, I decide on a rewrite, I'd prefer it to at least appear to be a work of fiction. Once I've transposed it into my own voice, I'd say few people could see too many correlations, even if they'd seen the original. Besides, I might choose to expurgate some of the more graphic details—those I consider too offensive and confronting."

"But honey, it's this very graphic 'in-your-face' quality that's its power," Neela replied, quite reasonably.

He was now getting seriously edgy. "Well, you may have a point there, but let's just not get ahead of ourselves. Can you leave all this to me? It's *me* who's going to have to write the damned thing, isn't it?"

He hadn't meant to shout. The shih tzu owner a few yards away turned her head, muttered something to the dog, and walked away, pulling at the leash impatiently.

"I'm sorry, Neels. You're right. I shouldn't let things get to me the way they do. It's the constant pressure of work and bills, and the thought I might have to write a novel I have no wish to write, based on events I find really repulsive. And then having to put my name on it."

"I understand that. Believe me. I do."

"So they never found him? Major, that is. He's still categorized as missing?"

"Right—'missing.' Unless what you saw in the tank was Major's head, he's missing."

"I don't think it was human. Actually, with the benefit of hindsight, I know it wasn't. It was a dead animal's head, no question," Dermot replied a little too quickly. "Next?"

"Abel Conway. The Flyer. They did find his body. He died exactly as Arnold says, falling from the seventeenth floor of a condemned building very close to our place. You know the building? It's the Gordon Building on South Broadway."

"I know the place. It's been empty for two years."

"Right. Well, the man was a cab driver. I read the police report online. It seems he had no reason to be in the building, let alone on the seventeenth floor, because no one's lived there since it was closed up. The cab company records state some guy called on a cell phone, asking the cab company to pick up his elderly grandmother and take her to a nursing home. Said his mother had asked for the cabbie by name. Anyway, it came out that he was terrified of heights, so what the hell would be so terrifying to make him jump out of a seventeenth-floor window?"

"How do they know he jumped? Maybe he was pushed?"

"Like Arnold?"

Dermot immediately felt a profound sense of irritation but didn't let it show. "Whatever."

"Someone saw him jump from an adjacent building," Neela continued. "Anyway, the Stakes Couple are next. Gareth Nash and his wife, Laura."

"Sure, what about them?"

"They went missing the same day, but at different locations. He was heavily in debt, and after their disappearance it was learned that she had been embezzling at the finance company she worked for, to the tune of over a hundred thousand dollars. The story at the time was that they left everything behind and went overseas to start afresh."

"You think that's likely?" Dermot asked. He was clutching at straws, hoping he might persuade Neela this was an option. "You think Arnold could have run across the story and concocted a different one—even going so far as to show me the setup with the stakes, together with the dried animal's blood?"

"Sure, why not? There's no other concrete evidence, is there? It's all simply speculation."

Dermot took a deep breath and tried to relax.

"The Plastic Bag Man's a mystery. I haven't been able to locate any reference to a Joey or a Joseph Farrell. Maybe he lived alone, went out of state someplace, and nobody noticed he was gone."

"Or maybe he never existed? Arnold made him up to pad out the story?" The lies were coming just a touch easier now.

"Yes, that's a possibility." She mulled this over. "You didn't find anything at the location you visited?"

Now he'd have to decide whether to lie to Neela or come clean. He had half a second.

"No, nothing." It was easier than he had thought.

Fortunately for Dermot, Neela had no reason to doubt him, so she never picked up on his expression—she was looking down at her notes again.

"That's a relief. It lends credence to my opinion that Arnold made it all up from missing person reports and newspaper clippings, and maybe some radio or television news stories when he came across them."

She paused and then looked at her final note. "The girl called Phoebe Blasé did go missing. She was actually a pretty well known model. I can see why Arnold dreamed up the dentist scenario—she could have been the Colgate girl. Amazing teeth. They had to be caps, though; far too perfect to be real."

Dermot thought of the fragments and made a mental note to destroy them as soon as he got home.

"Lucy Cowley, the Scorpion Girl, was murdered. Her body was found in her own bed. There was a long article in the *LA Times* about her. Quite a cause célèbre. I suppose it was the manner of her death. Cowley died of scorpion venom, though no trace of insects was ever found in her bedroom."

"Arnold says there were spiders, too."

"That's right. She had tarantula bites—not life-threatening—all over her stomach and neck. That apparently was unusual since spiders seldom strike humans unless provoked. But we have to remember that Arnold wrote that he took pleasure in goading the spiders with a straw before releasing them, so they *would* strike the moment they were free."

"Well, that's only what Arnold says. What actually happened to her at the hands of her murderer is another matter. I may have to consider what really happened if I'm ever to make his manuscript mine."

"You sound pretty convinced that Arnold had nothing to do with the deaths. What suddenly changed?"

Dermot opened his mouth, but words didn't come right away. "No, not at all. It's the lack of any real evidence, I suppose. The fact that it doesn't ring true in many respects."

"What doesn't ring true?"

"Oh, quite a few things. I won't go into it all right now. But as you rightly suggest, anyone could have researched the facts Arnold detailed in the diary. Anyone. So why not me?"

"It sounds to me like you've made your decision."

"Yes, but I'm not going to publish *Arnold's* novel. I'm going to write a whole new work using the murders. It won't be told as a second-by-second confession to abhorrent crimes, but rather told in the third person—in my own voice—as a depiction of the mind-set of a twisted psychopathic serial killer."

"You think it'll be as powerful told your way?"

Dermot couldn't help a glance of annoyance. "Well, I would hope so."

"I'm not saying otherwise, honey. I know you can do it. I'm just saying that what caught my imagination initially when I read Arnold's confessions was its immediate savagery."

"Well, let's hope I can match it."

Dermot laughed grimly. Then another thought struck him. "Derek Klein is the only person I can't check out because the diary doesn't state where he died—just that he was a paramedic and died of snake bites in an ambulance."

"Does it matter?"

"What?"

"That you don't know where the ambulance was at the time Klein was bitten to death?"

"It's just another anomaly I'll have to fix. Some victims are named, others aren't. Some crime scenes are detailed. Klein's is not. It's odd, but fixable."

"Dermot, Arnold is not a novelist so he has no sense of structure. You'll have to give the ambulance a geographical location, that's all. Place it on the road—somewhere."

There was a pause.

"I had a stroke of genius just now," Dermot replied.

"What?"

"How about I set the whole piece in Australia? It's the other side of the world, and the topography's similar—deserts, wide-open spaces. And who the hell is going to connect the American and Australian locations?"

"But you've never been there."

"What's that matter? I Google everything. Easy." Dermot continued, "And I was thinking of *Worst Nightmares* as a title. What do you think?"

Neela mouthed the phrase a couple of times. "*Worst Nightmares*. Yes, I like it. Keep it simple and to the point. Let's run it past Esther and she what she thinks." Neela stood up. "How about we go home?"

Dermot hugged her. He loved her with all his heart, but he knew he'd entered into a lonely world of his own now where she couldn't follow.

CHAPTER 28

Dermot typed the letters into the Google search bar. Seconds later he received the same message he'd seen before: *Sorry, no information is available for the URL www.worstnightmares.net*. Had Arnold closed down the site before he committed suicide? Presumably. Dermot made a mental note to check on the site regularly, just to make sure. Then a thought occurred to him and he called Neela on her cell.

"Neels? How do you register a website name? I'm wondering if we can track down Arnold's identity."

Neela's tone suggested the idea was a waste of time. "You mean a domain name?"

"I suppose so, yes."

"Well, I doubt very much he'd reveal his identity that easily to anyone. But it's worth a try. Try Register.com, they trade in domain names—they'll tell you if the name is still registered to anyone. But whether they'll tell you who registered it with them is another matter."

"Thanks, Neels."

He called Register and spoke to an employee, asking how to find out who had registered the domain name. A guy called Andy told him he could search for the name at a site called WHOIS. "That's what I'd do," Andy advised. "But if he's paid for a private domain, then it's a private generic data listing, and it's not available to the public at large. I expect the FBI and the police could find out. But otherwise . . ."

Dermot had no idea what the guy was talking about but thanked him anyway. Then he typed worstnightmares.net into the WHOIS search bar. A couple of seconds later he saw: *The domain extension you have entered is not supported.* He had no idea what that meant either. He'd ask Neela, the nerdier of the two of them.

He picked up Arnold's diary and studied the handwritten cover. He undid the stapled binding and spread out the pages by his computer keyboard. Then he slowly read the prologue again. *I will bring suffering to others, equal in measure to my own. Through suffering cometh salvation. You will never know true sorrow without suffering true loss.*

Dermot closed his eyes. Such garbage. Yet still riveting as ever. He started to type.

An hour later the doorbell rang. He instantly felt blessed—he now had a reason to stop.

It was Nick. "I was just on my way to Sotheby's. Thought I'd pop in, see if you'd like a break from whatever you're up to." He smiled cheerily. "Take you for a coffee?"

Nick and Dermot headed to Bill's Corner Place, where Dermot settled for a coffee and Nick ordered Bill's ricotta cheese pancakes with banana and honeycomb butter.

"For what it's worth, Dermot, I think you made the right decision," he told him, shoveling a forkful of pancakes into his mouth. "I know it's driving you nuts that you've got Esther on your back about pages, and worrying about money is simply going to make matters worse. Who knows, you may start rewriting this thing, and something similar but equally good will leap into your mind. That'd be even better."

It was a thought. Definitely. But the possibility of a similarly wonderful original idea born out of Arnold's canvas didn't seem likely. Nevertheless, Dermot smiled as he sipped his coffee.

"You realize that if I do rewrite the diary, it has to be 'in the vault'—"

"Naturally. I absolutely understand," Nick said. "No need to have mentioned it."

Dermot was embarrassed.

"My guess is that by the time you've finished with that manuscript it'll be so unlike the original even I'll find it difficult to see any similarity," Nick assured him. "That's the power of your gift. We simply have to reawaken that. It's been practically comatose for a year, hasn't it?"

Nick motioned to a waitress. "Another two coffees. Same as before, please."

"Have you thought about changing any of the plot details?" Nick asked.

"Of course. Why do you ask?"

"Well, I was mulling over some ideas on my way over here and a couple of things sprang to mind." He paused. "Mind if I share?"

"Not at all. Go ahead."

Nick leaned forward and lowered his voice—this wasn't a conversation one wished fellow late brunchers to pick up on. "Well, if you alter the details it'll distance you from any of the murders. But if you decide to change too much, you may lose the graphic intensity that Arnold achieved."

"I know that, believe me. My plan is to write Arnold's account in my own voice in the first person. I'll try to think like a psychiatrist, with Arnold confessing to the murders."

Nick made a face. "Mmm . . ."

"You don't think that approach will work?"

"I'm not a writer. That's your field. But the psychiatrist stuff may distance the reader from the horror. Either way, you should keep the original when you're through."

"No way! I'll shred it."

"Sound thinking probably. So many people just can't help themselves—they *have* to keep the evidence. It's a weird compulsion. No offense."

Dermot was immediately disconcerted. "You make me feel like a criminal."

"Sorry. I didn't mean to. Do you remember that novelist who wrote about someone flying a plane into the White House? Well, after nine-eleven, no one suggested the author actually trained the pilots—or planned the whole thing, did they? It was sheer coincidence. Fiction."

"Unless it gave the idea to al-Qaeda . . ."

"No way. That scenario has been around for years—the author simply used the premise in his own novel. And that's exactly how your novel will be seen—that is, if anyone should ever put any of the real crimes together with your outline. Which is highly unlikely. No one can prove otherwise. It was—" he paused, "coincidence. That's all."

"That's reassuring," Dermot replied. *More reassuring than you'll ever realize.*

"I thought I might set the crime scenes in Australia," he continued. "I'm sure there are horrors there that mirror our own."

The coffees arrived. Dermot waited for the girl to leave before he continued. "And I thought I might add a touch of my own," he said finally.

Nick looked quizzical. "What kind of touch?"

"A murder scenario. One not based on real-life events."

"You mean you're going to make up your own nightmare?"

"Why not? If ever some investigative journalist decides to investigate my novel he'll come up with at least one real blank wall."

"That's true."

"It'll be a personal challenge to attempt to get inside Arnold's brain and marry his cruelty to my creativity."

Nick looked puzzled. "But I thought you were convinced he wasn't the killer—that he merely based his diary on events he'd researched?"

"Well, that's right," Dermot answered, covering quickly. "What I'm really talking about is Arnold's spin on those events."

Nick nodded. "I see. So, have you come up with a nightmare?"

"Not yet, no," he replied, lying very easily. "But I'm sure there won't be any problem. We all have them—the question will be which nightmare instills the most fear in people; which nightmare is the most commercial."

"I think Arnold's covered most of those bases," Nick replied with a chuckle.

Dermot simply nodded.

"Maybe the nightmare could be close to home? Yours, for instance? What keeps Dermot Nolan up at night?"

Dermot looked at his friend for a minute and silently went back to his coffee.

CHAPTER 29

Dermot started on *Worst Nightmares* the moment he returned from breakfast with Nick. One approach that had just occurred to him was that he could subtly tweak the words of the text to make it clear that the banality of the language was a deliberate ploy to express the killer's inner mind-set. In any event, Dermot felt sure that with his name on the cover, three times the size of the title, every critic worth his salt would understand that the crude delivery of the text was intended, and not a sign of his own lack of writing skill.

Adding original material was an interesting notion. It'd be a real challenge. His own manufactured nightmare would have to match Arnold's in most respects. He'd have to begin with a fictional case history, continue with a made-up visit by the victim to the website, and end with a visit from the Dream Healer, as he put his own disturbing twist on the nightmare.

As the days of intense writing passed, Dermot's overwhelming sense of guilt did not. He wrote with a perpetual knot of apprehension in his stomach, similar to the feeling of unease he'd felt when he'd given up cigarettes—each hour a battle to rid his mind of the demon tobacco. Now, each time he paused from writing, he would recall images of Major's head drifting toward him underwater, or any of the other images he knew were all too real.

At night, as he slept, a new nightmare crept into his subconscious. In dreams, Dermot would turn on a digital camera, and one by one Arnold's victims would pop up on a screen and berate him for not bringing them peace. Each face was hideously scarred and mutilated to match their mode of death.

He never shared this new nighttime horror world with Neela. How could he? He'd lied about what he'd seen on his second field trip—and perhaps that was the worst aspect of his decision to rewrite this piece, that he now had to hide his new self from the love of his life, because he did not want her to see the monster he'd become. All for the sake of a best seller. It was a very lonely place to be.

Something that concerned Dermot was the nagging question about Arnold's particular choice of victims. Was it the nightmares that had intrigued him? Or was he searching for nightmares that fit into scenarios he had always wanted to bring to life—and death?

The more he thought about it, the more he concluded that Arnold had chosen well. Most common phobias were covered in the diary. Now he'd have to ask around to find something particularly original. He'd talk to friends, hoping they'd surprise him with their dark secrets.

Initially, it took Dermot some time to find his own voice and transpose Arnold's gratuitously brutal mind-set to his own prose style. Once he'd written the first page, a feat that took him a day and two nights, Dermot found that the pages flowed like molten gold. Arnold's cruel world became Dermot's own fantasy world, while his subconscious survival instinct had raised a protective wall to guard his sanity. He found he was no longer moved by the cries of anguish, the screams, the endless calls for pity, and the despair of the victims he was writing about—they now had different names and had died across the world in Australia. They weren't real anymore.

Dermot made one structural change. In his own *Worst Nightmares*, the substance of the story was delivered in conversations between a serial killer and his prison psychiatrist. The directions to crime scenes, however, were kept almost the same. Dermot simply changed road names, towns, hotels, and fast food joints as he came upon them. It was far simpler than he'd initially imagined. He just researched with the help of detailed maps of New South Wales, his state of choice in Australia. The online search engines were his new best friends.

In Dermot's version, the shrink was actually uncertain about whether or not his patient's confessions were real or figments of a warped imagination.

The bulk of each chapter was the conversation between the psychiatrist, Tom Sarris, and the serial killer, now named Lund. In this manner, Dermot could delve into Lund's depraved thoughts in some depth while leaving a great deal of the gore and revolting detail to the reader's imagination—where it belonged. In the final chapter, during an analysis session, Lund shows the psychiatrist actual grisly photographs he'd kept hidden, to prove he was the author of the crimes. Then Lund stabs the shrink through the ear with a homemade wooden shiv, killing him instantly.

Neela hadn't bothered to research Arnold's victims any further. She was comfortable with the conclusion that Arnold had merely done some research similar to hers, found missing people, evidence of murders, and had then made them his own. Now that Arnold was dead, surely the results of his research were fair game?

She did have one nagging thought, though. A part of her felt Arnold should share some of the credit for the book. But wouldn't that just complicate matters?

She also made it a point to stay on top of the status of the website. Every couple of days Neela searched for the worstnightmares.net site; each time it was unavailable.

Most importantly, Neela watched Dermot's progress with joy. Her husband was reborn. He was inspired. He had a role in life once again. He had stopped drinking to excess, he was no longer moody, he made love quite wonderfully, and was solicitous of her well-being. He ate like a trooper and sang in the shower. He worked fifteen-hour days, rising often at four in the morning to type away at the computer. Neither Nick nor Neela was allowed to read the pages—Dermot was adamant that he wanted the novel to be a surprise. The more he wrote, the more delighted he was with his results. Each time Neela or Nick tried to coax him to reveal story lines—and he was actually busting to do exactly that, such was his excitement about the project—he managed to refrain from telling them a single thing.

"It may be the best work I've ever done, Neels," he said one day, when he confided in her that he'd passed into the third and final act of the novel.

"When can I read it? I'll need to pretty soon if I'm to be of any use at all."

As his editor, Neela would get first dibs on the new manuscript. Then the pages would be passed to Esther, and ultimately to his publisher.

"Soon. Very soon."

"Can I at least share this wonderful news with Esther? I've been fielding her calls for three weeks now, and I don't know what to say anymore. I just tell her you're writing and you'll have something wonderful to show her soon. She invariably asks, 'When, honey?' and I don't have an answer."

Dermot hugged her. "I don't know how you were able to live with the old me. I really don't. It must have been—" he hesitated, deliberately, "a nightmare." He winked at her shyly, and she laughed. "Look, I'll call Esther myself. I'll tell her to expect the finished draft in ten days. How about that? At least she'll have something positive to tell Wasserman."

"Oh, please! Yes! Do that!" Neela urged. "If I hear her worried voice one more time, I'll go nuts. She loves you dearly, you know. You're her favorite protégé—she always expects great things of you and you've come good so many times. She'll never give up on you. I know that. But it has been hard for her to constantly fend off Dan."

Dermot reached for the phone, dialed, and switched it to speakerphone for Neela's benefit.

"Hi, Janey. It's Dermot Nolan. Is Esther available?"

"I'll put you through, Mr. Nolan. I'm sure she'll be delighted to hear from you."

"Thanks."

Dermot took Neela's hand and caressed it. Seconds later Esther was on the line.

"Dermot, my lovely man. Great to hear from you. Neela's been telling me day by day to expect something wonderful. I can't wait."

"The good news is I can give you the first draft in ten days. Unedited, except structurally by Neela. It's dynamite—even if I do say so myself."

Esther's tone changed from overly energized to wily cautious. "Dynamite, darling? Have we taken a one-eighty now into thriller territory?"

"It's pretty radical, yes. High-concept. A fundamental change of genres for me. But think Picasso! Suppose he'd remained in his Blue Period? We'd have missed out on his Analytical and Synthetic Cubism!"

Esther wasn't convinced. "But darling, I always loved your heart, the beauty of your line, the elegance of your voice—" She was about to wax praise still further when Dermot cut her short.

"Look, I know you don't care for anything that's too commercial. Nor do I. I feel this book will transcend that genre and possibly create its own. Besides, we both know what interests Dan. It's sales. This novel could put some serious money in all our accounts. Then I'll be free to take as long as I care to with the next novel—hopefully a sequel to *Incoming Tide*."

"Oh, I'd love that," Esther replied. "Not so much the money," she added quickly, "the sequel."

"I know what you mean. The thing is, I do need some money, and that's one of the reasons I started writing this book."

"What's the subject, lovely man? At least you can tell me that. Are we looking at an Edgar? It's a very different kettle of fish, but fish nonetheless."

"There's nothing wrong with an Edgar. It's as good as a Pulitzer when it comes to film options. But as for clues—I'd rather it was a total and complete surprise. I don't want you leaping to any conclusions as to whether you're going to like the book. Okay? And tell Dan it'll be like printing money. I'm sure that will appeal to him."

"Decidedly so, darling," Esther replied, a trifle grudgingly. "But can I actually call Dan Wasserman? Give him a time frame? Two weeks or so?"

"Sure, why not?" Dermot replied.

"What's it called? The least you can do is tell me that."

Dermot glanced at Neela. She nodded enthusiastically.

"*Worst Nightmares*. Get the picture?"

There was the slightest hiatus. "Sounds violent."

"In some respects it is."

"Well, get moving. I need those pages pronto."

"You'll have them. Ten days. Bye."

"Bye."

Dermot stared into space and took a long and very deep breath. His feelings were mixed, but Neela's were not. He was acutely aware of what he was about to embark on, as well as the dangers involved. He knew he'd crossed into a twilight world of moral delinquency by not revealing the truth of all the atrocities to the police. He couldn't bring closure to the grieving families. Above all, he'd lied horribly to Neela. Dermot's stomach turned over, while pure exhilaration flowed through Neela's veins.

CHAPTER 30

The next ten days passed with the speed of the Japanese Bullet Train for Dermot; for Neela, they dragged like an Amtrak freight. Dermot spent practically all day and most of the night in his office; Neela spent most days fending off the creditors and juggling credit cards so she could pay the utility bills. They both knew the stakes were high, but they were comforted by the knowledge that soon Dermot would have a finished manuscript. Given his credentials, it was more or less a given that the book would be published and sell well. After all, Dermot was still one of the hottest authors in America, and hundreds of thousands of devoted readers had been champing at the bit for another "Nolan."

At six o'clock on the ninth day, Dermot stepped out of his office and stood in the doorway to the living room. He smiled at Neela. She looked up from her book and knew at once he'd finished.

"Done?"

"Done."

"My God, that's wonderful. Can I read it now?"

"Go for it. But remember the rules. You love it, okay?"

"That's not fair."

"Sure, it is. You've loved all the others. Why should this one be any different?" Dermot replied playfully. He was pumped.

Neela just smiled back. *Maybe I'll hate it because you didn't really* write *it.* It was something that had worried her for over a week, but she had said nothing—with his voice and his craft it'd be wonderful. She felt certain about that.

"Well, get lost," Neela said, waving him toward the door.

"Where am I supposed to go?"

"Jesus, I don't know. Wherever writers go when their manuscripts are being read. I'm not having you hovering at my shoulder. Go on. And take the scraggy pooch with you."

"His name is Scarecrow and he's one of the family now. Please try to remember that. He's actually very fond of you. He told me."

"Sure he did. 'Cause it's usually me that fills his dish."

Dermot kissed her and fetched Scarecrow's leash.

It was a perfect day. Not too hot. Clear blue skies. Little or no wind. Dermot made his way to his private spot in Santa Monica—the pier.

He was staring out to sea with Scary sitting beside him, when the dog looked up, suddenly fixated by something he'd seen in the shallow water. The fact that Scary didn't move for over two minutes intrigued Dermot. He followed the dog's gaze.

It was then he saw the head.

"Fuck!!" he shouted, gasping. A young girl playing with a ball behind him shrieked at the noise and ran to her mother. The mother swept her up and shot Dermot a look, then strode off down the pier.

Dermot hardly noticed. It *was* a head. A *human* head. It was floating just beneath the surface and looked like it had been in the shallows for some time. It had that putrescent quality that Dermot had only seen once before—Bruce Major's head.

Dermot's mind was racing, yet his limbs were frozen.

What the hell do I do?

Panicked, he looked around. He would've liked to push the head down with a long stick, but there wasn't one around. But he *had* to push it away. He couldn't bear to look at it. A mental trigger was causing flashes of the water-tank head. He immediately found it hard to breathe. What the hell was happening? Was he becoming delirious? Was he asleep? His hands started to shake as he clung to his sanity, telling himself that he was both awake *and* sane, though he wasn't actually very certain of either.

"Scarecrow, *stay*!" he commanded, and began to unlace his boots. He peeled off his socks, rolled up his trousers, and clambered down from the pier into the shallows. Scarecrow watched him, curious.

The tide was out. The water was very shallow for a couple of yards. As he waded near to the head, it bobbed away, inch by inch, yet remained tantalizingly close to his outstretched hand.

He waded out a little farther, until the water was up to his waist. He didn't notice that water was flooding his pockets—his focus was on the cadaverous head, bobbing out into the Pacific.

That was when his right foot reached the end of a sand shelf and he dropped headlong into the deep water. He made one last lunge at the head and got hold of it. Clinging to it, he clawed his way to the surface, gasping for air.

"Here! Reach out! Give me your hand!" someone shouted from the shoreline.

A young man was stretching out a hand. "Come on. Reach out!" Dermot was soon being pulled out of the water.

Dermot lay gasping on the sand, Scarecrow licking at his face.

"Did you fall off the pier?" A short balding man stood over him. "You okay?"

"I think he dropped something into the water," someone else said, pointing to the honeydew melon Dermot still clutched in his left hand.

Dermot looked down. His fingers were stuck deep into the flesh of the fruit. Instantly, he shook his hand free with revulsion and cried out.

He then stared at the melon on the sand. It didn't look the least like a human head. It now hardly even looked like a melon. He felt a complete ass. One young boy was sniggering to his friend and pointing at the melon, then at Dermot's head.

"Better check your pockets, friend. Make sure you didn't lose your wallet, too," an elderly man advised him.

Dermot checked. It was there.

He stood up. "Thanks guys. I appreciate the help. I was standing on the edge of a shallow ledge, I suppose. Stupid really. Lost my balance. I'm fine. I'm fine."

The crowd began to melt away. It was clear from their expressions that most thought he had a screw loose. At this point, he almost had to agree with them.

A melon, for Christ's sake. But it had looked so much like Major's head. Each night the walking dead of the diary haunted his dreams. He'd tried Valium, sleeping tablets, Zoloft, too much booze—everything. Nothing worked. Every now and then he'd wake up screaming, and Neela would hug him till he went back to sleep. But she knew nothing of the demons that now controlled his brain as he slept.

Dermot sat down and Scarecrow sat dutifully by his feet. Gradually his breathing regained some normalcy as the sun dried out his clothes. He was oblivious to the looks he got from people passing. Scarecrow trotted off to relieve himself against the pier, then returned to lie and bask in the sun next to Dermot.

At three o'clock he and the dog drove home.

Neela was still in the office, making notes on a pad with a soft pencil when she saw him enter.

"What the—?"

"Don't ask. Scarecrow fell off the pier. I couldn't let him drown."

Neela looked at Scarecrow. He was dry as a bone, while Dermot was still damp and crumpled. "Okay. Right," she replied, a little confused. "You want to go change, then? When you come down we can chat about the novel."

Dermot's heart sank. He could read Neela like an open book. He knew something was seriously wrong here.

"What's the matter?"

He paused. She stared at him, searching for words. "You hate it, right?"

"Don't be silly, honey. Not at all. I don't hate it—shit, you can't ever help exaggerating, can you?"

"Okay. You don't actually hate it. But you don't like it? That's enough for me. As far as I'm concerned you hate it."

"Let me tell you what I think for heaven's sake, honey. Okay?"

"Okay, tell me. I'll sit down like a good boy and you can tell me. I promise not to interrupt."

Neela wasn't buying his story. "Sure, you won't," she muttered.

"Honest!"

Neela picked up her pad. "Look, I still have the last two chapters to go. But right now I feel it's somehow lost its edge. Maybe it's your voice? It's not Arnold's, after all."

"My 'voice'? That's the problem?"

"Thanks for your promise about no interruptions."

"Well, hell—you're telling me that the original was better, and now that it has *my* voice it's a piece of shit?"

"Calm down, Dermot. I am not saying that in the least. And don't shout at me."

Dermot took a deep breath. "Okay, I'm sorry. I apologize. Carry on."

Neela stared at him for a good twenty seconds—daring him to interrupt again. Then she continued. "It's genres fighting each other. Horror. Thriller. Documentary. Fiction. Reality. You are a gentle soul, not used to this kind of subject matter. Your voice lends itself to romantic, intelligent observation of humanity, not the brutal side of nature that Arnold depicted. You understand that point, surely?"

"Yes," Dermot grudgingly responded. "But it doesn't mean I can't imagine a side of human nature that is alien to my own disposition, and write about it? You see that point?"

"Of course I do. But the strength of the original was its hard, unemotional, amoral, vicious edge. Added to that, it was told as a diary—another strength. Arnold describes every last disgusting detail as if he were completely unable to respond emotionally to the terror, the screams, the bloodletting. Yet you have him recount his feelings to a psychiatrist. We have to view everything through the psychiatrist's eyes. It doesn't work."

"It worked for Peter Shaffer in *Equus*."

"Well, all I can tell you is that I don't think it works here."

She looked up at Dermot, tears welling in her eyes. This was the last thing she'd thought she'd have to tell him. She knew the pages were a very soft version of the original, and she knew that Esther would say exactly what she herself was thinking as she watched her husband: *Look, Dermot. Horror fiction just isn't you. I really don't think this is anywhere near your standard—people will be disappointed. Please don't put your name on this one.*

Dermot dropped heavily into an armchair. "So, I'm screwed, aren't I?"

Neela chose her words with care. "I don't think so. What Arnold had—because he had no skill as a writer—was minimal structure. A raw, vicious edge, combined with a horrifically dysfunctional, cruel voice. You have a hero in the form of the psychiatrist—someone we all can identify with. Someone who gives voice to our horror. Arnold was an antihero— a sadistic sociopath. I was hoping you'd give me 'stark unspeakable horror,' but instead got a precise clinical analysis." She paused. "Are you following me?"

"Yes. Of course I am." Dermot's tone was low and defensive.

"We must expurgate any literary style from the pages you send to Esther."

Dermot exploded. "Oh really? And what the hell will she think? Jesus, she'll think I've lost my marbles."

"No, she won't," Neela shouted back. "And that's because she'll know it's the most brilliant device you could use. A *literary* device!"

"A device?" Dermot wasn't quite following her.

"That's right. In your brilliance you have cut right to the heart of a man we have never come across before. You have crafted his speech, so we can actually hear his mind ticking over. We are able to listen to his unemotional exact descriptions of disgustingly vicious acts of torture and mayhem. We can look into his very *soul*. And that is the scariest thing we will ever do. *That's* what will be so fucking brilliant. *That's* what will scare the living shit out of Esther and your readers!"

Dermot struggled to take in what Neela was telling him, yet it made sense. He had found it utterly against his nature to do more than filter the horror through a third party—the shrink—so the author could have an excuse to practically apologize for the story he was telling. But Neela was right—it was the story itself, told very starkly and crudely, that was the horrific yet necessary element. The fact that a living breathing member of the human race could behave the way Arnold did was inconceivable.

They sat in silence for several minutes. "So what do I do now? I'm washed up." His voice sounded broken, beaten.

"No. You are *not*! I have the answer."

Dermot continued to stare at the floor. He didn't think for a second that she had any quick fix. "Okay. Shoot."

"You copy Arnold's manuscript. Word for word. No psychiatrist, no killer named Lund. The only addition is the nightmare you added."

Dermot looked up. "You *liked* it?"

"Sure, I liked it. It was very scary—especially when you put your own details into Arnold's mouth."

Dermot shook his head. "I don't know, Neels. I really don't know. Writing it my way at least made me feel I was contributing something to the piece. But if I just copy the pages . . ." He trailed off.

Neela knew he was right. She'd tried for hours to come up with a way Dermot could think of the book as his own but had no answer. She walked over to Dermot and sat on the edge of his armchair, wrapping her arms around him. She drew his head onto her chest.

"Look, honey. I've told you how I feel about your effort. The rest is up to you. I may be completely wrong with my take on it. Possibly Esther will love it the way you've changed it. But I have to give you my honest opinion, and in terms of horror, it's like giving a bondage freak a butterfly kiss."

Dermot laughed, despite his blue mood. "That's funny."

"Well, why not give my suggestion a try? Let me type it out. I'll include your special additions. Then read it and see what you think."

Dermot said nothing.

"The thing is, honey, you don't have a choice. I'm sorry to be so blunt, but you promised Esther. She in turn promised Dan. They'll be all over us in forty-eight hours and we've got to have something to give them. We could always revise it later, couldn't we?"

Dermot disentangled himself from Neela, and then held her hand. "Okay. Go copy. Do your thing."

"You think I might be right?"

"I know you're right. This kind of horseshit is quite beyond me. I knew that going in, but I tried to fool myself because I was so desperate. If you think we can get away with it—and that people will actually believe I was clever enough to use Arnold's voice as a literary device—let's go with it. It's our last option. Just be careful with all the new names and locations. And my additional nightmare."

"Consider it done."

He was still awake at six when Neela eventually decided to get some sleep. She looked exhausted. Neither was in any mood to make love; she was in the land of nod within ten minutes.

As he lay awake beside her, his eyes closed, Dermot considered what had happened to him that day. How was it possible that he'd misidentified a rotting melon as a human head? And if he had done so today, was it not also possible that what he thought was Bruce Major's head was also a fruit or an animal's head? And the tooth fragments? Wasn't it possible they were merely tiny shards of a ceramic vase?

His eyes snapped open and his heart began to race. The teeth. What had he done with them? He'd placed them in his plaid shirt pocket and buttoned the pocket down so they wouldn't fall out. But what if Neela had washed the shirt?

He quietly slid out of bed and padded to the wardrobe. He riffled through the clothes till he found the plaid shirt he'd worn the day he'd visited the dental shed. It had been laundered, just as he feared. He unbuttoned the pocket and felt inside. The fragments were still there! Miraculously unscathed by the washing machine and the iron.

One by one he pulled out the pieces. Glancing briefly at Neela to make sure she was still asleep, he tiptoed down to the office, and switched on a desk lamp. He stared at the tiny white chips in his hand. There was little doubt that they had once been either real teeth or caps. He pulled an envelope from a desk drawer and slipped the fragments inside, placing the envelope in the third drawer down in a box of crayons. Then he went up to bed. Luckily, Neela was still asleep.

Neela's alarm went off at seven-fifteen. By this time Dermot realized he simply had to share his burden with someone. Either that or he'd go completely mad. But telling Neela what he had discovered wasn't an option. It would have to be Nick.

Dermot met Nick at Bill's Corner Place at ten that morning. The time suited Nick because he had a meeting downtown with a big corporate customer looking for a massive bronze for their atrium. It suited Dermot because he was desperate to get away from the incessant cicada-like clicking of computer keys.

"How much?" Dermot asked as the coffee and pastries arrived.

"The Glassboro? Stephen wants a hundred thou, so I asked for half as much again. Makes it easier for him to shrug off my forty percent commission."

"Forty?" Dermot was surprised. "You're kidding!"

"No. It's normal. Besides, what would you prefer—zilch or sixty per cent of a hundred and fifty grand?"

Nick studied Dermot. Despite his attempt at showing calm, Nick could see he was anything but.

"So what exactly can I help you with?"

Dermot's awkward aura told the story. "Well, I'd need to ask your opinion on an . . ." he hesitated, "an ethical question."

"It's about the diary, isn't it?"

"Why do you say that?"

"Look, I know I'm no genius, but I'm not stupid. Ask me the question and I'll tell you what I'd do."

"That'd be great."

Dermot glanced around. The two closest tables were empty, but he still lowered his tone.

"Look, Nick. The thing is, I haven't even told Neela this, and it's been really bothering me."

"But you two share everything, right? So what are you holding back from her?"

"Up till now, there's never been anything I couldn't tell Neels. But something came up that I hesitated sharing with her because I was afraid I'd lose her respect. Once that's gone, you can never earn it back."

"I'm sure she'd respect you whatever you did. I've always respected you. There's not much you could do to alter that."

Dermot held up a hand. "Thanks. But let me just tell you first."

"Okay, I'm listening."

Dermot looked him straight in the eye. "I was lying to Neels when I told her I found nothing on the second field trip."

"What exactly did you lie about?" Nick now sounded more serious.

"I told her I hadn't found anything to make me believe Arnold's diary was fiction based on fact."

"But you *did* find something?"

"Yes."

Nick's expression became even more serious. "What did you find?"

"I was concerned . . . Well, Neela was concerned, that the Mouth Maiden might still be alive somewhere. Maybe locked in the shed that Arnold described."

"He didn't say he'd killed her, did he?"

"No, he didn't. So we both felt I'd better check it out."

"And?"

"Well, there were clear indications there that a prefabricated hut had once stood in the area Arnold described."

"So what?"

"I found some . . . fragments."

"Fragments? Fragments of what?"

"White fragments. To me they looked like fragments of human teeth or orthodontic caps. Now tell me that was just a coincidence."

"Do you still have the fragments?"

"Yes, I do. They're in a drawer in my desk."

"I'd get rid of them, if I were you. You don't want them coming back to bite you." Nick laughed at his accidental choice of words.

"Yes, I suppose I should do that."

"That all?"

"No. Next I went to check out the Plastic Bag Man. I found a shallow grave site. The earth was crusted on top but the actual digging wasn't hard at all—underneath it was soft.

"And there?"

"I found a bag. A *plastic* bag. Just like the one Arnold described. But the thing was—it stank to high heaven. And there was this . . . gunk inside it."

"What kind of gunk? Anything you could identify?"

Dermot was now sweating at the memory, his pupils dilated, his eyeballs twitching left to right. "Not really—it was almost some kind of visceral liquid."

Nick placed a hand on Dermot's arm. "Hey, steady. Calm down."

"Sure, okay."

There was a moment of silence as a middle-aged couple sat down at the next table. Dermot drew his chair closer to Nick's and lowered his voice to a whisper. "The long and short of it is this: I think Arnold *did* kill those people, and then he sent me his diary hoping I could arrange for it to be published, giving him some kind of cathartic expiation." He paused. "Is that a tautology?"

"Whatever. I get it. You're asking me if it's morally reprehensible to keep all these details to yourself, rather than doing the honorable thing and telling the authorities?" He made the words sound trite and empty. "Well, I can answer that right away. I'd have done the same thing you did. And why? Because you are in no position to do otherwise. Plain and simple. Tell the cops now and you put your whole life under the spotlight—the whole world will be asking why you didn't do the right thing *before*, rather than praising you for ultimately doing the right thing *now*. They'll be asking the real question: Why didn't he come clean right away?"

"So you think I should have come clean a long time ago?"

"Well, that's debatable," Nick replied evasively. "You have to admit you acted in an ethically questionable manner. There's little doubt about that. If Arnold was the author of all the horrific crimes detailed in the diary, then a lot of families need closure."

"You think I should tell Neels?"

"I wouldn't. But then I'm not married to her. There's always the chance she might freak out, and at some time along the road judge you. Maybe better she doesn't know. I mean, if there's ever an investigation down the line—and personally, I don't for a second think anyone will link you with the cases—then better for Neela to be able to state categorically that it's not in your nature to have done such a thing."

"But it is, isn't it? In my nature? I've proven that now, haven't I?"

Nick tried to lighten the moment by softly crooning the Chris Isaak lyric, *Baby did a bad bad thing*.

They both laughed. It seemed at least to thaw the ice, if not actually crack the surface.

Nick finished his own pastry, then eyed Dermot's untouched Danish. "You going to eat that?"

"No. Be my guest."

"So you're going to publish your version after all?"

"Not anymore."

Nick looked surprised.

"No?"

"I gave it a shot and it didn't work right. Neela said it was piss weak. So the plan now is to type the diary word for word and show it to Esther as if I wrote it. I'm still going to set it in Australia, though."

"That means you're going to have to give it an Aussie pass?"

"Sure, but the protagonist stays the way he is. His voice could easily be American, and everything remains in the first person. So only the other names and locations change. At least my readers will be able to identify with the bad guy. He'll be an American."

"Makes sense."

Dermot looked at his watch. "I'd better get back." He rose. "Thanks, Nick. For everything, as always."

"It was nothing. Nothing at all."

"No, you helped me a lot. I feel I'm not alone anymore."

"In the vault."

Dermot laughed and reached for his wallet, but Nick flipped a twenty onto the table ahead of him.

"Nah, it's mine. You can pick up lunch at Traxx when you hand the manuscript in."

"Be my pleasure," Dermot replied. "There's one location left I still have to visit."

"Which one's that?"

"Outside of Bakersfield. Mr. B."

"The agoraphobic? I remember him well. You're going to fly all the way to Bakersfield just to go walking in the red dust?"

"Sure. Why not? It's research."

"That's my boy," Nick replied with a broad grin.

The flight from Burbank to Meadows Field Airport didn't take too long. Dermot had booked a four-wheel drive from Hertz, and it was waiting for him at the airport. Ten minutes later he was heading into the city center.

Following Arnold's directions, the drive only took Dermot forty minutes. As the odometer clicked over to five miles, he stopped and looked around. Not a tree or bush in sight—nothing. He thought of Mr. B. This was agoraphobic hell on earth. He imagined what it must look like at night. Majestic, as far as any normal person was concerned—the peace and serenity, the vastness of the stars above. But to Mr. B?

There was no sign of a body. He could see right to the horizon, so it wasn't as if he was missing anything.

He walked forward a bit further. Then something glinted in the sun about twenty feet from him. It was a length of slim chain—the kind one might use for a dog collar. It was attached to a sturdier length of chain that was in turn secured to a low-lying block of concrete that had been buried into the parched earth sometime way back. Was this where Mr. B had died? If so, where was he? He could hardly have been buried anywhere close by. The ground was so hard it would break any shovel.

He had the worst case of agoraphobia I'd ever come across. The poor bastard had been housebound for years. For this guy, it was a nightmare to stand inside an open door! Imagine that! I knew I'd have a blast thinking of what to do with him.

The drive was sheer magic. It's a very long way to Bakersfield, but well worth the trip. Every few hours I'd stop someplace and give him another shot. The amusing part was that each time I opened the trunk, he freaked. He preferred it when I shut him in. But hey, that's agoraphobia!

Finally, Arnold had arrived at the spot where Dermot was now standing.

He was unconscious as I lifted him from the trunk. It was such a wonderful night. Cool, without the slightest breeze. The stars shone like a million fireflies. I attached a chain metal collar to Mr. B's neck and then attached twenty feet of thicker chain to it. Then I threaded the end of the chain to a link in the concrete and secured everything with padlocks—that way I could leave Mr. B's hands free and watch him try to release himself. I'd be able to watch him race to the end of his leash and be jerked off his feet!

Dermot stared at the rusting chain.

That's when I left him. No one was going to find him. Not out there. He could scream until his lungs burst.

Dermot looked around. It was true. If Mr. B had been chained here he could have screamed until he died of thirst. But why was there no body? Because there had been no victim, he assured himself. Because it was only a *scenario.*

The sun was beginning to become uncomfortably hot, so Dermot walked back to the SUV and climbed in. Two hours later he was back in Los Angeles—somewhat confused. Scarecrow came to the door to welcome him. The dog had clearly missed him. As had Neela.

CHAPTER 31

"I tell you, Esther," Wasserman said. "This is something else. *Worst Nightmares* is the most totally original high-concept book I've read since *Catch-22*—and look how much money *that* made!" In Wasserman's estimation, sales figures were the yardstick of a prize-winning novel. "It's like reading a weirdo's personal deviant diary. Sick as hell, yes, but a fascinating insight into the mind of a stone-cold killer. Only Nolan could have pulled this off."

"That's what makes him a genius," Esther replied.

Wasserman had little appreciation of intelligent writing, so this flip of Nolan's into sado-horror territory was the very best of news. "I got me a Booker prize winner writing schlock-horror, Jerome. Fucking A's what I say!" That's what he'd told his fresh young boyfriend in bed that morning as he finished the last page.

"I expect you're already thinking movies, Esther," he'd told her. "It's got dollar signs all over it. How about Geoffrey Rush for the lead? If you can *get* him. Or maybe Justin Timberlake!" Timberlake's appeal to young girls was the determining factor here. "They'd be my first picks. And the vics? All cameos. There's a heap of out of work ex-movie stars would snap up these roles like gators!"

Esther simply smiled, nodded agreeably, saying nothing.

"I'm going to fast-track this baby for Christmas," he continued. "I already had a conference call with Lou in London and Hal in Sydney." Gunning and Froggett had imprints around the world. "When we release Nolan's name on this puppy they'll all be licking their lips. And when I'm finished with the *press* release, you just wait—it'll explode!"

He held out a fat scented hand. "Congratulations, Esther. Looks like you've done it big again."

"I try to be of service," she replied with manufactured modesty, though she'd been born without that particular gene.

"And speaking of film rights—which we weren't—David's studio people want to know about them 'toot sweet,' as they say in Froggy land."

Esther presented her appalled expression. "Don't tell me you've shown . . ."

Wasserman waved a beautifully manicured paw. "Nah, just teased David with the concept, that's all. His tongue's dragging the carpet. Between you and me, he murmured two point five mil, with a clause when it hits the *NYT* list."

Esther gave Dan a wry smile—she was good at being everyone's best friend when it suited her. "It always amazes me that people openly discuss what they might offer third parties before they've even touched base with the agent in question."

"Hey, he's just putting out feelers! Thinks I may be able to help him cross the line when he makes you the offer. That's all."

"Well, just keep the manuscript in-house. Can you do that, Dan?"

"Of course, Esther. Consider it done!"

CHAPTER 32

Six months later, Dermot's world had turned from cold mist to blazing sunshine. He was a reborn award-winning writer, again pursued by the press, feted by talk-show hosts. The immediate prospect was millions in the bank.

Anyone else would have thought that Dermot would be the happiest man in the world. How could life be any better?

The real answer lay in Dermot's head—his conscience. He found it difficult to live with his guilt. He was now certain he had done a very bad thing indeed, and there was no way back.

Added to his guilt was a deep-seated fear that all would not run smoothly—he felt the "second shoe" hovering, waiting to drop. Each day when the phone rang, his heart leaped. Would it be Kandinski telling him they'd finally identified Arnold's body? Or worse, some crime desk journalist asking about the body of a young girl found with every tooth pulled from her jaws.

Every morning Dermot scanned the newspapers for news of bodies discovered overnight in the countryside—he constantly feared a dog might have unearthed one of Arnold's victims.

Hardest of all was masking his inner turmoil from Neela. He'd never seen her happier, and it was best for all concerned that she had no idea that he was mentally imploding.

Had it all been worthwhile? Possibly. The money was a godsend. Esther had sold the rights in twelve countries and the initial print run in America alone was three million copies.

Dermot's obsession with the phantom Peugeot 207 stalker continued, however. On one occasion he was driving Neela to an appointment when he passed a car similar to his on Pico and executed a very dangerous one-eighty before accelerating after the hapless motorist. "What the hell was that all about?" Neela said when the other car managed to slip away.

"The *car*! I thought it was the other damned car! The one that was stalking me before. I had to check it out."

"Jesus, Dermot. Put it out of your head. Get on with life."

But Dermot knew he would never be free of Arnold. Even dead, the old man was at his shoulder, chuckling to himself.

CHAPTER 33

Dermot hadn't fallen asleep until five that morning, and had dreamed yet again of falling into a stagnant pool of water, where he found himself swimming with ghouls.

"It's far too much money," Neela called out from the kitchen, interrupting his reverie. "Why not get the classic 1960s model? What do we need with a three-hundred-thousand-dollar car?"

"That was the idea, honey. I'd never buy the new Vantage—it doesn't matter how much money we have. The DB5'd be my pick." He was referring to the vintage Aston Martin he'd ordered.

"Oh, by the way, Greenwood Dental called. You missed your checkup."

Within a microsecond, visions of Phoebe Blasé invaded his mind like a virus. His heart skipped a beat. "Right, I'll call them," he replied, appearing casual. Then a chilling thought occurred. The tooth fragments! Nick had advised him to get rid of them and he'd forgotten about them.

He leaned down and opened the desk drawer, removing the box of crayons.

"You want salad?" Neela called from the kitchen.

"Whatever," Dermot replied as he opened the box.

He rummaged under the crayons—he couldn't exactly remember if he'd placed the envelope with or under the crayons. The envelope wasn't there.

"Honey?" he called loudly. "Have you used my crayons recently?"

"Crayons? What crayons? I didn't know you had any crayons."

"In the desk, third drawer down. Did you move an envelope?"

"No. Nothing. Haven't been in that drawer. You want shaved parmesan?"

"Sure. Whatever you like," Dermot replied. He stared hard at the box. Had he actually put the teeth inside? Then why weren't they still there?

He put the crayons back in the box and replaced them in the drawer. Either way, the teeth were gone. No need to worry.

As he stood up, the phone rang. Tentatively, he picked up the handset.

"Hi, it's me." Dermot exhaled. It was only Esther. "David finally got back to me. They've agreed to two point eight million. You get to write the first draft."

"Esther, I told you, I'm not interested in a movie. It's not a money thing—it's . . ." he stalled.

Esther interrupted quickly. "Then what is it?"

"I don't know, Esther. Maybe I think it works as a book and not as a film. The change in media would be a dramatic one. It wouldn't be a diary anymore. It'd end up some tawdry schlock-horror movie with a lot of blood and gore."

"Yes. Of course it would. That's the whole point. That's cinema, for heaven's sake. I don't understand your thinking."

"I . . ." He didn't know what to say to Esther.

"What the hell are we in this for, sweetheart? We agreed that this time the money was the issue. What's changed? Dan and I have moved mountains to get this deal going. What am I going to tell him? That you don't want to sign off on film rights because you think it might compromise the novel's integrity? Come *on*! It's a horror thriller. I can get Alex Rio to do the screenplay if you don't feel like doing it—that's no problem."

"Look, I'll get back to you this afternoon. Let me think about it. Okay?"

There was silence the other end of the line. Then Esther spoke. "Get back to me before close of play today. I need to call Dan and David." After a short pause she added, "By the way, I sold the Japan rights. You're going to be huge in Tokyo."

Dermot attempted a jolly laugh, but failed miserably.

"Call me this afternoon."

The line clicked off. Neela was standing at the door.

"What was that all about?" Her tone was severe.

"What was *what* about?"

"I was listening, okay? They want to make a movie and you're saying no? Are you for real?"

"Neels, I know it sounds crass, but you know the background and they don't. So go figure." His tone now mirrored hers.

"Don't get snotty, honey," she replied evenly. "Sure, I know about the background, and I thought you'd come to that conclusion a long time ago, way before I typed out Arnold's diary. But there was no evidence the killings were linked, let alone Arnold's handiwork."

Dermot began toying with an ornamental ceramic cat on the desk. "I know all that. The thought of a film just . . . well, it spooks me."

"Spooks you?" she exploded. "*Spooks* you! I hope it does, and that it will spook everyone from Beverly Hills to Katmandu. That's the point!"

Dermot held up his hand. "Enough. It's my book and I make the decisions about it. Anyway, we have plenty of cash without having to sell film rights."

"Jesus Christ! What the hell are you talking about? Plenty of cash? How much are they offering?"

"That's not the issue."

"It sure as hell is! Right now we have a bank balance plus an investment portfolio of just under two mil. That's enough? Suppose you never write another book? How long is that cash going to last? And then what? Get real, Dermot. The film rights issue is one of the major reasons we jumped on this insane merry-go-round." She paused for breath. "So. How much are they offering?"

"Two million. And some more. Plus points, I'd say."

"Jesus! That's fan-fucking-tastic!" She looked him straight in the eye. "How much more is 'some more'?"

"Point eight million."

"Eight hundred thousand dollars is 'some more'?"

"I guess."

"Right. Well, I just made a decision, and it's not the same as yours. And since we're going through this life together, everything I've got is yours and vice versa. I say we're making a movie. So get back on the phone to Esther right now and say you reconsidered and you're cool with the film rights. Okay? Am I making myself clear enough?"

Dermot was cornered. He had no argument, short of coming clean about keeping some nasty truths from Neela.

Neela softened and wrapped her arms around Dermot. "Honey, I want *babies*. And I know you do, too. It's been too long without them."

"We didn't have the money then."

"Sure, I know that, honey. I know that. But now we *do*. Don't you want a son? Or a little girl hanging around your neck, calling you Daddy? Don't you want to take her to ballet lessons, or take a little Elvis to a rock concert?"

"*Elvis?*"

"Somerset then, if you want him to be literary. Dashiell maybe?"

Dermot couldn't help but smile. "Sure, I'd like to take Elton to a concert."

"Elton, in your dreams!"

Neela sat on Dermot's lap and kissed him. It was long and sexy.

"I tell you what. You call Esther and tell her the good news, and I'll go upstairs and wait for you."

"Sounds good to me."

He laughed and kissed her again. He watched her leave and picked up the phone.

CHAPTER 34

The weeks that followed were blissful for Neela. The movie deal was cemented. The book had hit the *New York Times* best-seller list and remained there. But for Dermot, these weeks were filled with renewed angst. In a few short months he might be asked to visit a set featuring a water tower, another with a shed complete with a dentist's chair, drills, and several pints of makeup blood and gore in abundance, and all the other scenes that had become his worst nightmares. He wondered if he'd ever be able to cope emotionally, knowing they were all watching from the other side.

The press junkets continued endlessly. Dermot and Neela flew first class to New York, Chicago, and other big cities, where Dermot appeared on every imaginable morning, midday, and late-night talk show, quizzed about every conceivable aspect of *Worst Nightmares*. The most popular question had been whether he'd been inspired by actual events, to which he always replied, "I'm sure subconsciously I may have read about some pretty grizzly killings over the years, and maybe I included certain aspects of those incidents without realizing it as I wrote the novel. But not intentionally." He was often asked why he had chosen to set his new novel in Australia rather than America, and he usually made a joke of it: "Because they're catching up quickly to our level of urban violence."

He found his trips to Europe to be the most relaxing because the travel distanced him from the corpses that still haunted his dreams. Abroad, he and Neela were treated regally—the champagne flowed, the hotel suites were sumptuous, and the limousines were fifty feet long—or so it seemed to Neela. And at the end of each day they worked hard at making babies and enjoyed every second of it. On his return to LA, Dermot felt completely refreshed. He was no longer looking over his shoulder at cars that looked like his own, and he'd stopped scanning the daily newspapers for stories about newly found corpses.

The film was cast and the list of those who had showed interest in playing cameos was quite amazing—it was A-list everywhere.

They'd been home for about two weeks when Dermot's life began to unravel. He was the guest of honor at a literary lunch at the Hilton Hotel, and Dermot, Neela, Nick, and Esther sat at the head table. As his glass was being refilled by a waiter, Dermot's celebrated painter friend Neil Taylor stood at the lectern and made an amusing speech of introduction.

As Taylor finished, more than four hundred luncheon guests applauded, and Dermot made his way to the lectern.

Dermot's speech was the same one he'd given around Europe during the previous weeks and he was used to the reaction he received each time. Of course there weren't too many laughs due to the nature of the book, but where he did introduce a moment of levity, invariably everyone appreciated it. The speech had always gone smoothly in the past.

This day was to prove very different.

When Dermot had finished and the applause was done, Louise Fortall, a pretty young commissioning editor for Gunning and Froggett rose. "Now, let's get straight to the questions. Please raise your hands if you have one," she said.

A forest of hands went up. Fortall chose one at random.

"Was Truman Capote's *In Cold Blood* inspirational in any way?"

Nolan smiled. His mind went into autopilot as he replied. "Yes, that book scared me a lot. Of course I was practically a child when I read it."

A ripple of laughter.

"But it's in no way similar to *Worst Nightmares*. I like to think I've taken the genre to a different level. Not necessarily a better one—simply a different one. Okay . . . higher possibly."

Another ripple of laughter broke out.

"So you think your novel is *more* frightening?"

"Well, things have changed a lot in the past decades. If anything, life has become scarier. It doesn't matter who you are or where you are, you can die at any second of the day or night at the hands of a terrorist, a so-called freedom fighter, or a religious fundamentalist. Not to mention a serial killer." He winked and got another big laugh.

Fortall pointed. "The gentleman on the right. You have a question?"

"Good afternoon, Mr. Nolan. I enjoyed your book enormously— though perhaps that's not the most politically correct way to describe my exact feelings as I moved through the pages."

Another scatter of gentle laughter.

"I would hope not," Dermot replied with a wry smile.

Stronger laughter.

"My question is this: Did you find it a reach mutating the voice of the Dermot Nolan we have come to know and love—the gentle, fiercely romantic, cerebral voice—to accommodate the brutal nihilist mind-set of this savage man?"

"Well, that's what I do. I am a writer, after all. It's part of my craft to be able to sink into the minds of others and conjure up their thoughts and feelings."

"Next question?"

"Did you research any of the crimes? I'm wondering if—" he paused, "if you based any of the horrors in your book on real-life events?"

"The entire book is fiction. I conducted a great deal of general research, both psychological and otherwise, but the thrust of the story is pure fiction."

He was getting used to lying with a straight face—the words now came out easily and no longer set his nerves on edge.

Fortall picked another upraised hand.

"Alex Shand. *LA Times*. Good afternoon, Mr. Nolan."

"Good afternoon."

"First, my congratulations. All these weeks on the best-seller lists—and now the film."

"Thank you. I'm delighted with the way my book has been received. Your question?"

"Can you deny or confirm you'd initially had any reluctance to adapt the novel to film? And if so, could you tell us why?"

Instantly his nerves started jangling. How could the man have known that he'd been initially reluctant? Only Esther, Neela, and Nick had known.

The moments passed. Dermot shot a quick furtive glance at Neela, then another back to Shand, who had clearly picked up on his hesitation and was now searching Neela's face for some reaction.

Dermot cleared his throat. "Let me put it this way. I was never reluctant to entertain the possibility of a film. Yet, what's appropriate in one medium may not translate as well to another. One could posit that the canvases of Francis Bacon might be too disturbing if translated to film. It could be much the same with my novel—we do have impressionable minds to consider with film."

Fortall next called on an attractive girl seated near the front of the room.

"Gillian Hanna. *Guns and Ammo*. What made the killer choose his victims? It's not clear in the novel."

"Because, like Everest, they were there." The stock answer.

She pulled a disappointed face. "Don't you think you might have added another dimension if there'd been some reason? I felt sure that on the last page we'd be told why these victims had been targeted. I have to say that I was a little disappointed."

"I'm sorry to hear that, Ms. Hanna. However, I found during my research that most serial killers do have some reason to justify their killings—insane as their motives might appear to us. So I was intrigued, and ultimately chose to write about someone who killed at random *without* reason—the more unusual scenario."

The questions continued for some time. An older woman asked if anyone he knew had ever actually killed anyone, causing a gasp or two in the conference room. "I simply wondered if perhaps your father had ever seen active service and had explained to you what it was like to kill a human being? No offense, Mr. Nolan," she said.

"No, my father never served in any war. I had to imagine what killing one's fellow man might feel like," Dermot replied, then quickly added. "Actually, I'm delighted I never had any first-hand experience."

There was a big burst of laughter.

The last question came from a young hawk-nosed man right at the front. He had a twinkle in his eye. "Why set the novel in Australia? What's wrong with our own backyard? We have some of the best mass murderers around here in the U.S."

"No doubt we've got some weird guys hanging around here. And if you're privy to any *particular* information, please let the police know," Dermot replied.

"But why not set it here? In America."

"I thought perhaps America might be ready to read stories set in other people's backyards. There's a whole world out there."

Fortall wound up the session. "On behalf of Gunning and Froggett and all of us here today, I'd like to thank Dermot Nolan for his remarkable insights into his novel, *Worst Nightmares*."

Huge applause.

"Dermot Nolan will be signing copies in the Wills Room at three o'clock."

Dermot signed three hundred and forty books that afternoon. By six he was home and in the Jacuzzi with Neela and a vodka martini. Life was becoming easier every minute, and he'd finally decided he could relax a bit on the possible ramifications of his actions.

But he was very wrong.

CHAPTER 35

Dermot hadn't experienced a single nightmare since his return from Europe. He also believed his former bouts of depression were a thing of the past. His relationship with Neela was better now than it had been since they'd been married.

And then the second shoe dropped.

Dermot had just made a fresh pot of coffee and was casually leafing through the *LA Times* when a headline on page three caught his eye: POLICE REOPEN 'PLUNGE-DEATH' IN DOWNTOWN LA. Dermot immediately read the story.

It was the Gordon Building death. Abel Conway—the Flyer. The tightest of all knots pulled in Dermot's gut. His heart raced as he read. The police were reopening the case on the basis of new information that had recently come to light.

Dermot laid down the paper and called out to Neela. Alarmed by his decibel level, she appeared in seconds. Dermot's face was as white as Wonder Bread.

"Jesus, honey, what's up? I could have heard you in Santa Barbara."

"Read this," he said, pointing at the article.

She glanced through the story. "The police are reopening the Conway case? Big deal."

"What do you mean, big deal?" he shouted at her. "Of *course* it's a big deal! Arnold murdered him. I detailed the exact manner of his death in *Worst Nightmares*! There must be tens of thousands of people who have read my book, including a fair number of cops like Mike. Don't you think they might be murmuring to themselves, 'Hey, that's almost exactly like the guy that died in Nolan's book'?"

"I wouldn't think for one moment that readers of the *LA Times* would link Abel Conway's death with Dan Lasky's death in Australia. Why would they? It doesn't even mention any details in the article—just that the guy fell from the seventeenth floor of a building near here some time ago."

"People know I live here. They'll think it's a mighty big coincidence."

That evening Mike Kandinski watched hockey, while his wife, Dawn, sat down to read the paper.

"Mike? Have you read *Worst Nightmares* yet?"

The Sabres had just scored, so Mike only vaguely heard her.

"What's that?"

"Dermot Nolan's book. Have you had time to read it yet?"

"I work seventeen-hour days. When do I have time to read books?"

"Well, you should find time. After all, you helped him with his research. Your name's in the acknowledgments."

He didn't answer her. The Kings snatched a spectacular goal and Kandinski cheered.

"Well, maybe it's time you did take a look. Do you remember that taxi driver who fell from the seventeenth floor of the Gordon Building?"

"Sure do. It was my case."

"In Nolan's book, there's a man who falls from the seventeenth floor. He was a cab driver, too. Grabbed onto the fire escape and plunged down still holding it."

Kandinski turned toward his wife for a second and then looked back at the play-by-play.

"So what?"

"Well, the Nolans live just five minutes away from where that man fell."

Kandinski said nothing.

"I just wondered if Dermot had used the Abel Conway case for his book."

"Maybe he did. It was probably in the papers."

"Yes, probably. But here's the thing. Nolan says he made it all up. I wonder how many other deaths he pulled from the paper. Or the Internet. What do you think?"

The Sabres scored again and Kandinski clicked off the game—there were just three minutes left and the Kings were three goals down. A lost cause.

"Let's have a look at the book, babe. Where is it?"

CHAPTER 36

Jeff Schipp worked at the *LA Daily News*. He was twenty-eight, lean as a string bean, dressed badly, seldom took a bath, and smoked two packs of cigarettes a day. He loved his work with an almost crazy fervor. He was a results man. If there was a story to tell, Schipp would get to the nitty-gritty, no matter how long it took him. More often than not it didn't take him long at all.

He shared his small partitioned office with an associate, Angela Perito. On this day, his head was stuck out the window, his hand waving cigarette smoke to the winds with a manila file, when he heard his phone ring. He swore, stubbed out a newly lit cigarette, and ducked back inside. In turn, Perito cursed at him, too.

"Jesus, Jeff. Go downstairs if you want to smoke. I'm pregnant here!"

"Okay. Understood, Ange. Next time." He picked up the receiver. "Yes? Schipp here."

Schipp was used to hearing from complete strangers calling with information. It was how he got his best tips. He was good at judging who was genuine and who wasn't. But the voice at the other end of the line this day was hard to read. Guttural and a little scary.

"Have you read a book called *Worst Nightmares*, Mr. Schipp?"

He hadn't, but naturally he'd heard of it. Everyone knew that book by now.

"Why? You offering me pirated copies?"

"No, Mr. Schipp. Far from it."

"Call me Jeff. But get to the point, will you? I just wasted a cigarette to take your call."

"I prefer formality, if you don't mind, Mr. Schipp. I'll leave informalities to Karen."

Schipp's eyes widened. He was definitely listening now—his girlfriend was named Karen. How the hell did the scumbag know that?

"Have you got your trusty pen poised?" the voice continued. "If not, I'd pick it up. I'm about to give you some directions. Before you think of visiting the grave site I'm going to mention, I would advise you not to go alone."

Schipp's jaw dropped. *Grave site? What the fuck?*

"Perhaps you would be even better advised to take the LAPD with you. You see, there's a dead body involved. Not fresh by any means. It's been there for some time."

"What's your name, sir?" Schipp's brain was now firing on all cylinders.

"Please don't interrupt me or I'll talk to one of your fellow journalists. However, I feel sure you would prefer to have the . . ." He paused to emphasize the word, "*scoop* yourself?"

Schipp was definitely listening now.

"Before I give you precise directions, may I draw your attention to a chapter of the book I mentioned just now? Take a look at chapter twelve, and when you've finished reading, please follow these directions."

"I'll read the chapter, okay? Now tell me what you got."

Schipp waited for the man to speak again. He didn't for some time.

"You still there?" Schipp asked.

"Yes. Incidentally, I would take some smelling salts with you. They might be useful." The guttural voice chuckled. "Now, the directions."

"Shoot."

"Head to Topanga National Park. Take a right on Cedar Line Road. It's off Canyon Boulevard. Stop at the small lake. Park at the top right corner of the parking area. Walk exactly half a mile due east. You'll see two stakes. Twenty feet north of the taller stake is a grave. You will find two bodies buried there. Gareth and Laura Nash. Their names in Nolan's novel are Alan and Nancy Wood. Not very creative for a Booker Prize winner."

Schipp scribbled it all down, word for word.

The man stopped speaking but didn't hang up. "Don't forget to read that chapter carefully before you investigate. One last thing. Should you ever chat with Nolan, ask him if he's ever been to Shute."

"Hey, how did you know my girlfriend's name?"

The man ignored the question. "You have a personal e-mail address? A private one, not the company address. And a private cell-phone number. Give them both to me, and forget I ever asked for them."

With that, the line went dead. Schipp replaced the receiver. He smiled, despite the uncomfortable worry about how much the caller had known about his personal life. Most people would have been deeply disturbed by such a call, but Schipp was looking forward to checking out the lead— seeing if there was any truth to the caller's implied claim that Dermot Nolan had based his novel on real events.

He stood on his chair and looked over the partition.

"Ange, you still got that book handy? That *Worst Nightmares*?"

She looked up sourly at him. "I do. Just don't breathe stale smoke at me, okay?"

Schipp raised a hand and covered his mouth. "Can I borrow it for a few minutes?"

"Sure," she replied. "Catch!" She lobbed the book at him. Seconds later, Schipp was reading intently. Twenty-five minutes later, he was sitting in the editor in chief's office.

It wasn't an easy thing to access the editor in chief at such short notice, but if Schipp thought he had a huge story, it was more than likely that he *did.*

Schipp sat in a leather armchair that probably cost thousands of dollars, looking like a kid in a grown-up's chair. A gigantic Edwardian desk separated him from his editor in chief.

"This is very dangerous territory, Schipp. You're either sitting on the story of the year, or we're going to get sued to Saigon and back."

"I got a tip, sir. At this stage it's just that. The source could be genuine— he could be an asshole, for all I know."

"Mouth, Schipp," Melhuish murmured. The chief was sixty-three and treasured the English language. He didn't like jargon or swearing. "If we find evidence of dead bodies at this location, it'd be a pretty decent story in its own right. But if there's any link to Nolan's book, as the caller clearly suggests, then we'll have to move fast—we don't want any other paper breaking the story before we have first dibs."

"Of course not."

"You know this source? Is he reliable? Does he have a name?"

"No, I have no idea who he is—and I haven't dealt with him before."

"You're sure?"

"Without the aid of a voice analyzer, I can't say for certain. But he does have a very distinctive voice. Kind of Lee Marvin. It goes without saying of course that he could have been disguising his voice."

"Indeed." Melhuish steepled his short fat fingers as he collected his thoughts. "What this man is suggesting is that Nolan based his novel on real events, and then lied about it. Correct?"

"Yes."

"But why would he lie about what is obviously solid research?"

"My source is suggesting that if I go to the site he suggests, I should go with a police forensic team. I'm supposed to find a burial site. He's saying that if the cops do some digging, they'll uncover the bodies of two people—Gareth Nash and his wife, Laura. Before I called you, I did a bit of checking on the missing persons register. It appears that the two did go missing some months ago. They were never found."

"Just some missing people? That's pretty run-of-the-mill."

"Not if you read Dermot Nolan's *Worst Nightmares*. In the book the people are called Alan and Nancy Wood. They were tortured to death in Australia."

"So we know absolutely nothing about this source?"

"No, sir."

"If he knows where bodies are buried, and at the same time is suggesting they've been there some time and are going to stink when they're unearthed, it raises a lot of questions."

"It does indeed, sir."

"How would your source know where the bodies were buried unless he buried them himself?"

"Maybe he saw someone else burying them?"

"And thought about telling the cops all this time while they rotted? Not sure if I buy that one. It's just as possible that he read Nolan's book and it triggered his memory of seeing freshly tilled earth somewhere, and the topography of the book was just too coincidental."

"Do we know what happened to the Nash couple?"

"We should pretty soon, if the source is correct and there are bodies buried out there. Hopefully, the medical examiner can quickly confirm their identities. My source suggests that what we'll find is so similar to the fictional killing of the Wood couple it will be impossible not to see the correlation."

"Well, it would have to be coincidence if the bodies have yet to be dug up, wouldn't it? I mean, Nolan would've had to bury the couple himself to know all the details he put in his book—that is, if the details are substantially the same."

Schipp simply smiled at Melhuish. The seconds clicked by in silence.

"Are you suggesting what I think you are?"

"Possibly. It'd be some story if Nolan was actually a mass murderer, eh?"

"Be a great front page if the pope was one, too—but it's not likely. Call the police and tell them you know something they might be interested in, but you'll only help them out for a quid pro quo—a kickback, in your world. Ask for an exclusive. See what you come up with, and then get back to me personally. How do you intend to get matters started?"

"I'll drive out there on my own, make up my own mind about things, then make the call to the cops if it all looks kosher."

"Good luck, then. My bet's that it's a wild goose chase. It certainly does seem unlikely that a man of Nolan's standing would turn out to be a serial killer."

"Yes, but even if Nolan has nothing to do with the deaths, it might still turn out to be a very viable story. The book's as big as *The Da Vinci Code* was. Everyone's read it, so everyone'll have an opinion. I can see the lead now: *Buried bodies. The book of the decade? Is it coincidence? Or is fiction fact?* Just Nolan's name next to a shot of the cops lifting corpses out of the ground would be front page in my book."

"Why don't you leave the choice of the front page to me and just go move your butt."

At the same time Schipp was heading to check out his lead, Dermot was in the KABC studio answering questions on shock-jock Frank Vitek's show.

"All right. Next on the line is Jeannie from Sherman Oaks. Good morning, Jeannie. You have a question for Dermot?"

A frail voice came on the air. "Mr. Nolan? Am I really speaking to you?"

"You are now, Jeannie. Fire away."

"Such a lovely name—Dermot. My grandfather came from County Wicklow. He was a veterinarian at the Curragh racecourse in Ireland all his life. He had twelve sons and two daughters—"

Vitek cut her short. "Wonderful, Jeannie, but what's your question?"

"Oh, sorry. I just wanted to say that I really loved your book. I'll be eighty next Thursday, and I can tell you I have never read such a scary book before."

"I bet," Vitek answered with a chuckle.

"Here's my question: How did you ever think up such nasty things and not be a monster yourself?"

"You'll have to ask my wife about that," Dermot laughed. "She thinks I'm a halfway decent man. At least, I hope she still does."

Dermot could hear Jeannie laughing heartily on the other end of the line as he waited for the next question. For some reason, an image of Laura Nash's tongueless scream blew vividly into his mind. He reached for the glass of water that stood on the desk between him and Vitek.

Vitek took the next call. "I've got Arnold from Venice on the line. Hello, Arnold. You have a question for Dermot?"

"Good morning, Mr. Nolan." The tone was guttural—Jack Palance with bronchitis. Nolan stopped breathing and Vitek couldn't help but notice. He jumped in to fill the awkward silence.

"Good morning, Arnold."

"It's *Mr.* Arnold, actually. Arnold is my surname."

"Okay. You have a question for Dermot?"

"Indeed I do. My question is this. Is it your personal view that one can never know true sorrow without suffering extreme personal loss?"

Dermot abruptly needed air. The voice. It was the same voice! But Arnold was dead. He'd seen the man fall. He'd stood over the body!

Dermot took a deep breath. "In a way, I suppose . . . yes," he answered calmly. "Kids who have never experienced the loss of a loved one have no concept of how such a loss will affect them," he replied precisely and carefully. He didn't want to lose it on air.

"Same with car accidents," Vitek chipped in. "People'll drive like yahoos until a family member gets killed in a head-on and then the horror is brought home big time."

"I asked Mr. Nolan. Not you," Arnold snapped.

Vitek made a face at his producer through the glass and mouthed the words, Rude bastard.

"Is it appropriate that ordinary people learn the reality of extreme suffering as you detail in your book, Mr. Nolan?"

Dermot had to pull himself together, and damn quickly, or risk his reaction becoming a talking point on shows later that day. "I think shock tactics do work," he replied.

"So that we may appreciate the moment of our own death? Is that what you are suggesting?"

Another vile image leaped into Dermot's consciousness: Phoebe Blasé, her mouth cruelly wired open, a pair of pliers pulling out an embedded molar.

Vitek came to the rescue just as a bead of sweat started down Dermot's temple. "Maybe what Albert's saying is that you don't have to be confronted with the grizzly details of violent torture, as detailed in *Worst Nightmares*, to know that it's . . . well, savage and unspeakable."

Vitek nodded toward Dermot to suggest he run with the ball he'd just been thrown. But Dermot was having trouble ridding his mind of Phoebe's terrible mouth. And now joining it was Major's floating head.

"Er . . ." he tried, "I think it's the age we're living in. People are fascinated by crime. They witness violence every day. And filmgoers are increasingly fascinated by the macabre . . ."

"Thanks for your question," Vitek said, hanging up and switching to the next caller. "We now have Jeff on the line."

Dermot took a sip of his water.

"Good morning, Mr. Nolan. I was reading your book this morning. Great stuff."

"Thank you, Jeff," Dermot replied, relieved to take a normal question again. It was almost impossible to concentrate. All he could think about was Albert K. Arnold, back from the dead. But it couldn't be. Was it the accomplice? Was this really happening? A fresh nightmare began to unravel before his eyes. He pinched himself as he tried to focus on the new caller.

"A funny thing happened to a friend of mine yesterday. At Topanga National Park. Ever been there, Mr. Nolan? I hear it's really nice."

"No," Dermot replied, his mouth suddenly as dry as the Gobi Desert. "What's your question?"

"Well, a friend of mine told me he'd come across some stakes. Two of them—just like in your book. That couple in chapter . . . what chapter was it?"

"Twelve," Dermot replied like an automaton.

"Right. Well, it's an incredible coincidence, don't you think? I'm heading up there now to take a look for myself." He paused for a second. "You said you've never been there, right?"

"Right."

"Have you ever been to Shute?"

Dermot thought he was going to throw up. He took a deep breath and tried to look as though he was trying to remember. "Shute? Doesn't ring a bell. Nope."

"How about Van Nuys Airport? Two people fell from a plane out there—dead ringer to that couple you wrote about in Sydney."

"Really?"

"Yes, really," Schipp replied.

"Right, we'll leave it at that, Jeff. Have to share the air, fair and square. We'll take a break and be back after the news."

Dermot pulled off his headphones. His head was reeling and he knew he was sweating like a pig. The most important thing now was to at least appear calm.

"Thanks for coming in, Dermot," Vitek said, offering a hand. "Sheila will see you out. And thanks for the copy of the book. Haven't had a chance to read it yet—but I'm going on vacation soon so it'll be perfect for the flight."

"My pleasure." Dermot managed a weak smile. "These on-air interviews are harder than I thought," he said.

"Are you sure you're feeling well?" Vitek offered. "Anything Consuela can get you? You look a bit green."

"I think I ate something bad last night. It's probably a mild case of food poisoning. I thought a while back I might get sick on air. That's probably why I'm sweating. Sorry."

"Yes, well. Best to get home and get some rest. Nothing better than a good night's sleep. You know what I mean?"

"I do."

CHAPTER 37

Reggie Helpmann had not stepped outside his Glendale home for fifteen years. He'd had a tendency towards agoraphobia since childhood, but the condition had become worse as he grew older. That's when the dreams had started. Terrible dreams. So terrifying that within weeks of his thirtieth birthday he refused to do more than walk to and from the corner shop. But the dreams continued—ever more vivid and horrifying. On his forty-second birthday, Reggie decided he'd never leave his apartment again. It was a cause of great sadness to Alice, his devoted wife. After all, it was the end of any contemplated vacations, of dinner parties at friends' houses, of sunny days at the beach.

So the flyer she had found in her mailbox gave her hope. There was someone out there who could bring relief to nightmare sufferers, someone who could possibly help end Reggie's phobia. At least it was worth a try.

Sitting beside her husband at the computer, Alice typed in the domain name and within seconds they were on the site. She liked the home page—all those naked sinners in Bosch's artwork receiving their just desserts—but she was disturbed by the man's guttural tone when he identified himself as the Dream Healer and asked why he was talking to two people rather than one.

"My name is Alice Helpmann. I don't need your help personally. It's my husband, Reggie."

"Describe your nightmare, Reggie."

"I dream I'm walking on a lonely beach. There is no one in sight. I am petrified. It's the space. All the wide-open space."

The Dream Healer uttered a sigh of annoyance. "That's one form of agoraphobia, Reggie. It is a common nightmare. You clearly need to get out more."

Alice didn't think it was appropriate for him to be making fun of Reggie, but she bit her tongue. "My husband hasn't felt able to leave the house in fifteen years."

There was silence.

"Do you live near the sea, Mrs. Helpmann?"

"No, we live in Glendale. On Butler Street."

Somewhat surprisingly the connection was cut. Alice went back in to Internet Explorer and typed in the site name again, but all she saw was a message that the page she wanted could not be found. She was annoyed. So was Reggie.

"Don't worry, honey. We'll try him again later."

But Alice never did manage to dial up the worstnightmares.net site again. It was never available. Odder still was that a week later, Reggie decided to leave the house and go for a walk—at least that was the only conclusion Alice could make, as there was no sign of him when she returned from Ralph's Supermarket that day. Forty-eight hours later, when he had not yet returned home, she notified the police and they classified Reggie as a missing person.

CHAPTER 38

Dermot was pacing and wringing his hands. He was on his third scotch already. Neela was by the window, looking out. Nick was on the sofa.

"It's *him*! You heard him on air yourself!" Dermot's voice was shrill. "That voice—it's unmistakable. But a voice from the grave? I don't fucking *think* so!"

Neela turned from the window. "Dermot, calm down. Everyone in the street will hear you."

"What does it matter now, when this whole mess is about to implode? Jesus Christ. It's the same guy, or the greatest mimic the world has ever known."

"So who was the guy who fell from the Stratten Building? He told you he was going to kill himself."

"*Suggested* he would," Nick interceded.

"Whatever," Neela said. "*Suggested*, then. Anyway, you watched him fall to his death. And remember, it was the same guy who talked to you in the train—the actual man who delivered the diary."

"Okay, so Arnold's dead. So who's this guy on the air today who knew Arnold's name and clearly knew him personally because he mimicked his speech patterns exactly? He's out to hound me. Whoever the hell he is, he's waited all this time to come out of the woodwork and scare me shitless now the book's a best seller and soon to be a movie. He was toying with me today—and it isn't going to end there. I can tell you that, too!"

"Maybe he's after money," Neela suggested.

"Then why not contact you directly without involving the media?" Nick countered.

"That's the freaking sixty-four-thousand-dollar question, isn't it? And if this weirdo's not bad enough, what about the other guy from . . . where the hell was he from?"

"Don't remember," Neela murmured. She was getting the shakes, too. She knew they were in big trouble, but she was working major damage control because she was sure Dermot couldn't handle the stress.

Dermot slapped the wall hard. "It's happening. It's fucking *happening*! I'm going to get my literary ass nailed to the wall!"

"Dermot, I don't see how you think this is the catalyst for the end of the world," Nick said. "It was just one guy who asked a few dumb questions on a radio talk show."

"Come on, Nick. Stupid I'm not. He knew the exact location of the Stakes' burial site. How the fuck could he know that unless he'd read the original manuscript?"

"He could be the real killer," Nick replied, thoughtfully. "Have you considered that? You always preferred to think Arnold borrowed from news reports rather than being a serial killer himself. All this does is give weight to the theory that the killer was someone other than Arnold."

"But there *weren't* any news reports. I went through the papers online with a fine-tooth comb. So did Neels. Any reference to their deaths would have popped up on the microfiche finder. There weren't any. He either read the manuscript, or he's the killer instead of Arnold. And if he is . . ." His voiced trailed off.

They all sat in silence. Then Dermot started in again, his body shaking. "And Shute? How the fuck did he know that location? That's the Super-glue Lady. Her body was never found! How come we never came up with those news reports?"

He shot an accusing look at Neela.

"Oh right! Now it's my fault. It's *my* fault I missed something and we're all up shit creek on account of me!"

"Steady, Neels," Nick said soothingly. "We don't know how he found out about Shute. Maybe the motel guy recognized you and told him? Anyway, the only other cross-reference to your novel and real events was the mention of Van Nuys Airport, and that's quite understandable. Everyone knew about the people who died there—those killings were well reported."

"I know that, Nick, and I know you're trying to help. I appreciate that, believe me. I don't mean to shout at you, but you don't have to be Einstein to realize that whoever that guy was on the phone line at KABC, he knew a heck of a lot of details, and he had an agenda. It's going to get worse, no question."

Jeff Schipp crumpled up another empty pack of cigarettes and pulled a fresh one from his baggy trousers, all the while keeping his eyes on the twin stakes in front of him. His cell phone chirped and he flipped it open.

"Where are you now?" Schipp asked the cop on the other end. "Go park at the top right corner of the parking area. Walk exactly half a mile due east. You'll see two stakes. I'm right there. You brought a forensics team?"

He listened. "Shit, why not?" He listened some more. "Well, you're going to need one."

It took the forensic team several hours to arrive at the site Schipp had requested. It was the grave site that convinced Detective Sergeant Woo that Schipp's call was genuine. He'd arrived with a shovel and done some initial digging before unearthing some bones. Of course they could have been animal bones, but Woo thought it prudent to check more carefully. So he'd called back to dispatch for the forensics boys and taped off the area.

Within the hour, forensics had dug a hole seven by three feet and found enough bones for Woo to conclude that he was dealing with the remains of two humans. He called in the findings to his superiors, who were surprised, yet oddly delighted. Even more delighted, however, was Jeff Schipp, who called in the events to Melhuish.

"They found two bodies."

"Can any identification be made?" Melhuish asked. His voice had an excited tone.

"Not yet. It'll have to be dental records now 'cause there's scarcely any flesh on them. Until we have some idea who they are, DNA is a waste of time."

"How long will the dental stuff take?"

"Not long. A day, maybe two. But here's the interesting thing. Woo tells me—"

"Who's Woo?"

"The detective in charge. He says that someone's been here recently. There are clear tire tracks. The forensic guys have taken castings. And they're dusting both stakes for fingerprints."

"It could have been anyone. Right?"

"Right. Anyone could have stumbled on this site. It's a long shot that Nolan would have revisited the scene if he were personally involved in the killings. But stranger things have happened. Some murderers can't help themselves. Either way, my source has some genuine info about whether or not Nolan's involved in the murders. There *are* two bodies here and twin stakes, just like in Nolan's book."

"So the plot thickens?"

"It certainly does. I'd rather not release our insider info right now. Give me a few hours to do some real digging—literary digging, that is. I want to research other passages in *Worst Nightmares*. Then we can really beef up the front page."

"You got it. I'll get someone to report the incident to the electronic media—we're hours away from a front page and need to release a bit of info first. I'll get whoever it is to leave out any mention of the stakes— wouldn't want anyone to put two and two together. We have to bear in mind too that most of literate as well as illiterate America has read Nolan's book."

"That's four hundred people, sir." He paused. "I'm talking about the literate guys." He knew Melhuish enjoyed childish jokes.

"Nice one."

Schipp heard someone call him from behind. It was Woo. He was holding a skull in his gloved hands and he was smiling inscrutably.

CHAPTER 39

Dermot sat at his desk. It was half past eight at night. Nick was at the window, peering out into the street.

"Best thing to do, Dermot, is nothing," Nick said quietly.

Dermot's reply came in an exasperated tone. "How the hell can I do nothing?"

"Because it appears that someone is trying to draw you out. Haven't you ever seen *Columbo*? He feeds the bad guy just one seed of doubt, and before the guy realizes what he's doing, he's acting like a schmuck, revisiting the scene of the crime to remove evidence. Then he breaks down and confesses."

Dermot lifted his head and drilled Nick with a sharp look. "The scene of the crime? Confession? What the hell are you talking about?"

"In your case, it's better to wait until you know the exact extent of what they know. It may turn out they know very little. Don't even think about going public and telling the world you lied about the book being a product of your rich imagination. If need be, reveal it later with the addendum, 'So what's the big deal? It's research!'"

"Jeff Schipp doesn't bother me as much as the guy who says he's Arnold."

"He didn't say that, did he? That he's the same guy. He simply used the same name."

"Well, how the hell would he know that name? The inference is clear. If I ignore him, he'll just make matters worse for me. And I can't contact him because I've no fucking idea how to reach him. What's he want me to do anyway?"

"He wanted you to publish his diary, didn't he? The *real* Arnold, that is."

"Right. And I stole it and published it under my own name—you think that's what's made him so mad?"

"Who the hell are we talking about here? If the guy who now says he's Arnold *is* in fact Arnold, then who was the dead guy?"

They sat silently again.

"Look, sorry. I've got to get going. I'll call you in a couple of hours. Okay?"

"Sure. Thanks"

As Nick was leaving, Neela drove up. They hugged each other in the street.

"Did Nick have any good ideas?" Neela asked Dermot as she came in.

"Nah."

Neela looked at her husband. Dermot met her gaze and immediately knew she had bad news.

"What is it? Tell me."

"I answered my cell without thinking." She watched Dermot's frightened expression. "I know! We're screening. I'm sorry. I forgot."

"So who was it?"

"Esther."

"Oh shit. What did she say?"

"She said she'd been leaving messages for a day and a half, and asked why you hadn't got back to her. Some journalist called her, asking if *Worst Nightmares* was based on any real events in this country."

"Christ!"

"You're going to have to call her, honey."

"And say what?"

"Say you may have been subliminally influenced by newspaper reports—that's only human. The real question is whether you deliberately—that is, consciously—*used* those reports. To that you obviously say no."

"I don't think so. If it were one scenario, maybe. But the way things are shaping up, we're looking at several scenarios. Some coincidence."

The phone rang. Dermot's eyes were glued to the answering machine as the message kicked in.

"Mr. Nolan? Are you listening to me? I expect you are. But you're afraid to talk to me. I understand that."

Neela walked over to Dermot and stood behind him, wrapping her arms around him. She could feel his body shaking.

The guttural voice continued. "Do you remember a Derek Klein? I never left you details about where he died, did I?"

The voice hesitated, waiting for an answer. "That's because he's still alive. Well, just. Go find him—he's got less than an hour to live."

Dermot lurched forward. "How? Where? What do you mean?" he screamed at the answering machine.

"You have some swift thinking to do here if you are to avert a tragedy. Just remember his name and occupation. These are clues. He lives in Los Angeles . . . or *will* for another hour or so."

The answering machine clicked off. Dermot sat bolt upright. "What do we do, for Christ's sake?"

"You think he's for real?" Neela asked.

"We have to think he might be."

Dermot started to pace the room. "Oh God, what do we *do*?"

Neela tried to think logically. "In the diary, Klein was a paramedic, right?"

"The Snake Man. Yes! You researched him, remember? You said he wasn't missing at all. He was still alive and kicking."

"That's right. Never in a million years did it occur to me that he was only alive because the whacko hadn't decided to kill him yet. Oh Christ!"

"Come on—let's find him. He's with Schaefer's."

Dermot grabbed the phone and called directory assistance. A few seconds later, he made contact.

"Hello, this is an emergency." A look of exasperation crossed his face. "No, I don't need an ambulance. I need to contact a Derek Klein. Is he with Schaefer's Ambulance Service, or not?" Seconds passed as he listened and then hit speakerphone, so that Neela could hear, too.

"Why do you need to contact Mr. Klein, sir?"

"So there *is* a Mr. Derek Klein?"

"I didn't say that, sir. I asked why you wanted to contact him."

"It's an emergency. He may be in great danger."

"Oh really?" The female voice on the other end didn't sound convinced.

Neela spoke. "It's Derek's mother. She's had a stroke. She's old and asking for her son."

"Does she require an ambulance? If so, call the—"

"No, she doesn't! But we must contact Derek Klein. Does he work for your service?"

"Just a moment."

Neela looked at Dermot. *Success*, she mouthed silently.

"Yes, he works for us. He's out on a call right now. If you'd like to leave me a message I'll have him call you when he gets back to base."

"Is there any way you can contact him out on the road? Can you tell me where he is right now?"

"Give me a moment, okay?"

"Okay, thanks."

"Sure."

Neela was put on hold and happy mood music kicked in. A few seconds later the lady was back on the line.

"Look, they won't connect me directly to him on the road, but his shift's over at nine. Stewart says Derek and his partner usually stop off at Fatburger on West Sunset at the end of the day. It's almost nine now. You might catch him there."

"Thanks!" Neela slapped the handset down. "Let's move."

Dermot looked stunned. "What are we going to do?"

"We're going to find Derek Klein—see if his life actually needs saving, that's what."

"Hold it!" Dermot grasped her arm. "You don't really think the caller means business, do you?"

"I hope not. But I'm not prepared to take that risk."

"Don't do anything, Neels! Let's call the police and let them know someone's threatened to kill Klein. Let *them* do something!"

"Dermot. Listen to me. We do that and they're going to ask why the hell we think someone's going to kill him. And that's going to open the biggest can of worms in history. Then you'll have to come clean about everything and accept being a literary pariah for the rest of your life."

"What alternatives do we have? Go find the guy?"

Neela picked up her cell and punched in some numbers. "I'm calling Nick. I'm going to ask him to make a 9-1-1 call from a pay phone—they won't be able to trace it."

Dermot saw from her expression that she'd made contact.

"Nick? It's me. Can you do something for us? Call the police from a pay phone and tell them there's going to be an attempt on the life of a Derek Klein." Nick interrupted but she just talked over him. "Just listen, please. He's an ambulance paramedic, works out of Beverly Boulevard for Schaefer's. Somehow galvanize them—don't let them treat you like a loony caller—this is serious."

Dermot held open the door for her.

"Great. Do it now. I'll be in touch."

Once, as a child on a camping trip with his parents in Montana, Derek Klein woke up one night to find something inside his sleeping bag with him, tickling his stomach. It was clear even to a five-year-old that something small, alive, and wriggling should not be inside his cozy bag. He felt around with his hand to see what it was. When his hand finally made contact with a snake, he screamed so loudly that he threw up. His reaction upset the snake and it struck its fangs into the Derek's thigh. Fortunately, his father was a doctor and also knew a lot about snakes. He unzipped his son's sleeping bag and grabbed the snake, immediately identifying it as a copperhead—despite its large venom output, its bite was rarely fatal.

He threw the snake back into the trees and pacified his terrified son with an injection of antivenin. But the damage was done. Derek insisted on returning home and resolutely refused ever to leave the city again.

It was this incident that had sparked his terrible nightmares. So frequent and vivid were they, in fact, that on his twenty-first birthday he visited a psychiatrist, who gave him the obvious advice: "Confront your fears." Impossible as this seemed to Derek at the time, he'd decided to take the shrink's advice.

The first step was a visit to the Los Angeles Zoo in Griffith Park, where he gazed into various vivariums. On his first visit he again vomited with fear, upsetting a coachload of Japanese tourists. On his second visit, he'd been able to keep his food down. The fifth and sixth visits were a breeze. The final step of the process was to actually *touch* a snake.

Derek never thought he'd be able to get through this final stage, but his shrink impressed upon him that all the prior steps would have been in vain if he were to baulk at the final challenge. So he visited a small specialized reptile park near Monterey.

Although park policy was not to allow visitors to play with the larger snakes, Derek bribed an employee to allow him inside one of the houses so he could play with a python. Once a fifty-dollar bill had been exchanged, the park employee placed the snake around Derek's neck.

Derek surprised himself with his courage. He felt quite at ease with the reptile. That was, until it decided to "behave badly." Derek's screams started loudly, but due to the snake's constrictions and a subsequent lack of air, petered out quickly. The park employee did all he could to persuade the ten-foot snake to unravel, but was unsuccessful. He called for help from a supervisor who just happened to have a Stanley knife with him that day. Whether or not the reptile saw the knife was debatable. The handler told the media later he was certain it had. It uncoiled at once.

Derek suffered substantial neck bruises but was not permanently injured. However, he resolved never to visit the countryside again, nor get closer than a mile to a snake of any kind.

Fifteen years had passed since the incident at the reptile park, and Derek now worked as a successful paramedic. At the end of an intense day, he came home to find a flyer in his mailbox. It read: "Nightmares? Phobias? Banish these ogres forever!" Intrigued, he'd read the smaller print over a few beers and soon was chatting away to the Dream Healer online.

The day the Dream Healer came looking for Derek was a slow one. He was a compulsive reader and had spent most of the morning reading the passage about the murder of the paramedic in *Worst Nightmares*, and he'd been shocked at the similarities between his life and this other guy in Australia.

If Derek's partner, Stanley Bridges, wasn't eating and watching television he felt he was wasting time. Fortunately, the ambulance center's recreation room had recently been refurbished with a massive widescreen plasma TV. All that was missing was a Fatburger vending machine. The nearest outlet was two miles away on West Sunset, and each evening Stan would convince Derek to drive there for his late-night food fix. This night was no exception. Having had his fill of Stan supersizing himself silly, Derek headed out to the ambulance to get it ready for the next shift. Walking around to the rear, he opened the right-hand door and climbed in, closing the half door behind him. He never saw the gloved man walking after him to the rear of the vehicle, looping a cable tie over both door handles.

Derek had no idea that he was trapped inside the vehicle. He busied himself restocking supplies and doing a general tidy-up. As he moved to the rear doors he heard static on his Schaefer's headphones. Thinking it was base, he turned up the volume. That was when he heard the voice.

He remembered it immediately. It was the Dream Healer. But how had he found the emergency frequency? There were really only two ways. One was to be in the front cab in the driver or passenger seat and simply switch on. The other was to be in the radio room back at base. Just possibly he could be a really smart ham-radio hack.

"Have you thought about your nightmare recently, Mr. Klein?"

What the fuck?

He spoke sharply into his mike. "Hey, who the hell is this? What are you talking about?" But he knew.

"I am the Dream Healer, Derek. I have come to give you peace."

Derek was annoyed and unsettled that someone had accessed his ambulance frequency, but not frightened in the least.

"Get off this frequency. This is an emergency frequency."

"And this is soon to *become* one."

Derek moved to the back doors and tried the handle.

"'I see horrible stuff every day: body parts, dead kids. But it's part of the job,'" the voice cooed lazily. "Isn't that what you told me? 'But my worst nightmare? Know what that is?'"

The comment gained Derek's attention. His sphincter began to pucker.

"'Snakes. I hate them. They terrify me.'"

Derek tried fiddling with his headset in an attempt to talk to base, but nothing worked. Then a thought occurred to him. It was Stan! It had to be a practical joke.

"Stan, you bastard! Cut the crap, will you? It's been a long day!"

"And that day is about to come to an end."

"Who is this?"

"I told you. But you weren't listening. I have left you a present underneath the stretcher, Derek. Look and see."

Derek stared at the stretcher. "Okay, you bunch of jokers. I'll play along."

He crouched down.

As he peered under the stretcher, the cobra struck fast and hard—the twin fangs locking onto his upper lip. The pain was indescribable.

Derek reacted violently, staggering back, sending all his supplies flying. The cobra was still hanging from his face.

The rasping guttural voice continued in his ear. "When your worst nightmares come to life, there is nothing more to fear from sleep."

Derek pulled hard on the snake's head and ripped it off his face. It took a big piece of his lip with it. Falling to the floor of the cab, it spat out the lip flesh and reared up again. Derek tried to raise himself onto his knees and reach for a metal fire extinguisher to protect him from a second attack. He was so terrified he found a scream impossible. He was in huge pain. Then he saw two rattlesnakes drop from a shelf above. Both slithered toward him.

The first rattler struck his groin; the second lunged at his throat, sinking its fangs into his jugular.

As Stan walked toward the ambulance, he was vaguely aware that the main cabin was rocking back and forth. He chalked it up to Derek cleaning up. Reaching the driver's door, he opened it and climbed in. He smiled to himself, thinking he'd play a trick on Derek. He'd drive back to base at full speed with his partner in the rear and with the siren going. He fired up the ignition and switched on the siren.

As he pulled out of the exit and onto the main road he watched a black car turn into the Fatburger lot. It was going way too fast.

Someone must be really hungry.

Then to his surprise, the car did a one-eighty and started following him.

Stupid bastard. Some kid must think it's funny to tailgate an emergency vehicle.

He looked in his rearview mirror. It wasn't a kid at all. There was a woman driving and a man in the passenger seat. The man was waving his arms wildly.

Stan cut the siren and pulled over. He was angry. What did these people think they were doing? He pulled on the hand brake and saw the man in the car running toward him.

"Hey! What's your problem?" Stan called out.

"Where's your partner? Where's Klein!"

Stan was confused and taken aback by this man's crazy attitude.

"He's riding in the back. What the hell's your problem?"

"Go look!" Dermot screamed at him. "There's something wrong with the rear doors. They're practically hanging open!"

Stan looked at the doors. This guy was right. He quickly untied the knotted cable and pulled open the doors.

Klein was writhing in the back. His face was purple and bloated. He tried to say something but only froth emanated from his mouth. One rattler was still hanging off his neck; two others were sliding off his chest toward the door. Stan jumped backwards.

"Jesus Christ!" he said, slamming the doors closed. "What the fuck is going on? What do we do now?"

"You have any antivenin in the back?"

"Sure, but I'm not going in there. Not for nobody," Stan replied.

Dermot pulled open the doors. "Just tell me where it is! Now!" He climbed into the back.

"See that over there," Stan said, pointing to a clear plastic box that had fallen from a shelf. "Stick him with one of those."

Dermot kicked a snake aside and did what Stan had told him.

"Shall I stick him again?" Dermot asked.

"Nah, one's enough."

But it wasn't. Not nearly enough under the circumstances. And it was far too late. Derek Klein's heart stopped pumping that second. Dermot gave him mouth-to-mouth, despite half his top lip being missing. Then he started pumping on his chest.

Stan called the cops.

CHAPTER 40

Dermot and Neela were asked to accompany Stan to Parker Center to make a statement. It was a natural response by the lead detective—a wiry man in his sixties called Quin.

Although Quin was taking pains to make it clear everything was a formality, there were a lot of aspects of the incident that struck him as odd.

"Where were you going when you first saw the ambulance, Mr. Nolan?"

"We'd decided to go to the movies," Dermot replied, without thinking too much about what he was saying. He hesitated, then came up with a title: "*La Chatte*," he said.

Quin picked up on his hesitation and filed it away.

"Can you tell us exactly what drew your attention to the ambulance?"

Neela decided to answer this time. She could see Dermot wasn't thinking coherently. "The rear doors looked like they might spring open at any second. We couldn't see the ties at first, but we both thought the doors weren't secured properly."

"And that someone on a stretcher might fall into the roadway?"

"My exact thought," she replied.

Quin studied the pair. There was something quirky about Nolan's behavior. He was obviously on edge. His wife was going to great lengths to appear calm. But he didn't buy that calm. He had to figure out what was going on. He had a body in the morgue, killed by snakes that had been placed in the back of the ambulance, and the driver, Stanley Bridges, was in a state of shock and on tranquilizers. There was no way Bridges could have been involved unless he'd placed the snakes in the vehicle some time before Klein stepped in—but that was an option. Nolan and his wife had done all they could to *help* the dead man. Nolan had even risked his life getting into the back with the snakes. So why were they behaving like this now? Like they were hiding something from him?

"This may seem like a ridiculous question, but I have to ask it, Mr. Nolan. Had you ever met the dead man before?"

"No," Dermot replied.

"Nor have I," Neela added.

Quin pressed a button on the recording device, and the tape stopped.

"My thanks for taking the time to come over here."

"Not at all, detective. It's just a shame we didn't see the doors earlier maybe this whole tragedy could have been averted."

"Yes, a shame. What a devious mind to even think of killing someone that way."

Dermot was tempted to glance at Neela, but he didn't. His heart was pounding so loudly he felt sure Quin could see it beating in his chest.

CHAPTER 41

Nick saw them approaching through the window and opened the front door. Dermot looked like he was about to collapse.

"Shall I get a brandy?" he asked Neela.

"Yes, but not too large."

"I can walk on my own, honey," Dermot said tersely. "Did you make the call, Nick?"

"Of course. Took forever, though. They ask so many questions before committing to sending the troops. Imagine if you were being attacked by machete-wielding thugs. You'd be limbless before the cops piled into their patrol cars."

"Did you use a pay phone?"

"Yes, and I didn't give my name. They asked for it several times. My impression was they classify all calls where the caller refuses to give his name as nuisance calls."

"What did you say?"

"I said that there was a paramedic in an ambulance driving around near Beverly and I had information that his life might be in danger. They didn't pay too much attention, so I said I thought it might be a terrorist attack. That got them going. That's when I hung up."

Nick poured Dermot a brandy.

"So what happened?" Nick asked. "Can't give me the third degree, then tell me nothing."

"By the time we found the ambulance, the damage had been done. It looked like the rear doors had been tied together. The driver had no idea his partner was in the back being attacked by snakes."

"Snakes?"

Dermot sighed wearily. "Yes. Snakes."

"Just like in Arnold's diary?"

"Just like in my book, yes."

"Oh Christ."

"Oh Christ, indeed."

Nick handed Neela a brandy and finally poured one for himself. "This is getting out of hand," Nick said.

"Shut up!" Dermot screamed. Neela and Nick stared at him, shocked.

"What? I don't fucking need *you* to tell me things are out of hand. I know it. I'm royally fucked."

"Hey, Nick was just trying to help."

Dermot placed his head in his hands and was silent.

"I know, Nick. Look, I'm sorry. I have no idea what I should do. It seems suddenly everyone out there knows stuff about me, and it's only a matter of time before *Worst Nightmares* is blown out of the water."

Nick thought carefully before he spoke. "Surely the more important consideration right now is that someone—the man who called you today—is out there killing people. Isn't it?"

"I suppose so," Dermot grudgingly admitted. Quite frankly, he was far more concerned about his own welfare, and that bothered him, too.

"Damage control, Dermot. Don't wait to be asked the inevitable awkward questions by investigative journalists and detectives. Offer them whatever you think will keep them at bay and convince them your only crime was to lie about *what* scenarios inspired your book. You naturally leave out any mention of ever having been contacted by Arnold and never mention the diary."

"So how did I know how these victims died?" Dermot asked, a bit sarcastically.

"You admit you 'borrowed' case histories that are a matter of record, like the Van Nuys Free Fallers and the pilot. That was in the papers. Same with Lucy Cowley.

"But what about Shute? The Superglue Lady was never reported. She was simply missing. So why bring up Shute?"

"That was a fishing trip—that's all. Someone saw you there."

"Maybe. But you think it's a good idea to tell the world that I lied—that I couldn't actually think of these devious scenarios, but rather had to borrow them after I said they were conjured up by my sick brain?"

"Why not? Surely that's better than the alternative?"

"What's worse than saying I copied someone else's work, word for word?"

"Being a murder suspect."

Dermot stared. Staggered. "I guess you're right." He gestured to his glass. "How about another?"

Nick obliged.

"So what do I do about the second Arnold?" Dermot asked Nick.

"Wait for him to call again. Ask him how much he wants. Plead with him. That's all you can do. Remember, we don't know what his agenda is. One thing we do know—he's not the real author of the document because, like you say, that man died in the street."

"Which begs the question—who the hell is this new guy?"

Neela had been quiet up till then. "Who knows who Arnold knew? He could have shared his secret with a friend, someone who now believes you did the wrong thing by publishing *Worst Nightmares* under your own name."

"So you think this buddy of Arnold's is out to crucify me?"

"I don't see how," Nick replied. "After all, he doesn't have any proof unless there's a copy of Arnold's diary hanging around somewhere—and remember, it was written in long hand."

"It could have been photocopied," Neela offered.

"*Could* have been. But remember, Arnold was a vagrant. Where would he have found the cash to pay for photocopying?"

They sat in silence, thinking. Then Dermot looked up, terror in his eyes. "Oh my God!"

"What?" Neela was suddenly afraid.

"Who else isn't dead?"

"What do you mean, honey? I'm not following you."

"I think Dermot is referring to victims who didn't actually die in the diary."

"Let's go through the list," Nick started. "The Mouth Maiden? She *must* have died—if she was a victim at all. Mr. B? You never found a body or a grave, did you? And Arnold said he'd left him to die in the desert, chained by his neck to a concrete slab."

"So if you went there and there was no body," Neela chimed in, "chances are it never happened."

"Or he hasn't carried out the murder yet," said Dermot. "Like Klein. What if he still has it in mind to chain up Mr. B and leave him to die?"

"But we don't know who Mr. B is. He had no name—just the nickname. The Space Cadet." Neela replied. She was looking increasingly worried, not so much for herself and Dermot, but rather for people she didn't know who were possibly now in mortal danger.

Nick broke the silence. "We have to tell the police the location. Just in case."

"What are we going to say? That we think someone might be dying a few miles outside Bakersfield? How would we know that? Then tell them we don't, but go look anyway?"

"Okay, you have a point. But what about this. How about I call, again from a pay phone, and say I read your book. That I was fascinated by the death of the agoraphobic, and the story got me to thinking about a friend of mine who went missing."

"Why, though?" Neela said. "Why would you think that someone was dead?"

Nick thought for a second or two before logic came to his aid. "Maybe I was worried some sociopath might be doing copycat killings?"

Dermot and Neela pondered this concept. It seemed to make sense.

"You have to call Esther," Nick said. "It's just a matter of time before Schipp calls her and asks hard questions. Better if you call her first. Otherwise she's going to look pretty dumb—and she hates that. She'll blame you."

"And what do I say exactly?"

"Just that you may have been subliminally influenced by events you read in the media way back—but you don't believe it was tantamount to 'borrowing' the scenarios. Tell her you never did that."

"Pretty weak, Nick."

"What can I say? You don't have a lot of options here, but something has to be done and fast. Before disaster strikes."

CHAPTER 42

Melhuish was hugely impressed by Schipp. He fielded his protégé's report from the Stakes Couple's crime scene, but was still reluctant to point a finger at Nolan until he could raise the doubts of any "reasonable man." He needed to guard against possible libel suits—he knew Nolan now had stacks of money to keep his name clean. Still, all that was necessary for an exclusive banner headline was to raise doubt . . .

It took Schipp just an hour and fifty-five minutes to beat a path to his editor's door.

"What do you figure about Nolan and the ambulance?" Melhuish asked. "We have to dance cleverly here."

"The way this Klein guy died is almost word for word the same as what happened in Nolan's book, which was published months ago. Coincidence? I say no way. Add to that the Stakes Couple and the Van Nuys Free Fallers and we've got a dynamite front page. I'll use my connections to see if the police suspect Nolan has some hands-on involvement in the killings, and if so, I can raise the same question in my story: Shakespeare a serial killer? Scott Fitzgerald a mass murderer?"

Melhuish was now very excited indeed. "Are you sure the *Times* hasn't gotten wind of this story yet?"

"The ambulance story, sure. But the bigger picture? No way. No one else showed up at Cedar Line Road. If my source had told another journalist, he'd have been there, too. Without a tip, there's no way anyone else would have put the book, the forensic dig, and the ambulance incident together."

"What did the detectives say to you?"

"Not a lot. They don't want to share anything with me—they just want me to share everything with them. They've got two decomposed bodies on the way to the medical examiner, and they want to know who told me where to look."

"That's easy—you don't know who the hell your source is, because he won't tell you."

"Right. But they want to tap my phone line. So they can trace him next time."

"No way anyone's tapping a journalist's telephone line without a court order. We'll fight that one."

"That's what I told them. They looked at me like I was a criminal. Said I was impeding their investigation. I told them to talk to our lawyers. Right?"

"Right."

Melhuish stared off for a couple of seconds.

"Okay, Jeff." It was first names now that Schipp had performed so well. "You get onto your police buddies and I'll hold the front page." He paused, and then looked Jeff in the eye. "But Nolan a serial killer? You really think so?"

"Remember Bundy? Anything's possible. Just because you have everything doesn't mean you're not a psycho at heart."

As Schipp closed the door behind him, Melhuish poured himself a congratulatory scotch.

At that precise moment, in his Linley Place warehouse, Dermot picked up the phone and dialed Esther. It was going to be a high-wire act that would require immense skill. He wondered if he could pull it off. "Esther Bloom," she answered.

"Good morning, Esther. It's Dermot," he said, giving his best impersonation of "carefree best-selling novelist."

"Dermot—thank heavens you finally got back to me. I just received the most bizarre call." She sounded anxious.

"What's up?"

"A man named Jeff Schipp just called me. He's a journalist for the *Daily News*."

"Arts page?" It was worth a try, he figured.

"Hardly. He works the crime pages."

"Well, as far as *Worst Nightmares* is concerned, they're one and the same right now." He laughed nervously, desperately trying to spin the reasoning behind Schipp's call. "What did he want?"

"A statement from me."

"Look, I'm glad to offer you any help I can. But what's all this got to do with me?"

"He wanted to know if *Worst Nightmares* is based on real-life criminal histories here in America, or if it's entirely an original work of fiction."

She let Dermot take in her words, fully expecting an immediate derisive denial. But one second led to another, and another after that.

"I told him you'd answered that question a million times—of *course* the novel is one hundred percent fiction. I was quite cross with the man. I told him to be very careful before he suggested otherwise in his newspaper."

That must have gone down really well, thought Dermot. The last thing he needed was for Esther to get Schipp's back up. But it was too late now.

"Esther, what can I tell you? You've known me a long time—"

"And I love you dearly—"

"And I love you too for protecting me."

"Just tell me, Dermot. Did I do the right thing?"

"Of course you did, Esther. This man Schipp also called me on air on the Frank Vitek show."

"I know. I was listening."

"Then you'll know there's nothing whatsoever to be concerned about. The fact is that there are some similarities between recent murders and some of the scenarios in *Worst Nightmares*. That was bound to happen. How would Perry Mason have fared, for heaven's sake? A woman strangled with her dressing gown cord? Happens all the time."

He could hear Esther laugh on the other end of the phone, but there was something a little hollow about it, as though she was far from convinced.

"I reread the chapters he mentioned. The Woods couple? Those are the people tied to the stakes? Right? And the girl called Barbara Rush. Schipp says a woman named Lucy Cowley died here in Los Angeles in a pretty similar way. He was very convincing, in an argumentative kind of way."

"Relax, Esther. Every day authors file away information into their brains without thinking about it. When they sit down to write, out pop those subconscious thoughts. If some television news program subliminally influenced me, then . . ." he paused, ". . . then that's what happened. Certainly I wasn't conscious of any real events. As far as I was concerned, the pages came straight from my own twisted mind."

He could hear Esther breathing hard, clearly upset. "We've reached a very delicate stage in the final negotiations on the film. We don't need a scandal like this. For once there *is* such a thing as bad publicity."

"Maybe so."

"Can I tell Dan and the film people not to worry any further?"

"You can. Bye for now," Dermot replied. He hung up and reached for a drink. He looked up. Neela was standing in the doorway. She'd been listening to the conversation.

"Honey, I think you made the wrong move. Sorry, but there it is. I think Nick's got the best handle on what to do here."

Dermot threw his shot glass against the wall. "Okay, Neela! Let Nick handle this shit. What did he suggest anyway? That I come clean and say, 'Yes. I did lie. Since I couldn't think of anything original to write, I became a third-rate hack. I resorted to stealing real events and disguising them as fiction. Sorry.' Sure. Great idea, Neela. Real career-ender."

"I think you may have to say something along those lines. Appropriately watered down, of course."

"Such as?"

"Well, Schipp thinks you based the Stakes Couple on the Nash deaths, and he's put together some similarities of the Free Fallers' deaths with the Van Nuys couple. But remember, there is someone on trial for that crime. The only other bizarre coincidence is the Snake Man."

"Oh, give me a break, honey! Schipp's a journalist—he knows about that already. And he knows about the others. He even mentioned Lucy Cowley by name—the Scorpion Girl!"

"But everyone else is a missing person! So he can't dig up anyone and point the finger at you!"

"Unless the man masquerading as Arnold has it in mind to tell him? How did Schipp get his initial piece of information, for Christ's sake?"

Neela was silent. The information could only have come from one source—the killer, or his accomplice if there was one.

"Call Esther back. Tell her you did base some of the stories on real events. Apologize. That's better than her finding out in the newspapers somewhere down the line that you did. lie to her."

"You really think that Schipp's informant is going to take me down?" His tone was starting to sound desperate.

"We can only wait and see. In the end, everything will turn out to be circumstantial. There's no more diary; it was destroyed. So it's whoever's word against yours. In the meantime you *must* have Esther on your side, rather than her feeling let down by you."

Dermot started toward the phone as it rang. He picked up.

"Yes?"

It was Esther.

"Dermot? What's this about you and an ambulance?"

CHAPTER 43

Mike Kandinski heard the news report on his way home. The story of a paramedic being bitten to death by snakes in an ambulance was startling in and of itself; that Dermot Nolan's name was attached was downright disturbing.

So while the last thing Mike wanted to do when he arrived home was work, he felt he had to touch base with fellow detective Richard Quin, who was on the case. "Richard? It's Mike Kandinski. North Hollywood. Heard about your Snakes case. Hope you don't mind my interfering just a smidge?"

"Interfere away."

"You questioned some people I know personally this afternoon. Dermot Nolan and his wife, Neela."

"That's right. They're the ones who noticed the ambulance doors were open and tried to help."

"Heard it on the news. Thing is, I know the Nolans pretty well. And my wife was concerned about them, but didn't want to intrude by calling them. They okay? Not too shocked?"

"They'll be fine. She's a tough cookie, the wife. Not in a bad way, just capable. You know? Nolan looked pretty freaked when we arrived. But then most people would be, wouldn't they, seeing what they saw?"

"Yeah, I suppose." Kandinski paused. "Have you got any angle on who did this snake thing? Or why?"

"Not yet. We recovered five snakes. All potential killers. Whoever put them in the back of that ambulance wasn't taking too many chances—any one of them would have killed the guy. As it was, four had a go."

Dawn looked at her husband and mouthed two words: *Tell him*.

"Look, Richard. It's probably nothing . . ." He hesitated.

"What's nothing?"

"What I'm going to say here. I think you ought to know something— just so you can think about it and then probably dismiss it. It's likely nothing at all."

"What do you have? Spit it out."

"Have you read Nolan's book, *Worst Nightmares*?"

"No, I must be the last person in the world who hasn't. What about it?"

"Well it was Dawn who thought of it initially." Mike's wife made a face at her husband. She didn't want to be the one pointing the accusing finger at Nolan. "There was a chapter in the book about some guy who fell to his death from the seventeenth floor in a building in Sydney, Australia. Reminded her of a case I handled some months back. The circumstances were real similar, she thought. I had to agree with her."

"So?"

"Well, I did some legwork and the cases did prove a lot alike. But hey, that could just be coincidence."

"Okay . . ."

"But it's not the only one."

"So where does the dead paramedic come in? Wait—let me guess. Someone in Nolan's book was bitten to death by snakes?"

"Not only that, but it happened in the back of an ambulance."

"And the guy that died?"

"A paramedic."

"I see," Quin replied slowly. His mind was in overdrive.

"I only bring this up because one death is coincidence. More than that seems like it should be followed up."

"Seems to me these events are connected."

"I'd say so, too. But keep in mind that I know Dermot Nolan, and he's not an evil guy. I'm in no way suggesting he had anything to do with these crimes. I just want to know where he got his stories from."

"I got it. Let's catch up tomorrow. I start at midday."

"Sure thing," Kandinski replied, as Dawn placed an ovenproof dish on the table in front of him and lifted the lid. He clicked off his cell and smiled at his wife. She's made his favorite, Andalusian Lamb. And it smelled like heaven.

CHAPTER 44

When Mr. B, otherwise known as Reggie Helpmann, regained consciousness, a wave of intense terror surged through his body. That man at the door! The man who had stabbed him with a syringe! He'd been kidnapped! Oh, Jesus, what was happening to him?

His brain took some minutes to adjust to his surroundings. It was pitch black. Finally, when some semblance of rational thought returned to him, he realized he wasn't in bed, but in some dark confined space. The pain in his head was different from the ones in his joints.

He tried moving his arms and legs and immediately discovered they were tightly bound by ropes. A rocking motion, coupled with continuous engine noise, told him he was in a vehicle—the trunk of a car!

His thought processes were slow. His eyes felt like they were glued together. He remembered this feeling from his childhood, when he was once awakened by his mother, arriving home after a long car ride. He forced his eyes open as wide as possible—it took some effort.

How long had he been trapped like this? He had no way of knowing. His muscles screamed discomfort at him.

A flash of pain almost blinded him when he attempted to straighten his head—he hadn't moved his neck in hours. The same with his legs and arms.

He tried to focus on sounds other than the engine, but could hear little or no traffic. That told him he wasn't in a big city. Possibly on a highway. Cars came by at intervals of no more than thirty seconds. He had to be way out in the country.

He finally managed to fully open his eyes and gradually became accustomed to what light there was. It wasn't a lot, which told him he was in a relatively new or expensive car that was well manufactured, allowing little light in through the cracks. The engine noise led him to believe he was in a European car—he'd owned many.

The really scary question was, why was he here anyway? What would anyone really want with him? He hadn't socialized for years. He knew nobody. He *was* a nobody! He wracked his brain for an explanation. Surely Alice hadn't been driven desperate by his condition, taken out an insurance policy, and hired a hit man to kill him? The idea was almost laughable.

At least he was in a dark confined space—that was a relief.

The vehicle slowed, lurched to the right, and then sped up again. Reggie presumed from the bumps that he was now off-road. Logic dictated they were now close to their destination.

But this logic was flawed—in reality he had a long, long way to go.

"Esther," Dermot began, hardly able to counter a faltering tone in his voice. "I've had a long chat with Neela, and I think I need to make myself clearer regarding the details in *Worst Nightmares.*"

Esther cleared her throat and took a deep breath. "Oh lord, Dermot. What are you going to tell me now?"

"Don't jump to any conclusions yet. All I'm saying is that Neela remembered she drew my attention to the Van Nuys killings while I was writing."

"The Free Fallers?"

"Them. Well, I didn't give the case much thought at the time, but it must have made an impression on me. The long and short of it, Esther, is that I must have factored some of the details into my book."

"Some? Schipp says the details are almost exactly the same."

Dermot was taken aback and wasn't sure how to respond.

"Dermot, please level with me. Were there other chapters?" Esther asked gloomily.

"Well, yes. The Scorpion Girl. Neela told me she'd read the details when she was browsing the *LA Times* online. She thinks I must have I picked up on the idea and then used it later without thinking too much about it."

"Dermot, can I ask you a question? This may be ridiculous, and maybe it's a question you can't answer." She paused for effect. "Or maybe you won't."

"Sure, anything. Go ahead."

"The incident you were involved in with that ambulance man. It was all over the news last night."

"I know, Esther. It was a real nightmare for me."

"Of course. Well . . . I'd like to believe—no, let's put it this way—I *know* that there is no connection between the man's death in your novel and the death of that man yesterday. It was very brave for you to have put your own life at risk to save that man. But here's the thing. What kind of serendipity was at work for you to be tailing the very ambulance in which this poor guy died at that precise moment in time? The coincidence of it all really bugs me."

Nolan was shocked. It was a very good question.

"I'm sorry, Esther, I don't quite follow you here. I tried my best to save that man's life."

"I know you did, Dermot. But what were the chances of your noticing the doors of this particular ambulance hanging open at that exact moment, and at that very place?"

"We were on our way to the movies."

"So no one had alerted you to what was about to happen?"

It was hopeless trying to lie to Esther. Dermot knew that. She could smell a lie at a thousand yards in a swamp.

The line stayed quiet for several moments as Dermot debated on what to say now.

Reggie heard the crunch of boots on hard earth coming around to the rear of the car and then a voice. "I'm about to open the trunk, Reggie. Close your eyes, I don't want to give you a scare." It was deep, guttural, and familiar. Where had he heard that voice before?

He did as he was told just as a key was inserted in the lock—he was now terrified. When he felt the scorching heat of the sun on his skin he lost control of his bladder.

"Do I know you?" he gasped as strong arms lifted him from his prison. "Have I done something to you?"

There was no reply. He wanted so much to open his eyes to see who was carrying him across what sounded like hard pebbly ground. But of course he couldn't—if he did, he'd be looking into the void and become even more terror-stricken than he was already.

"This has nothing to do with you, Reggie," the guttural voice stated matter of factly. "Nothing at all."

The man continued to carry him forward.

"But it does! It has everything to do with me!"

The man didn't speak for a bit. Then he explained. "Well, of course, insofar as you will die, I suppose it has a bit to do with you. But we must all die at some stage. Right? Right. And your time has come. It's that simple."

Reggie now knew he had to reason with an insane person.

"Why do you say it has nothing to do with me?"

"Because you are a random victim, Reggie. Most of the others were not. They 'offended' me. You didn't do that."

"Then why do you want to . . ." he could hardly bring himself to say the two words, ". . . kill me? Just for fun?"

"Because you are part of my story."

"What story?"

"You will never know. You'll be dead. Unless, of course you read my diary."

"Diary? What diary?"

"*Worst Nightmares*. Have you read the book?"

Reggie wracked his brains. He had to think, and think fast! If he established a rapport of sorts with his assailant, it might help him. Was this a Stockholm syndrome situation? Or was that the other way around, when victims came to love their assailants?

"*Worst Nightmares*? Yes, I've heard of that book, sure. But I haven't read it."

"You are part of that book. It's such a shame you haven't read it. You would know what to expect—but possibly it's just as well."

"Your voice . . . I remember your voice from somewhere."

"You do indeed. We've spoken before."

"Can you tell me when? Where? Can you tell me who you are?"

"I am the Dream Healer, Reggie. And I am about to put your worst nightmares to rest. I am going to bring you eternal peace."

Reggie screamed. He couldn't help himself. He now knew his tormentor intended to torture him until he died a terrible death.

The man stopped abruptly and laid him down on the parched red earth. Reggie Helpmann opened his eyes wide and screamed in pain. The baked earth beneath him was scalding his body—it was as hot as a grill rack. Immediately Reggie screwed his eyes tight shut again—this *was* his worst nightmare, but magnified a hundredfold.

He continued to scream as a slim yet strong chain was placed around his neck and padlocked to a much thicker chain that led to a concrete boulder.

"I'm not of a mind to inflict any more pain on you today. I just want to watch you for a while. I am conducting an experiment, you see."

At that moment Reggie felt a huge surge of relief. He'd been expecting to feel a knife at his throat.

"I shall now cut your arms and legs free. If you try to fight me, I will have to kill you. So don't even think about that course of action."

"I promise . . ." Reggie replied.

The Dream Healer cut the straps around his wrists and ankles. The relief was delicious. The blood flowed freely into his limbs. He did not struggle.

Then he heard footsteps, walking away. They became fainter and fainter until he could hear nothing. Absolutely nothing. Not even a bird. He'd never experienced such stillness.

Ten minutes later he heard a car's engine start up. It engaged into gear. Then the sound grew fainter and fainter until Reggie was back in his silent hell.

The terror of what he might see if he opened his eyes prevailed for two hours. By then he was so parched he knew he'd die if he couldn't find water—and it was possible, yet unlikely, that the man had left him some. Anything was worth a try.

He opened his eyes.

He knew at once that he was going to die. The red landscape reached to the horizon in every direction. There was not a tree, nor a building— no structure of any kind. Not even an electricity pylon. Nor was there any water at his side. He curled into a fetal ball and wept.

CHAPTER 45

Nick had called late the night before to suggest they all take in a movie the following day. Anything that would take Dermot out of the house, away from the telephone, would be a good distraction. Dermot had reluctantly agreed, after some persuasion from Neela.

"You have to take your mind off Klein. It wasn't your fault. We did all we could to save his life," Neela said, attempting to console him.

"But we didn't tell the police why we were so worried."

"What difference would that have made, honey? Do you really think the LAPD would have reacted any faster if Nick or I had told them there was a madman out there—a serial killer who'd called us before? Or if we'd told the police this maniac had told us that Derek Klein had less than an hour to live?" She begged Dermot with her eyes to say no. But he looked down and said nothing. "Tell me honestly, did you really think he'd die?"

"Yes, I did."

Neela tried to make sense of things. "Okay, tell me one last time. Do you believe that Arnold killed all those people?"

"All the people in his diary, you mean?"

"Yes."

He looked at her and thought he could feel his heart break. He just couldn't bring himself to tell her he'd lied all along.

"No," he lied.

"Who killed the Snake Man?"

"Someone who read my book. A copycat killer."

"Honey," she began soothingly, mindful of his fragile mental state. "I don't see how that makes any sense. Whoever telephoned you about Klein sounded exactly like the voice of the man we called Mr. Arnold. How would that caller have known how to replicate Arnold's guttural tones if he hadn't met Arnold, or God forbid, actually *was* Arnold?"

Dermot gaped at her. "How on earth could he be Arnold? We established weeks ago that he was dead. No one could survive without half a head."

"Then he had to have had an accomplice, Dermot. And that means he *and* Arnold committed all the crimes."

"Or the accomplice committed all the crimes and Arnold found out about them."

Neela stared at him. Was he really serious?

"Some other person is waiting to see if you did the right thing?"

"And of course we all know that I didn't!"

"The question now is how do we handle this situation? Do you think that Arnold's 'little helper' has done his dash? Or will he keep trying to drive you mad by threatening to kill more people? If he does that, then we have no option but to share the entire story with the authorities."

Dermot put his head in his hands. She had no option but to continue.

"Honey. I'm simply thinking of the worst possible scenario, so that we are prepared. We don't know things'll get worse. But we do have to take stock of our position. Then we can sit tight and see what happens. Ultimately, we may have to do the right thing and risk everything. But until then, let's pull ourselves together, support each other, and hang tough."

"Oh God, I can't sit in this house all fucking day waiting for the phone to ring."

"So let's join Nick. He's been trapped in a boring meeting at Sotheby's. Let's take in a movie and escape for a few hours."

They waited for Nick outside the movie house for fifteen minutes. He called just minutes before the beginning of the movie to beg off. He had to visit a client.

Inside, Neela received a call from her mother's neighbor in Brentwood, telling her someone was shouting from the yard next door. He was afraid Neela's mother may fallen and hurt herself. He'd gone to look but couldn't see anyone.

"I have to go check this out, honey. Why don't you stay and watch the movie? You take the car and I'll take a cab home. I'll see you later." She gave him a small kiss and with that she was gone.

Dermot got home just before eight. He'd stopped for a few beers in a bar on Grand Avenue. When the car turned onto Linley, he saw there were about fifty people gathered outside his house. The crowd was so big the traffic had come to a complete standstill. Drivers were leaning on their horns, and one helpful man was trying to persuade a bunch of journalists with cameras, as well as TV news crews, to part to allow the traffic through. Dermot's stomach turned over.

"That's him! It's Nolan!"

It took Dermot a second or two to react because of the booze. He put his head down and walked purposefully toward the house. Somewhere ahead he could hear Neela calling his name. He shouldered his way through the press crush. It was practically impossible.

"Mr. Nolan!" a young man shouted. "Alan Gibson. KCAL 9. Is it true that you based *Worst Nightmares* on the ravings of a serial killer who actually exists?"

Another TV journalist elbowed his way forward and stuck out a mike. "Mr. Nolan. How did you know that the Snake Man would die, weeks before he did?"

He pressed further forward. "Let my husband through! Get out of the way!" Neela demanded. But the media paid no attention.

"Did you plagiarize the entire novel, Mr. Nolan? Or just parts of it?"

Dermot could hardly breathe.

"Have you ever been charged with any sex offenses, Nolan?"

He could see Neela a few feet away now, her hand outstretched. "Let my husband pass! This is disgraceful!"

"Have you engaged an attorney? Will the film still go ahead, Mr. Nolan?"

Dermot grabbed at Neela's hand. She pulled him past the last few journalists. Still the flood of people pushed them relentlessly toward the front door.

"Do you have a criminal history, Mr. Nolan? Would you say you're a violent man by nature?"

In a flash of anger and exasperation, Neela slapped the face of the man who had asked that question. Another big mistake. Several of the paparazzi caught the image, with Dermot clearly visible in the background. The man whose face she had slapped recovered quickly. "Mrs. Nolan, would you care to comment on the allegations of plagiarism leveled at your husband?"

"Plagiarism?" Neela responded angrily. "Don't be ridiculous. What are you suggesting?"

"It's happened before," a middle-aged woman, holding a KLSX radio mike yelled out.

"Well, it hasn't happened here! My husband is one of America's most respected novelists, for heaven's sake!"

Neela had lost her momentum in getting them both inside. She was furious and responding to questions right and left before she realized how the press had tricked her. The questions now came thicker and faster.

"Can you respond to comments that your husband is actually involved in the slayings?"

"Did your husband have anything to do with placing those snakes in the ambulance?"

Neela was astonished at the insinuations. "Who exactly is making these allegations?"

Behind her she heard Dermot shouting at her. "Don't say a word. Get in the house! Now!"

Neela strode to the door, her key in hand.

When she closed the front door she had to lean against it to make sure that no one was still trying to push through.

"I tried calling you," she said, shakily.

Scarecrow ran to Dermot from the kitchen, wagging his tail like a propeller, jumping up at his legs. Cheesecake jumped from the sofa and hissed at the terrier, swiping at his muzzle with a paw. Scarecrow yelped and ran for cover in the kitchen.

"I had the cell switched off. I was at the *movies*!"

"I know. But I thought you'd call when the show was over."

"I went for a couple of drinks."

"I can see that."

No sooner had she said the words than she wished she hadn't.

"I am not drunk!" he replied. But he knew most drunks said that when they knew they'd reached their limit.

"Come into the kitchen and I'll make some coffee."

"Jesus, the entire press corps is here," he said. "I guess now I *have* to come clean!"

"No, you don't. Better to say absolutely nothing. Don't give them anything. We'll call Esther and ask her for the name of the best attorney in town. That's what we'll do."

"Every radio and television station in Los Angeles is out there. And all the newspapers. I think I saw CNN. Christ, those people move fast!"

Neela handed the phone to her husband. "You have to call her. Now. We need an attorney immediately. And don't forget to grovel—now you have to tell her the truth." Dermot stared at her, ashen faced.

"Just tell her you did base all your stories—albeit subliminally—on actual events. You're sorry, and you don't think it's a big deal. Ask her to suggest an attorney."

Dermot punched in the numbers.

The conversation wasn't pleasant. Esther had been expecting the shit would hit the fan for a couple of days now, but she was pretty angry that Dermot had placed her in such a completely untenable position.

"It's unforgivable, I know that, Esther. I never for one second thought—"

"That you'd be found out?" Esther interrupted coldly.

"I didn't think it'd ever become such a big issue. It was research, nothing more. All writers research their novels—why should I be any different?"

"No reason you should be. But once you tell the press that all the ideas are original, you're riding for a fall. I have my own integrity to think of, you know, and you've made me look ridiculous."

"I apologize, hugely. But now's the time to play down this angle; give a statement and find some closure. It only affects three characters anyway."

"Can you lay your hand on your heart and tell me there are no more skeletons in this closet, Dermot? It's imperative I know all of it now. Everything!"

Dermot looked at Neela. The conversation was on speakerphone, so she'd heard it all. She nodded vehemently.

"No more, Esther. That's my solemn promise."

"Well thank heavens for small mercies at least," she replied.

"Just one thing. I think I need a lawyer."

"What on earth for, darling? I have Brennan for all our legal literary matters. He's the best."

"I need an attorney who handles personal matters in case they crop up here. I have an ugly crowd of journalists outside my front door—people who refuse to leave without a statement. I'm not going to give them one, but I need to know my rights."

"Are you talking a criminal attorney, darling?" Esther said—her tone had hardened a bit.

"I suppose so, yes. I wouldn't need a corporate attorney, would I?" Dermot replied, trying to make light of his request.

"Call Harold Fountain. He's one of my oldest friends and the best legal mind in town." She gave him the number.

The obese manager of Dusty's Motor Inn staggered from the back room where the *Sopranos* theme tune was pounding away.

"You want a room?"

"No, I want a license to drill for crude oil," Jeff Schipp replied.

Schipp pulled out a snapshot he'd printed off the Internet. It was a photo of Nolan. "Is this face familiar?" he asked.

The fat slob chuckled. "Is now. Wasn't before. See, I don't read much."

Schipp couldn't have guessed.

"I watch the box." He looked at the snap. "Isn't that the writer who's got himself in a shitload of trouble?"

"Maybe. Have you ever seen him here?"

"Sure have. Been in here a few times over the last couple of years."

"He's been around here before?" Schipp asked.

"Oh, I think so. Yep, pretty sure of it." He paused for a second, as though recollecting. "Yeah, I know so. Why do you ask? You a detective?"

"No. I'm with the *Daily News*."

"You be sure to mention my name in the story? That'd make my mother smile."

"Sure, why not." It was always good to keep the sources happy. "What's your name?"

"Rod Beamon. Looks like this writer guy has stepped in a fair pile of cow poop, huh?" Beamon said, chuckling. "What's the matter—his wife not giving him enough?"

"Thanks for your help, Mr. Beamon. Look for your name in the paper tomorrow. By the way, how far's Shute?"

Beamon smirked. "You mean the Lizard? Ten minutes. Ask for Honey—she's cute."

Schipp forced a smile and left quickly.

CHAPTER 46

"I'm afraid things are more serious than you imagine, Mr. Nolan," Fountain advised, stirring his Earl Grey tea in the Nolans' living room. "However, there's no need to worry too much yet."

Fountain was a man in his early fifties. Good looking in a craggy lean way, with wavy silver hair. Women had been dropping at his feet for close to forty years. His looks and charismatic demeanor also stood him in great stead with a jury that generally had more women than men.

"Please, call me Dermot. Mr. Nolan's a bit formal."

"Without appearing to be too dull here, I do prefer to remain formal with my clients. I hope you won't take offense."

"Of course not, Harold," Dermot replied pointedly.

Fountain stirred in the single dot of sugar.

"I assure you, I appreciate the gravity of my situation. After all, what could be more fundamentally serious than to be publicly declared a liar? If

I'm tarred with the brush of plagiarism, it could mean the end of my career as a novelist."

"Mr. Nolan, while I don't wish to alarm you at this early stage, we must remember you are now a 'celebrity,' and as such you'll be the focus of the media's attention twenty-four/seven. So I have to reiterate—since you still seem to be missing my point. At this very moment the district attorney is gathering information about you. Details of your recent whereabouts over the past few months. In short you are 'a person of interest.'"

"If that's the case," Neela interceded, "then I'm missing your point, too. How can the authorities think of my husband as a 'person of interest'? What reason would they possibly have? That he arrived too late at Derek Klein's murder scene in an attempt to save his life? While putting his own at risk?"

"Mrs. Nolan, I have to tell you bluntly that in the past few days a pretty substantial forensic file has been put together by the LAPD. It placed your husband in the immediate vicinity of at least two murders—murders that bear an uncanny resemblance to those featured in his novel. This forensic evidence places your husband in a rather bad light."

"Places him? Bad light? Where? Where has he *been*, for God's sake?" Neela shot back.

"Well, Shute for one, Mrs. Nolan. The prosecuting counsel may even draw a very long bow taut and suggest you went to Van Nuys Airport on your husband's behalf to protect him."

Dermot looked directly at Fountain. "Is it a crime to go to Shute? No one can seriously be suggesting—"

Fountain cut him short. "It is not I who is suggesting anything. I am here to counter these kinds of suggestions. That's what you're paying me to do."

"May I ask another question, Mr. Fountain?" Neela asked.

"Ask away, Mrs. Nolan."

"Am I right in thinking that anything I say in this room today is covered by the 'without prejudice' rule?"

"Of course. Anything you tell me is privileged. You are Mr. Nolan's wife, and consequently you are also covered by the rules of evidence regarding spouses. You cannot incriminate your husband."

"Mr. Fountain, I have no intention of incriminating my husband because he has done nothing wrong."

Fountain could see he'd put her back up, so he smiled his best smile. "I'm sorry, Mrs. Nolan. I was simply summarizing the law. What do you wish to ask me?"

"Let me put it this way. If my husband were to admit that certain passages of *Worst Nightmares* were—how can I put it delicately—based on case histories that are freely available in the printed media, would that be sufficient to call off these dogs of war?"

"The press? Never. But the authorities? That's debatable. I think our best bet is for your husband to answer my questions frankly so I can see how tricky it's going to be persuading the police to back off."

"Seems like a plan," Dermot offered.

"Right. Well, let's get at it. First of all, was it really chance that placed you behind that speeding ambulance in which Derek Klein died? Or did someone tip you off that his life was in danger? I need to know the truth here. The exact truth."

Neela watched Dermot struggle with an answer.

"We must tell Mr. Fountain, Dermot. He's our attorney," Neela placed a comforting arm around Dermot's shoulders.

"There is a man," Dermot began, and then faltered. Fountain said nothing. He knew that to respond would let Nolan off the hook. "He told me his name was Arnold."

"The same name as the character in your novel, *Worst Nightmares*?"

"Correct. He simply suggested that he had it in mind to kill someone in exactly the same way as I had recounted the death of my character in the novel, Jon Hartog. He gave me a name and told me the man was a paramedic, again just like in my novel, and that he worked for Schaefer in the Beverly Boulevard district, and . . ." he hesitated, ". . . he told me Derek Klein had an hour to live."

"And you believed him?"

What could Dermot say? He desperately hoped he could still, somehow, with Fountain's unwitting assistance, keep the authorship of the original manuscript a secret.

"I was horrified by what this man said. So, I suppose . . . yes, I *did* believe him. Why would he make up such a thing?"

"So you immediately dialed 9-1-1?"

Dermot looked at Neela, a glance not lost on Fountain.

"I called a friend of ours," Neela explained, "and asked him to make the emergency call while we left the house immediately to do our best to locate the ambulance. We called Schaefer and they told us where Klein and his partner usually went at the end of their shift. We didn't tell them why we were so worried because we didn't want to get bogged down with bureaucrats asking a lot of dumb questions. It was imperative that we get to Klein quickly."

There was something about what she'd said—logical though it was—that didn't sit particularly well with Fountain. *What is she keeping to herself?* he wondered.

"Who made the call?" he asked.

"One of our oldest friends, Nick Hoyle."

"And he actually made that call?"

"He told us he did—yes."

"Did you confirm that with the police?"

"No, I didn't. But it stands to reason—someone must have made that call because the police arrived at the scene less than ten minutes later and told us that they'd been alerted by a citizen call."

Fountain wrote down Nick's name in an expensive notebook with a black Montblanc pen. "Has this man ever called you before?"

Neela was about to answer when Dermot interrupted. "No. Never." She shot him the smallest of glances—again Fountain noticed. "The people murdered by the killer in *Worst Nightmares,* did you borrow any of those details from real-life crimes?"

"Yes. I know I initially denied it, but I was simply being vain, not deceptive. It's a flaw in my character, I'm afraid. So, yes—I lied. I *did* borrow some real case histories. Just a few."

"Which few?" Fountain let the question hang in the air.

"Have you ever visited Shute, where the woman died of suffocation?" the lawyer continued.

"Yes, I have. It's a nice area."

"Really? I passed by it once and wasn't impressed. But maybe I prefer 'lush' while you prefer 'arid.' Do you like the desert?"

Dermot couldn't see where Fountain was leading him, so he just replied truthfully. "Yes, as a matter of fact I do love open spaces."

"You're clearly not an agoraphobic, as was Mr. B in your book."

Fountain had obviously done his homework.

"I prefer the wide open spaces to English hedgerows. Why do you ask?"

"No reason in particular," Fountain replied. But Neela could see there had been a reason—the question was, what was it?

"What's our next step, Mr. Fountain?" Neela asked—she was damned if she'd call him by his first name while he referred to them both so formally.

"Well, I'm going to have some of my team ascertain the present mind-set of the authorities. As soon as we have an idea of that, I'll do my best to put an end to any thoughts they might have that you are at all involved with the crimes they are investigating. Clearly it's a ridiculous notion." He smiled at Neela. "Your husband's a great storyteller, isn't he?" It was a purely rhetorical question, though one mixed with a certain edge.

He looked at Nolan and saw only angst. Then he looked at Neela and observed a concerned calm. *She's the strong one. Good. We may need her.*

CHAPTER 47

Police Commander Victoria Willis stood at the front of the conference room on the fifth floor at Parker Center. On the whiteboard behind her were the names of those confirmed dead and their locations, dates of demise, and so on. Underneath were the names of all the fictional characters in *Worst Nightmares*. Arrows led from the real to the character names.

As Willis gave her first major briefing to the team drawn from all over Los Angeles, a dozen of the best detectives in the city faced her: Kandinski, Quin, and Woo among them.

"I want this investigation to be conducted in the spirit of minute-by-minute cooperation. There is little doubt in my mind that many, if not all, of these deaths are linked. So we will begin with this premise and put aside investigations that prove otherwise. I will handle the press and only me. Understood?"

Kandinski raised a hand.

"I think I know what you're going to say, Detective Kandinski, and the answer is no, I don't think you should recuse yourself from this investigation purely on account of your personal relationship with Mr. Nolan. As far as the LAPD is concerned, Nolan is simply a person of interest at this stage. Your insight on the Conway case is integral to this investigation. However, I am sure I don't need to impress upon you that from this moment on you are to have no personal contact with Mr. Nolan."

Kandinski nodded, but he felt bad about it. Nolan had always been a good friend, and now, in his time of need, he couldn't be there for him.

"There's no way of knowing at this early stage whether or not we are looking at the work of a serial killer who is responsible for *all* the deaths we have noted here on the board," she continued, indicating the whiteboard. "Or whether the most recent killer is simply taking credit for murders committed by others. That will be our first objective—proof of linkage. As for any involvement by Dermot Nolan, we need to tread carefully because of his celebrity. Believe me, we will not treat him any differently than we do any ordinary Joe, but we do have the media to consider here.

"One last thing. There are characters in Nolan's book we haven't been able to identify as having died in this country yet. Of course they may not exist in real life—that's always a possibility. But experience tells us that where one finds a list of targets, and all but a few have been killed, it's simply a matter of time before we find the rest. So, let's get on and find them, shall we?"

Woo raised a hand.

"Yes?"

"What about Schipp?"

"Our one link to the source. I'm not expecting Schipp to offer up his name—even if he knew it, which I very much doubt. Still, we need to make sure that Schipp handles all further communications with the utmost delicacy. If we can convince him to agree to a police presence in his office when he fields calls, we can trace them, and that would be the best-case scenario."

Woo ground his teeth. He knew Schipp would never agree to a wiretap.

Willis noticed his doubtful expression and zeroed in on him. "Jeff Schipp called *you*, Detective Woo. I suggest you keep a very tight rein on him to make sure that we at least know of any calls from his source as soon as he is contacted."

"Right, ma'am."

"I suggest we get on with our work and get some results ASAP. We need a few touchdowns double quick. The last thing we need here is for the opposition to score—and that's always a possibility. The DC is expecting the best from us. And quickly. I know you won't let him or me down."

CHAPTER 48

Schipp was exuberant. He'd nailed his first national headline: WORST NIGHTMARES—THE REAL DEAL? And the best part about it was that he'd scooped every other journalist in America. And they all knew it.

"You've done well," Melhuish said. "But the story's out there now, and we have to be first every day on new facts until Nolan is charged, convicted, and jailed for life. If he's guilty, it goes without saying."

"Aren't we getting ahead of ourselves a bit here?" Schipp replied with a thin smile.

"Maybe. Maybe not. Let's see where your source leads you. I don't actually want any quick resolution to this. We were the first to break this story, so LA will be reading our sheet first. We have to stay one jump ahead."

"With the source on our side, we should," Schipp replied.

His cell phone rang and Schipp snatched it out of his pocket, apologizing with his eyes to his boss.

"Schipp here."

"Mr. Schipp. I can't stay on long. While I'm sure you wouldn't jeopardize your 'exclusive' by ratting me out, there must be no attempts whatsoever to trace this call."

"No problem," Schipp assured him.

"Right to the point then. I have another location for you. There's a man—a very thirsty man. He may at this stage be far too thirsty for you to quench his cravings. Be that as it may, I think there's a slim chance he might still be alive. His name is Reggie Helpmann. In Mr. Nolan's book his name is Leif Crane."

"Where is he?"

"Look up the directions in Nolan's book. But start at the Four Points Sheraton on New Stine Road in Bakersfield. I have to go now."

"Will you call me again?"

"Oh, yes. I'm sure I shall," the guttural voice almost laughed.

A click signaled the end of the conversation.

Schipp immediately got Woo on the phone, and twenty minutes later they were in a helicopter on their way to Bakersfield. Also on board were a police doctor and a forensic specialist, as well as a pilot.

The temperature there was just under a hundred and five degrees, so if the poor bastard didn't have any water, he'd be dead in a matter of hours. The odds weren't good.

The sun-baked earth below seemed to stretch out forever. Even at a thousand feet, the ground felt like the surface of Mars. "Should be there in a few minutes, detective," the pilot called over the mike. "There's the road. I'll have to judge the rest with the compass."

The chopper dipped and fell to five hundred feet. It then leveled and cruised forward at a slower speed.

"It looks shit hot down there," the forensic guy observed.

"More than you know," echoed the pilot. "I wouldn't give a man without water more than six hours. How long has he been there?"

"Not exactly sure. We're not even sure if he's actually down there. Could be a hoax."

Schipp shot Woo a glance. He didn't care for his lack of faith.

"Look!" the police doctor shouted. "Down there!"

The pilot slowed and dipped even further to sweep the ground at a height of around fifty feet.

"There," the doctor said, pointing. But everyone in the chopper had already seen it. It was a man, lying sprawled on the red earth like a dog at the end of its chain. His skin was black; the figure inert.

When they touched down twenty feet from the crime scene, there were two words written in small stones at the end of the body's right hand: *Worst Nightmares*.

CHAPTER 49

Sitting in his temporary space in the partitioned Task Force Tower operations room, Mike Kandinski called to mind all the details he could remember about the Conway homicide. There had to be something there that might give him a clue about why Conway had been targeted—there had to be a motive. If it had been a random killing, and all the other deaths seemed random, then the only link would be the book.

Because of his well-known fear of heights and the neighborhood, Conway might have passed on the job, but he didn't. A lucky break for his killer.

Another odd fact was that electricity to that building had been shut off some two months before, yet the elevator showed signs of having recently functioned. The energy company suggested that possibly an electronic feeder line had been run from some adjacent building. Other than that, they had no idea how the elevator could have been operational.

Kandinski read through the other statements. Everyone agreed Conway was a nice guy with no enemies, so a motive for his murder had been hard to find. His marriage was in decent shape, despite his frequent extramarital liaisons. So if he couldn't find a motive for Conway's death, possibly the right approach was to try to link Conway to one of the other people who had died. But he couldn't find any kind of connection at all. As far as he could tell, none of the victims had even met.

The telephone rang.

"Mike? It's Neela Nolan."

His heart sank. Not only could he not help them out, he wasn't even supposed to be talking to them.

"Hi, Neela. Nice to hear from you. Listen, I wish I could help you, but—"

"Mike, please. I'm not asking you to put your job on the line, or influence anyone—"

"I couldn't even if I wanted to, Neela," he replied kindly and sincerely. "I'm on the team investigating a series of recent deaths that may be linked to Dermot. I'm sorry but—"

"But he's your friend! You really can't believe he's done anything bad," Neela pleaded.

"Of course I don't, Neela. But I'm obliged to do my job. I'm under strict instruction *not* to contact your husband. All I can advise is for Dermot to get a lawyer—as a precautionary measure."

"This is not going to go away is it, Mike?"

"No. I'd say not."

There was a long pause. He could hear Neela crying. Then she spoke.

"Thank you, Mike. I understand your position. You'll always be our friend."

"I appreciate you seeing things this way, Neela."

Neela hung up just as the door to the large operations room opened. Willis entered and stood by the massive whiteboard. "Detectives? May I have everyone's attention?"

Within moments, the room was focused entirely on her. "I have just received news from Detective Woo that the body of a dead man, identified as Reginald Helpmann, has been found a few miles outside Bakersfield in the desert. Lesions around his wrists and ankles suggest a person or persons took him there bound and against his will. He died of dehydration only a few hours before Woo and his team reached the scene. I have not yet released details to the media. However, I'm going to do that at the appropriate time.

Quin raised a hand.

Willis already knew the question. "Yes, the crime scene is exactly the same as the one detailed in *Worst Nightmares*."

Quin smiled and put down his hand. "Any more questions?" She paused and looked around the room, but none of the detectives were game enough to ask anything. They all knew she'd answer before they'd asked it.

"Detective Kandinski, I need a word with you, please," she said with a light smile, then disappeared through the door into her office.

CHAPTER 50

Schipp had called in his story on the way back from Bakersfield. He'd been told he had to fly back on a commercial helicopter, as the police chopper was required in situ. What the hell did he care? A chopper ride was a chopper ride; it was fun, and he wasn't paying.

He now sat in the editor's suite facing a beaming James Melhuish.

"The opposition has hardly any idea what's really going down here—which I find marvelous," Melhuish said. "We'll have another screamer headline tomorrow morning. Do you foresee any problems?"

"No. Just the normal legal read. Nolan probably has a bunch of attorneys by now, so we have to be careful."

"Of course. The Bakersfield crime scene really got the cops going. Woo's generally tight-lipped when it comes to opinions, but seems like he's thinking this is the work of a copycat killer, using Nolan's book to recreate the murders we haven't stumbled on yet."

"So Woo's thinking that since Nolan wrote his book before the victim was killed, it could have been anyone?

"More or less. Yes."

"Same with Klein?"

"Yes. But not some of the others. They can place Nolan at the scene of those crimes—"

"But not at the time they were murdered, surely?"

"No," Schipp replied carefully. "But it's a major coincidence that he was in both places and lived around the corner from where Conway died."

CHAPTER 51

Neela answered Dermot's cell phone. "Yes?" she asked.

"Mrs. Nolan? Hi, it's Mike Kandinski. Is Dermot around?"

"Mike, hi. Good to hear from you. But I thought you weren't supposed to be . . ."

"I need to come over for a chat. I just wanted to make sure you and Dermot were home."

"Yes, we're home."

"It's Mike," she said to Dermot, handing him the cell.

"Mike, hi."

"How's it going?"

"Well, frankly, it's not much fun when the general public thinks you're a mass murderer, and you have no idea what's going on in the investigation."

"I know. The best thing would be to clear up this whole thing ASAP. I'm on my way over. Just wanted to give you a heads-up in case any of the press recognizes me as a detective and thinks you're being arrested."

"Arrested?" Nolan was taken by surprise. "Jesus, Mike. Arrested for what, for Christ's sake?"

"Hey, take it easy. I'm not coming to arrest you. They just want you to come in and answer a few questions." He paused. "You have a lawyer? You know, just as a precaution?"

"Of course."

"Then maybe you should give him a quick call."

"Where are you now?"

"On Figueroa."

"Okay, see you shortly."

Dermot turned to Neela. "They want me to 'come downtown,' as they say in the movies."

"Well, we kind of knew that was eventually going to happen, honey. But it doesn't mean things have gotten any worse."

There was a *ping* at the door. Neela pressed a switch on the video entry monitor. It was Nick. She let him in, as thirty or so reporters shouted questions from the street.

"Have you heard?" Nick asked.

Dermot stared at him. "What the hell now?"

"A journalist from the *Daily News* took a team somewhere outside of Bakersfield. They found another body. He was chained by the neck to a buried cement block. Died of dehydration."

"Mr. B . . ." Neela whispered. She could barely breathe.

"Right. That's the connection the police are making right now."

Dermot collected his thoughts. "Do they know when he was killed?"

"Two days ago, they say. Why?"

"Because I couldn't possibly have had anything to do with his death—I was here in Los Angeles!"

"That's right," Nick replied smiling. "Of course! This might turn everything around. We were all going to the movies, right? I begged off at the last minute and you and Neela went alone."

Dermot's smile turned into a frown.

"What's wrong?"

"Well, the fact is, Neela couldn't make it either. She had to check on her mother. So I went alone. Then I had a few drinks on the way home. I didn't get back till late."

"Surely someone at the movie theater or the bar will be able to say they saw you?" Nick suggested encouragingly.

"I hope so. But that's not the only problem here."

"What?" Nick and Neela asked, nearly in unison.

"I've been to that exact spot before. There may be evidence. They'll want to know why."

His wife and best friend's silence spoke volumes.

He picked up his phone and punched in Fountain's number.

"Harold? It's Dermot Nolan. Listen, my police friend Detective Kandinski just called. He wants me to come down to Parker with him to meet with his superiors and answer some questions. Is this a good idea?"

"Providing I'm there, yes. It shows good faith. When are you going?"

"Mike said he'd be here in about five minutes. Are you free?"

"I'll make myself free, Mr. Nolan. I do have to justify my fees." It was a joke, but Dermot wasn't laughing. "Go with him when he arrives. But wait till I arrive before saying anything other than 'hi, there.' Okay?"

"Okay." Dermot saw Neela signaling to him with a hand. He knew what she was going to ask. "Can Neela come?"

"I'd imagine there'd be no problem. That'd be up to the police. But take her with you, and we'll see. Oh, one more thing."

"What's that?"

"Dress casually. Try not to look rich. It's always good if the general public thinks you're a true upright citizen."

"Right."

"Also, try not to look grim when you leave the house with your detective friend. Look as if he's just that—a detective friend. Same goes for your wife. Remember: You're helping the police, you're not under suspicion. Okay?"

"Okay." Dermot flipped the cell shut.

When Kandinski double-parked outside the Nolan home, the press crowded his car so tightly he couldn't get the driver's door open. He had to flash his police badge to get them to move aside. Once he'd done that, the camera lights went on and the various radio journalists shoved their mikes in his face. He pushed his way forcibly to the front door.

"Have you come to arrest Nolan?" a young man asked.

"Mister Nolan to you, son," Kandinski replied gruffly and continued to push forward.

"You think he had a hand in the Bakersfield murder?"

The flurry of the media outside announced Kandinski's arrival.

As Neela opened the door, thirty questions fired through like incoming artillery shells. She slammed it shut.

Kandinski attempted a weary smile and took a deep breath. "Hi Neela. Hi Dermot. I had to double-park. But that's the joy of being a cop—no one's going to book you." He laughed, but no one else did.

"Hi Mike. You remember Nick Hoyle?" Dermot said, gesturing towards Nick.

"Sure," Mike said, extending a hand.

"Nice to see you again, detective," said Nick, accepting the gesture.

Mike turned his attention to Dermot. "So, were you able to get ahold of your attorney?"

"Yes. He'll meet us at Parker Center. Is it okay if Neela comes with us?"

"Absolutely," Mike replied.

A few minutes later, Nick held open the front door, and together with Kandinski, did his best to part the waves of journalists for Neela and Dermot. Neela pretended to joke with Dermot, a relaxed yet fixed smile on her face. Dermot's amiable expression didn't fool anyone.

A couple of minutes later Dermot, Neela, Mike, and the entire press corps were on their way to Parker. Twenty minutes later three police vehicles drove up to Linley Place.

CHAPTER 52

Fountain was waiting at the station when the Nolans and Kandinski arrived. Fountain shook hands with both of them and gave Kandinski a look. Kandinski got the hint and left them alone.

"I've been told Commander Willis will be joining us shortly," Fountain advised with an easy smile. "I think you should say as little as possible today, but at the same time show good faith. After all, you are doing your best to help the police with their investigation. You have nothing to hide and have done no more than tell a few white lies about the research for your novel. I foresee no real problems."

"That's a relief, Mr. Fountain," Neela said.

"That being said, you must understand that the police are investigating a very serious matter, and may ask some very direct questions. But do *not* take offense. They have to follow up all leads. Do not take anything they say personally."

"Of course," Dermot replied.

"If I feel you should not answer a question, I will interrupt on some pretense, and then encourage you to continue with your answer. That's the cue to say nothing. Do you understand?"

"I do," Dermot replied.

The door opened and Willis entered, followed by Detective Woo. She smiled at Dermot, and extended a hand to him and then to Neela. She and Woo sat opposite the Nolans and Fountain.

"Thank you for taking the time to come in this afternoon."

She focused on Dermot. "This past week must have seemed like a personal nightmare for you, Mr. Nolan, and we're not looking to prolong that. So the sooner we can clear up some anomalies that have come to light concerning your book, the sooner we can go after the person or persons responsible for the crimes we now have to solve here in LA."

Relief surged through Dermot's veins.

"Well, I certainly would like to clear my name publicly," Dermot replied with a hesitant smile. "And you're not wrong about my nightmare—but that's the tabloid press, I guess," he said, doing his best to bond with Willis.

"I hope you won't mind if we record our conversation?" She asked. "It's standard procedure."

"Of course I don't mind."

Willis clicked on the recorder and identified the date, time, and those present.

"First, in the broadest terms, can you clarify whether or not you did use news reports of crimes that took place in California as research for your current novel *Worst Nightmares*?"

"I did," Dermot replied. "I admit I did tell some white lies about the book early on, and I would like to add that it wasn't intentional. My wife told me of various incidents and I carried them subconsciously in my psyche."

"You're saying then that the Flyer in your novel—Dan Lasky—was really a subliminal issue suggested by the death of Abel Conway two blocks from your house a while ago? Is that correct?"

"Yes."

"And the Free Fallers in your novel, Joan and Thomas Foster, were modeled on Meredith and Noam Zersky, who died at Van Nuys Airport; together with Corey Hamilton, their pilot—a man you simply renamed Mike Roper?"

"Yes. That's correct."

Dermot smiled. He was pleased she'd mentioned the Free Fallers so early on. "I believe that someone is currently about to stand trial for their murders. Is that so?"

"The district attorney is reviewing the case in view of the Tower investigations, but you're right, a suspect *was* charged some months ago."

She consulted her notes.

"I believe you recently visited Shute?"

"Yes, that's right," Dermot replied. What else could he say?

"Can you tell me why?"

"I felt like a driving trip into the country. Nothing more."

"I wish I could get out more often, but when I leave the office it's nearly always to visit some very depressing crime scene." Willis paused. "Did your trip take you to other locations?"

Dermot pretended not to understand. "Like where?"

"Topanga State Park?"

Willis's eyes bore into his like lasers. Dermot knew he'd have to admit to having been in the vicinity of the Stakes Couple—someone may have seen him. If he didn't come clean he'd be in deep trouble.

"Yes, I believe I did drive through the park."

"Does Cedar Line Road ring any bells?"

Dermot pretended to think. "No, I don't think so."

"You do remember the Woods couple in your novel?"

"Of course I do."

"The remains of two people were uncovered near Cedar Line Road two days ago—Gareth and Laura Nash. They were buried not far from two stakes embedded in the ground—the distance between them was exactly that mentioned in *Worst Nightmares*. There were rope marks at neck height and blood stains at the foot of each stake."

She stared at Dermot. He stared back like a dead blowfish.

"Are their names familiar to you at all?"

"No. Not at all."

"The manner of their deaths is so similar to the way you described the Woods' deaths, one would have to think that whoever murdered these two unfortunate people must have read your book."

Dermot nodded—he hoped against hope this was her line of thinking.

"Yet forensics concluded that they died well before the publication of *Worst Nightmares*," she continued.

Fountain interrupted. "Have you an exact time of death yet?"

"No, not yet, Mr. Fountain. But shortly we *will*. In the meantime could you tell me, Mr. Nolan, of anyone you might have shown your manuscript to?"

"You mean *before* it was published?"

"Exactly."

"Just my wife. My agent, of course. Oh, and my best friend, Nick Hoyle."

She made a note.

There was a lull in the conversation.

"You also visited the Lazy Lizard Bar. Had you heard of this bar before?"

"Yes," Dermot replied. How could he say otherwise? Neela managed not to look at him.

"It's quite a rough establishment, wouldn't you say?" Willis continued.

"True. However, I had no idea that was the case before I stepped inside, that it was—"

Willis cut him short. "Doubling as a brothel? Of course you didn't." She smiled reassuringly at Neela.

"I asked the manager of Dusty's Motel where I could get a drink and he suggested the Lazy Lizard."

"I see," she said, and scribbled some more notes.

Another hiatus. Dermot sweated. Fountain looked relaxed. Neela tried to breathe normally.

"I know you've been asked this before by Detective Quin, but bear with me. It was quite a coincidence that you happened to be driving behind the ambulance in which Derek Klein was bitten by snakes."

Fountain interjected. "It may very well be that whoever placed the snakes in the ambulance engineered Mr. Nolan's presence close to the crime scene so that the death might implicate him."

"Yes, that's certainly a possibility. You mean that someone familiar with Mr. Nolan's novel decided to recreate the death of . . ." she looked down at her notes, ". . . Jon Hartog, and throw suspicion on Mr. Nolan. Perhaps that person managed to lead Mr. Nolan to the scene of the crime?"

"That's *exactly* what I'm suggesting," Fountain continued. "As you know, an unknown party called Mr. Nolan and told him Mr. Klein had less than an hour to live. Mr. Nolan behaved in an exemplary way, risking his own life to save Mr. Klein's."

"You're a brave man, Mr. Nolan."

She again looked at her notes. "The Scorpion Girl, Barbara Rush in the novel and Lucy Cowley in real life . . ." Willis let the two names hang in the air, hoping Dermot would say something. He didn't.

"The similarities between the real cases and your book are almost spooky, wouldn't you say?"

"What exactly is your point here, commander?" Fountain asked.

"Well, I am sure I don't need to go any further, Mr. Fountain. These deaths were described almost word for word the way our crime team determined they unfolded. Very curious, wouldn't you say?"

"'*Determined*'? That's the point here, I think. Meaning this is how your crime team imagined their deaths occurred. The discrepancies might well be many. Depending on further forensic examinations."

"True. But the coincidences are baffling. Wouldn't you agree, Mr. Fountain?"

She waved a dismissive yet polite hand as Fountain opened his mouth to respond. "Let's move on. I'm sure both of you are tired."

Neela took Dermot's hand and smiled gratefully. "Yes, we are. As you might imagine."

"Leif Crane." Willis said no more—she just eyeballed Dermot. He couldn't meet her eyes. "The Space Cadet, you called him in the novel. Because he was agoraphobic."

"Yes, that's right."

"I believe you visited Bakersfield recently."

Dermot knew he wouldn't be able to keep his visit a secret if the cops did some real digging—the airline reservations were there for all to see.

"Yes, I did."

"Why exactly?"

"Because I have been thinking about locations for the film of my book. I thought that the bleak sun-baked open countryside outside Bakersfield would replicate the desert outside Broken Hill in New South Wales wonderfully."

"I've never been there, but it certainly sounds similar." She flicked a glance at Fountain. "But again it's curious that you should visit Bakersfield only days before the body of Reginald Helpmann—your Leif Crane—was found murdered in that same area. Did you visit the site where we found the body?"

"I have no idea where you found him, Ms. Willis."

"But of course you do. It was exactly detailed in your novel."

"I'd say the incident only reinforces my proposition that Helpmann's murderer is trying to implicate my client for some reason."

"Yes, that's a possibility. Yet how did he know Mr. Nolan would go there? And at that time? How could he have set up such complicated scenarios at such short notice?"

"Must be a very ingenious killer," Fountain replied easily.

Willis carried on as if Fountain hadn't interjected. "Because he or she would have to have already targeted a suitable victim, known his particular phobia, and then been able to arrange an abduction. He'd also have to have arranged all the logistics of getting Mr. Helpmann to Bakersfield and killing him in the exact way described in *Worst Nightmares*. Very ingenious, indeed."

Fountain stood. He could smell her tone. Dermot was a very real person of interest.

"Just one more thing, Mr. Nolan. You must have known about the website. Right?"

It was the one detail Dermot hoped she'd avoid.

"Initially no, I didn't. But I was told when I was well into writing the novel that one existed. I borrowed the name—the Dream Healer—and various weird aspects of the site. But not until I had done all I could to track down the identity of the person who had set it up. As a courtesy. Yet each time I attempted to log on it was 'unavailable,' as they say. So that was a disappointment."

"Then how did you know the website used Bosch's triptych detail as the home page?"

Dermot opened his mouth to speak but couldn't. Fountain interrupted forcibly. "Quite possibly Nick Hoyle visited the site and mentioned it to my client. Any number of people clearly logged on. Hundreds, if not many thousands. So that can be no big mystery. Someone must have told my client all about it."

"I'd sooner have heard that from your client," Willis replied. "This is what happened?"

"Yes, most probably. I can't remember who exactly."

Fountain put a hand on Dermot's arm. Dermot took the cue and stood.

"Someone told me today that the website is up and running again, Mr. Nolan." It wasn't true, but she wanted to see what reaction these words would generate. Dermot flinched noticeably. "Did you know that? You might want to take a look and see how eerily similar it is to the site you describe in your novel."

"I think you've been misinformed, commander," Fountain said.

"Possibly. I shall have to check," she replied.

Had it not been tantamount to admitting his guilt, Dermot would have at that moment gladly vomited on Willis's shoes.

The arrival of the police convoy took Nick completely by surprise. He'd just sat down to watch the news when the doorbell sounded. At first, thinking it was the press, he ignored it. Then he heard shouting outside, and was so angry that he opened the door to shout back. It was then that he saw twelve police officers standing at the door, some in uniform, others in a police version of blue jumpsuits with the letters LAPD across their backs. A tall man in a suit appeared to be the leader of the group.

"Excuse me, sir. My name is Detective Quin. I have a warrant to search the house. Also the immediate environs. Are you alone in this home at present?" Quin asked, holding up a sheet of paper. Nick took it.

"Yes, I am. I suppose you can come in," he replied.

The men filed past Nick and fanned out into the various rooms of the house. The men in the blue jumpsuits carried plastic bags and wore latex gloves.

Nick pulled out his cell phone and punched in Dermot's number, but the call went right to voicemail. He then tried Neela, then called Harold Fountain's office. Nick could only sit and watch as the police scoured the house. He noticed three policemen busy in Dermot's office; one had the computer up and running, the other two were going through the desk very thoroughly. Through the window, Nick could see a forensics officer taking samples from the wheel rim of Dermot's Peugeot, while another was inside the car sucking up evidence with a small vacuum cleaner. All were put individually into evidence bags and identified.

While the search team combed the Nolan home, Kandinski continued with his investigation. He was still convinced there was no way Dermot Nolan was involved in any killings. Clearly someone was out there feeding some pretty inflammatory information to both Schipp and the authorities to frame him, and Kandinski was determined he'd do all he could to provide Willis with an alternative theory.

By why Nolan? Who had gone to all this trouble to nail him for a series of terrible killings he had not committed. He began making a list of names of all Nolan's associates, friends, and rival authors. Then his phone rang.

"Mr. Kandinski?"

It had to be the same voice that Schipp had described to the police. Kandinski flicked a switch on his desk and an automatic trace began—as did a tape recorder. He flicked another switch. Red lights on all the other detectives' phones lit up alerting them to pick up their phones and listen. But Quin was on the search detail, and Woo was with Willis and Nolan.

"There's no future in a trace, Mr. Kandinski. It's pointless."

"Who's this?"

"You know very well."

"Why are you calling me? I thought Mr. Schipp had the exclusive?"

"He did. But I suspect you are smarter than Mr. Schipp. And I must say, this is becoming a delightful game. You see, I know how Mr. Nolan executed all those people. I know where they lie. And I feel they should be avenged. Properly, of course. By the authorities. Yet I feel you still believe Mr. Nolan to be innocent? Am I right?"

"You are."

"Then you must visit the grave site of the Mouth Maiden. Take your police colleagues and count the teeth. You'll find there are several missing."

"Missing?"

"Yes, missing. I know for a fact that Mr. Nolan took them as a trophy. I watched him do it."

"Who is the Mouth Maiden?"

"Her name is Phoebe Blasé. She is buried near Kemps Creek. Have you a pen? I will tell you only once how to get there."

Kandinski scribbled frantically as the voice gave him directions. Then the line went dead.

CHAPTER 53

Dermot was already shaken to the core when he returned home to find the police searching through his and Neela's belongings. Cheesecake was sitting in the lounge, daring any policeman to touch her. Scarecrow was skulking in the garden, curled up in his favorite hollow behind the garden shed.

"I'm afraid we're going to have to take your hard drive with us, Mr. Nolan," a policewoman informed him pleasantly.

"Well, you can't. I have my life's work on it. It's extremely confidential. My novels, ideas, concepts. I can't work without it."

She raised the warrant so Dermot could see it. "I'm sorry about any inconvenience, but this warrant allows me to remove any article from your home that we believe might have pertinent evidence. We will make copies of all the files and return your hard drive within twelve hours. I assure you that all personal information not relevant to the cases we are investigating will remain intact and confidential."

Neela was in the bedroom. She watched a police officer wearing latex gloves go through her clothes. He parted her dresses in the wardrobe one by one, looking behind each one for anything that might be concealed there. Neela was seething with anger but said nothing. Then a police-woman started in on the lower drawers of the dresser, rummaging through her underwear.

She watched as another officer placed two pairs of Dermot's boots into a plastic evidence bag. Then the same officer found the hamper, and rum-maged through that, selecting certain shirts and socks. He tagged them, placing all of the items in a big plastic bag.

Downstairs, Dermot was on the phone to Fountain.

"It's normal procedure, Mr. Nolan. If I were Commander Willis I would have done the same thing as a matter of good procedure. It's more a process of elimination—one designed to rule out evidence of the victims' DNA in your home."

Dermot felt his knees wobble slightly. He was getting light-headed. DNA? These days one could identify the DNA of a flea on a pinhead. He'd been to so many of the murder sites. He'd picked through them with his bare hands, touched the stakes, the tower, the wheelchair. Was it time to come clean with the whole story? No. Better to wait and see what the search actually revealed. After all, apart from the teeth, which were no longer in their hiding place and had probably been thrown away, there was nothing in his home that linked him to any of the murder sites.

He watched a forensic cop walk past him, holding a black plastic bag. He could clearly see the outline of his boots inside—the ones he had worn on both field trips. He swallowed hard. Examination might prove he was in the vicinity, but surely that was all. Besides, ultimately the question would be whether he was at the murder sites when the victims breathed their last—not days, weeks, or months later.

Detective Quin approached him and apologized again for any incon-venience. Then he informed Dermot that they had almost finished. A po-lice officer was out in the back garden looking through the shed, but he'd be finished shortly, too. He held up a clipboard and tore a carbon copy of his list for Dermot.

"This is a detailed list of all the items we will be taking with us. They will be returned to you as soon as all the requisite forensic tests have been completed." He handed Dermot the sheet.

"I'd like to thank you very much for your cooperation," he said as he was leaving. "I wish everyone were so helpful."

The following day, a hiker found the body of Wanda Bell. The police estimated that she'd only been dead a few hours. Her heart had failed. Of course there were other serious complications that caused her entire system to break down—mostly associated with the constriction of blood to her limbs. A classic case of rapid onset dry gangrene. It had been a merciful release at the end. At the autopsy, the pathologist observed that during her final few hours the pain would have been beyond comprehension.

News of her death reached Task Force Tower within an hour. Willis added Bell's name to the others on the whiteboard and checked her off against the list of characters in Dermot Nolan's novel.

CHAPTER 54

The area around the tree line where the informant said the body of Phoebe Blasé had been buried was a hive of activity within two hours. Kandinski had the task of following through on the Mouth Maiden because the source had called him personally.

Within a few minutes, the indentations became apparent and Kandinski was speculating where he would find what remained of the temporary dental surgery. Tire marks in the general vicinity suggested a flatbed truck had been used to remove the hardware. Impressions were taken.

A careful dig was instigated at the far side of the tree line, just where the source had indicated, and within four hours body parts appeared. She'd been dead a long time; very little tissue remained on the skeleton. By late afternoon, the entire area had been searched. It would be up to the medical examiner to count the teeth and match them with the fragments that had been found in Nolan's office.

As Kandinski drove back to town he was filled with an overwhelming feeling of sadness. How far had the world progressed since barbarians roamed Europe with lances and bludgeons, and humans cannibalized each other in countries such as New Guinea? People relaxing in LA, Sydney, New York, Moscow, and London might think they were living in a privileged part of a civilized world community, yet only minutes away from any one of them, suicide bombers were entering theaters, crazed killers were loading guns to kill students, Serbs and Muslims were ethnically cleansing their environments, Palestinians and Israelis were killing each other in the name of their respective religions, and fundamentalists were strapping explosives to their bodies in Iraq so that they could be united with the seventy virgins they'd been promised by their prophets. The world was an ugly place where people did horrible things to one another. So why was he still so certain that Nolan could not have committed these crimes?

He couldn't shake the feeling that he'd let down a good friend. They'd shared many a good lunch, joked together, chatted about hockey over a few beers. Then, when Dermot had needed him most, he hadn't been able to be there for him. He decided it was time to do some research on Nolan's mental state. Had he ever seen a psychiatrist? Did Dermot have mental problems that few people knew about? It was a possibility. Of course doctor-patient confidentiality would, as usual, be a problem.

The following day, Willis, along with Quin, Kandinski, and Woo, were in the lab of Medical Examiner Colin M. Meaney, staring at the individually bagged objects taken from the Nolan house. Meaney was looking at his written report—the protocol.

"It's almost as if Nolan had no fear whatsoever of being implicated in these crimes," Meaney said, as he reviewed their contents. "Of course that's often the case. People with his celebrity never suppose for an instant that anyone would think ill of them."

Meaney held up the bag of small white shards. "These items were recovered from a drawer in Nolan's office, hidden under a box of colored crayons. There is no doubt that these fragments came from the mouth of Phoebe Blasé. Three items were *actual* fragments of her teeth. There is no DNA of her attacker on the fragments other than recent finger smudges. When Ms. Blasé's body is properly retrieved, we'll examine her jaw for more evidence. I'm sure we'll find it."

Meaney placed the bag of teeth on the table and lifted the next bag.

"It was a very simple task to match this rope sample to the sections unearthed from the grave containing the bodies of Mr. and Mrs. Nash. It had been found with some cloth behind Dermot Nolan's garden shed. The rope has the same DNA as the body of the man we are currently supposing to be Gareth Nash, as well as the DNA of a dog."

Meaney lifted the third bag. "This sample of cloth has the same DNA as the rope."

Meaney placed the bag back down on the table. "I have matched fingerprints from the wood of Gareth Nash's stake, and his wife's. I have also lifted a partial palm print from the wheelchair in which Ms. Bell was found. There are also fingerprints and blood smudges at the top of the water tower. They all match the fingerprints on the computer confiscated during the search of the Nolan home. Since we have not fingerprinted Mr. Nolan, we may presume that they will match his. But they could also belong to Mrs. Nolan, since we must suppose she also used the computer."

The detectives shared knowing glances; a new lead had presented itself that they'd never before considered.

CHAPTER 55

It was the anniversary of the death of his twins. Nick was staring down quietly at the small headstones that flanked Giselle's at the Inglewood Park Cemetery when he became aware of a presence some distance behind him. Nick didn't turn around. Instead, he placed three small wreaths in front of the headstones, talking softly to his family as he always did on this day of remembrance. Then he turned and walked slowly toward Mike Kandinski.

"Kandinski, how are you? This has to be more than a coincidence, given all the present circumstances?" he suggested with a forced smile. He was in no mood this day for a casual chat. Kandinski held out a hand. "I just got off the phone with Neela, wondering where I might find you. She told me that you'd be here today," he said, sheepish. "I had no intention of coming, but she seemed so desperate. She assured me you'd understand the urgency. Please accept my apologies."

There was a labored pause. Nick left the next move to Kandinski.

"You were visiting family?"

"My wife and children," Nick replied.

Kandinski was taken aback—he hadn't known that a tragedy of this magnitude had struck Nick Hoyle. Of course, it wasn't the kind of information that Dermot would have shared with him over a few beers and a pastrami sandwich. "I'm sorry for your loss."

"Thanks." They stood in silence for several seconds.

"Mr. Hoyle, I see now that it was inappropriate to come here to ask you questions—despite Mrs. Nolan's assurances. I wanted to do all I could to help Mr. Nolan."

"My car's over there," Nick said, pointing. "Let's walk. You can quiz me all you like on the way."

"You've known Dermot ever since you were at college—right?"

"Correct."

"And you've been close friends since then."

"That's right."

"Could you say you've noticed anything radically different in his general demeanor over the past year? Anything out of the ordinary?"

"You mean, have I noticed him howling at the full moon? Or playing with sharp knives?"

"I'm just trying to help here, Mr. Hoyle. That's all."

Nick glanced at him and smiled. "I know—and I apologize for being glib. A Booker Prize is a hard act to follow. Over the past eighteen months, he had absolutely no inspiration, and I know it's been a depressing time. Hence the medication."

"Medication?"

"It's no big deal. I've been on the pills for years myself. Depression is becoming an ever-increasing problem. It's been a stressful time for Dermot—not knowing if he'll ever come up with anything as good as *Incoming Tide*. And, of course, there were the financial pressures. But hey, most people have those."

They walked on in silence.

"Have you ever witnessed a violent side to Dermot?"

Nick stopped cold and looked at Kandinski. "No. Never. He's pretty stable. He's probably more subject to fear than I am, but I did a tour of duty in Iraq. Not much scares me these days, if you know what I mean."

"Sure."

"He's also had his share of dark moments. But we all have those."

"Dark moments?" Kandinski asked.

"Nothing big. A few years back, he became so distressed about his work that he disappeared for a couple of weeks or so. But when he came back, he was fine and had a wonderful manuscript to show us. Of course, at the time, the disappearance scared Neela to death because she thought he might have . . ."

"Taken his own life?"

"Well, yes. But he was back to his old self again and had pretty much stayed that way until this whole mess." He stopped and looked at Mike. "I know your investigation is disturbing him immensely, and I can't wait until you all do your job, and he can put it behind him."

"Let's hope soon."

They reached the car. Nick handed him a business card.

"I know you want the best for Dermot, the same as I do. If there's anything I can do to help, call me."

"Oh, one more thing, Mr. Hoyle. Do you know if Mr. Nolan has any personal enemies?"

"Personal?"

"Someone who might bear him a grudge—another writer, a family member, an acquaintance, a friend from way back in his university days? My instinct tells me someone's gone to a great deal of effort to implicate him in these murders. I just need to find out why."

Nick opened his car door and leaned his cane against it.

"Great cane," Kandinski said. "An antique?"

"Yes. English. Over a hundred years old." Nick slid into the driver's seat and pulled his cane in after him. "I made it through a full tour in Iraq without a scratch, then messed up my leg up two days before I came home."

"Murphy's Law. That's tough."

Nick smiled and started the engine.

"Let me know if there's any other way I can help you, Kandinski."

"Of course. Very grateful."

CHAPTER 56

Tim Leadbeater's office in Beverly Hills was magnificent. Every wall was wood paneled. Every piece of furniture should have been classified a national treasure and cordoned off to the general public; but since these belonged to the most experienced criminal attorney in California, they were there purely for comfort.

Leadbeater and Fountain often worked as a team. When Fountain felt his client could afford Leadbeater, he leaned on Tim to come to his aid. Good as Fountain was in court, Leadbeater was better. Together, they were formidable.

Two days after the forensic team turned over his home, Fountain advised Dermot to meet Tim Leadbeater in his office. He was quietly certain that there was no way to make the current "unpleasantness" go away.

Dermot and Neela sat in matching English Jacobean armchairs opposite Leadbeater; Fountain sat on Dermot's right.

"Harold and I spoke at length earlier today," Leadbeater began, "and we agree that it seems likely, yet by no means certain, that an arrest warrant will be served on you within the next twenty-four hours."

"I can't believe it," Neela said. "On the basis of what evidence, if you don't mind my asking?"

Leadbeater turned and faced her. "On rather a lot of evidence, as it happens." His tone was coolly logical and quite matter-of-fact. Though born and raised in New York of American parents, Leadbeater spoke like an English politician. He had trained himself to do so because he felt it gave him a more imposing air in the courtroom. "However, every atom is circumstantial in my opinion. If I were district attorney, I wouldn't consider such a move at this stage. But of course, I'm not."

"What have they found that could possibly implicate my husband, Mr. Leadbeater?"

"A great deal of forensic evidence that places your husband at various crime scenes." His hawkish eyes swiveled to lock onto Dermot. "Of course this merely shows that you visited several locations where crimes had been committed some time ago. As far as I am aware, none of the forensic evidence places you at the crime scenes at the time the murders occurred. And this," he smiled, "is pivotal to our case."

"Should the case proceed, will you represent me, Mr. Leadbeater?" Dermot asked.

"I should be delighted to assist, Mr. Nolan. I have admired your work for some years—*Incoming Tide* in particular. I'm not quite as certain that I enjoyed the speed-read I made of *Worst Nightmares* last night." He smiled at his own little joke, then continued. "Which brings me to a few pertinent questions I should ask you without undue delay. They may cause you some embarrassment, but there must be *no* skeletons in the closet. You do follow me? My reputation hangs on no one ever being able to pull a rabbit out of a hat, unless it was placed there by either Mr. Fountain here or myself."

"Ask away."

"First of all. The characters in *Worst Nightmares* were based on actual events in this country. Correct?"

"Yes, sir."

Dermot stared at Leadbeater and then at Fountain. He had the best imaginable legal team. If he could possibly convince them of his innocence without admitting to the existence of Arnold, he would. Neela had begged him to come clean, but Dermot was still clinging to a last ray of hope that he might be able to salvage his integrity.

"And you have nothing else you wish to share with me?" Leadbeater drilled Dermot. "Your life may depend on it."

Dermot hung tough, but Neela was breaking. "Honey, we have to tell him."

Dermot looked as if he'd been slapped in the face. He turned sharply to face her—his expression cold as ice. "What are you talking about?"

But it was too late, as far as Leadbeater was concerned anyway. He picked up the papers Fountain had given him and handed them back. "Harold, I'm afraid I can no longer represent your client. It's clear he intends keeping pertinent facts, perhaps even explosive facts, from me."

"Please, Mr. Leadbeater," Neela begged. "My husband has been under incredible stress these past weeks. There *is* something he felt he couldn't share with Mr. Fountain before, but that's because he felt it wasn't anything that would compromise your position. I implore you to hear us out."

Leadbeater sat. "Well, I'm prepared to listen a while longer. However, I must insist that it is your husband who shares this information with me, rather than yourself." He paused. "Let him use his own words—that's what he's good at. And I ask you, Mrs. Nolan, to reassure me as we proceed that what he says is not an equivocation."

He turned his eyes to Dermot. "I can only defend you if you are absolutely frank with me."

Everyone in the room looked toward Dermot. His jaw muscles were working hard. He knew he was trapped. It was time to bite the bullet. The time to reveal the diary had come. But that wasn't all he had to reveal now. What about all those details he had kept from Neela? She'd be devastated if she knew he'd been lying to her all this time about what he had found.

"A man left a manuscript in my mailbox," Dermot began. "It purported to be the diary of a serial killer. He asked me to get the damn thing published."

"I see," Leadbeater smiled. A Pavlovian technique—a chewy treat for each correct statement.

"And you read this . . . diary?"

"I did."

"And did you think it was based on real events, or simply a work of fiction?"

"I wasn't sure, so Neela and I conducted some research."

"What kind of research?" The smiley face now beamed fully at him.

"Well, Neela tried to find out if those mentioned . . ."

"There were names? The victims were *identified?*"

"Yes. There were names."

"I see. And what were the results of your wife's research?"

"She found out that many of the people mentioned had gone missing, and that several had indeed been murdered in the manner described by the author."

"He used his name?"

"No. He referred to himself as Mr. Arnold. Albert K. Arnold—a pen name, I suppose."

"Referred to himself?" Leadbeater interceded quickly. He missed nothing. "You actually *talked* to this person at some point?"

"He telephoned me. At home. Mr. Hoyle was with me at the time."

"What exactly did Mr. Arnold say?" Leadbeater continued. He cut each word slowly and crisply like a scalpel.

"He claimed he had done everything he described in his 'moment-by-moment diary.' That's what he called it. He confessed to killing all those men and women. His tone was tough, but he seemed remorseful. So much so that he stated he was going to commit suicide."

"And did he?"

"Yes. Twenty minutes or so later. He leaped off the People's Bank Building."

Leadbeater allowed Dermot a brief respite as he digested the information.

"Did you read about his suicide the following day? Or see it on the television news?"

"Neither." Dermot shifted in his seat, awkwardly. "Arnold had indicated that he would commit suicide at the bank, so I raced there to see if I could prevent him from killing himself."

Neela glanced at Dermot. Of course what he was saying wasn't *exactly* true, but she decided to let it pass. Leadbeater didn't miss the furtive glance; his smile disappeared.

"So you called the police at once. Right?" His tone was hard now.

Dermot licked his lips—they were parchment dry. "Well, no. I didn't. You see, he intimated that he had kidnapped Neela and that he might harm her . . ."

"I would imagine that would be an even greater reason to call 9-1-1, surely?"

"I left it to my friend Nick Hoyle to call the emergency number. I raced to the building to see what I could do. You know, personally."

"Well, that makes sense." The smile was back. "But just how did he threaten your wife?"

"He said he would 'make his final statement' at the People's Bank Building. That's what I took to be his threat to kill himself. Then he said that possibly Neela would make a similar statement alongside him. He said it as if she was there with him—his prisoner."

"He mentioned her by name? He knew her name?"

"Yes, he did."

"And you feared he may have kidnapped her?"

"That's right. I mean, he was kind of old looking, but—"

"You *saw* this man?"

"Yes. When he delivered the manuscript."

"You knew at this time that he was the author of a manuscript—as opposed to perhaps just the delivery boy?"

"No, not at that time."

"Describe him."

"I'd say sixtyish and maybe a bit frail. Sunken cheeks. Stubble. Bright orange hair. And he wore a dirty brown long-rider's coat."

"Doesn't sound very strong to me. Yet you believed he could have kidnapped your wife?"

"I was scared. I didn't consider the rationale at the time. He seemed to know where Neela was, and was threatening her."

"I take it you arrived too late to prevent him from committing suicide."

"That's right. As I arrived, I saw him standing on the roof, and well . . . he jumped."

"Did the police arrive quickly? After Mr. Hoyle called them, that is."

"Yes, they did. They sealed off the area."

"And you told them of the conversation you'd had on the telephone minutes prior to the man's death?"

"No, I didn't."

"Why not?"

"Because I didn't want anyone to know about Mr. Arnold, *or* the existence of the diary." Dermot was talking too fast now. He was rattled.

"Because by this time you had read it, and were seriously thinking of plagiarizing the work? Am I right?"

Dermot's stomach turned over. "That's correct. It was a spur of the moment decision and I'm ashamed I made it."

"What did you tell the police when they arrived?"

"That I had been there by chance."

"Oh dear," Leadbeater replied throwing a disappointed glance at Fountain. "That's a shame."

"How could the police know it wasn't true, Mr. Leadbeater?" Neela offered, weakly.

Leadbeater turned toward her, surprised at her question. "Are you suggesting that we only share the information we choose with the court, Mrs. Nolan? I hope not. In order to defend your husband successfully, it is essential that I, and the police, know everything. Only then will the truth be revealed. I am not one of those attorneys you read about in the *National Enquirer* who makes a career out of defending guilty criminals by using deception. There are aspects of any defense that we prefer not to dwell on, of course—matters that we feel have no bearing on our client's guilt. Previous reprehensible behavior, for instance. But I would never hold back evidence that could clearly demonstrate the guilt of my client."

"Of course," she replied swiftly. "I think you misunderstood me."

"I would like to think so, Mrs. Nolan. However, it is never a good idea to lie to the police. About anything. Lies follow you—they are a matter of record that can be raised at any time. For instance, at a trial. To have failed to reveal the truth is one thing—to lie is another matter entirely."

Neela cast her eyes down. "I understand, Mr. Leadbeater."

Leadbeater smiled, then continued questioning Dermot. "So, you convinced yourself that the man who died as a result of this fall was the author of the work of 'faction' that you used as the basis of your book?"

"That's right. No one else could have known all the stuff he did."

"Other than an accomplice. Have you ever considered that?"

Neela and Dermot spoke in tandem.

"No," said Dermot.

"Yes," Neela replied.

Leadbeater knew right then it was going to be a grueling trial.

"Tell me about *your* research, Neela."

"I looked into the names in Arnold's diary, and found that some of the people had already been found dead, while others were still missing. Some I could never track down."

"So some had already been killed when the diary was delivered by Mr. Arnold?"

"Yes. But there's a suspect in custody for the murder of the Free Fallers."

"I believe his attorney is suggesting that, in view of the new evidence, he has no case to answer."

Both Neela and Nolan looked shocked to the core.

The phone rang. Clearly annoyed at the interruption, Leadbeater picked up.

"Yes."

He listened and his attitude softened slightly. "Please ask them to wait a few minutes." He replaced the receiver.

"I have to be swift, I'm afraid," he continued. "You'll have to forgive me."

"Of course," Dermot answered.

"Did you visit the crime scenes of those victims who died in this country?"

"Yes. I consulted the directions that Arnold detailed on the loose pages I found in the back of the book. I wanted to see if he was for real or if he was pulling my leg."

Both Fountain and Leadbeater raised their eyebrows.

"Pulling your leg? As in 'joking'?" Leadbeater's tone was becoming close to insulting. "You thought a man capable of dreaming up such terrible scenarios was doing so simply to *jest* with you?"

"Not at all," Dermot replied. "I was curious about whether he'd simply taken details of crimes committed by others and called them his own. So I went to the places he wrote down as being the actual crime scenes."

"And did you find any evidence that lead you to suppose that bodies had been buried at these various locations?"

"No. I did not," Dermot replied with a poker face. This time, Neela didn't quibble.

"Who else knew of this manuscript? Anyone other than your wife?"

"My oldest friend, Nick Hoyle. No one else. Unless Arnold shared the document with a third party before he killed himself."

"I see. And since the story in the *Daily News*, has anyone contacted you regarding the murders? I am thinking here of a possible accomplice."

Dermot took the time to carefully gather his thoughts.

"Yes. Someone with exactly the same gravelly voice as Arnold called me when I was on the Frank Vitek radio show. He was the perfect mimic—of Arnold's voice, that is. He quoted certain passages of the diary as if he had not only read it, but committed it to memory."

"That's a great help, Mr. Nolan. It certainly raises sufficient question as to who might have committed these crimes. Clearly the person on the radio program . . ." he paused, then changed his line of thought. "He didn't, by any chance, identify himself, did he?"

"He called himself Arnold—but of course, he wasn't."

"Good. Clearly this person had all the knowledge you had, and could have been Arnold's accessory, if indeed the man known as Arnold *was* a serial killer rather than someone seeking fifteen minutes of fame. And I have your word then that you visited many of the crime scenes and found no evidence of body parts?"

"That's correct."

Neela couldn't help but clear her throat. Leadbeater closed his eyes.

"I mean . . . I found certain props left by the man to try and convince me he was genuine."

"Such as?"

"The twin stakes of the Stakes Couple. A wheelchair that he said belonged to Wheelchair Wanda—that kind of thing."

"And you felt sufficiently happy with the logic that he could have organized delivering this kind of lumber and other heavy objects to the sight he detailed—even though he was a frail old man?"

Dermot had no time to answer—the phone rang again. Once more Leadbeater picked up.

"All right, Kate. Send them in."

Leadbeater turned to Dermot. "I am afraid an arrest warrant has been issued for you. Two detectives are here to take you into custody. Mr. Fountain will accompany you downtown."

Detective Woo and a uniformed cop entered into the room. Woo flipped his badge at Leadbeater, turned to face Dermot, and read him his rights. Then he took out the cuffs.

CHAPTER 57

Bail was set at three million dollars. Dermot and Neela returned home, where Nick waited—in a place that now resembled a medieval castle under siege. At first, the police attempted to clear the roadway outside the Nolan home, but when it became clear that wouldn't be possible for more than an hour at a time, they ended up cordoning off Linley at Fifth and Sixth.

Dermot called Esther the evening he was released on bail—as soon as the Valium kicked in.

"Before you say a word, I know you didn't kill anyone," Esther said. "But I'm not sure I can ever forgive you for lying to me in such a horrible way."

"I know, Esther. It was unforgivable." He had never felt this low. "But I had nothing to give you. My mind was a literary desert. Then God threw this manuscript in my face."

"He did nothing of the kind, Dermot. A madman, possibly. But not God."

Dermot didn't know exactly what to say.

"I expect they'll suggest I wrote the original myself, disguising my handwriting."

"We'll have to see. But things aren't looking good for your career right now. You're a pariah. The film's been canceled and they've pulled copies of *Worst Nightmares* worldwide. And if you think your career's in trouble? My top five writers have asked to leave the agency. So, next time you lie to me, consider the consequences. For everyone."

"There's nothing I can say—"

She cut him short. "You have the best legal team in the world. I'd imagine Leadbeater could get Hannibal Lecter released on bail even while he was still masticating raw human liver."

There was a pregnant silence at Dermot's end.

"I'm finished, Esther."

"As a writer? Possibly. Let's try to keep you out of prison, shall we?" She blew a kiss down the line and hung up.

Nick peeked through the venetian blinds at the reporters camped outside. "Enterprising. I'll say that for him," Nick muttered.

"What?" Dermot asked?

"That catering truck. It's been parked outside for a day and a night now. Making a fortune."

Neela walked into the living room from the kitchen, carrying sandwiches.

"You feed Scarecrow?"

"Of course. He's asleep. And Cheesecake's out on the town," she replied.

They ate in silence—they both knew Dermot was fortunate not to be locked up, but the future looked very bleak. It was now a question of guarding his sanity.

Dermot finished his sandwich, stood, and walked over to Neela. He hugged her. "Neels, I want you to think seriously about leaving the country. Consider somewhere with no extradition treaty. If I go down, they might come after you, saying you knew what was going on and lied about Arnold, too."

"Don't be ridiculous."

"I'm not going anywhere either," Nick interjected. "No way. And I fully intend to tell them I saw the diary. That's evidence, surely."

"But you never actually *read* it. And you never actually saw Arnold."

"I heard him on the speakerphone, didn't I?"

"Hell, they'll have an answer for that, too. Look, I have money stashed in Bermuda. Neels knows how to access it. It's not a lot, but she can start a new life there if things turn bad."

"They won't, honey. Please be more positive. You are an innocent man and that will become increasingly apparent when the case goes to trial. And thanks to Leadbeater we have an early date. Fountain is very upbeat and has asked us to conduct our lives as if this is all a terrible nightmare—one from which we're going to emerge very soon. We can't appear to be afraid."

CHAPTER 58

When Tim Leadbeater reviewed the forensics list, he was appalled to learn that his client had lied yet again. He immediately called Fountain to tell him he was off the case, but Fountain begged him to reconsider. They arranged another meeting with Nolan at his home three days later, this time with Nick present. The atmosphere was tense, to say the least.

"Mr. Nolan," Leadbeater began. "Subsequent to my receiving the forensics list from the district attorney's office, I have sadly come to the conclusion that you are still not being frank with me. The reason for the meeting today is to establish whether you still want me to represent you. If you do, then I will need to have direct and honest answers to all my questions here. If I feel you are being truthful, I shall do all I can to make your case. If, however, I feel you are keeping important germane facts from me, I shall have to ask you to find another lead attorney. Do you understand me?"

Dermot croaked an affirmation.

"Good. Then let's get right to the point. It appears that some teeth fragments were found during the recent police search of your house. These fragments have been identified as belonging to Ms. Phoebe Blasé, whose remains were unearthed recently. Please explain precisely how these fragments found their way into your desk."

"They were found in my desk?" Dermot was incredulous.

"Correct. In a box of crayons in a drawer."

"But they weren't there when I last looked."

Leadbeater and Fountain exchanged glances. This was not the answer they were expecting.

"So you *knew* they had once been there?" Leadbeater asked.

"I brought them back from my second field trip."

Neela stared at Dermot. He had never told her this detail. Why not?

Dermot was more than aware of Neela's gaze, but refused to meet it. As it turned out, Fountain asked the question for her.

"Did you tell your wife you had found evidence of this slain girl—this Mouth Maiden?"

Dermot hesitated.

"You must answer all our questions truthfully, Mr. Nolan. That is of paramount importance. It may cause you pain—but that's the way it must be in order to establish your innocence," Fountain continued.

"No. I didn't," Dermot replied.

"I see," Leadbeater continued. "Can you tell us why?"

"Because I preferred her to think I had found nothing. That way I could still convince her that the diary was a work of fiction."

"When in fact you thought otherwise by then?" Leadbeater prompted.

"That's right."

"And you felt that your wife might insist you report your findings to the authorities?"

"Yes."

"Let me try to understand this. You thought that Phoebe Blasé had indeed been murdered at the site Mr. Arnold detailed. You also thought that the diary was genuine. Yet you chose to keep silent, and plagiarize the book, rather than offer any chance of closure to Ms. Blasé's family?"

Dermot barely nodded, and then hung his head in shame. Neela stared at him—astonished. She wiped perspiration from her forehead, though it wasn't in the least hot in the room.

"Then you hid the tooth fragments in your desk. Why?"

"I don't exactly know why. It was stupid, I suppose. Possibly so I would have something to show the police if I decided to change my mind about writing the book."

"The prosecution will of course maintain the fragments were a trophy of some kind. A remembrance of the crime."

"I thought I got rid of the teeth."

"Mr. Nolan, while I am happy to believe that you found the teeth while attempting to ascertain whether Mr. Arnold was in fact a killer rather than a bad writer, a jury might view that phrase 'I thought I had got rid of them' as the words of a killer who had tried to divest himself of incriminating evidence. Do you see my point?"

Dermot nodded his head.

"So you thought the teeth were disposed of, when in fact they were still where you had left them?"

"No. I looked for them in the crayon container and they were gone! I don't understand."

"Are you suggesting that someone else took them and then replaced them? Who could that be?"

Dermot looked at Neela for help. "Perhaps someone broke into the house and bypassed the alarm? It's possible."

"Or you simply didn't see them? That's also possible, isn't it? We often search drawers for items and they are plain to see, yet we miss them."

He looked at Dermot's confused expression.

"Which brings me to another item on the forensics list. A piece of cloth was found buried behind the shed you have in your back garden."

"Cloth? What cloth?" Dermot's mouth hung open. Nick watched his expression—it seemed quite genuine. Clearly Dermot had no idea what Leadbeater was talking about.

"The DNA found on the cloth belonged to Laura Nash. Can you tell me how this piece of cloth could have ended up in your garden?"

"Mr. Leadbeater," Dermot began in a rush, "I have no *idea* how it could have got there. I told you, I visited the site but I found nothing."

"Dermot told me he saw black stains on the ground." It was Neela who spoke. Her tone was less sympathetic, somewhat staccato—as if she were short of breath. "But he told me he was certain they were not human blood stains."

"Did you take a shovel and dig around that area? Where you believed the couple was buried?"

"Yes, I did."

"And did you stop digging after a few minutes?"

"That's right." Dermot knew what was coming, and his eyes searched for Neela's, but she was looking into her lap.

"Did you in fact stop digging because the shovel you had brought with you struck organic matter you believed to be the remains of the Nash couple?"

Dermot looked at Neela again but she still avoided his glance. He looked to Nick for support.

Nick's face said it clearly: *I can't help you here, buddy.*

"Yes," Dermot said finally, "I thought I had come across bodies. I thought I could smell them. So I left before I actually unearthed them."

"I see," Leadbeater said. At last he was getting somewhere—his client appeared to be telling the truth.

"And did you find any evidence at the water tower?"

Dermot's stomach turned over. "I did, but it was an animal's head."

"I certainly hope it was. The police will surely find whatever is in there."

Leadbeater paused, and then drilled Dermot with an earnest look.

"But you preferred not to share this devastating information with your wife?"

"I didn't want to involve her further."

"You mean you didn't want her to know you were now certain that more than one body lay out there in the countryside, and you were going to write a book about it all and make money out of it."

The comment stung. Dermot looked at Leadbeater with hatred. Leadbeater merely smiled back.

"You'd better get used to this manner of questioning—I can assure you my words are very tame compared to what I envisage you'll be facing in court very soon."

The expression of hatred turned to one of contrition. "I'm sorry, Mr. Leadbeater, I know you're doing your best."

"Tim, Mr. Nolan. Tim."

"Tim."

"So you kept Mrs. Nolan out of the loop because you felt she might ruin everything and force you to tell the police what you'd found?"

"I suppose so. Yes," Dermot replied.

Dermot looked again at Neela. Tears were running down her cheeks.

"But did you take the piece of cloth with you? As a memento?"

"No, I did not. I have no idea how it got to where it was found. Maybe the dog took it. Now that you bring up the subject, I did see Scarecrow with a piece of cloth."

"Scarecrow is the name of the stray dog you found—the one you took with you on your field trips?"

"That's right."

"And you think the dog was responsible for that piece of cloth being buried behind the shed?"

"Maybe. Maybe not. All this evidence could easily be the result of someone placing the cloth where it would be found to incriminate me."

"That's exactly what I shall maintain in court." Leadbeater paused deliberately, then continued very slowly. "If I am satisfied with all the answers you've given me today. We shall see."

Leadbeater gathered his thoughts. "Which brings us to one item of forensic evidence I have particular problems with."

"What's that?" Dermot asked—what was coming now?

"A small piece of plastic was found with the material belonging to Joey Farrell behind your garden shed. Evidence of human tissue was found clinging to it. His tissue. We're talking here about the similarities of Mr. Farrell's death and the death of the man you call Roger Tennyson in your book. Have you any idea how this tissue, clinging to the plastic material, may have got into your garden?"

Dermot could hardly breathe. Plastic? The Plastic Bag Man's *mask*? Neela's eyes were like needles—asking the question, *Did you lie to me?*— What could he say?

"On my second field trip I followed the directions to the place Arnold stated was the grave site of the man Joey Farrell—the Plastic Bag Man. I'm afraid I did come across a small piece of plastic material, which at the time horrified me."

"Because at that time your thinking was that it was in fact part of the plastic bag that had covered Mr. Farrell's head?"

"That's right."

"Did you take home any part of the plastic bag you found?"

"No, I didn't. Absolutely not."

"Then how can you explain its presence in your garden?"

Dermot was shaking. He'd developed a nervous tick in one eye. "The dog?" he began, falteringly. "Maybe Scary picked it up."

"Dermot . . . please." It was the first time Neela had spoken for some time. She knew she had been lied to all this time, but would nevertheless defend Dermot to the last. She knew he was no killer, yet he was now up to his neck in lies and dubious logic. But the dog took it? It was an almost laughable alibi.

Dermot turned to her. "How else? I did not take any putrescent material away with me. It would be revolting! I swear!"

"Let us be clear here. Again, you did not tell your wife of this discovery?"

"No."

"For the same reasons as before?"

"Of course. I love her too much to involve her in anything sordid. I love her even more for standing by me now."

"Well, sad to say, you have done exactly the opposite here with your actions. You have involved her in a very sordid story indeed."

Leadbeater looked toward Fountain. Was there a final question he'd forgotten to ask?

"Arnold. The question about Arnold," Fountain prompted.

"That's right, Harold. There's Mr. Arnold." He turned to Dermot. "You met Mr. Arnold how many times?"

"I met him once. Well, that's a matter of semantics, I guess. I saw him when he delivered the manuscript. He ran away before I could speak to him. Then he sat next to me on a train once. I suppose that qualifies as 'met.'"

"It was the same man? No doubts there?"

"None."

"Then you saw him dead?"

"Yes, in the street."

"You are sure it was him, not someone disguised as the man you'd met before?"

"I'm certain."

"When you spoke to Mr. Arnold on the telephone, what was your opinion of him? Intellectually that is."

"What do you mean?"

"I mean, was he intelligent? Or not so intelligent? What would you imagine his background to be? A working man? Or a middle-class man who'd fallen on hard times?"

"I'd say the latter. He spoke with a strangely guttural accent, but what he said was intelligent—even if the delivery of the words was odd."

"Odd?"

"Yes, staccato. No rhythm. No cadence to them."

"Did you actually see the man you knew as Mr. Arnold fall from the top of the People's Bank, Mr. Nolan?"

A slight hesitation. "Yes, I did."

"Were you in the street when it happened?"

A second hesitation.

"No, you were on the roof. Weren't you, honey?"

Dermot locked eyes with Neela.

"I saw someone on the roof when I arrived at the bank. I could see a shadow behind him. I wasn't sure if it was Neela, so I was terrified. Okay? I raced up the fire escape, but when I got to the roof all I could hear was the man screaming as he fell. I looked over the edge and saw him just before he made contact with the ground."

"He screamed? Interesting."

"Why," Neela asked.

"Not too many suicides scream. But those who have been pushed . . ."

He let everyone absorb his observation, then continued.

"Then you raced down to see if he was dead?"

"Well, more to see if Neela was anywhere close by. I was still terrified that her life was in danger."

"When you reached street level and saw the body—was anyone else in the street?"

"No. But people were looking out windows."

The seconds passed. Leadbeater said nothing. He just stared into space, thinking.

"I'm glad your wife volunteered that you were on the roof at the time of Mr. Arnold's death. You seemed reticent to share this fact with me."

"Not so," Dermot replied, lying.

"Well, it's just as well. Because someone from the building opposite— an office building—did see you on the roof. That will be part of the evidence against you. You see, the prosecution will suggest that it was you who threw Mr. Arnold off the roof. The office worker in question has identified you. And the fact that you lied to the police about your identity won't help matters."

"But I . . ." Dermot stuttered.

Leadbeater held up a hand. "I know. I have listened to your recollection of the events of the day, and you've given me your side of the story. It's quite possible that there was another person on the roof. It will naturally be an option to suggest that it was this person that pushed Mr. Arnold just before your arrival on the roof. The difficult part of this suggested line of thinking will be to answer the question, *Why would anyone do such a thing?* Who dislikes you sufficiently to go to all this trouble to set you up?"

He let the words hang in the air.

"One final question. Did you at any stage tell him you would not help him publish the manuscript?"

"Well . . . yes, I did."

"And did he say—" Leadbeater pulled a sheet of paper from his jacket pocket. He read from the page. "'You call me Arnold Kent once more and you and your pretty wife will live to regret it. Respect me. My name is Arnold. As must be obvious to you, it is a pen name—and besides, my feeling is that you refer to me this way because you are patronizing me. Do not do so.'"

Both Dermot and Nick's expressions told it all. They were amazed.

"Yes, that's almost exactly what I remember."

Leadbeater turned to Nick. "Do you agree with Mr. Nolan? This is your recollection of the speeches?"

"Yes, it's what the man said—almost word for word. But how can you know that?"

"Because the police found a sheet of paper on the roof of the People's Bank Building on which these words were written in capital letters. Each sentence is numbered, as if whoever was speaking should speak the first line first, then move on to sentence two, and so forth."

Dermot looked completely confused. "I don't understand. You mean the police think the man who made the call was in some way coached to say those words to me?"

"That is exactly so. You see, the copy has an asterisk at the base. It states, 'If Mr. Nolan refuses to do what he's told, you must say the following.' Those are the words I just read out to you aloud."

Neela was now crying openly, her shoulders heaving. She was wrapping her arms around herself, as if in great pain. "It's not possible," she muttered, "not possible."

"Sadly it is, Neela. We shall contend that this was the work of some third party who was trying to get Dermot onto the roof to implicate him in the subsequent murder, and all the serial killings as well. Of course the prosecution will contend that it was you who coached this man, in order to have Mr. Hoyle witness your telephone conversation with Mr. Arnold—and that you then raced over to the People's Bank to kill the one man who knew too much."

Dermot stood and waved his arms frantically. "But what did he know?"

"Nothing. Because—and now please understand that I am suggesting to you the prosecution's line of thought, rather than mine—there was no Mr. Arnold. They will suggest Arnold was a smokescreen—that in fact you were the killer from the outset. That the diary was yours all along."

It was then that Neela started to bleed.

CHAPTER 59

Neela hadn't been that far along; she hadn't even known she was pregnant. Sure, she had missed a period, but she'd just chalked it up to all the stress.

Dermot was crushed by the situation—more affected than he imagined he could be. After all, it was Neela who had wanted babies so badly. But that he'd finally given her what she wanted, only to bring on her such horrible stress to cause her to lose it . . . He couldn't hate himself more.

Dermot stroked Neela's forehead as he sat by her bedside at Cedars-Sinai. "We'll get through this," he assured her. "All of this. When Leadbeater proves me innocent, we'll move far away and make all the babies you ever wanted to have. I promise. I'll give you the most wonderful life you can ever imagine."

She managed a weak smile and drifted off to sleep.

With the trial date set some weeks away, the press eventually drifted away from Linley Place and a modicum of sanity returned to the street. Dermot and Neela's relationship strengthened during the wait; the miscarriage had in a strange way brought them closer together.

Dermot had several more meetings with Leadbeater and Fountain. Now that he'd come clean about almost all of his darkest secrets, his attorneys were inclined to believe his story—and this made their work easier. The thrust of the defense would be that the prosecution's case was based entirely on circumstantial evidence.

After a good deal of discussion, Leadbeater convinced Fountain that the defense should not point to the "second man" theory too heavily, unless the prosecution forced their hand by suggesting Nolan had pushed Arnold off the People's Bank Building. Far better, they concluded, was the simplicity of the *existence* of Arnold—the real killer— the man who had written the diary about his own heinous crimes. It was fact that he had visited the Nolan home; it was also on the record that he had delivered the manuscript. Nick had actually been a witness to the conversation between Nolan and Arnold just minutes before the old man committed suicide.

All in all, Leadbeater felt very confident, and told Dermot so on many occasions.

However, Dashiell Goode, the prosecutor in the Nolan murder case, was as confident as Leadbeater, that he could achieve a conviction. The circumstantial evidence garnered by the police was more than any prosecutor could have wished for. And on top of everything else, the accused had such an overweening ego that he actually boasted to the world of his killings by dressing them up in the guise of a work of fiction set in another country. Who in the world would not convict this monster? He was a cold-blooded killer of the worst kind. A living, breathing "worst nightmare."

As the trial date approached, the embers of media interest reignited, and newspapers all around the world began to drum up enthusiasm for what was becoming the most celebrated case since O. J. Simpson. One journalist ringing the doorbell soon became five, all camped out in the street taking turns. The catering guy somehow obtained a resident's parking permit—even though he actually lived in Canoga Park—so he could park right outside the Nolan home to provide sustenance to reporters and camera crews.

Neela spent hours each day on the Internet looking for anything she could find that would make sense of who was persecuting her husband. To no avail.

Dermot no longer noticed black Peugeots passing along Linley. He was more concerned for those mentioned in *Worst Nightmares* that had not yet been killed, including the victim of the nightmare he himself created . . .

During the long wait for his trial, Dermot was approached by several publishing houses to write his autobiography, regardless of the outcome. Neela called them "reality vultures." Dermot refused to deal with any of them. Esther stopped calling him a week after the bail hearing. Her secretary fielded all her calls. Esther was always in meetings when he rang.

It didn't matter that much to Dermot—to know who his true friends were. As long as he had Neela and Nick, he'd be okay.

CHAPTER 60

It was getting near time to put to bed another edition of the *Daily News*, but Melhuish had nothing to offer his readers—other than the copy everyone else was reading in rival newspapers. Schipp had stopped delivering, and the glow that had surrounded him when the story had broken was starting to fade.

"It's been too long, Schipp," Melhuish growled. "*We* broke the story. *We* were on the fast track. Now we've got nada."

Schipp took a breath. "The cops are trying almost as hard as I am to track the bastard, but all I have is a voice. What can I do if my source dries up and won't call me?"

"No more excuses, Schipp. Give me headlines."

Schipp sulked, thinking of ways out of his dilemma.

"When do we get started on the meat of this trial?" Melhuish asked offhandedly.

"The prosecution is going to be feeding on the murders one by one beginning this Friday."

"How long's each going to take before the prosecutor moves on to the next?"

"A day. Maybe two."

"Right. We'll save the front page each day for a screamer. Just the names Nolan gave to his victims—with a graphic underneath depicting how they died. Make sure you get the best artwork. I want the pictures to look scary as hell."

Melhuish waved him away. "Now go do your thing."

Schipp walked to the door.

"And let me know the minute that voice contacts you."

"I will, sir."

The trial began with a whimper. The jury was chosen without too many challenges from either Goode or Leadbeater. Each day the gallery was packed with ghouls, and each day Neela, Nick sitting beside her, endured the grueling testimony. The only ray of hope was the presence of Esther, who sat behind Neela in the same seat each day.

The proceedings seemed endless. Beginning with two days of a general introduction from the prosecution, Goode spoke directly to the jury, trying to feed them undeniable proof of Dermot's guilt—and many looked as though they were biting. When he was done, he returned to his seat and turned to face the jury once again.

Then it was Leadbeater's time to shine. "I shall go into greater detail later, but for now let me tell you a fact the defense will not be disputing. The accused visited the scene where the bodies of Gareth and Laura Nash were buried and later found. But how many times had he been there before—and was he revisiting the scene of his crime, or had he simply been doing his research to authenticate his novel? The prosecution will give you many grisly details of circumstantial evidence against my client, but it will be up to you to decide whether there's reasonable doubt."

But despite Leadbeater's skillful arguments, Goode continued to have a field day, horrifying everyone in the courtroom. It soon became clear that a new picture of Dermot Nolan was crystallizing in their minds minute by minute. The defendant was disturbed, prone to violence and road rage, with a prurient compulsion to visit bars frequented by prostitutes.

During the latter part of the day Goode introduced damning forensic evidence: the fingerprints and blood samples found on the rim of the water tower in which Bruce Major's head had been found; soil samples taken from Dermot's boots that proved he had driven to the water tower at some time. Of course, this by no means proved that Dermot had been there when Major had been murdered, but it further strengthened the prosecution's case.

Leadbeater countered that the forensic material merely confirmed the defense's contention that Nolan was seeking to establish whether the details in the diary were fact or fiction. Of course there would be fingerprint evidence proving that Nolan had been there at one time or another. And soil samples on the tires identical to the soil at the tower. But this proved no more than that Nolan had been there—once. There was no proof as to exactly when.

The judge called a recess early. Leadbeater took Dermot and Neela to an anteroom where they discussed the day's events with Harold Fountain. Both Fountain and Leadbeater thought the session had gone as well as could be expected.

But good as Leadbeater and Fountain were, they didn't notice the rabbit jumping into Goode's hat.

CHAPTER 61

Even though all of Mike Kandinski's work on the Nolan case was now in the murder book, he continued to have a nagging feeling he hadn't done nearly enough to help his friend. Of course it wasn't the function of LAPD detectives to attempt to vindicate criminals, but Mike just couldn't believe Dermot was guilty of these crimes. He was sure someone had set him up, had manipulated the man known as Arnold. And that this someone was still out there watching an innocent man get persecuted.

Mike reviewed the victims list again, determined to find a motive. He knew serial killers took pleasure in their victim selection, and in over ninety per cent of such cases the selection pointed the way to their particular psychosis and led to their eventual capture.

Each evening Mike took files home with him. He studied the background of each victim over and over again hoping that something would connect one of them to a previous profile. He believed it was only a matter of time before some small seed of information linked one victim to another.

Across town, each evening Dermot, Neela, and Nick deflected the press, first outside the courthouse, then at Linley Place. Once inside the sanctuary of their home they did their best to live as normal a life as possible. Dermot refused to discuss the day's developments, so if anyone had issues with the testimony, they discussed them out of his earshot.

Because of Neela's condition, everyone tried to remain upbeat and positive. Nick attempted to be amusing when he could, and often succeeded in making everyone laugh despite the circumstances. They never read the newspapers, or listened to the radio, or watched the news on television.

The days continued, and both Goode and Leadbeater painstakingly sifted through the evidence. Each morning the general public breakfasted on the tabloid news with horrific banner headlines. Melhuish persevered with his one-liners, coupled with disgustingly graphic drawings. Other newspapers were more circumspect, and as a result suffered in the circulation battle. The day the evidence of the Mouth Maiden was introduced, the drawing was particularly shocking. Melhuish had finally acceded to the expense of color—red, naturally. The drawing took up two-thirds of the front page. It was a female face, staring at the reader, the mouth a circle of red, and captioned: *The Mouth Maiden*.

In court, Goode dwelled a great deal on pointing to the horrific nature of each murder. "These innocent victims were not murdered—they were butchered, tortured, abused in the foulest way!" One by one, the characters in Dermot's *Worst Nightmares* were examined. Goode linked each fictional character to their real-life counterparts. He then placed Dermot at the scene of the crime, courtesy of forensic evidence, and asked the jury if they could come to a conclusion other than "lightning has a tendency not to strike ten times in the same place." And judging by the expression on the faces of the jurors, they agreed wholeheartedly.

Leadbeater continued with his line of argument that the real murderer was still "out there." He sought to frighten the jury members with an almost storybook scenario, reminiscent of Jack the Ripper, that a boogeyman was stalking through the night alleys of the City of Angels, selecting future victims.

Schipp practically never took his eyes off the telephone on his desk, but each time it rang it was someone other than his source. He saw his career on the decline—he had to get back in touch with his man. The question was, how?

Nick was always there for Neela and Dermot—always insisting there was no way in the world that any twelve women and men would even entertain a conviction without at least some concrete evidence.

Kandinski worked at home after his shift, often deep into the night, to find a connection between the victims—a connection that might offer up a motive for the crimes; some kind of reason for the current public and private madness.

At the end of the tenth week of the trial, Kandinski at last chanced upon the link he had been looking for—just as Goode and Leadbeater were about to begin their closing arguments. He shouted so loudly in triumph from downstairs that Dawn thought something terrible had happened to him. Before she could get out of bed, he was upstairs at her side.

"I think I've found the connection" he said, breathless.

"That's nice, honey," Dawn replied drowsily. "But will it clear Nolan?"

"Well, I don't exactly know yet. First up, I linked two of the victims. Then, when I knew what I was looking for, I found I could link three of them. Now it's four." He was almost joyous in his enthusiasm. "You know, honey, I've always thought Dermot was innocent."

"Yes . . . I know that." She was fully awake now.

"Well, if I can establish this link—and thus a motive—maybe I can get to the bottom of it all and find out who the real killer is!"

"Well, that's marvelous, honey. Now please let me get back to sleep."

A few hours later, Mike and Dawn were sitting down to breakfast. "I need you to do something important for me this morning," he asked.

"What is it?"

"I want you to call the Nolans. Right now, so you'll catch them before they leave for the courthouse. Ask to speak to Neela. Be sure to speak to her personally."

"And what do I tell her?"

"Tell her who you are. Say I asked you to contact her privately—unofficially."

"Is this wise, Mike? This stuff's not going to get you into trouble at work, is it?"

"Frankly, I don't care. But I don't think so. Just tell her I've come across some new evidence on my own, and I've linked some of the vics. Tell her I'm excited because I've got an idea now about who to look for. Tell her to keep her chin up, too, 'cause I may be cracking this case really soon." He strapped on his weapon. "You got all that? Tell Neela Nolan only!"

"Sure. I'll do it right away. But you have to leave now! Go!"

As he sped down the street, Dawn was already talking to Neela.

CHAPTER 62

In the pressroom, Schipp was watching Leadbeater parade a line of impressive character witnesses on the plasma screen. All professed that Dermot was a quiet, gentle, intelligent, kind, and amusing man, and that he could not have done it because it was out of character. It was then Schipp's cell phone rang.

"Mr. Schipp?"

It was him! The voice. Schipp's adrenaline kicked in as he prayed for another tip.

"What have you got for me today?"

"I have some interesting information. But before I confide in you, you must promise me something."

"I'll do what I can—that I *can* promise," Schipp replied.

"Promises are broken every day. But let me put it another way. I can continue to give you useful information for some time, but if you do not use this information as I suggest, you will never hear from me again. Rather, I shall offer even more intriguing information to your rivals."

"No need for that. Just let me know what you have in mind."

"You have all been attempting to establish the identity of the man who threw himself off the People's Bank Building—the man Mr. Nolan refers to as Mr. Arnold."

"Yes, that's true. We couldn't even find matching dental records."

"Well, I know why," the voice replied.

"Can you tell me?"

"Of course. But if I reveal Mr. Arnold's real identity, you must never divulge it was a source that informed you. You must always maintain that finding the key to his identity was due diligence on your part."

This sounded fine to Schipp—to hell with how this lie might damage Nolan's chances of a fair trial. Anyway, he'd simply be offering information to the police. "Okay. That's fine with me."

"You must tell the police that it occurred to you this dead man might at one time or another have been institutionalized. So you very painstakingly searched for him in the health records of each and every hospital in California. This took many weeks of arduous work. Finally you visited the Universal Psychiatric Hospital in LA. Their staff was very helpful and told you that a man fitting the description you gave them had been released from the unit. His name was Christopher Sheldon. He was sixty-eight, but had the mental capacity of a ten-year-old. The only reason he was released was lack of bed space." The gravelly voice paused. "Come to think of it, that could be another wonderful angle for a political story on the health system. What do you say?"

"Yes, it could. But you're saying that the man who fell was named Christopher Sheldon, and was recently released from Universal?"

"Precisely."

"But a man with the mental age of a preteen could never have written that manuscript."

"Look, I have many various pressing appointments today, so I will have to leave you with this thought. But remember, it did not come as a tip from an informant—it was you who was the super sleuth. Make sure the detectives match the DNA of the dead man—they'll have plenty of dried blood available, I'm sure. Then let them match it to the hospital records. Oh, by the way, Sheldon also had a thing about his teeth. He never allowed any dentist to tamper with them. That's why there were never any dental records."

That's when the cell phone went dead.

As Schipp made his way down the corridors of power to share his investigative brilliance with Melhuish, Kandinski was at his desk pretending to work on a series of burglaries as he ran leads on more of the victims, using the linkage he had found in the murder book. That was when his phone rang.

The call he fielded was from a man who spoke in whispers. He said he had information. It was to change the course of his life. Dramatically.

CHAPTER 63

Schipp delivered the news of his discovery personally. He took a staff photographer with him to Parker Center and insisted he would only hand over the breakthrough material identifying Mr. Arnold if Willis would allow the photo op of him personally giving her the info outside Parker Center.

Of course he had to rely on the facts given to him by his source, but the psych hospital did confirm that Sheldon had had bright red almost orange hair, was the right age, and had never allowed anyone to take a look at his teeth. Willis allowed herself to be photographed by the *Daily News* photographer in the full knowledge it would only be printed in the paper if the information were correct—besides, she needed the identification badly.

Willis had her top scientists fast-track the DNA, and within hours she had a positive match. The man who had jumped to his death—or been pushed—was indeed Christopher Sheldon, and this revelation raised a whole raft of new questions.

If Sheldon was mentally challenged, he could hardly have written the manuscript himself, so he had to have been assisted, perhaps by the real killer. Or an accomplice. An alternative theory was that Nolan had been lying all along. He had paid Sheldon to deliver the manuscript to his home, a manuscript he had previously written himself, thereby attempting to prove the diary was originally written by someone else. He had then murdered Sheldon to cover his tracks—and the truth.

Her first priority, after establishing that Arnold was Sheldon, was to inform the DA. A message was also immediately sent to Goode. It caused a sensation in court, and of course in the pressroom. The plasma screens showed the clerk of the court delivering a note to Goode. It was immediately evident that something major had occurred. The journalists reached for their cell phones.

Goode stood and asked permission to approach the bench. He then asked for a recess, based on fresh evidence having just come to light—evidence that he felt duty bound to share with the defense team.

As the journalists in the pressroom chattered into their cells, Schipp's scoop was already on all the television stations, both free to air and cable. The implications were obvious. Nolan had to have been lying all along. In interview tapes Nolan had indicated that Arnold was intellectually astute, though he spoke strangely—that was a lie. "Arnold" was a man by the name of Sheldon, a mental child.

Leadbeater and Fountain held a crisis meeting. Their main defense was no longer credible, and the identification of Sheldon raised some very worrisome issues. Their client was on record as having told the police he had met this Sheldon person and found him normal, if a little eccentric. And during the first phone call, he'd actually found him "intellectually bright." But this couldn't be true. So had Nolan been lying, simply mistaken, or could they prove the man on the phone was someone other than Arnold? This would be hard to achieve at this late stage of the trial. Would the jury believe that a man as bright as Nolan could meet a man as mentally challenged as Sheldon, a man who had spent the greater portion of his life institutionalized, and not realize at once that the man had the mental capacity of a child?

Leadbeater immediately concluded that Schipp had been gifted the information, quite possibly by the serial killer himself, but there was no way Schipp would ever admit it because he had too much to lose. So how could he and Fountain radically alter their strategy to handle these new developments?

While Fountain and Leadbeater went into instant damage control, Goode licked his lips in expectation of what lay ahead. He did a little homework, and went home early—tomorrow he would deliver the coup de grâce.

Dermot Nolan was done.

CHAPTER 64

Kandinski had tried to get Hansen on the police radio, and then on his private cell. No luck. So, against all standard practices, he decided to check out the information he'd received from the man who spoke in whispers. Alone.

"I can show you why Nolan did what he did," the voice told him. "Meet me on the rooftop of the Stratten Building."

The Stratten Building had been derelict for several years. It had at one time been part of a hospital complex. But when the hospital moved into the new buildings, the Stratten had simply been locked up and left to deteriorate. It wasn't lost on the detective that the empty building was close to Nolan's house.

From the street Kandinski glanced at Dermot's front door, then up toward the roof of the Stratten Building. He then started up the fire escape—it was going to be a long climb, but hopefully well worth it.

It was gusty up on the roof—a stiff southerly wind had kicked in and the temperature had dropped ten degrees in as many minutes.

He walked the full length of the roof, to the side of the building that faced the Nolan home, passing as he did a small shed that looked locked. There was no sign of anyone on the roof. Perhaps he'd made the drive from Parker Center too quickly and his informant hadn't arrived yet; perhaps the informant had gotten cold feet. He glanced up at the vast Fuji sign, blinking its own bizarre red alert.

The detective looked down through the trees at Nolan's house. Had the curtains not been drawn he could have looked right through the tree canopy and into the living room.

He turned back and scanned the rooftop again. No one. He looked at his watch—how long was he going to wait?

He paced up and down for several minutes, until his curiosity got the better of him, and he strolled over to the prefabricated shed that stood near the fire stairs. To his surprise the door was unlocked—the padlock that had once secured it now hung open. Kandinski pulled the door open and looked inside.

It was so dark that almost nothing was discernible. He felt for a switch and found one, but it didn't work. He took out his flashlight and turned it on.

That's when he saw the digital photos, nailed to the walls.

The first one made him catch his breath. It was a close-up of a young girl's mouth. Phoebe Blasé. Although the photo looked old and had faded a little, the blood was still vivid red. The eyes looked dead.

Kandinski instinctively glanced behind him. Even for a seasoned detective this was strong stuff. He focused the light on the next photo. A man's head—a plastic bag almost glued to his face, the eyes staring out through the bag in panic. The Plastic Bag Man.

Kandinski didn't need to see all of the other shots. Not now. Now it was far more important to establish who had pinned these photos to the walls of this shed.

He turned and shone his Maglite on the opposite wall. Here there was a host of surveillance shots of the victims before they were abducted. Lucy Cowley looked to be laughing in her photo. Joey Farrell was eating an apple he'd just bought at a corner fruit market in the city. Under each shot were scribbled notes.

Kandinski reached for his cell—it was time to call this in. He punched in the numbers, and then thought twice about hitting the Send button.

Maybe it was better to see if his informant had arrived. After all, he still didn't have an absolute lock on who had taken these photos. But if his hunch was right, he now knew the identity of the killer. But proof was going to be imperative. It was possible forensics might help, but it was by no means a certainty. So he held off calling back to base. Instead he stepped out on the roof once more to see if his informant was there.

He had just enough time to register an outline against the setting sun before he was struck in the head with a length of wood.

When he regained consciousness, Kandinski was aware that his limbs were numb. He was lying propped up against the side of the shed, and a man dressed in a dark blue Nike jogging suit, wearing a motorcycle helmet with a dark visor down to obscure his face, was holding Kandinski's cell phone.

"Just about to call it in, huh? Guess I caught you just in time," the gravelly voice muttered.

"I know who you are," Kandinski managed, despite the terrible pain in his head.

The man in the motorcycle helmet chuckled, bent down to Kandinski, and whispered in his ear.

"I felt sure you *did*," the man replied. "That's why I asked you up here. Anyway, now is the time to get Mr. Nolan off the hook."

So saying, he pulled six inches of duct tape off the roll, pressing it over Kandinski's mouth. Then he took out his Flip video camera, one that was almost as slim as a credit card. He turned it on and laid it down on the rooftop, facing Kandinski. He then switched the camera to Record.

Kandinski could do no more than look up at his attacker. His torso and limbs felt lifeless—presumably he'd been injected with sux like all the other victims. Possibly a smaller dose, which was why he'd been able to get out a word or two. The thought of what was to come made his blood run cold.

"Framing Mr. Nolan has been exhilarating for me. It has given me the utmost pleasure. You know why? Because it was a work of pure genius. It took me years of research and months of planning. I didn't think the actual execution of the plan would be such fun. You see, initially I didn't think I'd *enjoy* making people suffer. But the manuscript had to be sufficiently abhorrent to interest a man of Dermot Nolan's standing. But—I'm going to surprise you here—I found killing the innocent parties just as much fun as killing the guilty. Imagine! The innocent didn't deserve to die, but that didn't bother me at all!" The man in the helmet crouched down, and whispered softly in Kandinski's ear—this was private, not for Schipp's ears. "The guys and girls that you linked—*they* certainly deserved to perish. Because they had caused me so much sorrow. The others were just . . . well . . . to keep you guessing."

He repositioned the Flip camera, so that it pointed at Kandinski, but now included the shed in the background. "Now watch up, Schipp—this is one big mother of a scoop. Maybe right this second you're desperately trying to find out my location? But remember, by the time I e-mail this to you, it'll all be over. But now I have something to do."

The helmeted man stood and walked around the side of the shed, lifting a plastic container and unscrewing the top.

Kandinski smelled gasoline. He tried to speak through the tape over his mouth, but couldn't. Even had he been able to, he knew that pleading for his life would have attracted no mercy.

Gasoline was splashed on his face and hair, then on his torso.

"All has gone according to plan, detective. I'm sorry you have to die so painfully, but you must."

The man pulled out a box of matches and struck one. He tossed it at Kandinski. Immediately Kandinski was engulfed in flames. Within seconds the flesh of his cheeks was crisping, like a suckling pig. There was remarkably little smoke. This was a blessing; the killer didn't want the corpse visited too quickly. As far as he was concerned, a few hours' delay would be perfect.

The flesh burned hot. Only the head convulsed for a few seconds—the limbs and torso were already anaesthetized. When the flesh was charred black, the killer retrieved two buckets of water from the shed and doused the body. Then he covered Kandinski with a tarpaulin to reduce any residual smoke.

A gloved hand retrieved the Flip camera.

Schipp was trying to read a magazine in his partitioned office, but his real concentration was on his laptop. He felt certain that his source wouldn't let him down. It was a sixth sense. That's when his open laptop trilled to alert him to new e-mail. This one had no message—simply an attachment.

A video.

He immediately looked to see who had sent the e-mail. But no surprises there—it was the kind of gobbledygook address that one got from scam artists. It made no sense at all. Except for one part of it—the letters *WN* in caps in among the other stuff.

Schipp clicked on the attachment. One second later, he knew he was watching something terrible. There was a man lying on some rooftop, and it looked as though another man, the man who was speaking but was not visible, was about to do the guy on the ground great harm. Schipp couldn't move. He had to watch; he had to listen to the appalling voiceover.

As he watched the gas poured over the detective, Schipp couldn't help screaming out, loudly. He knew he was watching an execution, one that had taken place recently. He listened in horror to the words—the confession. Then flames engulfed the man on the ground. The video stopped.

Half a dozen staffers were now poking their heads into his office. He waved them away.

Within seconds Schipp was connected with Parker Center.

The problem was that Kandinski had failed to follow correct procedure, which was to tell someone where he was going, so no one knew where Kandinski went when he'd left the Center. An all points bulletin was put out at once, every available chopper lifted into the skies to scour the rooftops, but the remains were not found for over an hour.

CHAPTER 65

Following the public revelation of Sheldon's background, Leadbeater was given the option of a long adjournment. However, he felt that if the defense opted for more time, it would lead the jury to the conclusion that the Nolan camp was in trouble. So he brazened it out and went with plan B—he always made certain he had several such plans up his sleeve.

Needless to say, the press was salivating at the prospect of hearing what new evidence was to be introduced when the session continued. Some were making bets in the pressroom that the evidence would be such dynamite that the defense would open with a guilty plea, having come to some kind of sentencing deal with the district attorney's office. All hoped for photos of more dead bodies, or a deviant sexual slant to the case—prurience always sold papers and made for high ratings on the news.

"Members of the jury," Goode began, "this has been a long, taxing trial. During the course of it, the defense has introduced little evidence other than some character witnesses, and a long convoluted story—one that you will be asked to believe when the time comes to make your decision about Mr. Nolan's guilt or innocence.

"It must seem that the defense case rests entirely on the premise that Mr. Nolan was handed a manuscript, a diary if you will, of the day-by-day conduct of a cruel and unusual psychopath who called himself 'Mr. Arnold.' This man, we are asked to believe, was in his late sixties, and I doubt if the prosecution would argue with the fact that he was reasonably infirm. He had the appearance of a street person, and as far as anyone knows he *did* live rough on the streets of Los Angeles. Yet it was this man, you are asked to believe, who carried two heavy twin stakes of lumber on his back to his vehicle, and then drove them into the country, embedded them firmly into hard ground, kidnapped two able-bodied people, tied them to these stakes, tortured them, and finally dug a huge grave and buried them.

"They will maintain that it was this frail old man who rigged a very complicated windmill apparatus on top of a tall water tower, kidnapped Bruce Major, dragged him up a rickety ladder over his shoulder, and secured him to a chain so that his head was positioned only inches from the water. It was this man who pulled every tooth from the head of Phoebe Blasé with a pair of pliers." He paused for effect. "I could go on, but I am sure you get my point here. How was an old man possibly capable of such tasks?"

Goode walked closer to the jury and continued. "I contend that it was Mr. Nolan who performed these feats—for feats they are indeed. Mr. Nolan is a fit, strong, young man. Could he have done these horrible things? Most certainly.

"The defense would have you believe that Mr. Nolan did no more than plagiarize Mr. Arnold's diary. He tells us he is very sorry he acted the way he did—he's sorry for ignoring the feelings of all those families affected by his refusal to divulge the locations of the graves of these victims. He's also 'very sorry' to have lied to his wife. And very possibly even sorry for lying to his counsel."

Leadbeater stood. "Objection, Your Honor."

"I agree," the judge replied. "Let the last remark be stricken from the record."

"I apologize," Goode added—though he wasn't in the least sorry.

"So, we have a defendant who has the interesting and creative propensity for telling lies. We *know* he lied to the police, over and over again, and even lied about the most fundamentally important matters of this case to his own wife. The question remains: Is he lying now? Most certainly.

"When Mr. Arnold fell—or more likely was pushed—from the roof of the People's Bank Building, where was Mr. Nolan?"

Goode met the eyes of each jury member one by one. "Well, wouldn't you know—he was up there, right behind Mr. Arnold." Goode smiled. "He didn't push him to his death, of course. Oh no! He was simply there because Mr. Arnold rang him and told him he would be committing suicide that day. So Mr. Nolan was there to change his mind. I say, nonsense."

Another objection by Leadbeater. Upheld.

"Withdrawn," Goode conceded, a wry smirk on his face. "So, we come to the news of the day." He leaned against his chair and drew a deep slow breath.

"We now know who this Mr. Arnold really *was*. An investigative journalist by the name of Jeffrey Schipp discovered that Mr. Arnold was in fact an old man by the name of Christopher Sheldon, who had been released from the custody of a mental health facility only recently—and where he had been since he was twenty-five. But here's the thing—Mr. Sheldon had the mental age of a ten-year-old!"

Leadbeater's expression was stoic.

"So? Will the defense still maintain that this simpleton wrote this treatise? Or will they contend that someone else wrote the diary? An accomplice perhaps? Because if they do, I feel certain you'll find this defense laughable, too."

Goode's speech lasted a full forty minutes before the door of the courtroom opened and the ADA took a seat behind Goode's chair and urgently signaled to him.

"Your Honor, may I consult with my associate?" Goode asked politely.

"You may. You have one minute, Mr. Goode."

There was a murmur in the gallery. Goode turned back to the judge. "Permission to approach the bench, Your Honor."

Crowe beckoned Goode and Leadbeater forward, and Goode delivered the news of Detective Michael Kandinski's murder to Justice Crowe. "In view of this development, may I ask for a brief adjournment, Your Honor?"

Goode and Leadbeater returned to the courtroom within the hour. Goode told Justice Crowe that all charges against Dermot Nolan had been withdrawn. Crowe pronounced Dermot a free man. Upon hearing the words, Neela began to sob. Nolan smiled at Tim Leadbeater and hugged him. He had no idea at the time to whom he owed his biggest debt of gratitude.

CHAPTER 66

The media frenzy that greeted the dismissal of all charges against Dermot Nolan was even greater than when he'd been arrested. Networked TV shows and cable channels drew their own conclusions—having charges dropped was a very different thing from an acquittal.

Of course Dermot's legal team immediately convened a press conference and went to great pains to explain that the revelations following the death of Detective Kandinski—at the hands of the real killer—completely exonerated their client.

Of course it was a massive relief to Dermot and Neela. But they knew their lives would never be the same again. They knew they'd have little or no money left after Leadbeater and Fountain had submitted their invoices. And most frightening was that Kandinski's killer, the real killer, was still out there. The immediate post-trial celebrations at the Nolan home were very subdued. They all knew that to break out the champagne would be in the poorest of taste because of what had happened to Mike.

But it was the cue for Neela at last to share a secret with Dermot. She was pregnant again.

Several weeks passed. Each day Dermot and Neela lived in fear of the unknown. They checked the locks on all the doors and windows each morning and evening. Neither slept well. They hardly ever let each other out of their sight. They shopped together and walked Scarecrow together. They had actually considered hiring some security, but decided bodyguards would be too intrusive.

As the weeks passed, the initial adrenaline rush of being a free man morphed into a dull feeling of uselessness. Dermot became bored and listless. His depression medication failed to cope with his mood swings. His doctor suggested upping the dosage. Nick did all he could to cheer them both up—arranging a seaplane trip to Catalina Island and a chopper ride to Mammoth. They would have already gone abroad to escape the limelight had it not been for medical considerations concerning the new pregnancy. As it was, these short escapes from the dreary life of a social pariah only warmed the tip of the iceberg. Dermot's core was black ice.

One evening, Neela found Dermot in his office late, staring into space. He hadn't shaved that morning, and she knew it was a bad sign.

"How are we ever going to leave here and establish ourselves anywhere else? The real estate market is so depressed we'll walk away with only a million or so if we sell now. But I have to get away. What are we going to do?"

"We have to think of Virginia," Neela replied. The tests had confirmed that the child she was carrying was a girl. "We only have a few months before she enters our world. We must be strong when she arrives."

She sat in Dermot's lap and he hugged her.

"I have so much to apologize for. Most of all to you."

"There's no need, honey. I understand the desperation you felt—I know you lied to protect me."

"Well, I'm glad of that."

He stroked her hair.

"I want so much for Virginia to be proud of me, Neels."

"But you didn't do a terrible thing."

"I behaved like a moral bankrupt."

"People simply don't understand the pressures you were under."

"Neels. I'd like to apologize publicly. I've been thinking about doing so for some time. Quite often people in the public eye have done it, but not many of them succeeded in gaining much sympathy. But that's not what I'm after. I just want to tell everyone how terribly sorry I am for what I did. Doing that, for me anyway, would be a catharsis. Then I may be able to move on and become a better person."

Neela thought about the idea for a couple of days and then contacted someone she knew at CNN. That person suggested Dermot be interviewed by Jack Duggan on his program, *Up Very Close*. There, he could apologize to the families of all the victims and show the world he was genuine in his sorrow. Perhaps the world might forgive him.

The interview was scheduled, completed, and it aired two weeks later. The exchange was tough, yet honest—that was Duggan's style. Dermot pointed to the pressure that had been on him to write. Duggan countered with the bald statement that "pressure" was surely not sufficient reason to steal someone else's work and keep the locations of dead people from the police. Dermot admitted it was not.

"I can hardly believe now, looking back, that I did what I did. I couldn't be more sorry—to those victims and to their families."

"What are your plans for the future, Mr. Nolan? Will you continue to write?"

"I very much doubt it. I can't imagine many people would want to read any of my work—and I fully understand why."

Six more weeks passed. A Greek businessman came and visited the house with a view toward buying it. He made an offer, which was way too short of the asking price. Dermot and Neela declined.

It was the night the Greek called to say he was returning to Athens and was thus withdrawing his miserable offer, that Dermot got the call from *The New Yorker*. The magazine had made an editorial decision to reach out to Nolan. They asked him to write a series of articles called *Dealing with Solitude*. They'd heard the story about Dermot disappearing without a trace before returning later with the seeds of a best-selling novel. They wondered if he could do it again—kick-start his career once more if they recreated a similar environment to the last time he'd disappeared. He would deliver articles to the magazine once a month for several months and write about living alone in a remote area of Papua New Guinea—far from any other Caucasians. Each month a messenger in a helicopter would go and pick up the handwritten articles.

"It's a fantastic idea, Neels! Imagine. *The New Yorker*!"

Neela managed a smile—she was really happy for Dermot, but there was the question of Virginia.

"Honey, I'm having a baby, remember?"

He wrapped her in his arms, taking care not to squeeze the baby. "I'll be back in plenty of time. Trust me—I wouldn't miss that moment for the Nobel Prize."

CHAPTER 67

Dermot was in a cab just minutes from LAX when he received the phone call. Neela had planned to see him off, but was feeling off-color that morning, so she'd stayed home promising Dermot she'd call her obstetrician if she felt any worse. When his cell phone rang, he answered it without looking at the caller ID, fully expecting the call to be Neela wishing him well.

It wasn't.

"Mister Nolan? It's time," the guttural voice said coldly.

To Dermot it was like listening to the voice of the dead. He felt like his brain had been hit by a stun gun.

"What do you want, you barbarian?" he replied, with very little composure. Every muscle in his body was fibrillating.

"I want to talk about Neela."

The word struck like a poison arrow fired into his chest. *Neela.*

"And about little Virginia," the guttural voice of the dead continued.

Virginia! A second shaft entered his heart.

"What have you done to them?"

"Me?" the voice replied. "I haven't done anything to either of them."

The voice paused to allow a little relief to invade his victim's psyche. Then he continued. "But there are five good ol' boys who are very eager to meet with her in the elevator you described in such a delightful fashion in your book."

Dermot couldn't speak.

"That was her nightmare, I believe. Wasn't it? Incidentally, it was such a jolly read. *Worst Nightmares*, that is. I was impressed by the final product."

The voice hung up.

Dermot immediately called out to the cabbie. "Turn around! Now! Go back downtown."

"But—"

"*Do it!* Right now!" Dermot screamed. "I'll pay double!"

The cabbie obliged. Dermot immediately called Neela.

"Neela. Pick up!" he prayed. "Please! Pick up!"

But the call went to voicemail. He called Nick. Nick picked up right away.

"Nick! Thank God I reached you. Neela's in danger. At least I think so. The killer with the guttural voice. He just called me. Where's Neels? She isn't answering her cell. Where has she gone?"

"Neela felt a bit worse—not much, but enough. She's gone to see her obstetrician."

"The Sibley Building? I'm on my way there now. Call the police right away! Okay? Tell them to get over there—that madman has threatened to assault her."

Dermot hung up and directed the cabbie. "The Sibley Building! South Broadway! Five hundred bucks says you can get me there in fifteen minutes!"

Dermot continued to call Neela's mobile—but there was no answer.

The cabbie drove like a NASCAR champion, but he still took longer than Dermot had hoped to get to the building. The cab pulled up outside. Dermot tossed the cabbie his VISA card.

"Stay here! The five hundred's yours. Another hundred if you wait."

Dermot jumped out and ran into the foyer of the building. The last golden rays of twilight sun reflected off the glass panels.

Minutes before, Neela had stepped into one of a bank of elevators and pressed the button for floor twenty-seven, where her obstetrician had his office. The floor number lit up and the elevator rose.

Neela marveled at the city spread out before her—it was one of the features of this newly built building. The elevators were on one corner, affording the most spectacular views of LA, all the way to the ocean.

The elevator slid to a premature halt on the eighth floor. The doors opened and a muscled young man with a shaven head stepped in. He was wearing overalls. Despite his confronting appearance, Neela wasn't afraid. The man smiled and turned away to face the doors.

As the elevator continued upward, the guy turned and stared at her. He was still smiling—but this time his expression had a tinge of menace. He slowly circled her, his eyes locked with hers.

Neela was now frightened. She reached for her cell phone.

In the foyer, Dermot was stabbing all the elevator buttons frantically. "Come ON!" he screamed at the metal doors.

The skinhead in Neela's elevator finished his circle, and stood with his back to the elevator doors, watching her. The elevator slowed and stopped. It was the twentieth floor. The doors slid open. Four more young men stood there, all wearing similar overalls. All had rings pierced through various parts of their faces. Neela's blood ran cold when they stepped into the elevator and crowded her back into a corner. She tried to punch 9-1-1 into her cell, but the lead skinhead grasped her hand and took the phone from her.

"What the hell do you think you're doing?" she said.

The man didn't reply. He dropped the phone and stomped it under a work boot.

On the ground floor, the doors of an elevator opened and Dermot leaped inside. He immediately punched floor twenty-seven. The doors closed agonizingly slowly. The elevator began to rise.

Dermot's elevator reached the tenth floor, slowed, and then stopped. The doors slid open. Nick was standing there, smiling.

"Hey! Get in here!" Dermot shouted. "We'll be there in a few seconds. Thanks for getting here so quick—you're a lifesaver!"

That was when Nick pulled what looked like a cell phone from his trouser pocket and thrust it at Dermot's chest.

Dermot felt a shocking pain and fell to the floor. Nick studied the stun gun in his hand, impressed with how well it actually had worked.

"Hell, that was something else! What do you say, Dermot? A Stun-master cell phone stun gun. Eight hundred thousand volts of power! Wow!"

Nick stepped into the elevator and leaned his cane against a side wall. He inserted a security elevator key. The doors closed behind him.

Dermot gasped with pain. "What the hell's going on? Jesus, Nick. You just electrocuted me or something!"

"Just a stun gun," Nick replied. "Come on! Be a man, Dermot."

He crouched next to Dermot and slipped a woolen ski mask over his head. "I have to give you credit, you know. You sure came running to Neela's rescue. Great job, by the way."

Dermot was still trying to recover from the high voltage shock. "What the hell are you talking about? Where's Neela?"

"You want to see Neela? Okay, let's go see her. My treat." Nick punched in the button for the top floor. The car rose.

In her car, Neela now had all five men in a tight circle around her. Hands were searching her body, fondling her breasts and buttocks, attempting to feel under her blouse and under her skirt. In desperation, she looked at the CCTV and began to scream. The scream was short-lived, however—the palm of a massive hand was clamped over her mouth, followed by a length of duct tape.

When Dermot's car passed Neela's, he could look right into his wife's elevator. For a couple of seconds, their two faces were a mere yard from each other. Neela caught the most fleeting glimpse of Dermot as his elevator passed. She blinked, trying to refocus, but it was too late—he'd gone. Could it have been Dermot? Slumped on the floor at the feet of someone in a Nike tracksuit and ski mask?

When Dermot registered what was happening to his wife, something snapped. He found he was suddenly capable of strength he never knew he had. With a primal roar, he lunged for Nick.

As the elevator continued to rise, they struggled for the stun gun, but Dermot was no match for Nick.

In her car, Neela too found a new strength. She slapped the face of the skinhead as hard as she could.

"Fuck you!" she screamed at him. His head snapped back. But it had all the effect of water flowing off a duck's back. The man leered at her and cupped one of her breasts. "Easy, bitch. Just having a bit of fun," he replied.

At that precise moment the skinhead hit the elevator button—it rose a few feet to the next floor, and the doors opened.

To Neela's surprise, and huge relief, all but the skinhead exited. The ringleader stared at her and smiled. "By the way, the clinic's closed—looks like you missed your appointment. Try again tomorrow?"

The massive tattooed bully pulled the tape off her mouth and pressed the button for parking station level two. He stepped out of the car, and the doors closed.

As the elevator fell, Neela slumped against the glass opposite the doors. She was shattered, dripping with sweat. She'd been spared. But why? What was going on? She had to find Dermot.

As Dermot's elevator reached roof level, the doors opened and the two struggling men tumbled out, still clawing each other. The elevator doors closed behind them; Nick's stun gun spun away onto the roof.

The pair disengaged and scrambled to their feet. They circled each other like a pair of jackals.

"I fight okay for a cripple, wouldn't you say, Dermot?"

It hadn't occurred to Dermot until now—the cane was still in the elevator, but Nick was as agile as a circus performer.

"That cane? I never needed it. The second operation was a complete success, but I needed the prop. How could a cripple be responsible for so many spectacular killings? A killer has to be agile. Isn't that right? Right!"

"Where's Neela?" Dermot still felt extremely weak, but he knew he'd have little chance unless he played for time and Nick allowed him time to recover.

"Oh, she's just fine. Nothing's going to happen to her. I've seen to that. You see, you keep forgetting—I *like* Neela. The fact is, I've loved her always. In fact, if it hadn't been for Giselle . . ." His voice trailed off for a second. "When I've removed you from sight, and she feels you have deserted her, I shall woo her cleverly and she'll be mine—as Giselle was yours that evening long ago."

Dermot swung a right at Nick, his fist just glancing off Nick's jaw.

"That's the spirit, Dermot. That's *great*! You've got to fight! Because this is the last chance you'll ever have!"

Dermot lunged again—this time for the stun gun, but Nick grabbed one of his legs and he fell heavily.

Nick then grasped the stun gun and slipped it into a pocket, taking out a second cell phone device. "Takes too long to recharge—always best to travel with a backup."

As Dermot regained his footing, Nick rushed Dermot, shoving him hard toward the retaining wall of the roof. Nick pressed Dermot backwards so far that his upper torso practically hung over the abyss—the street was hundreds of feet below.

"I have to hand it to you," Nick breathed into Dermot's ear. "You've got balls putting your name to that garbage. You writers have some sort of a fantastic twisted vanity."

Dermot eyes fixed on Nick's.

"Seems I was a natural, though. We wrote a best seller—together!"

Dermot made one last move but Nick jabbed him in the throat and the fight went out of him instantly. Then he zapped Dermot's body again with the second stun gun. Dermot spasmed for a good five seconds and then lay still.

"Well, that's enough of this fighting shit," Nick said, towering over him.

Dermot could hardly breathe, yet he knew he had to keep some inter-action going. So he spoke.

"All those innocent people, Nick. How could you?"

Nick crouched down beside Dermot. "Innocent?" he asked with a large measure of incredulity. "Innocent?"

Nick reached under Dermot's armpits and sat him upright against the retaining wall at the edge of the roof. Playtime was over. Now Nick was deadly serious.

He began using the affected guttural voice. "I shall bring suffering to others, equal in measure to my own. You like the accent? Creepy, isn't it?" He sat cross-legged in front of Dermot.

"Through suffering cometh salvation. You will never know true sorrow without suffering true loss." He paused, then reverted to his normal voice. "And I have suffered, Dermot. How I have suffered. You had no idea."

Dermot couldn't move a muscle—only his eyes revealed he could still hear. He managed just a word.

"Why?"

Nick took a deep breath.

"Giselle and I never anticipated complications with the birth of the twins. Why would we? We were assured everything was nicely on track."

Nick stared out across downtown LA toward Long Beach, just as the last rays of sun disappeared. "When her water broke early, we knew we had to hurry. But this was no big deal. A few minutes here and there. That was all. She wasn't about to die. But I drove as fast as I could to the hospital.

"I laid her in the backseat, making her as comfortable as possible. She looked so radiant. I can see her now; in pain of course, yet sublimely happy, relying on me to keep her and our babies safe."

He stopped speaking. All Dermot could hear was the wind blowing the twin radio cables together above their heads—it sounded like the halyards of a yacht far out at sea in a strong wind.

"We could've made it, you know. We could've made it in time. Had it not been for a certain cab driver by the name of Abel Conway."

Nick searched Dermot's eyes.

"He ran a red light. There was no need. He was an idiot. Conway ran a red light. I was forced to avoid him, and we got nailed by a Range Rover."

Dermot tried to open his mouth, but couldn't.

"I wish we'd both died there. Because Conway set in motion a chain of events that was too brutal to imagine."

Dermot's lips moved a fraction of an inch—he desperately wanted to speak. Nick ignored him, now deep in his own memory—*his* story.

"Twenty minutes! Can you believe it? Twenty. That's how long it took the ambulance to reach us. I could have carried Giselle on my back to the hospital in less time—but how was I to know? It was more important to keep her still—she was losing so much blood."

Nick stared off into the sunset and recalled those terrible moments.

"When the ambulance reached us, I screamed at the paramedic. 'Move! Get her in the back. Get her to the E.R. She's dying!'" He turned to Dermot. "But the young buck told me to back off—said *he* was in control."

Nick stood and flexed his legs. "Giselle's life was slipping away while this arrogant prick played George Clooney in some medical drama."

Nick smiled down at Dermot. "Can you guess?"

Dermot managed to mouth the name. "Derek Klein?"

"He paid for his arrogance." Nick winked at Dermot. "You actually had me on my toes there for a while, Dermot. Had to move real quick. But a motorbike's always quicker in traffic, you know. You came so close to saving the bastard. But his death was fated—along with those who killed my babies."

Nick reached into a pocket and pulled out a syringe.

"We don't want any more fisticuffs, as you English put it. Better to relax you a little. We can't stay here much longer, anyway. Neela will surely be bringing people here to search for you. I think she saw you. That was the idea, anyway. Besides, it's been ten minutes, and I do have a deadline."

He injected an exact measure of succinylcholine into Dermot and continued speaking.

"Giselle bled to death before we reached the emergency room. But as if her death wasn't terrible enough, there was more suffering to come. Unimaginable suffering. Suffering on such a scale I lost contact with the human race. I became a monster—the monster I am now."

Nick broke the needle off the syringe and placed all the pieces in his pocket.

"The twins were born alive. An incredible achievement by the obstetrician. They were premature, of course. I watched them fight for life for several days and nights. But they survived! Incredible as it may seem, these tiny people survived. They even began putting on weight!"

Dermot knew what was coming. The fire. The final catastrophe.

"A nurse named Lucy Cowley was on duty that night." Nick saw Dermot's mouth twitch. "She had several jars of ammonia on a trolley headed for a storeroom. But she was too concerned with her damned cell phone to watch where she was going. The cart hit a wall, and the ammonia jar fell. It broke."

"But you killed her . . ." Dermot could manage only a couple of words.

"I did. It was her fault the ammonia was there to light. But the ammonia didn't kill my darlings. It was the fire. It took a careless idiot sneaking a cigarette in a storeroom. Result? *Whoosh!* Guess who? Right. That imbecile of a security officer, Bruce Major. He killed them."

There were tears in Nick's eyes. "The fire spread to the neonatal wards where my twin treasures were sleeping." His expression was one of calm despair. Nick chuckled.

With a superhuman effort Dermot managed a few more words.

"Blasé. Why her? What had she done?"

"Well, I had to add some others, you know, some innocents to avoid any obvious linkage. The police can be very smart at times. Blasé was killed simply to make you squirm. But here's the rub, as Shakespeare might have put it. As my 'killing spree,' for want of a better term, continued I became aware of a dark side to my nature that I never knew existed. I discovered I found it amazingly thrilling to be the final arbiter of life and death." He gave Dermot a wry sad smile. "Possibly experiencing the killing fields of Iraq awakened some grotesque primal side of my nature? I'm not sure. As a soldier I had initially found random butchery of civilians disgusting. But within weeks I was killing with abandon, amazed by my bloodlust. When I returned home I was two distinct people. I could switch from good to evil at will, as a driver might click from manual drive to cruise control."

Dermot's ability to speak was returning, but his limbs still had no function.

"You wanted to see me die in prison?"

Nick looked surprised. "Oh *no*! Not at all! My, we are being the simpleton today. I was the one who delivered the evidence that set you free! I was always going to do that, one way or another. Then Detective Kandinski made matters so much easier for me by stumbling on the links between five of the victims—the hospital where Giselle died, and where the twins were burnt to death."

Dermot knew he had one chance. Keep Nick talking until Neela could bring help.

"How could you have killed Arnold? You were with me when he called?"

"Ah! Yes, I was. That is, I was with you until the second you left the house. Then I was on my motorbike. I was faster than you—all the side streets and cut-throughs. Worked very well, if I do say so."

"But how did Arnold . . . ?" The effort was almost too much for him. He faltered.

"How could an idiot speak so cogently? With a great many hours of tutoring, Dermot. Days of it. Weeks actually. Fueled by many, *many* cases of beer. We almost became friends. He saw me as a father figure. The deep accent was actually his—it was me who affected his voice. We spent hours together drinking beer. He read the lines I wrote for him aloud. I'd tell him that if you ever asked a question he didn't understand, he should start speaking at the cues at the bottom of the page. It's quite amazing what you can get from a homeless soul with an empty stomach. I was his savior, you see. He couldn't write at all, but he could read passably well—for a ten-year-old mind, that is. I had to write my instructions in capitals. He performed his tasks wonderfully. He even waited for me obediently on the roof of the People's Bank. He was expecting a case of beer—as usual. But instead I treated him to a case of eternity." He laughed.

Nick looked at his watch. "Enough of this chitchat. We must make a move before Neela returns with the cavalry."

He used a fireman's lift to carry Dermot back to the elevator. He'd used his stolen caretaker's key to make sure the elevator wasn't accessed by anyone else. Within two minutes they were on the lower parking level. Nick carried Dermot toward a Peugeot 207, black with tinted windows.

He lay Dermot down by the trunk. "Good-looking car, don't you think? I just love it. It's my second car. There are so *few* nice cars around." He laughed again, clearly enjoying himself. "Of course! I'm forgetting—you have one, too. Very handy, placing you at crime scenes."

Nick opened the trunk, lifted Dermot, and slung him inside—not worrying about sharp edges.

"Oh, one thing I must tell you. I have every intention of continuing to do what I enjoy best. I fear I am addicted to death. Call it an obsession. I enjoy 'curing' people's worst nightmares in my own particularly amusing way. But I like to take my depravity one step further. So consider this. What could be more fascinating and challenging for me than to kill the one person I still love? Someone who trusts me with her life?"

Nick brought his face close to Dermot's, curious as to how he'd react. Dermot's eyeballs buzzed, as if an electric current had been run through his brain.

"That's right. You got it."

Nick took the precaution of taping Dermot's mouth in case he summoned up sufficient energy to shout. Of course, that wouldn't be possible. Nick was by now very familiar with the correct dosage of succinylcholine.

Nick drove Dermot to a warehouse in Inglewood. He'd rented the space months before. It had cooking facilities in one corner, and a toilet and washroom in another. It also had a small room that Nick had soundproofed and secured with deadbolts.

Within a few minutes of arrival, Dermot was chained to a wall inside the secure room and Nick continued his monologue, reveling in his moment of vengeance.

"So, is there any other question I can clear up for you, Dermot? Feel free to ask—you're going to be here for some time. I have to arrange more suitable lodgings a little closer to home."

Dermot stared at the man he had called a friend for so many years. The Ted Bundy principle was truer than anyone could have believed. He'd never have thought Nick could harm a living soul.

"Why me? What did I do to you?"

Nick was very quiet for some seconds. "Are you serious, Dermot? Do you still feel you can play this game after so many years? You are a writer. You should know where the story starts, and with whom it ends. The answer to both questions is, with you, of course."

Dermot's brow furrowed. He struggled to make sense of Nick's words. Was it conceivable that all this madness was the direct result of one occasion where he and Giselle had, in a moment of inebriated madness, made love? It wasn't possible.

"You know, don't you, Dermot? I can see by your face you do."

Dermot closed his eyes to shut out the memory. But he couldn't. Within a fraction of a second he was back at his publisher's, the edited sheets on the table next to an empty bottle of red wine, and he and Giselle were in each other's arms.

"This shouldn't . . ." he'd begun. But Giselle had held him still closer.

"I know. This can never happen again," she'd replied, as she lifted her skirt. "Never again."

They had made love that evening, but had never done so again. In fact they never mentioned it again. It was too painful for each of them to love two people at the same time.

"It was a single moment of bad judgment. Neela never knew," Dermot was just able to say.

"And I shall never tell her. Why punish her for your crimes? However, I shall do to her as you did to me. That's only fair."

Nick walked to a spot underneath a high window. "I expect you'd like to know how I found out."

"Giselle would never have told you."

"Of course not. It was the DNA. The autopsy reports on my beautiful babies. I was told I wasn't their father."

He looked down at Dermot with a look of extreme venom.

"My wife lay dead. My children had been burned to death, and now I was informed that my oldest and dearest friend, my quasi-bother, had fucked my wife when he'd felt horny one day. You'd actually chosen not to give your *own* wife children, and then had been so careless, you gave my wife *twins*!"

He paused, then spoke very slowly and deliberately. "You visited upon me my worst nightmare. So I will shortly visit you with yours."

CHAPTER 68

When Neela staggered into the empty foyer of the Sibley Building she looked around desperately for anyone who might let her use a cell phone to call 9-1-1, but the building was deserted. She buzzed herself out and ran into the street. Her clothes were disheveled, her hair was a mess.

She was shaking with fear and her limbs were not functioning properly. She was also now unsure whether she had actually seen Dermot sitting on the floor in the elevator next to hers. Why would he have been there at all?

She grabbed at a passing man. "Hey, can I use your phone? It's an emergency! I've just been attacked! Please!"

The young guy pretended he hadn't heard her and hurried on, clearly thinking Neela was trouble he didn't need.

At the corner of West Fourth Street, Neela stumbled into the center of the street, waving her arms wildly. Cars stopped at once and a crowd soon formed around her, though still everyone kept their distance.

She screamed. "For God's sake, someone call the police! I've been attacked!"

Several people did call, and within five minutes a patrol car appeared and two uniformed cops approached her.

By the time they had asked their fifty questions, called back to base for support, and detectives had been dispatched to the Sibley Building, the young men were long gone. And Neela's suffering had just begun.

Dermot never arrived at the airport. He was not seen there, nor had he checked in. He never made it to the dark jungles of Papua New Guinea to reinvent his career. He was nowhere to be found. The cabbie had stayed for a while for Dermot to return, then had called the cops.

The disappearance of Dermot Nolan became a cause célèbre all around the world. As if his trial had not been spectacular enough, now the notorious author had disappeared. Detectives stationed a police truck on South Broadway the day following Dermot's disappearance, and interviewed every member of the public that passed. All to no avail.

Each week, Dermot would be sighted somewhere—a game lodge in Africa, a bazaar in Tunis, a brothel in the Bronx, a checkpoint in Iran, he was even spotted fighting with the Taliban in Afghanistan.

It was a miracle that Neela didn't have a second miscarriage. Nick moved into the spare room to look after her, and assured her that Dermot would return. After all, hadn't he before?

But weeks passed with no sign of Dermot. After her initial mental meltdown, Neela sank into a state of despair. However, she knew she had to look after her health for the sake of her unborn daughter, so she somehow managed to convince herself that Dermot would stumble back into their lives.

But he didn't.

Months later, Neela's water broke prematurely. Nick drove her to Cedars-Sinai, where tiny Virginia took her first gulp of air.

Four days after the birth, Nick suggested Neela go and stay with her mother for a few weeks. He would man the fort at Linley Place.

The next day, Neela left for her mother's house, while Nick went out to make over Neela's small rear garden—something she had always wanted to do, but never seemed to have the time.

CHAPTER 69

Nick kept Dermot bound at the hands and feet and chained to a wall in the Inglewood warehouse for two further weeks while he created his new designer garden for Neela. Each day when his prisoner had been fed and watered, Nick left him alone so that he could continue work on the new garden at Linley Place. In a couple of days he'd pulled down the old Nolan shed and built a brand new one. That done, he began to dig—inside, away from prying eyes.

It took Nick four days to get down eight feet. At that stage he climbed back to the floor of the shed from the bottom of the pit and began to assemble the coffin.

He thought of most things. An air vent was a must, as well as an almost silent electric motor to power the ventilation system. Then there was the question of nutrients. Rather than have to hand feed his nemesis every day, Nick came up with the idea of a composter. In this way, Neela could do the feeding without her knowing. The chute worked automatically. When there was a certain weight of rotting organic matter on the base plate, the food fell down, allowing two days of decomposing scraps to fall directly onto Dermot's face. It was his choice to eat whichever morsels he chose. Nick had done some research into the lengths human beings would go to stay alive. Most drink their own urine if they are sufficiently dehydrated, and will even consider killing a fellow human when truly desperate for food. So Nick concluded that fresh water sucked from a stoutly constructed plastic bag through a rubber hose, together with the meal scraps and garden clippings, and the worms already inside the composter, were really quite a generous diet.

One of the most unpleasant aspects of being buried alive is the lack of a toilet, but plumbing simply was not an option. Nevertheless, Nick organized a pit just below where Dermot rested his naked hips, so that his urine and excrement would fall directly downward into a custom-made septic tank. Without this waste-management system, Dermot would soon die of infection and/or drown in his own urine. And that would spoil everything.

Nick also equipped Dermot's coffin with a light source so Dermot could see where he was, and what was happening to him. That was all part of the torture. The light would also allow him to decide which scraps of food he cared to eat first, a move Nick actually considered a gesture of compassion. Also he'd be able to turn the light off when he wanted to sleep— another act of kindness. Nick's one little practical joke was to place a small handbell inside the coffin.

The question Nick often pondered as he shared dinners with Neela in the Nolan home in the weeks that followed was, how long should he let Dermot linger underground. A year? No, not nearly long enough! Finally, he settled on three years. Then he'd poison Dermot with rat bait in the food scraps.

The day Nick took Dermot home to Linley Place was a very special one for the Dream Healer. He found he couldn't stop whistling sunny Broadway show tunes—a sure sign he was supremely happy. Neela was due home the next day, and he couldn't wait to surprise her with the new garden.

During his captivity at the Inglewood warehouse, Dermot never ceased to think of ways to escape. But Nick had thought of everything. Dermot was always securely chained to a metal ring beside the mattress, bound, spoon-fed, and kept hydrated via a plastic suction tube near the mattress. Nick had thought to soundproof the warehouse, so screaming was pointless.

As he lay on his crude bed, Dermot tried desperately to figure out what horrors Nick had in mind for him. The first day he was sure Nick meant to kill him. But as the days progressed he wasn't so certain.

Then one day, Dermot saw Nick preparing a syringe. A few seconds later the liquid was in his arm. When he awoke he found himself trussed like a chicken, duct tape covering his mouth, sitting on a chair in his own kitchen.

He'd been moved.

He felt an initial huge surge of relief. *But what now?*

Dermot tried to move, but realized at once that a relaxant drug had deadened his muscles. Then the living room door opened and Nick entered, wearing the broadest smile.

Nick placed one arm under Dermot's shoulders, the other under his knees, and carried him like a child out into the garden and into his newly constructed shed. As Nick kicked open the door, Dermot saw the coffin. He immediately lost control of his bladder.

"Hey! That's disgusting." Nick said in mock anger, like a parent chiding a small child for some nighttime incontinence. Secretly, he'd expected this reaction. He grinned at Dermot. "While we're on the subject, try to control your bowels until you're inside the box."

Nick noticed that Dermot couldn't take his eyes off the coffin. He was transfixed! It was very gratifying.

"Pretty neat carpentry, eh?"

He then waited patiently for Dermot to notice the burial pit, with the hoist standing above it. But the seconds passed and still Dermot didn't look away from the box. For Nick it was exasperating—it was like waiting for a child to spot the second equally special present that lay at the base of the Christmas tree.

"Look at the pit. The *pit!*"

Seconds passed. Then very slowly Dermot's eyes swiveled toward the stout winch that stood over the black hole in the dirt. "Buried alive! Isn't that your worst nightmare? That's what sets you off screaming, isn't it? Well, once Neela told me about it, I simply couldn't resist! Don't blame her, she was so worried about you." He chuckled. "Welcome to your new home, Dermot," Nick said. "I call it my reverse penthouse, because it's so deep." Nick laughed aloud.

If his muscles had been capable of any function, Dermot would have vomited. Somehow he managed to maintain control of his sphincter.

"Want to take a closer look-see? Be my guest."

Nick carried Dermot to the edge of the pit to allow him to look directly downwards at the eight-foot deep hole in the earth—his grave. Then he pivoted slightly so Dermot could look right into his custom-built sarcophagus.

"You'll be snug as the proverbial bug in a rug," he said quite gently.

Then with exquisite cruelty he lowered Dermot very slowly, an inch every second, into the box, watching Dermot's chest pound like a pile driver.

When Dermot had been laid out, Nick untied him and spread his limbs to make him comfortable. Nick knew the drug's effect wouldn't wear off for at least ten minutes, so he took care to make sure everything was just as it should be. All the while, Dermot's eyes never left his tormentor's.

Dermot knew his very worst nightmare was about to come to life. Or more accurately put—*come to death*.

He looked upwards. Nick was attaching the ropes to the box, ropes that would hold the coffin securely when it was lowered into the ground.

A moment later Nick stood over Dermot, a hammer in one hand and some nails in the other. He placed the nails in his mouth and reached for the lid.

"Time for bed."

Dermot's eyelids pulsed and flicked faster than a hummingbird's wing as Nick lifted a pair of sturdy seamstress's scissors and began to cut away all Dermot's clothes. He then extracted every last vestige of cloth from the box. Dermot was sweating like a fat man in a sauna. He couldn't speak. He could hardly breathe. Only his tear ducts were working; the tears bled down his hot cheeks.

Nick lifted the heavy lid and, again with the utmost cruelty, slid it agonizingly slowly across the top of the coffin until only Dermot's eyes were visible.

"Bet you wish you hadn't done 'the wrong thing' all those years ago. Bet you wish you'd kept your dick in your trousers, ol' buddy."

The insane panic engendered by the pounding of the long galvanized nails into the lid of one's coffin is a matter for conjecture. For Dermot it couldn't have been other than heart-stopping.

"Oh, one more thing," Nick shouted as the final nail was driven into the wood. "There's a bell there if you want anything. Oh! And a light! Sayonara!"

It didn't take Nick long to lower Dermot's coffin down to its final resting place above the septic pit. As he began to fill in the earth, he became aware of a distant ringing. Dermot was actually ringing the bell! It was too funny for words! And Nick could also just make out a low groaning. This became more of a shriek as the drugs wore off. But when the grave was full and Nick was patting down the earth, he could hear nothing.

His justice was complete.

Nick chose to remain in the shed for several hours. He was contemplating—enjoying the moment, so to speak. After an hour, he pulled a stethoscope from his pocket and placed it on the earth and listened carefully. Though the coffin was virtually soundproofed for all but such sound-enhancing equipment, Nick was amused to hear the bell still tinkling—as though Dermot really believed his tormentor would let him out if he rang a bell!

Naturally, the bell ringing was coupled with perpetual screaming. This also gratified Nick. As did the incessant rodentlike clawing sounds from inside the coffin. Well, who wouldn't try to scratch their way out of such a predicament when all else had failed?

CHAPTER 70

Two months to the day after Nick had nailed down Dermot's coffin, Neela invited Nick to join her and baby Virginia for dinner at Linley Place. Nick offered to cook and Neela gratefully accepted his kind offer. He had moved back to his own duplex apartment, but was still visiting her every day.

As the pot roast cooked in the kitchen, Neela nursed baby Virginia in her lap in the living room. She and Nick were watching Jerry Springer while the meat cooked. The baby at her breast was soothing and relaxing—it was one of the few moments of the day when she could go into a mental holding pattern. Dermot didn't exist.

"You won't believe this, Neela—the guy actually married his ex-wife's grandmother!" He chugalugged another long neck beer.

But Neela wasn't listening—Virginia was at her breast, and that was all that mattered right then.

"Yes," she muttered on autopilot, "there are some seriously weird people out there."

As the Springer crowd started to chant his name like some insane mantra, Nick stood up. "I'll go see if the pot roast is done."

An hour later Nick had served Neela a fabulously tasty meal in the kitchen. The potatoes were just right, the meat perfectly cooked, the vegetables just the way Neela loved them. The gravy was also not too thick, yet had a rich, deep flavor.

Virginia lay in a cot beside the table, fast asleep. Neela found that if her little girl was close, she slept—but when she was left alone in the nursery, she tended to cry.

"You've been so wonderful to me, Nick. I couldn't have made it through Dermot's disappearance without your support. You know that, don't you?"

"That's what I'm here for. If Dermot should ever walk back through that door, he'll see I've been looking after you both."

Nick collected the plates and scraped the food off them into a bucket. They were ready to feed into the composter.

"The incredible thing is that I've never felt Dermot isn't still with me."

"You mean in your heart?" Nick asked.

"No, in a strange way I feel his presence all around me—as though he's very close." She smiled at Nick, almost embarrassed by her words. "It's silly, I know. But hey, that's the way I feel; and oddly it's a comfort to me."

"Well, stranger things have been known to happen," Nick replied, as he picked up the plastic bucket of food scraps and carried it out.

In the garden he opened the door of the shed and stepped inside, clicked on the light, and lifted the lid of the composter.

"Good evening, Dermot," he whispered, more to himself than the undead beneath his feet. "It's feeding time."

He could just make out the sound of the automated chute opening at the base of the composter. It allowed the bottom layer of rotting food scraps to fall downward. He poured a pint of water through a funnel into a length of plastic tubing at the left hand side of the composter. He'd told Neela that the water was a necessary part of the composting operation. A concealed catchment tray at the rear of the shed was usually enough to feed a sufficient amount of water down to the box and support life. The warm water gurgled its way down.

"*Santé, et bon appétit!*" Nick quipped with a chuckle.

He made sure the air vent was still completely unclogged. Satisfied, he relocked the shed and returned to the house. Neela was filling the dishwasher.

"You'll soon have some decent-sized worms, Neels. That's when you know the composter's working really well."

"I wish Dermot was here to see them."

"We have to remain positive." Nick gave her a hug. "With any luck, I can unite Dermot with his worms really soon. He'll get a kick out of nourishing the garden with kitchen waste."

Neela smiled. "Let's hope."

CHAPTER 71

The chances of a mutt like Scarecrow ever digging a hole deep enough to reach the treated pine coffin had always been slim. But the dog had never given up. He was made of the right stuff. He quite possibly would have made it on his own had the workmen not helped him out.

The day the municipal workers hit an obstacle they hadn't anticipated, Scarecrow was down two feet and still burrowing like fury. Nick had never noticed the canine archaeologist at work before because Scarecrow had chosen a spot between the shed and the rear wall, a position no one would have noticed unless the shed was moved from its foundations.

When the drill hit the obstruction—a massive stone just two feet from Dermot's coffin—the work detail had the luxury of having a very sturdy drill bit, one sufficiently powerful to cope with practically all unforeseen objects.

Jon Brackenhoff barked into his walkie-talkie to his supervisor. "Hey, Don. We hit something. Check the survey sheets? Could be granite."

"Shit. That's all we need. Hold off with the drill! Gimme a second."

"Sure, boss," came the answer.

A full minute passed while the foreman checked his blueprints.

"Jon? You listening?"

"Sure, boss."

"Two options. One is to drill a secondary and hook up behind."

"Nah, that'd be a bastard. What's option two?"

"Find out what you hit and make a decision. Make damn sure it's nothing that matters—then drill right through. Okay?"

"You got it! Any problem with utilities to the left and right?"

"No. Nothing where you are—should be virgin. Let's get done and get outta here."

"Roger and out," Jon replied. He hit the power switch on the drill, and it started its staccato rhythm as it pounded through the rock.

Four minutes later the drill shot forward. It hit the far side of the rock and sliced through some soft wood. The drill bit missed Dermot's temple by two inches.

Curious as to whether he'd hit some buried treasure, Jon killed the drill motor and scraped away at the hole he'd made in the box.

It was then he heard the faintest clawing sound, coupled with the faintest feeble cry. "Jesus . . . help me . . ."

"Shit," the worker mouthed as he stared through the hole the drill had made. "Boss!" Jon shouted into the walkie-talkie. "You'd better call for an ambulance. There's someone down here."

CHAPTER 72

"Just some bits of potato and cabbage, and a few Brussels sprouts. It's amazing how delicious simple things can be."

Nick had just served a post-movie supper of cabbage and potato hash to Neela at his home in Studio City. Neela had no way of knowing that this fodder had been Dermot's day-to-day sustenance for months—served raw and fetid.

"My worst nightmare was always losing Giselle," Nick began as he sat down next to Neela on the sofa. "Now it's a fear of rejection."

Neela's heart went out to her friend. She put a friendly comforting arm around him. "Is that why you've never looked for another partner?"

Nick stared off blankly. "Possibly."

Neela drew him to her.

"I expect your worst nightmare now is losing Virginia?" he commented.

"I don't *have* a worst nightmare," Neela replied quickly. "I never had one."

Nick looked directly at her. "Dermot told me your nightmare was the one he added to the novel. The elevator."

"No. That's not it." Immediately, she wished she'd said nothing.

Nick studied her expression closely. Was she going to tell?

"I knew that," he replied softly.

Neela met his eyes. "Really? You're very intuitive." She smiled. "I'm never going to tell anyone about my nightmare. I'd prefer no one ever know. Not even you, Nicky." She smiled again at him. "No offense. It'd spook me if I knew that anyone knew."

"Yours was one not included by Arnold?" Nick asked. It was a rhetorical question. She didn't answer. However, her expression changed slightly, confirming that his assumption was true, but she tried as hard as she could to mask it.

Ever since his conversation with Dermot, when he'd remarked that there were nightmares missing from the diary—those associated with the five senses—he'd known Neela's nightmare lay there somewhere. And it didn't take a genius to discard taste and smell. Most probably touch, too. That only left two. He knew which would be his pick.

Nick laughed and hugged her again. "You see? I knew!"

"Knew what?"

"I always knew what your real nightmare was."

"You couldn't have known," she replied, with an expression that told him she hoped he had no idea what her secret might be.

"Your nightmare is nothing sexual, is it?" He studied her face.

No it wasn't. He could see that now.

"It concerns the loss of something fundamental. Right?"

"Please, Nick. Enough. This isn't funny."

"Not the loss of a loved one," Nick continued in a low tone.

Neela's face was now a blank mask. She would never reveal her nightmare to anyone—it was too terrifying. She blinked a couple of times, rapidly. It was purely instinctive.

Nick studied her. That was it!

"O! Let me not be blind," Nick whispered in her ear. "Not blind, sweet heaven."

Neela's eyes dilated and her breathing quickened. Yet she said nothing.

Nick searched her eyes. "*King Lear*."

Still Neela remained silent.

"That's it, isn't it? You see? I knew all along."

She turned toward him at last. "The word is 'mad.' Not blind. 'Let me not be mad.' It's the Duke of Gloucester that is blinded."

Nick tried not to let his internal triumph show. He'd guessed correctly. It had been blindness all along! She hadn't denied it. Not at all. Rather she'd corrected his deliberate misquote from the play.

"How? How did you know?" she asked, so softly he could barely hear the words.

"Maybe I have a sixth sense," he replied easily. "Perhaps we're kindred spirits. We are, aren't we?"

Nick leaned closer to her, so close they were eye to eye—their lips barely an inch apart.

The seconds passed. First two. Then ten. Then twenty.

He moved imperceptibly closer until his lips barely brushed hers—like the kiss of a butterfly.

Neela instinctively drew back, surprised and suddenly more than a little confused. "Nick, what are you doing?"

He looked deep into her eyes for several seconds, then the moment was gone and his expression became vacant. He stood and walked slowly toward the door.

"Nick?" Neela pleaded. "I hope I haven't offended you. It's simply that . . ." she hesitated, speaking to his back. "It's simply that we are the dearest of friends, and can never be any more than that. You know that, don't you?"

Nick turned and held out a hand. His face was as cold and expressionless as Carrera marble. "Yes, Neela. Of course I know that."

She stood, grasped his hand, tears in her eyes. She was about to add something else when he cut her short, his expression again gentle and kind.

"I have something to show you, Neela. It's upstairs. A surprise. Can you wait here—just for a couple of minutes?"

A wave of relief surged through Neela. "Of course I can, Nick."

Nick smiled a bit sadly. Neela studied his eyes—there was something oddly removed, even distant, in his expression.

As Nick slowly climbed the stairs, Neela sat on the sofa. It was just as the bedroom door upstairs closed that Neela's cell rang. She flipped it open.

As she listened, the blood drained from her face. Then she began to gasp.

"It's Detective Jim Hansen, Mrs. Nolan. We've found your husband. He's alive. In a very serious condition, of course. But he's going to make it.

He's been taken to hospital where he's currently in intensive care. Can you tell us where you are right now and we'll pick you up."

Neela found it hard to breathe, let alone speak.

Eventually she filled her lungs and spoke. "I'm at my friend's house. Nick Hoyle."

"I see." A pause. "Yes, I remember his name. We have that address on record. I'll send a patrol car immediately. It should be there in a matter of minutes. We want to take you to your husband."

Neela caught her breath. "Can Dermot speak? I mean, is he coherent?"

"Not at the moment, Mrs. Nolan. He's drifting in and out of a coma. Not making much sense. He's lost a huge amount of weight, and his body's a mess of sores, infection, that kind of thing. But physically, the attending doctors think he'll recover eventually. We found him buried alive."

"Buried alive?" Neela felt the shock of that revelation. "Oh, my God! Where? In a collapsed building or something?"

"Not exactly. Look, the patrol car should be with you very soon."

"I can't thank you enough, Detective Hansen."

She clicked the phone off, and then screamed hysterically for Nick upstairs. "Nick! There's wonderful news! He's alive! They've found Dermot!"

But there was no reply to her joyous news. She called again, louder this time. There was still no answer from upstairs.

Confusion crossed her face—Nick must have heard her. If not her exact words, surely her loud shouts.

The house was so quiet. Neela felt she could hear her pulse quickening. Why had Nick not responded? What had happened to him?

A sudden wave of terror flooded every fiber of her body. The killer! Was he in the house? Was he upstairs? Had he . . . ?

She stood very still, took a few deep breaths, and quickly looked around. No one was in the room. Perhaps Arnold had been lying in wait for Nick upstairs all along. Of course! That's why Nick hadn't replied. Arnold was in the house . . .

She pulled her cell open to dial 9-1-1. Then she heard Nick's voice from upstairs. A wave of joy and relief flowed through her body.

"It's okay," she could hear him shouting. "Come up. I want to show you something. Everything's ready now."

"Nick! Thank God!" she called back. "I thought it was him! In the house!"

"Come on, silly. Get up here, Neela. Everything's ready!"

Upstairs in his bedroom Nick expertly tapped the needle of the syringe just once. A small amount of succinylcholine spurted from the end and fell to the carpet. Nick had heard Neela's shouts from downstairs, but he wasn't listening. It was no longer important. He was in the zone now. Nothing she said interested nor moved him—his blood had run cold for so many years that now nothing could change that. She had rejected him.

As he heard Neela's footsteps on the stairs, Nick placed the syringe on the bed. He then lifted a vial of sulphuric acid from the nightstand and gently poured the contents on a pair of airline slumber shades that he'd backed with several sheets of protective foil so the material would not disintegrate too quickly. The material hissed its own peculiar pain as the acid soaked the face of the eyeshades.

Nick turned toward the bedroom door. Neela's footsteps were now just feet away. The doorknob turned. He raised the slumber shades to match Neela's head height.

Then, for the first time, Nick became aware of a loud persistent knocking at the front door. He could clearly hear the strident calls of the uniformed cops.

He hesitated. Discretion was paramount now. So they'd found Dermot. And alive, too! Now was an appropriate time to vanish into the mist. The ultimate retribution would have to wait. But it wasn't all bad—planning and executing another delightful game of horrors would be so totally delicious.

He lowered the slumber shades and held them behind his back.

The bedroom door opened. Neela's expression was one of ecstatic relief.

"He's alive! Can you believe it, Nick? It's a miracle!" she shouted, exploding with total joy, wrapping her arms around Nick's neck, hugging him tightly.

Had she known what the future held, her heart would have stopped beating.